# CHASING LIBBY

## BASED ON A TRUE STORY

## PS TEAL

❀ Created with Vellum

# CONTENTS

*Thank you, Miller, Dutton, Martin and Brown.*

*Special thank you, Heidi*

# CHAPTER ONE

*"How many times will I have to lie, Jesus?"*

I felt the exhaustion of lying about what I did, what I liked, and who I was developing into as a person. I prayed that I would not have to lie or play a role very often because that first time was too much and too heavy, but the moment I met Frank Hudson, I knew my life was about to change. I was about to become a habitual liar, my efforts eclipsed only by the woman I learned to lie from—my own mother.

Six months into my relationship with Jesus Christ, I came to the realization that right and wrong are not always black and white, and sometimes the people meant to teach us how to tell the difference are just as broken as we are.

* * *

I ENTERED MY HOUSE THROUGH THE FRONT DOOR OF OUR BIG, GREEN Victorian for the first time at the insistence of our mother, who was already home with a visitor in the dining room toward the back of the house. My siblings and I had been at my older brother's football game, where my older sister was a cheerleader. That previous week there had been cheer camp for the little girls my age, which was six, and we had danced at halftime to "Great Balls of Fire" with my sister's varsity squad.

I remember wondering why my mom wasn't there. She had never before missed anything that was important to me. What's more, we had never entered the house this way. We had always pulled into the garage and gone into our house through the back door. Once inside, my two sisters and I were rushed by our mom through the parlor and up the stairs to our older sister's bedroom.

There, our mom told us, "Be quiet. Don't talk about ballet, dance, or cheerleading. Don't play any loud music."

I was confused. I knew there was a man in my dining room. I had seen him. But I didn't understand why we were pretending to be people we were not. My teenage sister turned on her CD player at a low volume as my mom changed me out of my cheerleading uniform into a church dress. It was a Friday night, and I had never changed out of my cheerleading uniform into anything but pajamas.

"Turn that music off," my mom snapped at my sister.

Mellissa obeyed but replied, "But it's Christian music."

"It doesn't matter. It sounds like rock n roll," Mom explained.

It was one of the first times that our mom would explain to us that, although DC Talk's "Red Letters" was not evil, my cheering in a homemade uniform for my brother playing football was not evil, my older sister being a high school cheerleader was not evil, ballet and the earrings in my ears were not evil, but the man downstairs strongly believed that they were, so we had to pretend that too. He believed they were ungodly.

We could still do those things, but only if we hid them and lied about them.

Whether the way rock music versus other genres sounds was sinful, and whether cheering, dancing, and jewelry were sinful or not was beside the point and did not matter. What mattered was that a child should not have to lie in order for an adult relationship to develop. A child should not have to feel the weight of adult consequences if they slip up, are caught doing those things, or are found in a lie. What mattered was that children should not have to pose and fill the gap where a woman was not right for a man, especially when those children were filling that gap with a false narrative about themselves. A grown man did not pick a woman to marry because she was willing to change her entire life or teach her children to change who they are or who they were becoming. A grown man found a woman who was right for him, or he went without.

Unfortunately, Libby didn't see it that way, so neither could I.

## CHAPTER TWO

Shortly after that night, within months, we were moving into the house of the man to whom we were being taught to lie. My little sister Ruby, who was three years old, my mom, and I moved in with Frank Hudson. Our two older siblings, Jordan and Mellissa, had to find other places to live when Frank broke up our home. My mom and dad were already divorced, but for almost two years we had lived happily with our mother. Our dad was involved in our lives and lived two blocks away, and we were well-adjusted.

Ruby and I went from living in a house where we had a normal-sized bedroom to being shoved into a room that was about four by five feet and could only fit a bunk bed. Our toys were not allowed to come with us because Frank considered most of our toys evil. My sister Ruby and I went from playing dress up, Barbies, Ninja Turtles, and Power Rangers throughout our house to being told to keep the one or two toys we'd been allowed to keep in our room. Our Barbies were considered extremely evil in our new home, so our mom made sure we only had one or two, and they had to stay hidden. I had emotional ties to some of my Barbies, and I never saw them again.

Baby dolls were allowed because Frank wanted us to learn to become mothers, but anything else was thrown away. Our mom told us he had chopped our Christmas-themed stuffed animal's heads off with an axe because he considered Christmas to be evil. No one ever explained why any of these things were evil. Ruby was too young to really understand what was going on, but for me, a six-year-old who was trying to build a relationship with Jesus, there was incredible confusion in being told that everything I liked was evil.

The worst part of that time in our lives was not the loss of material possessions or the changing of our entire lives. Ruby and I had to stop playing basketball with our dad as our coach. We had to stop attending football games, cheerleading, gymnastics, and ballet classes, and we even had to stop going to the church we had gone to since we were born. Those activities, our entire community, and everything we had ever known had been taken away from us overnight, but that still was not the worst part.

The worst part was the separation from our dad, our two older siblings, and our grandma.

For four months, my mom's new husband kept us away from our family. We were not allowed to see anyone, not even our dad. My dad didn't see me and my baby sister for four months, which I later found out caused him to have panic attacks, and his already ailing heart became weaker. My dad was born with two holes in his heart, and going without seeing his babies caused him unimaginable pain. He even ended up in the hospital for a period.

When I started school in a nearby town, my dad came to eat lunch with me. He asked me the types of questions you would ask a six-year-old, simple questions about puppies and whether I liked my new teacher. He didn't ask me anything that would upset my school day.

I asked him why we couldn't see him anymore. I told him how much I missed him, Grandma, my brother and sister, old friends, school, activities, and my old life. He told me he was working very hard on something called "custody," of my sister and me and to keep talking to Jesus.

My dad came to school to eat lunch with me several times, but other than those visits, for four months, I went without him. The ache in my heart for my dad and my grandma turned me from a child into a woman on a mission.

Soon, at home, my mom's new husband Frank began trying to separate Ruby and me from our mom. He told us to go outside every evening until dark even though it was very cold in late autumn, and we were no longer allowed to wear pants or jeans. We had to go out in the cold in dresses. According to Frank, pants or jeans on women were evil. Again, this perplexed me because I knew many very kind, Jesus-loving women who wore jeans.

Every morning before school, my mom would place earrings in my little hand and tell me to put them in my ears on the school bus and take them out on the way home from school so that the holes in my ears didn't close up. Petrified, I would forget to put them in or forget to take them out, all my six-year-old heart could muster was that the Jesus I knew could never be superficial enough to care about earrings or pants, but a man who keeps children away from their father, siblings, and even most days, their mother, was the true evil.

# CHAPTER THREE

Every night for hours when I was trying to sleep, on the other side of the wall, my mom's new husband Frank would lecture her. Well into the night, he would read scripture and preach to her about what wives should be like and what women should and should not do. Women should not wear makeup or jewelry. Their clothes should be modest. Nail polish was evil. Women should not speak in church or ever teach a man anything under any circumstances. A woman should not need the right to vote because, if she was a good wife, she'd vote the way her husband voted anyway. Women should always be paying attention to how their clothing, their words, and their tone of voice affected the men around them. They should be meek, quiet, and humble.

Frank said he was lecturing my mom on how to be a woman not solely for her own benefit, but so she would know how to properly raise Ruby and me. Every day there were new rules. One night while getting ready for bed, the new rule was no more bare feet. My sister and I were not allowed to be barefoot around him because he was a man. To a six-year-old, this was mind-boggling. I knew nothing about sex and had barely even heard the word, "sex," and now I was being told that my six-year-old feet and my sister's three-year-old feet were, what, too provocative for this man? A man who was supposed to be my stepfather?

The girls in my first-grade class were in the habit of coloring our nails with our washable markers. Just for fun, we would color our fingernails in rainbow colors. When I came home from school with purple, green, and blue nails, my mom's husband sat me down, preached to me, and read to me from the Bible about how having painted or colorful fingernails was evil. Having painted or colorful eyelids, lips, or fingernails was for one reason and one reason only, and that was to entice men. Only loose women and prostitutes wore makeup and nail polish, according to Frank.

I spent most of my time trying to avoid him, but we lived in a single-wide trailer with a makeshift closet as my bedroom. It was not easy to avoid him, and it was not easy to forget how mean he was, even when he was not speaking.

Frank looked like a mean person. I tried to tell myself that people could not look mean or kind because people couldn't control every-thing about their outward appearance, but he did actually look mean. He looked like a vulture, with a long nose and beady eyes. His skin was bumpy, and most of his fingernails were missing. I was not only scared every time he spoke to me but also scared if he even looked at me.

Another day when I got home from school, my mom and her husband were waiting in the living room to talk to me. They told me to sit down, and I began to tremble. I had no idea what I had done or what was coming. "Do you know anything about sex?" Frank asked me.

My eyes filled with tears. I did not want to talk to this man. I did not want to look at his goblin face any more or hear his voice ever again. Not knowing what else to do, and thinking that because of my fingernails or earrings or maybe even my feet, these two adults were going to accuse me of having done something sexual with someone, I shook my head.

"No," I said frantically.

They both laughed at me as though this was a fun, light hearted conversation. Fortunately, that day was not about them explaining sex or accusing me of having done something wrong, but unfortunately, it was so that Frank could explain to me that having sex before marriage was wrong and that even though they had been living together for weeks, they had not yet had sex. Frank told me that he and my mom were planning to get married soon. I was so young and bewildered by everything going on, I had not even realized they were not yet married.

Why a grown man felt the need to explain to a six-year-old his sexual relationship with her mother is still beyond me, thirty years later. My boundaries were constantly being crossed. I did not feel safe or happy unless I was at school.

Under the guise of my sister and me needing to be more independent, one evening, Frank told my mom she was no longer allowed to help us with our bath. He told her that I was old enough to do bath time. He told me, "Just take your sister and go take a bath. It's not that big of a deal. Just go do it."

With my sister and I both being girls, my mom had always just bathed us together, and it probably wouldn't have been a big deal if I had ever been paying attention to things like how to turn the water on and how to make sure it was not too hot or too cold, but I hadn't.

Ruby and I went into the bathroom and closed the door, and as I write this my hand shakes because my sister and I did not know what was going to happen. We didn't know how to do any of this, and I didn't know what he would do if we had a problem because we could hear him in the other room telling our mom that she could not help.

Being a very sensitive child as it were, a child who cried any time she was separated from our mom, Ruby started to cry. I started to beg her to stop, and not looking at the faucet or even taking time to register that there even were hot and cold options because I was more focused on keeping her from crying, I turned the water on and got Ruby undressed. I kept begging her to stop crying because every time she'd cried over the past few weeks living with Frank, he would become angry and start yelling at everyone. I knew if she cried for long enough we would be in trouble, and I did not want to be naked and in trouble. Naked and in trouble with a man who looked like what I imagined demons looked like, who scolded us for having bare feet, seemed like Hell.

I filled up the tub, got undressed, and got in. Muffling my own scream from the heat of the water while trying to keep Ruby from even putting her foot in, while trying to find where the cold water knob was, proved too much for a six-year-old. Ruby put her little baby foot in and shrieked.

Boots in the hallway. Not my mother's shoes. Boots.

*He's coming in here, and I'm naked. I don't have time to jump up and cover myself with a towel. I don't have a towel or a washcloth or long hair or even soap bubbles to cover myself. I have to be completely naked in front of a man who implied I was a whore for wearing marker colors on my fingernails.*

He opened the door, walked in, yelled at us that it wasn't rocket science, fixed the water temperature, slammed the door, and left.

I had my arms straight down over my chest and my fists over my lower private parts. I was vulnerable, horrified, embarrassed, and never the same. I had not only been violated, but I had been violated with my mother in the other room sitting in a chair.

Had he touched me or my sister? No. He had not. Did he have to physically touch us in order for that incident to rob me of my innocence and my childhood? Also, no.

I left that bathroom knowing three things. This man was not safe to be around, I was leaving, and my mother was a coward.

# CHAPTER FOUR

My sister and I, being so young and resilient, often forgot how scared we were, and we would be playing and start giggling. Giggling was another thing my mom's husband had a rule against.

"No giggling!" he would yell.

It's difficult to remember not to laugh when you are six or three. I am still, to this day, very confused about why we were not allowed to giggle or "be silly," as he put it. We had no TV and were not allowed to watch TV or movies. It was as though every small treasure or joy we had was being cut off from us.

One thing we did enjoy were the puppies. Frank had a few bird dogs, and one of them, Dolly, had just had puppies. She had four male puppies, and they were my pride and joy. I named them and played with them as often as I was allowed. Dolly's pen was a quarter of a mile away from the house through a field, and I would walk to her, sit in her pen, and play with her puppies. I would miss my mom when we were "down at the barn," as we called the end of the property with the barn and dog pens.

One day, I asked if I could bring one of the puppies to the house with me. I can't remember if my mom said I could or if I completely disobeyed and did it anyway, but I do remember standing in front of the pen trying to decide if I wanted to take the solid liver puppy I called Hershey or the white and ticked puppy I called Fred. I started to look for a solution and thought, "If only I had a basket. I could bring all four of them home with me."

So, I ran home and got a laundry basket, ran back to the dog pen, scooped up all four squirmy puppies, and then slowly made my way home. The trip back home through the field proved difficult. I remember they were too heavy for me to carry, and they were all four trying to get out of the basket, but I made it, and I was so proud of myself when I got back to where my mom was working on something outside with my stepfather.

I was not met with proud smiles or accolades. They were both furious. I was disappointed and upset because I knew that I would have to figure out how to take the puppies back to their pen, and I was already worn out.

The whole journey back after dropping the puppies off with Dolly, I was terrified. What would my punishment be when I had actually done something wrong if I got scolded for giggling? What would happen when I had actually disobeyed?

Fortunately, Frank had instructed my mom about how to administer my punishment. She took me where he could not see us and with tears in her eyes, she said, "If he asks you what I'm doing, tell him I squeezed the fire out of your arm."

"Why?" I was confused and didn't understand anything about the situation, and she could tell.

"Those puppies are for sale. If you drop or hurt one, we can't sell it, and Frank will be out a lot of money. Look what he did to my arm." She rolled up her sleeve and showed me the handprint. The blue and purple bruise had already begun to form on her bicep. "This is what he wants me to do to you. I'm not going to, but if he asks you, you have to tell him I did."

I realized that this man was to be lied to because he was actually physically hurting her at this point.

He was also very reckless with our physical safety. He had a very old, small, tractor from the 1950s that did not have anywhere for my little sister and I to sit with him. It would have been more than fine with both of us if we did not sit on the tractor with him or interact with him at all, but he not only insisted that we ride on the tractor with him, but that both of us did at the same time.

That meant Ruby sat on his lap, and I sat on the hood, the piece of metal over the engine, at the front of the tractor. I had to straddle it, and once, I burned my leg severely. The real problem was that if I had fallen off, I would've been crushed to death by one of the huge back tires. No one had ever explained to me that if he hit a bump, and I fell, I should quickly roll out of the way. I'm sure if I had fallen, I would've tried to jump up and run out of the way, but there would not have been enough time. From the nose of the tractor to its back hitch it was only about five feet long. Even if it was going slowly, I would've had only a second or two before the back tires, which were about five feet tall, crushed me. My mom begged him not to put me up there and to just let me walk. He always snickered a sarcastic laugh and told her she was worrying about nothing.

I suppose to him, I was nothing.

All four of us had to ride on the tractor one time. My mom and I begged him to just let us walk. He could drive the tractor back to the house, and we would follow on foot. He insisted he would hold Ruby on his lap, I would sit on the front, and my mom would perch on the foothold next to the enormous tire. If she had fallen, she would've died.

I had already learned that crying and begging did not work with this man and that we had to do everything the exact way he wanted, no matter how infantile the idea. I sat quietly on the tractor's engine. I don't remember whether Ruby was crying or not, but I do remember exactly the way my mom's facial expression and tone of voice screamed terror. She was scared. She didn't want to die.

"Please let me get down! Just let me walk! Just stop! Stop! Stop! I want down!" She was pleading, and then he did it. He did the thing that is forever sealed in my memory as not only the most childish but the most unforgivable, infuriating thing anyone could ever do.

He pushed my mom. He pushed her left shoulder as if to say,

"Fine, if you want down so badly, get down," the way an eight-year-old would speak. She faltered and almost fell. In her eyes, I could see she was beyond afraid.

The next time my mom and I were alone together I asked her, "If you are afraid of him, too, and he is hurting you, why don't we just leave?"

"It doesn't work like that, Amelia," she said.

"Why not?" I was completely confused. She'd always seemed like such a confident woman to me. She had never even taken anyone's verbal abuse, let alone let someone physically bully her.

"Because he is dangerous, and where am I gonna go? Where will I take you? Where will we go that he doesn't know where to find us?" she asked.

"How is he dangerous?" I was still only six, but I could sense in her fear that she was talking about more than the things I had seen.

"He has killed people, Amelia," she said with daggers for pupils.

"What? Who has he killed?" I was starting to cry.

"He has killed more than one person, but one of them was his son."

"What?" I was sobbing.

"Yeah, he backed over him with his car."

"What? How old was he?"

"I don't know. He was a baby, one or two," she answered.

The only real information or help I received from that conversation with my mom was that out of the four of us living in this single wide I, at six, was the only adult.

At six, thirty years ago, I remember thinking *"How do you move your young children into a house with a man that you know has killed a young child without finding out the details? Why are you choosing this man you barely know over your children? Now I have to get my sister and me out of here without my mom."*

# CHAPTER FIVE

Every night before falling asleep, listening to my mom's husband drone on in the next room about how he didn't even listen to the women at church pray if they had short hair or how you could tell by looking at someone if they were a Christian, I would pray.

I prayed about one thing and one thing only and that was how to take Ruby and escape. I was always paying attention to directions and roads. I knew how to get to my dad's house, and I knew it would be very far and very cold if we walked. As an adult, I now know it would've been close to twenty miles and incredibly dangerous, but back then, I was willing to try. I just didn't know how or when, and so I prayed.

In the meantime, my mom spent her evenings trying to get me to interact more with her husband. She wanted us to be friends, and I did not want to get in any more trouble, so I obeyed when she told me to ask him questions. Before dinner one evening she told me to ask him how he trained the bird dogs he raised.

His answer is still the most disturbing thing anyone has ever said to me.

My six-year-old voice at the dinner table asked, "How do you train a dog to hunt quail?"

Frank's forty-year-old grown man's voice answered. "What would you do, Amelia, if I dug a hole out here in the yard," he said, motioning to the yard outside the front door, "and put you inside of a box, poked holes in it so you could breathe, threw some dirt on top, and left you in the box in the hole for a week?"

I was stunned and did not move. I did not answer, so he continued.

"And you were poopin' and peein' all over yourself for about a week, and then I dug up the box. What would you do?" he asked.

I was frozen. I had no idea what he was talking about. My mom was sitting next to me. He was saying this in front of her three-year-old and to her six-year-old. I looked to my mom for help and got nothing.

I got nothing from her.

"You would do anything I said after that, wouldn't you?" he asked.

As an adult, I vaguely understand how his example correlates to breaking a bird dog, but as a very young and confused child, I was screaming inside for Jesus to rescue us.

## CHAPTER SIX

When I was a child, I didn't know much about my mother's childhood. After having spent more time with her as an adult, I found out that she had just as traumatic a childhood as I had, only in a different way.

My mom's mother had a baby when she was sixteen, a product of rape and incest. This child was severely developmentally delayed and had anger issues. My mom has a scar on her arm where her older brother, known to his younger siblings as "Crazy Larry," stabbed her with scissors when she was three or four. With an absent father, a neglectful mother, and eventually six more siblings, my mother had really never been shown what love was in her youth.

I was blessed enough to have a wonderful father who had been raised and loved by a reverend and a teacher. He had only one sibling. He was the youngest, was the only boy, and so my dad was not only cherished and taught to be kind and loving, but he was also charismatic and intelligent, and he demanded respect. Even at the age of six, I knew that how I was being treated by my stepfather was not going to fly with me, and that was due mostly to my dad's personality and how he taught me to accept nothing less than what I deserved.

My older siblings worried about the well-being of Ruby and me as well, and on Halloween, our eighteen-year-old brother, who had always taken us trick-or-treating, braved coming to visit us. My mom's husband let our brother drop off Halloween cupcakes but would not let him in the house or let us see him.

"You deal with it," my mom's husband told her as he sat in the house with us and had my mom go outside and tell her son that he could not see his own little sisters.

I could hear my brother, whom I missed so much, loudly asking my mom so that her husband could hear, "Why can't I just see them so I know they're okay?" It had been months since he'd seen us. "Why are you doing this? You can just leave! You don't have to stay here!"

Mom told him to leave, and we didn't even get to see him that night, let alone go trick-or-treating with him.

Later in life, my stepfather told me this story from his perspective. He made fun of my brother for always carrying a baseball bat when he came to try to see us or protect us.

"A baseball bat," he scoffed. "What's he gonna do with a baseball bat?"

I was in my thirties for that conversation, and by then I had realized you don't answer crazy people aloud. But inside, my response was that if you'd ever seen what Jordan Boyd could do with a baseball bat, you'd be much more scared. More importantly, why should a child or a very young man have to arm himself with a baseball bat, or any other weapon, when visiting his mother and his sisters?

## CHAPTER SEVEN

I was so young when my mom met Frank that I didn't have many memories of her before she started to change. The very first thing he did when they met was something every controlling narcissist does—he changed her name.

Everyone in the county we lived in, which was small, rural, and tightly knit, knew my mom as Libby. She had been Libby since she moved there when she was thirteen, and now, he wanted her to go by Elizabeth.

She was thirty-eight when she met Frank. At the time, she owned a home and ran a very profitable daycare business. She and my dad had been divorced for about a year and a half, and they were able to afford for us to live comfortably.

My mom had an incredibly strong work ethic throughout her entire life. Before she met my stepfather, my mom was Libby who sang at church, taught Bible study and aerobics classes, wore lavender or light green eye shadow, rouge, and a vibrant lip. She played softball, had a lot of friends, and was quick-witted and very smart.

The longer she stayed with him, the more friends she lost. It was impossible for her to go anywhere or see anyone. Everything was evil and outlawed. There was no more makeup for her. Dresses went from sparkly to plain. There was no more softball, aerobics, or friends. The light in her eyes dulled, and the jokes and laughter faded away.

I spent my entire adolescence and adult life trying to win her back from him, but in my heart, I knew when I was six that it was within those first few weeks that he had already killed that person.

He'd killed Libby.

Another thing that was overly difficult was my terror when it came to asking my mom for help. When one lives with a controlling narcissist, they never know how that person will react to anything. As I studied him and his reactions so as not to anger him or get in trouble, I could usually guess whether or not he'd let me ask for Mom's help.

If she was doing something for him, or he needed her attention, I knew not to ask, but when a person is hurt, sick, or desperate, we often don't have the capacity to think about what someone else will say about asking our mother for help.

And no one should have to worry about that when they are a child.

One evening, my mom made spaghetti for dinner. After helping her with the dinner dishes, I told my mom my stomach was in pain. Her husband told me to go sit in the chair she usually sat in when he lectured her so that he could, "See what 'The Word' says about feeling sick."

After reading from the Bible, he determined that a six-year-old with an upset stomach full of spaghetti needed to drink an entire glass of burgundy wine. It was not when she poured it for me, and he told me to sip from the wine, but when she started to pour it out, replacing it with grape juice when he wasn't looking, that I saw exactly what would eventually change her brain composition.

*How long can she play this brain-rotting game where she hides, lies, and tricks this devastatingly immature joke of a man rather than just standing up for herself?* I sat in the chair contemplating how I had been lying for mere weeks and already felt physically, mentally, and emotionally exhausted. I could not handle it, and I saw it changing my mom into someone else.

That night I threw up in my bed and had no energy to estimate what the Beast's reaction would be if I called for my mother's help.

I whimpered, "Mom," so quietly, she must've been awake, waiting for me to call for her, knowing I would be sick. She knew that, if he were awake, he would force me to figure out how to clean myself and my bed. She had fresh bedding and pajamas ready to go, motioning to me to be silent. She cleaned up the mess silently and by herself.

"If he had known about it, he would've thrown a fit," she told me as she put me on the school bus the next morning. "So, you did a good job of being quiet."

My mother was telling me that I did a good job of hiding the fact that she was mothering me for the first time, and it would be nowhere near the last time I'd be praised for our deception.

# CHAPTER EIGHT

I knew that if I had to think about my mom's husband's reactions to things and predict them ahead of time in order to know what to hide, what to say, what not say, and what to lie about, my mom must have been playing those mental games constantly.

She and Ruby had to stay home with him all day every day as he ran a business from home, so they never got the break from him that I was blessed with while I was at school. This constant state of trying to predict his reactions, trick him, and lie to him would end up later costing my mother her sanity. This man had even changed the things that brought her happiness, down to her beverage of choice.

My mom had always been a Pepsi girl. My entire childhood, she had a Pepsi nearby. Only now, she had to hide them. When they first met, Frank didn't allow her to have Pepsi at all, so she hid them in her closet and drank them warm. She hid other treats like chocolate bars and candy because her husband would lecture her about gluttony and tell her she was overweight.

Not that it mattered, but she was not overweight, and at the time, she was in much better shape than he was. He smoked a pack of cigarettes or two a day. I genuinely can't remember how much he smoked, but it was always indoors, and Ruby and I had never been around cigarette smoke before. He was a man so full of himself that he smoked with her young children in the house and in the car, but she was not allowed to have a Pepsi.

A day or two before Thanksgiving, my dad came to eat lunch with me at school. He was excited to tell me that they were working on going to court and that his lawyer had a judge issue an order saying he would be able to pick Ruby and me up for Thanksgiving.

He said a policeman or two would be with him but not to be afraid. I was very happy that we would be getting to see our dad, our older siblings Jordan and Mellissa, and our grandma for Thanksgiving, but my spirits dropped on Thanksgiving morning when, before daylight, Ruby and I were dressed and ushered by our mom into our stepfather's car. My mom and Frank drove us three hours to Frank's mom's house in another state.

I knew that Frank thought he was above the law and wasn't shocked in the least to see that he didn't think court orders applied to him. I tried not to think about how my dad would feel when he got there to pick us up, and we were not home. I tried not to think about how my dad knew Frank was dangerous and how my dad had told me Frank was what was called a "felon," asking me if he had ever hurt me or touched me. I tried not to think about how my dad would be heartbroken, worried, or even scared that he would never see us again.

We spent Thanksgiving with Frank's mom, Norma. He and my mom helped her cook while my sister and I played outside. Later in my life, I would learn more about Frank's mother. She had married his father twice. Both times, the man had cheated on her, the second time with her best friend. Both times, she was left to raise two little boys alone.

When Frank was eight, she married his stepfather. That man was on antipsychotics and other barbiturates for anger management issues in the 1960s when medicine, especially for mental illness, was new and undeveloped. Frank told me that when he and his brother were still grade school age, they would open their mother's husband's pills and snort the powder inside of them, refill them with flour or sugar so that they didn't get caught, and put them back in the bottle. They were taking 1960s antipsychotics straight through their noses at ages eight and ten.

The more stories Frank told me about his past life when I was an adult, the more his personality, mental instability, and emotional issues would make sense. His stepfather was physically violent with him, his brother, and their mother. One time when Frank was eleven, the man was raging naked in the living room threatening to kill Frank and his family. That night, Frank had to pull a gun on his own stepfather to get him to leave.

Eventually, Norma's third marriage would end, too. Her husband cheated on her with one of his psych ward nurses. Her oldest son, Frank's brother, died very young of a cocaine-induced heart attack in a hotel room with a hooker, even though he had a wife at home. Frank had a long list of felonies and had taken multiple human lives.

Norma could've been paying more attention to her sons. Maybe so many families wouldn't have had to hurt so badly if she had been. She eventually died of dementia in a nursing home alone.

So, on Thanksgiving in 1993, we were court-ordered to spend the day with our dad, but instead, a couple of cowards drove us three hours away from him to spend the day with a stranger.

# CHAPTER NINE

Christmas, if one celebrates the holiday, is one of the most special seasons of the year. When we are children, we look forward to that morning for weeks, and the whole month of December leading up to it is filled with sparkles, songs, and different events designed for kids.

I think when we are children we also get a glimpse into the aspect of Christmas that causes even adults to become childlike. Even children can tell that grown-ups need Christmas by that time of year as something to look forward to and to take their minds off of the fast-approaching winter.

When my mom was a child, Christmas was pitiful. She had the kind of mother who didn't cook or clean on regular days, let alone create holiday joy. Their bathtub was black, my mom told me.

"You didn't even want to get in that thing."

I asked, "So, where did you take a bath?"

"We didn't," she responded without even blinking.

Her facial expression was that of someone who had lived her childhood in fight or flight mode, surviving from moment to moment because no one was paying any attention to her. Her dad would come home long enough to get her mother pregnant again and then be back working on the road.

My mom grew up in the slums of Chicago where she said her mother would clean their house only once a month.

"When the welfare lady would come to check on us, she'd clean with a shovel," she explained. "My mom would shovel the floors, and everything got thrown out the back door."

"Even your toys?" I asked.

"We didn't have any toys," she said with that same blankness on her face, her tired green eyes with no pain left behind them. There was nothing left behind them.

Remarkably, before she met Frank, my mom made Christmas the most magical season for us. Libby loved sparkles. She always chose the sparkliest dress or earrings. She loved our ballet costumes with all the sequins, and she absolutely loved Christmas lights. She would always be the first to comment on the Christmas lights on people's houses when we were driving in December. She loved Christmas music, giving creative presents, helping us write letters to Santa, and always having everything we asked for–and then some–under the tree.

The year before she met Frank, the Christmas when I was five and Ruby was two, my mom's dad came to visit us. She and her dad had always had friendly conversations. I could tell from the memories she'd told me of her childhood that even though he was not at all the father he should have been, she had no ill feelings toward him. I didn't realize it then, but as an adult, I saw that my mom had never even unpacked any of the baggage she carried around with her dad inside.

This particular Christmas, he brought Ruby and me two stuffed animals–Scottish terriers wearing plaid hats and kilts. When we pressed a button on their foot, much to our delight, they barked to the tune of "Jingle Bells." I think those stuffed animals were my most memorable Christmas gift ever because I later found out that Frank had chopped their heads off with an axe.

Frank's hatred of Christmas was not explained to us at all at that age. We were simply told that, this year, we would not be participating in our absolute favorite events of the whole year. Later in my life, he would give me enough lectures about how Christmas is a pagan holiday, how it has nothing to do with Jesus, and how Jesus would disapprove of the holiday, to understand his position and opinion on Christmas.

For me, Christmas is every day of the year. For me, Christmas is love and kindness. I ask Jesus to give me opportunities to be kind and show love, and I look for those opportunities every day. If we believe Jesus is who He says He is, we should be celebrating His birth every day, and if one doesn't believe He is who He says He is, I'm sure one would still choose kindness and love over ugliness and hate too. The speech Bill Murray gives at the end of the movie *Scrooged*–set this book down for a minute and listen to him give that speech–that's it! That is what Christmas is, and who doesn't want that for all of us? So, I believe Jesus would love that aspect of Christmas. He loves joy, kindness, generosity, and hope, and that's what Christmas inspires in our hearts.

The commercialism and the unfortunate way people are over-worked during the Christmas season, paired with the fact that everyone's stressed out because they're trying to spend more money than they have on the holiday, has caused that part of Christmas to become tragic. Jesus would flip over food court tables and sit down and braid a whip, or maybe He would just ask us to remember that the number of gifts under the tree is not at all what Christmas is about.

Christmas can become whatever we want to make of it, and it can be every day.

My sixth Christmas was approaching, and I was dreading it. I didn't know what it would feel like to wake up that morning and treat it like it was just another day, but what was worse was knowing that both of my parents would be sad to see Ruby and me sad on Christmas. In my dad's case, it was gut-wrenching to know that he wouldn't get to see us on Christmas at all.

One cold December day, I asked Ruby if she wanted to run away.

"Yes." She emphatically nodded. "We will have to get our coats on, sneak out the back door, and walk all the way to Dad's house," I explained.

She was agreeable, as I knew she would be. Anything was better than living here around this man. Ruby and I hid our coats under our bunk bed and waited for our mom and her husband to go to bed. We waited for hours, and he was still lecturing.

I couldn't take listening anymore, so we crawled out of bed, got our coats on, and peeked our heads out of our bedroom door. It wasn't going to work tonight. They were both awake and sitting where they could see the front and back doors of the single-wide trailer.

"Go back to bed, girls," my mom said.

It's always been interesting to me that neither of them noticed we were wearing our coats. Did they even realize we were unhappy? I understood then that we would never be able to stay awake long enough to run away in the middle of the night, so all I could do was pray. I prayed for Ruby and me to have a way out.

A day or two later, for seemingly no reason, my mom and her husband drove us in the car down to the barn at the opposite end of Frank's property. He parked his car near a large tree, and they told us to go inside the barn and wait there. Ruby and I always did as we were told no matter how strange the instruction because we feared the punishments would be even stranger and much worse.

We went into the barn, and I watched what Frank and my mom were doing. He was smoking a cigarette beside the tree, and she was sitting in the car. Everything that was happening seemed fishy to me. I thought, *"Either someone is meeting us down here for some reason, he brought us down here to hurt us, or we are hiding. We are hiding!"*

I prayed, *"What do I do, Lord? I don't want my dad to not be able to find us."*

I heard a car driving down the dirt road and felt inspired to run down the driveway toward the car.

*"I don't even care if it's my dad in the car! I don't even care if I get in trouble! I don't care anymore!"*

A police car and my dad's car behind it pulled into the driveway that led to the barn.

My dad jumped out of his car and hugged me. "Do you know what day it is? Do you know what we are going to get to do?" He always crouched down to talk to us at eye level. Ruby had run out of the barn too. "It's Christmas Eve, and you get to spend the night with us and have Christmas tomorrow!" We were hugging him and crying happy tears and also tears of such relief.

My mom and her husband were arguing with the policeman, who was handing them papers and shaking his head. When we were driving to our dad's house, he turned to my stepmom in the passenger seat and said, "If she hadn't run out like that when she did, we might not have known where they were."

I still believe the Holy Spirit moved me.

We spent the next day enthralled in Christmas joy. My dad's wife was amazing at Christmas presents and decorating cookies. They took us to see the Christmas lights and sing songs. We got to see our grandma, Jordan, and Mellissa. Then on Christmas night, our hearts were broken when we had to go back to Frank's house.

CHAPTER TEN

As I reflect on the inattentive parenting of my mom's mother, Mary, and Frank's mother, Norma, I can't help but see why they had difficulties. Mary and Norma were both born in the 1920s, the very decade women were finally recognized as adults and human enough to deserve the right to vote in a country they helped grow, build, shape, and produce for over one hundred and fifty years.

Women born in the 1920s, raising families in the 1940s and 50s, were taught to be wives above all else. We can find examples everywhere throughout history of brilliant women who were educated, warriors, inventors, rich, and in power. But more commonly, unless they were born wealthy or very fortunate, until very recently, women were born to be wives and mothers.

Motherhood was expected to be second nature to all of them. If you had to ask how to be a mother, you were doing it wrong and would sound incompetent, so no one discussed it, and everyone assumed that every woman was simply born knowing how to be a mother. Society focused on teaching little girls how to be good, meek, humble, obedient wives. If you flip through an early American census, you may commonly see the name Obedience as a female name.

Mary's and Norma's mothers would have been completely dependent on their husbands. The lessons Mary and Norma would have learned as children during the Great Depression would not have so much been, "Here is how to love, honor, and keep your husband." More likely, the message would have been, "You need a man to survive!"

By the time the Second World War was over, and Mary and Norma were old enough to start looking for a man to marry, Mary had already been impregnated by a family member and left to raise a baby alone at age sixteen. Norma's adolescence is a part of her life that I'm unfamiliar with, but knowing that she married Frank's unfaithful and abusive dad twice and his stepdad, who was also abusive, my conclusion is that she, too, thought having a husband was more important than health, happiness, and even her own children.

These women were inattentive mothers because they were trying to make childlike men into husbands and fathers. Their focus was husband first, children second, themselves last, and this process never has, and will, never work. A woman and her children should not suffer or be neglected in any way. If the men in their lives, or the men who created them, are not up to the task, they must go! They can go sort themselves out and possibly have a second chance if they have proven themselves to be changed men, but if the man of the house is interfering with the well-being of his family, he doesn't get to stay.

Mary thought she needed my mother's dad. Norma thought she needed her husbands. Would it have been difficult to raise children alone back then? Absolutely, but Mary was already doing it alone anyway, and Norma could have found the time to do it alone, too, if she had put her energy and focus into herself and her children.

However, society had brainwashed them into thinking they could not survive without a husband and that a husband comes first. More-over, these women believed they had to do everything their husbands said, which was why Mary ended up with eight or nine children.

A husband who contributes to his family and treats everyone in the household with kindness and respect should most definitely be treated as a priority by his wife. If a woman has not found that man yet, she should focus on herself. Norma and Mary never once in their entire lives even looked at themselves. Each of them died of dementia, a disease that robs a person of any shred of dignity or sanity they may have once clutched. May we forgive the women who were trapped in that cycle and break it... stomp it.

When Ruby and I came back from Christmas at our dad's house, I feared I would be in trouble for running out of the barn and giving away our hiding place. Frank did not mention it to me, and I assumed that was because he didn't want a six-year-old to call him out for being a coward who was trying to hide from legal documents and court orders. My parents were in a full-blown, 1990s-style custody battle. No matter the evidence of being the safer, more secure, non-felon, cooperative parent, my dad was still a dad trying to get custody of his two very young girls in 1993 when such things were unheard of.

My dad visited me at school for lunch a couple of times a week. That January, Ruby and I were court-ordered to go to his house every other weekend. My mom's husband was compliant when my dad would pick us up and drop us off with a police escort, but when we were at our dad's house, Frank would call and threaten our dad with physical violence if he did not bring us back immediately. My dad recorded these phone conversations on a tape recorder to use in court while my baby sister and I sat wide-eyed on the couch, listening.

As he left the cafeteria after lunch one day, my dad hugged me and said, "Don't forget, you can always write me a letter. I gave Mrs. Phillips stamps and envelopes."

As I was seeing the custody battle unfold, it started to become clear to me how Ruby and I would be able to leave. My dad had to *win* us in a battle. I went home after school that day, took my notebook paper out of my backpack, and began to cry as I wrote. The letter to my dad was really a letter to judges and lawyers I had never and would never meet.

*We hate it here. It is dangerous. He already killed a child. We are scared. We cry every night.*

I remember a tear hitting the sheet of paper, and I circled it.

*These are my tears,* I wrote. *Please let us live with you, Dad.*

The tears I was crying were mixed in three parts. Some of them were out of the pain, frustration, and confusion we had already endured. Some of them were because I felt like I was betraying my mother. It was the first time I had ever done that, and I knew I could not bring her with me. Mostly, I was crying with relief because I knew it was finally almost over.

At least this part of it was almost over. Ruby and I would be safe soon. I could feel it.

The next morning, I handed the letter to Mrs. Phillips. She was more than just my teacher. She had been a family friend of my mom and dad's when they were still married, and she was my older brother's best friend's mom. Mrs. Phillips knew everything that was going on in my life at the time, and she was very helpful, understanding, and kind.

She did not read my letter. She folded it neatly so it would fit in the envelope because I was six and had waded it up and crammed it in, but she did not read it. She put it in the self-addressed envelope my dad had given her and dropped it in the mail for me.

Mrs. Phillips is an angel on Earth.

# CHAPTER ELEVEN

A few days after Mrs. Phillips had mailed my letter, my dad came to have lunch with me at school. "You are a very brave and clever girl. I thought you were going to write to me about puppies or school."

He was happier than I'd seen him in a long time.

"When do we get to come and live with you?" I asked.

I can't remember what my dad's response was, but it wasn't very many days later that Frank and my mom came to my school in the middle of the day to talk with Mrs. Phillips. I had been worried about this possibility, but I was in fight-or-flight mode, so I could not worry too much about what would happen if Mrs. Phillips got in trouble for helping me, and I knew that I had not asked her to do anything wrong or illegal.

I had prayed that she would mail my letter without invading my privacy and reading it first, and I wholeheartedly believed that she was the kind of woman who would do just that. I also knew that if she did read my letter, she was a teacher and would, therefore, have to report any abuse or violence that was occurring in my home, so either way, we would be rescued. I knew that Mrs. Phillips was intelligent and that she'd be able to hold her own when speaking with Frank.

My class was at recess when I saw my mom's husband's truck in the school parking lot. I snuck back into the school without the teachers who were on recess duty noticing and stood quietly in the hallway listening to the conversation between my stepfather and my teacher.

My mom was there, but as usual, when Frank was around, she was silent. My mom's husband was yelling at my teacher that she had no right to interfere in any of their business and that he was going to have her fired.

Mrs. Phillips was clearly shaken, as anyone who has ever had to deal with this man's violence would be. He was never in control of his emotions. He lacked even a drop of empathy, and usually, his argument, because it was based solely on the desires of a narcissist and never on facts or logic, never made any sense. It was one of the first arguments I had ever heard an intelligent person have with him, and Mrs. Phillips was far too professional and far too kind to argue with anything more than, "Sir, I did not read the letter. I simply dropped it in the mailbox."

When Frank could not withdraw terror from Mrs. Phillips, it frustrated him. He got louder and made less sense. When intelligent people would argue with him, they would leave in frustration from the struggle, not with this man but with themselves for having exerted any energy arguing with a man-child.

Mrs. Phillips not only impressed me with being noble enough to mail my letter but also because she held her own against Frank. She could emotionally afford to stand firm. She had backup. This man was not her husband. She did not have to go home with this man. She got to go home to a loving husband and a kind and supportive family. Her co-workers, the school counselor, and everyone else involved would surely back her up, and she had them to turn to if Frank became physically violent.

When this bully came to yell at Mrs. Phillips in the middle of an already stressful workday where she was teaching six-year-olds, my mom just sat there. Mrs. Phillips had been a friend to my mom for over twenty years, much longer than my mom had even known her new husband of a couple of months. Never once did my mom come to her friend's defense, and even at that age, I knew that this was who my mom had become.

*"She will never defend you against him either,"* I told myself.

I went back to recess and saw my mom and her husband drive away in his filthy white Bronco. When my class came back to Mrs. Phillips' classroom, I could tell that she had been crying. The sheer size of the man and his goblin-like features, paired with the evil one could feel radiating from him, would always cause me to cry after he'd berate me, too. I knew that this was what my teacher was feeling.

She did not look at me with any facial expression except for kindness and love. She did not mention the scene to me, and we went on with our day. I believe that God put that woman in my life for all the lessons she taught me in such a short amount of time. She showed me how a true lady and a woman of strength of character would treat people.

Very soon after that day, my mom told me to get off the school bus at the little old neighbor lady's house across the street because no one would be home after school.

"Where are you going?" I asked.

"We have to go to court so we can get custody of you and your sister, so your dad will leave us alone," she replied.

I tried not to think about how shocked my mom would be when that did not happen. There was no doubt in my mind that Ruby and I would soon go live with our dad. I had to make sure she and I were safe and away from Frank, and then I would worry about how to rescue my mom.

When I got to Mrs. Taylor's house, Ruby was already there. Mrs. Taylor was always very kind, but we knew that she loathed and despised Frank. She had lived across the street from him long enough to know that he was despicable. She often asked us if we were all right and would give us lots of snacks, love, and hugs when we were at her house.

When my mom and Frank pulled into Mrs. Taylor's driveway, they did not get out, come in, and thank her for watching us, or exchange pleasantries. He simply honked the horn repeatedly until we realized he wanted us to come out.

I thanked Mrs. Taylor, said goodbye, got my little sister's coat on her, and walked down the icy steps to the car while the most immature of men continued to honk the car horn loudly. We got in the back seat, and my mom was in the front seat, sobbing.

I had never in my life ever even seen my mother cry. I had recently heard her scream, yell, argue, and beg, but I had never heard her cry, and now she was crying with her entire body. Her husband was staring at me through the rearview mirror as though I had just murdered his entire family.

The whole thirty-minute drive to my dad's house, Frank lectured me about the word loyalty and how disloyal I had been to my mother. He said how she was heartbroken and how I had betrayed her. He told me to go into my dad's house, get a dictionary and look up the word, loyalty. When he pulled into my dad's driveway, Frank told us, at three and six years old, to, "Get out!"

Then he peeled out and left. He rushed us so much that when we were stepping out of the car, Ruby tripped and fell and scraped her hands and knees. She was tiny, and she was scared. She was crying and physically hurt. My mom did not get out and kiss us goodbye or brush Ruby off. She didn't walk us to the door or explain what was happening. They pulled up, literally dumped us off, and then left.

I gathered Ruby up, held her hand, walked up the sidewalk and steps, and knocked on our dad's door. He and his wife were surprised to see us. They were celebrating winning in court and were overjoyed to see us, but they were also shocked. They had won custody of us, but we were supposed to spend a couple more nights with our mom, pack our things, have everything explained to us, and then we would hug her goodbye. It was supposed to be a smoother transition, so we were not overly confused.

I sat on the couch and began to laugh hysterically. My dad asked me why I was laughing. I laughed until I had a stitch in my side and was crying. I was laughing because, even though Frank was forty and I was a child, the entire lecture, tantrum, performance, everything that had just been said to me during that car ride, was a grown man throwing a baby fit because he'd lost. He lost, and he wanted to win, and that was the entire issue. It had nothing to do with loyalty.

If he wanted loyalty, he would not have separated a mother from her four children. If he didn't want her to feel heartbroken or betrayed, he wouldn't have separated us from her in the first place. I laughed because I understood that, in the end, men like him always lose because they always have to live with themselves, and we got to escape.

I could tell that my dad was concerned by my reaction, my laughter, so I simply said, "Frank told me to look up the word loyalty in the dictionary."

My dad laughed too. "What an idiot," he said.

We went to the store to buy toothbrushes and new clothes since we had to leave all of our belongings behind, and that was as far as Ruby and I ever got with recuperation or counseling of any sort. No one ever asked us what had happened in those six months that we lived in fear. No one ever asked us how we felt or if we wanted to talk about it. We were just dumped off and ushered into our new lives with nothing but new toothbrushes.

Later, when I was an adult, my mom told me a story about the year she turned nine and went to live with the lady who owned the neighborhood grocery store for a year.

"What?! You have never said anything about this before. Weren't you sad? Didn't you miss your mom?" I asked.

"No, my mom wasn't the type of person you'd miss," she said. "Plus, I got to take a bath every night and have real meals instead of just peanut butter."

My mom's mother couldn't afford the grocery bill, and she'd charged too much, so the solution was that my mom, at nine years old, would live with the owner of the store for a year and work at the store every day after school. Apparently, the owner was a very kind older woman, and she taught my mom how to act like a lady. When it was time to go back, my mom didn't even want to return home.

The first night I spent under my dad's roof knowing that Ruby and I were finally safe was the first night that I was worried that my mom's husband was going to kill her and that I wouldn't be there to stop him, call 911, or help.

Every night for far too many years, I would close my eyes to the anxiety of, "Brace yourself. Tomorrow could be the morning you wake up to the news that he's done it. He could kill her."

Those very real concerns started when I was six. Maybe my mom didn't think that she was the kind of mom worth pining away for because she didn't have a mother that she missed when she was little, but I did.

My mom was worth missing, and she missed so much, too much. Everything.

# CHAPTER TWELVE

When Frank was twelve, the abuse of his stepfather had angered him so much that he ran away from home. After years of anger issues and rebellion in school, sports, and the community, Frank had been in so much trouble that the school counselors and city police officers knew him by name.

They suggested that his mother and her husband have him seen by a psychologist. This was in the 1960s, and even though this boy was doing things like shooting out street lights with a BB gun, poking sleeping hobos in train yards with sticks and almost getting strangled by one, busting out the glass of everyone's gas meter on his block, climbing on and sneaking into neighborhood houses, stealing and drinking booze from liquor and grocery stores, snorting antipsychotics, petty theft, and endless fights with other boys, everyone's diagnoses was that he was "just a very angry boy."

Having listened, in my thirties, to Frank tell me story after story about his life, many of them more than once, it was clear to me that he had been abused, traumatized, at times neglected, and more. When he was twelve, he ran away to his maternal uncle's house where he hid in the barn for weeks stealing food from his aunt and uncle's house at night. He somehow remained unnoticed until one night, he heard his uncle fire a shotgun and yell, "I know there's someone in my barn, and the police are on their way! I have no problem shooting a man! I have killed men before!"

Frank knew this to be true and that his uncle didn't know it was him who was in the barn. Terrified, he didn't move until the police got there and checked the barn with their flashlights and everyone was surprised to find a scared little boy. The next morning, his uncle drove him back to his mother, and she called her ex-husband, Frank's dad, to come and get him.

Frank's real dad was a narcissistic, womanizing swine with anger issues. The next few years of this boy's life proved to be even more dreadful, and now he was causing sorrow in other people's lives. When Frank first got to his dad's house, his dad was living with a woman and her children in a trailer house, and Frank's bedroom was underneath the trailer on some blankets on the dirt.

By the time Frank was sixteen, he was driving vehicles under the influence of narcotics and alcohol. He'd become the county drug dealer. In 1969, he was driving down the highway on "some sort of pills," as he told me. He couldn't remember what the pills were, but he could vividly remember the highway number and the exact part of the two-lane highway he was driving on when he saw his friend driving toward him in the opposite lane.

He flagged his friend down, and they both pulled over. They stood on the shoulder, talking and drinking whiskey for a few minutes, and then they both got back in their cars. His friend pulled away and drove off. Frank decided he was going to pull a U-turn in the middle of the highway and did so without looking, causing a head-on collision between two semi-trucks and trailers. As Frank told me this story, he focused on the details like how the wreck was so loud.

"It was so loud that I didn't know what was happening at first. They both came out of nowhere."

"What happened to your car? Were you hurt?" I asked.

"No, I didn't get hit at all. They both swerved to miss me and hit each other," he said. "There was fire everywhere. I just got out of my car and sat on my hood and watched this big, huge, fire." He described it, emotionless, as though the fire were the focus of the story.

"Did anyone get hurt? Did the drivers make it?" I asked.

"Oh, they all got hurt. The one driver died instantly. He was thrown through the windshield. The other driver was walking around. He had his little boy with him, and at first, he was saying, 'My boy! My boy!' like he was looking for him, but then we both saw him. He was dead, but he was on fire," Frank told me as though he were reading the grocery list.

"His son was on fire, and you watched all of this happen?! How old was the little boy?" I was shaken.

"He was eight or nine," he said.

The story was being shared with me because he was a narcissist who wanted to talk about himself no matter the topic. Today's topic was not the horrendous tragedies he caused or the lives he took. It was not a confession of guilt. The only reason this horrible story was being shared with me was because Frank wanted to brag about how he was the first minor arrested and imprisoned on a drug charge in that county.

This was how I learned so many traumatically sad memories this creature carried around inside of himself.

When I was six, and I was living under a safer roof because I did not have to live with him any longer, I knew that he had killed people before, but I did not know how many or how he had caused their deaths. I didn't have to know the details at that age because I could feel the hatred, anger, and selfishness, paired with narcissism, expertly aged with this man who had never had to pay any real consequences for anything he had ever done.

The ego—I could feel the most evil ego when I was around him. It would take me years to uncover the beasts that fed his ego, but the way he had treated my teacher, my sister, my mother, my brother, my father, and myself was enough to have me praying for my mother's life every night.

# CHAPTER THIRTEEN

After Ruby and I moved in with our dad, we did not see our mom for a long time. I missed her so badly that I cried every night in bed. Ruby experienced much more severe separation anxiety than I did since she was only three and had never spent more than a day or two away from our mom at a time.

Eventually, we were allowed to see our mom on the weekends we asked to go to her house, but we had to forfeit our comfort and safety. I could tell my mom was utterly miserable. She talked about leaving her husband all the time. She told us she hated him and was trying to figure out how she could leave.

The only places my mom was allowed to go were church and the grocery store. Sometimes, she would pick us up on her way to the grocery store and take us with her so she could see us for a few minutes and then take us home because she wanted to see us, but she didn't want to make us be around her husband.

Every time Ruby and I would go anywhere with anyone, we would look for our mom. "Maybe we'll see her car, or maybe she'll be at the grocery store too," we would think, looking out the window and around every aisle. My heart never let go of the pain of her absence, and my brain had trained itself to search for her.

When I was in my thirties, Frank told me a story about the first few weeks we left and went to live with our dad. I had vaguely heard part of this story when it had happened when I was six, but to hear it in its entirety from someone who had been there was completely different.

"She has always been goofy, you know." He wanted me to agree, but my face remained stoic. "She was really an idiot when we first got married. Did I tell you about the first time she got the law called on me?" He was asking me, but I didn't answer. "She was all in a dither over something," he said.

"*Maybe it's that her babies had been taken away from her,*" I thought, but I didn't suggest it. One doesn't suggest things aloud to a crazy person.

"And she was bound and determined to leave," he went on. "And you know, she was never my type. I always thought that. Even before we got married, I thought she wasn't my type because she was always arguing with everything I told her to do or not to do," he explained.

I thought, "*She wasn't your type because she wanted free will, and you wanted to control her.*" But I sat silently, listening to his story.

"She just would not listen," he continued. "She didn't realize yet how much stronger I was than her, and I was used to…. If I said something to a woman, that was it. That was how it was, no ifs, ands, or buts about it. So, she's telling me she's going to leave, and I'm chuckling and laughing at her, which only made her madder, and I'm saying, "You're not gonna leave. You're not gonna leave." And she picked up the car keys and started to walk out the door. So, I just stood up, grabbed ahold of her hair like this–"

He demonstrated on himself by pulling on the back of his own head. "And I just body slammed her, hard too. Knocked the wind out of her. You should've seen her face. It was like, 'Okay, I'm scared now. This guy's not messing around.' I had to get rough with your mom at times."

He was telling me this expecting me to be on his side. He was telling me this so that I would know that it was all right for him to treat my mom this way because as he had said thousands of times before, "Men are the heads of the household, and women don't need an opinion or a say. Everything the man says is the way it should be."

The story was actually about a man who had physically abused his emotionally traumatized wife, who was mentally in fight-or-flight mode. She was exhausted, missing her children, scared, and desperate, and so with his six-foot-five-inch frame looming over her five foot nothing, unsuspecting body, he grabbed her by the back of the head and body slammed her to the floor.

My mom waited until the middle of the night when Frank was asleep to call 911. When the police got to their house, they cuffed him and took him to jail for the night. The next day, she called, dropped the charges, and picked him up from jail. Once again, his narcissism was fed a healthy dose of "rules don't apply to me."

As for me, I would watch her try to run the clock out on this game for twenty-eight years and lose everything.

# CHAPTER FOURTEEN

When I was a kid, my dad kept us busy and out of trouble by involving us in every sport our school offered. He was our basketball coach from the time we were big enough to shoot the ball, and by the time I was nine, I was obsessed with the sport. Although I was never the quickest, tallest, or best, I had a pretty good jump shot, and I loved the game so much that I wanted to be good.

More than anything, I benefited from the bond my dad and I shared with basketball. He took me to basketball camps every summer, and when I was twelve, he drove me to my mom's dad's house in Indiana so I could attend the Indiana State University basketball camp. That was the first and only time I ever really got to talk with my maternal grandfather.

Since we had never really spoken before, I took that opportunity to ask him questions about my mom's childhood. I knew she had a mother who seemed to be neglectful, and her dad was almost never home, that they were on welfare, that there were eight or nine kids in the home, but that was basically all I knew. So I asked Grandpa Jake, "What was my mom like as a little girl?"

He told me when she was little, everyone had always called my mom Sissy until they moved to a small town in Iowa, and that was when people started to call her Libby. "I still call her Sissy, though," he continued. "She was always very scrappy and smart. She didn't let anyone mess with her, even when she was small, but back then, when your mom was little, I was a butthead. I was a turkey. I was never home. I was always out working and drank my money or threw it away on junk. There was a night when your mom was little, and you know, she was raised in Chicago, right? And we was in a bad part of town in Chicago. I shouldn't have been there. No one should have been there. I was partying with some bad guys. It was about two or three o'clock in the morning. I was driving, getting out of that terrible neighborhood, when I stopped at a stop sign and looked over, and there standing on the corner was your mom and Aunt Cathy. They couldn't have been more than… oh, your mom was probably nine or ten, and your aunt was probably seven or eight. They were out there at night in the freezing cold, bare feet, walking around in a part of town where a grown man should not have been."

"What happened? Why were they there?" I asked.

"They had just snuck out. Little kids, you know, and their mother was never paying attention to them, and I was never home, you know. So, I picked them up in my car and took them home to their mother, threatening to beat them within an inch of their lives if they ever left the house at night or went to that part of town again.

"That was when I decided to change my life. I got a good job, and it took me a year or two, but I got a house in Iowa and divorced your grandma. I met my wife, Cheryl, and married her, and then I came back for your mom and Cathy, and let's see, I took Jimmy, John, and Timmy with me. That's when we moved to Iowa, but that night, when I saw your mom and your aunt Cathy out there on the street, that was when I decided to come home and be a dad."

Grandpa's story was over, but it would remain with me forever. I couldn't imagine being the kind of mother my grandmother was or the kind of father my grandpa was, but I could also feel the despair they must have felt as very young parents with so many children and so many obstacles. People made so many mistakes because, back then, they did not know how to cope. I could relate.

When my grandpa bought a house and moved his new wife and half of his children to Iowa, my mom was thirteen. Her life seemed to improve, but she still had issues. Her stepmother did not like her and spent most of their money on herself and her own children.

My mom and Aunt Cathy had five dresses each, one for each day of the school week, and I know that bothered my mom. My mom loved fashion and clothes. Shopping was one of her favorite things to do when she was Libby. So, as a young teenager, not having any money for outfits, dresses for dances, or even just something new to wear, it was a disappointment for her. But at least she was no longer being neglected. She had food to eat, and someone was paying enough attention to her that she was in bed at night and at school every day.

In high school, my mom began to excel. It was clear that she was gifted and intelligent. She was taking advanced classes, getting A's, and was in National Honors Society. By the time she was a senior, she had a full ride scholarship to Kansas City Missouri University and planned to be a doctor.

How proud of her I am any time I think about this great ambitious feat! Here was a kid who, eight years prior, had been running barefoot through the Chicago slums in the middle of the night by herself. Here was a kid who couldn't take a bath or eat a hot meal for lack of a mother to provide such necessities, and she clawed her way out of that putrescence and was heading to college. A girl, with a full ride scholarship in 1973? A dirt poor kid in 1973 with a full ride scholarship? Can we all stop here and take a moment to marvel at a that? Every time I look at her college ID, I can't help but wonder who she could have been, who she could have become, if someone, somewhere along the way had taught her to love herself.

## CHAPTER FIFTEEN

The verbal and physical abuse my mom's husband inflicted on her became worse and worse the more she fought back. About a month after Ruby and I had moved into our dad's house, Dad asked us if we wanted to go see our mom at our old house, the house we had lived in before she had met Frank.

I was instantly confused, and a fire began to burn in my stomach. I had just turned seven, and that fire in my gut had been present a few times before, but never as fiercely as when I thought about our lives in that house with my mom when she was still Libby. I must have zoned out and not responded because my dad began to explain that my mom had left Frank and was back in "the green house," as we all had always called it.

My parents bought that house together when I was four. We lived there for about a year and a half before my parents got divorced and then another year and a half before moving in with Frank. Most of my serene childhood memories take place in the green house, and now, I was being told that my mom was there, and Ruby and I were going to spend the weekend with her.

I should've been elated. I should've jumped up and down with glee, but even at seven, I had a fire in my gut because I knew that nothing any adults had ever told us was the whole deal or the real deal.

When we got to the green house, it was nearly empty. Our furniture and belongings were either in a storage unit or at Frank's house. It was quiet and dark. My mom was still my mom, but she was no longer herself. Her spirit had become broken with body slams, slaps in the face, bruises on her biceps, and lectures into the night about how Libbys were to become Elizabeths if they didn't want to burn in Hell.

We went out to the backyard where I had not played in nine months. My eagle's nest that my dad had built me used to be my fort, and now it was painful even to glance at it. My mom pushed Ruby in the swing while I stood next to her and asked a million questions.

"So can we come back and live with you here?" I asked first.

"I already sold this house. Some other people are moving into it soon," she replied.

"So then, when can we live with you? Where can we live with you? We can live with you somewhere else, anywhere else. Where are we going to live?" I was scared of the answers, and in my heart, I knew them already.

"I don't know, Amelia. Let's just take it one day at a time," she said.

"Are you going back to him?" I asked. I wanted to ask why she didn't love us anymore, but I knew this was just as difficult for her as it was for me.

That night we watched *The Last of the Mohicans* and *Curly Sue* on the couch in the green house with our mom, and I felt like she was a different person. Therefore, I felt like I was a different person. Most of my heart still wanted to rescue her. I was stubborn, so I never gave up trying, but a tiny bit of my heart knew she was already gone.

The utter confusion and emotional roller coaster that my parents both put Ruby and me through with that trip back to the green house was incredibly irresponsible. Neither of them should have thought that was acceptable. For one thing, The Angry Goblin knew where the house was located and that my mom was there, and for another, it blew our hearts into smithereens.

## CHAPTER SIXTEEN

After our weekend at the green house with our mom, the next time we saw her, she was back with her husband. We had to go to their house to see her and have dinner with them. The physical abuse, and the fact that my mom was clearly disturbed enough by her husband to have already run away from him once, had caused my dad to insist that we not spend the night with them, so we went for dinner, and then our mom was to bring us back to our dad. Mom would pick us up without her husband and drive us home without him so we could at least have an hour to speak freely.

Usually, on the way to their house, she would re-explain all of the rules we already knew—no giggling, no talking about basketball because girls shouldn't play sports, no talking about dance class or dancing of any kind. If we had earrings in our ears, we took them out and put them in our pockets, and she kept nail polish remover and cotton balls in the armrest of her car so I could take my polish off on the way. Then she would give us Oreos as a reward for censoring ourselves for the control freak.

The weekend following the weekend at the green house, I could tell my mom had been crying. She looked more depressed every time I saw her.

"What's the matter?" I asked with a lump in my throat, afraid of the answer. I was seven going on thirty now, and this was the first time my mom would use me as her therapist.

"He beats me, Amelia." She was pissed—not sad, but furious.

"What do you mean? What does he do?" I was asking these questions for so many reasons… so I could put together a portfolio, so I would know how to rescue her, so I would know how to protect myself or anyone else from him, so I could learn exactly who not to grow up and marry, so every cell in my body could stop buzzing with rage.

"He gets drunk. He drinks too much." My mom was talking, and I was looking at the floorboard of her car where two jugs of burgundy wine sat. She always stopped at the grocery store and got him two gallons before picking us up.

*Why feed a dragon?* I thought, but I didn't ask because one doesn't ask for answers about a crazy person.

"He pushed me into the shower and started slapping my face," she said.

"What did you do?" I asked.

"I went to the barn and stayed down there all night," she said.

How miserable it had to have been to live with such an incredibly cruel man. When I was an adult, and my mother got sick, I had to allow this man access to me in order to help her. This was when he told me all the stories from his perspective. He told me a story that took place around the same time he was knocking her into the shower and slapping her face. This story was about a pecan log.

"Your mom has always been goofy." All of his stories about my mom started the same way—an insult, a shot to her character, so everything he did to her in the story was justified. "She was never right in the head." He didn't mean goofy like silly or funny. When he called her goofy, he meant she was stupid.

"It was right after you and your sister went to live with your dad. We hadn't been married for a year yet. She had lied to me, no doubt, one-hundred-percent lied, and I don't do that lyin' crap. If there's anything I hate, it's a liar. So I had one of those pecan log things, you know, the candy bar? I really like those, so any time I see them, I buy two or three. So I had eaten one and put the other two in the cabinet. Then a day or two later, I remembered I still had two of those pecan logs up in the cabinet, so I go to get them and there's only one left. So I think well, okay, she must like them too, so I ask her if she ate one, and she said no, and I knew she had to have been lyin' 'cos we was the only two people in the house. So I tell her, 'It's okay if you ate it, sweetheart. Just, did you eat the pecan log?' And she still said no. By this point, I'm beginning to lose my temper. I'm getting mad because I won't have no woman lyin' to me. So we talk about it all afternoon, and that goofy woman would still not admit, no matter what, to eating that pecan log. So you know what I did?" He was asking me although I rarely ever responded to him when he was telling me stories about belittling or abusing my mother.

"You'd be proud of me," he said. "I didn't smack her around like I wanted to. I picked up the phone and I called our pastor and asked him to come over."

This was so stupid that I had to break my rule and respond. "You called your pastor over a pecan log?" I asked.

"Well no." He was confused. "It was over the lying," he said.

"Your pastor actually came over? About lying about eating a pecan log?" I asked.

As you can imagine, the rest of his story was one of a man and his pastor berating a woman who was being emotionally, mentally, and physically terrorized. She needed help, and they brought her humiliation and more stress. Why lie about eating a snack? This woman had struggled with body issues and self-esteem her entire life. Her stepmother had called her fat every day from ages thirteen to eighteen, and in high school, she was a size eight. She did not allow herself to ever eat anything guilt-free in her entire life. Everything she'd put in her mouth was accompanied by self-deprivation.

When she was eighteen and enrolled at KCMU, she came home to visit her family and my dad. A few weeks later, she went back to Kansas City and found out she was pregnant. My mom had to quit school and move in with my dad and his parents. My dad was only sixteen and still had two years of high school left, but they got married anyway.

A few months later, my brother was born, and my parents moved into a house that they rented from my dad's parents. My mom and dad had my brother and sister and were married for five years. One of the struggles she had in that marriage was that my dad complained often about my mom's weight. He was a musician who played in bars. It was the late 1970s when very, very, thin was 'in,' not just for women, but for men as well. My dad made sure he stayed very thin at the time with long hair, bell bottoms, and a Fender Telecaster.

He, however, had not given birth to two kids in four years. My mom was naturally curvy, and for her to be as thin as 1977 was demanding required a very small caloric intake. Her body needed fuel to run around chasing two toddlers and working a full-time job.

After five years, my dad left her for bars, clubs, and another woman. My parents married each other again years later, and once again, my mom, who even from childhood had never had a good relationship with food, struggled with her body image. My dad, again, would say hurtful things to her about being overweight, which was never true at any point in her life.

Although it was not the reason for their divorce, it certainly did not help that she never received any help for her food issues. Never in her life would she have a chance to stop, reflect on herself, and look at her own issues. She had grown up in a house where there was no food. She moved to a house where she was told she was eating too much and was called fat by her stepmom. She went through two marriages where her weight was an issue for both her and the man, and now she was married a third time to someone who, from the very first conversation they had about getting married, had told her she did not have the body type he preferred.

At this time, in her mid-forties, after four babies and years of stress, my mom was a size twelve, and from the beginning, Frank told her that he preferred very, very thin women and that she was not his type physically. He married her anyway, let her children be taken away from her, and then began to beat the body he loathed so much.

She wasn't lying about a snack. She was in fight-or-flight mode about everything and everyone, all of the time.

Ruby, Mom, and I arrived for dinner after she'd told us her husband had been beating her. We helped her set the table anyway. She checked the baked chicken she'd put in the oven before leaving to pick us up and realized it had not been set high enough to cook and that it was still raw. Her facial expression instantly changed to fear.

"Oh shoot," she said. "Now he's going to be pissed when he gets in the house."

She put the chicken back in the oven and turned the heat up to higher than normal, hoping it would cook faster before he came inside from training dogs. All too soon, he was inside demanding dinner. He prayed to Jesus and then made his plate.

"What is this?" he asked her, already losing his temper.

*"Is he really going to do this in front of us?"* I thought. *"Is he really going to throw a baby fit in front of us about the way his dinner is cooked, in front of children who know better than to act that way?"*

"This is chicken that's burnt on the outside but still bloody and raw on the inside?" he asked her as though she was the scum of the Earth, never mind the fact that, because of him, she had to drive an hour to pick up her own children in the middle of making his dinner, and that shortly after him throwing a temper tantrum about the dinner, she'd have to clean up the kitchen and drive her children home.

He continued to belittle her, throwing his plate in the sink completely full of food. Ruby and I sat silently eating the mashed potatoes, homemade biscuits, and salad on our plates. My mom sat next to me, tears streaming down her cheeks. She wore the face of someone who was trying to hold it all together but just could not catch a break. My stepfather sat in the next room, continuing to gripe about how women should be good cooks and how it did not take a rocket scientist to bake chicken.

At seven years old, listening to this man who was always quoting scripture, I wanted to stand up. I had to force myself to stay seated. I had to choke on my words. I wanted to get up, hand him his Bible, and ask Frank to turn to the passage where it says, "Husbands, belittle your wives. Mock them in front of their young, impressionable children. Teach the children not only how to lose their temper over something as silly as chicken, but teach them to mock and belittle. Simultaneously, teach them how to accept a husband who has no control over himself, mocks, and belittles."

But I knew better than to interrupt crazy, so we listened to his fit about chicken, and then twenty years later, I listened to him ask me why someone would lie about a pecan log.

# CHAPTER SEVENTEEN

Before my mom and dad got divorced, when Ruby was a baby, my mom opened a daycare so she could stay home with us. She was a very dedicated mother. Up until she met her new husband, Ruby and I had never been away from our mom. She took us everywhere with her except for aerobics and softball, and when she went to those two places, Ruby cried the entire time Mom was gone no matter who was watching us.

The trauma of having our mother ripped away from us at only three years old paired with the terror we had endured at the hand of our stepfather had caused Ruby to go backward, reverting to past behaviors she had already outgrown. At three, she was finally starting to stop crying every time Mom was out of her sight, and now that we had gone through all that we had, Ruby cried all the time. This confused and frustrated all of the adults around us, and she was in trouble for many years for being unable to control her emotions. Due to the stress of being in trouble all the time, the enormous stress of being around Frank, and then being separated from our mom, Ruby's body developed a health issue.

Our dad and stepmother took Ruby to many different doctors who had many suggestions but no real answers. She needed patience, kindness, love, comfort, time, and her mother back. She received nothing but a spoonful of this and a spoonful of that, poking and prodding and being made to feel unacceptable.

I was now seven, and she was now four. We were expected to act like the other children, the ones who went home to hugs from their mothers. We simply could not act like we were not hurting. We were too young.

Ruby's story is her own, and it's not my place to tell it. She is now the most dedicated, strong, and wonderfully intuitive mother I have ever seen. She inspires me every day to mother my own children better with the patience and love she shows her own kids. Indescribably, and with only the help of the mothers of our childhood friends to guide us, we have both become the mothers we never had growing up.

As a kid, every holiday, every year, I was in trouble. Every family vacation we went on and every special family occasion, I spent either scowling and being mocked for it or scowling and my dad reprimanding and punishing me. In my childhood, this was all subconscious. I did not realize at the time that I was acting out, that I was scowling or frowning, that I was saying angry or derogatory things on our family outings. I just knew that I wanted to have fun but that I couldn't. I knew that I wanted to have a wonderful Christmas or trip to the zoo and that I would start out excited, but before I knew it, I was in time out or sitting in the car crying with one parent while the others went into the gift shop with the other parent.

No one ever asked me, "Do you miss your mom?" Not on a regular day. Not on a holiday. Not on a special day. There were never any questions. The adults in my life assumed that I was just a crabby child with selfish tendencies and that I wanted to ruin everyone's fun.

As a mother, looking back, I realize now that I deeply missed my mom on special days and at special places. I wanted her to see me open my gifts. She was supposed to be at the zoo, too, so I could look at her reaction to the baby kangaroo. I desperately needed her to see me make a layup. I needed her to hear me play trumpet and drums. I needed her to be there at award ceremonies. I needed her to hear me sing the National Anthem and see me serve all fifteen points at my junior varsity volleyball game, but she was not there, and therefore, I was not fully there.

The part of me that missed her had to turn into something. It was energy. It was love that turned into anger.

*I'm pining for my mother*
   *Not acting out or pouting*
   *Sour for reasons I do not see*
   *I'm just little, and I miss her*
   *Especially on days like today*
   *Where there are cannons to pose for photos near*
   *I turn around, and she's not there*
   *She's not in the photos, so I throw a fit*
   *But I don't know that yet*
   *Thinking I was feeling sorry for myself*
   *Red and green lights*
   *Wrapping paper, some of hers, no less*
   *How could anyone miss that I was such a mess?*
   *Mistaken for disobedience, love, with nowhere to go*

At Christmastime, my mom would send us presents. She would buy them on days she went to the grocery and department store and then leave them in different places so we could have them at Christmas. She left some with our grandma and some with our dad. She had to sneak around to buy us anything, hide everything, and tear up every receipt. Not only did our mom miss everything, and Ruby and I had to carry her absence like a ball and chain, but we also had to worry about her.

She was still not safe.

When I was eight, my mom ran away from Frank and spent a few weeks in Indiana at her dad's house. This time, her departure was planned. She had found out that she was eight weeks pregnant, and her husband was still being violent with her.

One of the weekends leading up to her leaving, she had picked Ruby and me up to take us with her to the grocery store, and there was a green bruise on her cheekbone. I had stopped asking about her bruises, and Ruby and I had stopped going to her house for dinner. By now, she, too, was insistent that we be kept away from her husband.

At around eight weeks pregnant, she ran away to her dad's house. I assume she wanted to keep her baby and did not want any violence to disrupt her pregnancy. Unfortunately, every time her husband went looking for her, she was in obvious places. Even more unfortunately, every time he found her, she let him come in, sit down, and talk to her. He would find her and be in a calm state of mind, serene. He never yelled at her when he would find her hiding spots.

My mom's husband had been a salesman for most of his life, and being so erratic, selfish, and rude by nature, he spent his life not changing those qualities about himself but masking them, selling himself and his actions. Every time he would find her, he would convince her that she was special. He would convince her that she was the one who had tamed the dragon. She was the magnificent one who had calmed the storm. He spoke of promises of change that had already taken place and growth that was inspired by love that was yet to come. He would complement her, which was something new she'd never heard in her entire life. The endorphins and false sense of security would bring her back. Trauma-bonded to him, and terrified of raising another baby alone, she took his hand. He took her suitcase, and they went back to Iowa.

Four weeks later, she was hiding out in the barn after he had been beating her, and she began to bleed. Now the number of children he had taken from her was up to five.

# CHAPTER EIGHTEEN

Nina met Frank in 1971 when she was thirteen, and he was eighteen. She was from a very large, devout Catholic family, and he had just spent the last two years in prison for a car accident he had caused while under the influence of narcotics and alcohol resulting in the death of a man and a child.

Nina's mother forbade her to be around Frank at first, but after she had snuck out too many times, her mother took her to buy birth control instead. This always perplexed me a bit because, as I understood it, especially back then, Catholicism was anti-birth control, but the way Frank told it, her mother was just sick of dealing with Nina. Frank Hudson did not respect boundaries or listen to people, so Nina's mother gave up and let her child go.

For years, Nina traveled around with Frank from state to state as he sold drugs. When she was fourteen, he took her to South Dakota where he was incarcerated for a few months, so she went back home to Nebraska to her mother. When he was in prison or jail, Nina would call and find him wherever he was when he was released. She did everything he said, no matter how risky. He would have her knock on people's doors so she could ask to use their restrooms, and then she would raid their medicine cabinets for drugs he could either use or sell. He would party incessantly and often leave Nina at random people's houses. He was too high to know who he was with or where he would end up.

Frank described Nina as short and small, not even weighing a hundred pounds. She never ate anything, and she didn't do drugs or drink with him. She just followed him around and did everything he said. At one point, they found themselves in Florida living in a bungalow with part of a Mexican drug cartel. The boss's girlfriend would walk around completely nude and out of her mind stoned all day and night. She would often do outrageous things. There was a very large glass window, and the nude woman walked over to it and started slamming the back of her forearm into it, causing the glass to break and her arm to bleed.

The men in the house thought Frank had hurt her, and guns were pulled. The chaos caused the neighbors to call the police, and when they showed up, the police were more concerned about the drug cartel and didn't bother with Frank or Nina and let them go. The danger he put Nina in was insurmountable. She was a child. She must have been terrified.

For years, Nina would hitchhike back to her parents' house when Frank would abandon her either for prison or a bigger, better, party. He put her in danger. She did not have her nutritional or hygienic needs met. She did not have a home or a stable life. They were nomadic hippies with no purpose, and yet, she followed him and found him again and again. He even forced her to marry him so authorities would stop asking her if he had abducted her. Every time he would get arrested or go party with strangers, she searched for him until she found him, and they would meet back up hundreds of times.

When she was seventeen, she found out she was pregnant. When she told him, he seemed happy, but he did not stop doing drugs, losing his temper, getting into bar fights, or running around. Nina asked Frank how they could bring a baby into a life like theirs. He had no plan but said it would be fine. He seemed to know even less about babies than she did.

The baby was premature. Nina went into labor eight weeks early and had a brutal labor and delivery, considering she was such a small, malnourished child--barely a woman. They had been on their way to Iowa to see Frank's dad and had only made it to a city about four hours away when she went into labor.

She had her baby, and he was so small and underdeveloped, he needed to remain in the hospital for the first twelve weeks of his life. Frank decided that he and Nina should go ahead and go to his dad's house, four hours away, and leave their baby at the hospital. He insisted the baby would be fine. He never let her go visit her baby even once in three months. Nina was not allowed to call long distance and ask about the baby either, so she was left to wonder and worry.

Finally, the hospital called to tell Frank and Nina they could come and pick up their baby. Frank did try to live his hippie, druggie life-style now that he had the baby. Nina could not nurse her son because she had been away from him for so long, so they gave their baby formula and left him with this person and then that person. Families they had just met would watch their baby while Frank partied, and Nina was forced to go along.

The full-grown baby needed her attention more.

Still trying to live the nomadic lifestyle and go wherever he wanted, Frank decided they'd move to Phoenix, Arizona, when their baby was two. On their way to Arizona, Frank was drinking whiskey while driving, and he wrecked their truck, knocking Nina and the baby around, and injuring her as she tried to protect her son. There was glass in her hair, arm, and face. She rode the rest of the way shielding her toddler from the wind blowing through the broken window.

A thirteen, fourteen, or even seventeen-year-old girl having sex with a grown man who is completely in control of every single move she made and every thought she had–it was disturbing. Horrendous. Listening to Frank tell me stories about his time with Nina would always make me physically ill. I would watch myself leave my body in order to strangle him and claw his eyes out. So many people have asked me, "How did no one kill this man early in his life?"

In Arizona, when Nina's baby was two, he liked to play outside with their kitten. She would follow him around watching him toddle and carry the cat.

"Come inside. Mommy needs to start dinner, then we'll come back outside and play with the kitty." Nina started to pick up the boy.

"He'll be all right out here," Frank said, and Nina knew better than to argue and better than to not start dinner and have it ready when he was done fixing his motorcycle.

Nina ran into the house and put something in the oven, and that was all the time it took for Frank to forget he was supposed to be watching his son. He needed a part from the auto parts store for his bike, so he jumped in the truck and backed out. He never checked to see where his baby was, and he backed over him with his truck, pulled forward off his child, and yelled Nina's name.

Nina sat in truck with the broken window on the way to the hospital, holding her lifeless child whose ears were pouring blood.

After the death of their son, Nina tried to stay loyal to Frank, who moved to Las Vegas, Nevada. They tried to make it work, but Nina ended up going home to her mother. Nina was robbed of her childhood and her motherhood all by the same man.

Years later, Frank tried to reach out to Nina and heard she had developed an alcohol dependency, and eventually, committed suicide.

CHAPTER NINETEEN

After my mom's miscarriage, we did not see or even hear from her for months. She was undoubtedly exhausted, physically, mentally, and emotionally drained from the toll of losing five children. My older brother was a grown man by this time. He was twenty, so he was not a child, but he was her child. Their relationship would never be the same as before she met her husband.

My older sister was finishing high school, motherless. Both of my older siblings had to finish raising themselves because a man had stepped between them and their mother. My mom then lost her two tiny girls and then a baby—the tremendous guilt she must have felt, the tragically heavy loss she must have spent so much energy stifling. She was busy trying to find a way out, and Jordan, Mellissa, Ruby, and I were busy trying to move on without her. We all had to choke down that we had lost her to a monster. What hold he had over her was still so mysterious to all of us.

Before I had even seen my mom again, my dad was asking me a new question. I was nine, and he was asking me if I had ever heard of a women's shelter or if I knew what the word "battered" meant. Having watched too much *Law and Order*, putting together contextual clues, and associating my mom with domestic violence every time I thought about her, I asked, "Is she in a battered women's shelter?"

My dad always looked dismayed when I gave him adult responses at my age, but I had already lived what felt like thousands of adult lives.

"She was in one, yes. But she's back with him now," my dad said.

I wondered why he had even told me at all. Why tell me she had to flee in terror having only strangers to ask for help, especially if she was already back with her abuser? Somehow, I knew it was my dad's first time dealing with insanely messed up circumstances as well, and that in these instances, he had no idea how to parent his children through the turbulence of their mother's horrible choices.

A few months later, when I saw my mom again, I was able to ask her about it myself. She had reverted back to picking us up before she went shopping and dropping us off again before she went back home so we did not have to see her husband. Having to sneak around to see our own mother was another mysterious feeling with which Ruby and I would have to contend. It was shame mixed with jealousy, for Mom was clearly choosing him if we were the ones being hidden. The shame was questionable, for we were children who were simply missing their mother, and yet, we knew that we were supposed to hide our relationship with her, and that felt like shame.

Mixed together, it all felt like confusion and pain.

She would tell us to watch for his Bronco just in case he had decided to come to town, too. She would search every parking lot before getting out of her car to make sure he was not there. Our mom would tell us that if he were to ever stumble upon us at the store, we were to tell him that we were there with our stepmom and had just bumped into our mom and asked if we could walk around with her.

"What if that actually happens? How will we get home if he wants to follow you home?" I asked, and she never gave me an answer. Those were among the things I had to wonder and worry about. I should've been worrying and wondering about multiplication tables and basketball practice, but I was looking over my shoulder making sure the big bad wolf, as my mom referred to him, was not there.

I fell behind in certain areas academically and had more trouble than I should have learning basic, everyday things because my whole body was stressed and preoccupied with my mom and her situation. I was robbed of my childhood in infinite aspects, and I can never have any of that tranquility or self-worth back. The peace and self-value that one cultivates in childhood when one is fed beautiful things like security, safety, love, kindness, accolades, and patience can never be replaced. We can grow up and focus on putting those things into place in our hearts, but it is never the same as when we are given them without a price, as children.

"Did you have to go to a battered women's shelter?" I asked in the car on the way to the store.

"Yes." She was brief.

"What was it like? Did they help you? Why did you go back to him?" I wanted to know the real reasons, but the part of her that told the truth to anyone, including herself, had long ago deserted her.

"They didn't help me. I slept on a cot in a room with a whole bunch of other women. I stayed for two weeks, but I couldn't go back to my dad's, and I didn't have anywhere else to go." She almost seemed to make sense, but I knew that she used to be the type of person who, when she really wanted something, she would get it, make it, do it, become it, if she had to. I was still missing something. Either she wanted to stay with him, or she had completely changed.

A few months later, we were riding to the store again when she told me about her second miscarriage. This time she had driven herself to the doctor in tremendous pain. She rarely asked for help or even acknowledged physical pain, and she had to fight with Frank, to plead and beg to go to the doctor.

The doctor told her she was simply getting older and that at her age of forty-one, if she wasn't bleeding, she was fine, but to expect some discomfort. On her way back out to the waiting area to leave, she passed out. The doctor's staff took her to a bed to lie down, and she was having an incredibly intense miscarriage. Child number six, ripped out of her heart by this man.

After this story, I asked, "Did you have this miscarriage because he was hitting you again?"

"No. This time it was just because I'm old," she said.

"Why wouldn't he just drive his wife to the doctor if she was in that much pain?" I asked her. Sometimes I liked to word things as though we were not talking about my mom. I thought she might see the situation as though we were talking about someone else, to show her how distorted her view was. I had learned that "trick" from episodes of *Oprah*, which I would devour every day after school, especially if the episode was about domestic violence.

"He doesn't believe in doctors. Doctors are evil, Amelia," she explained. When she would call something evil, I knew that she didn't agree that it was evil. The way she said it was in a mocking tone, mocking the big bad wolf.

"He thinks doctors are evil too?" I asked. It was exhausting keeping up with all the things her new life had outlawed. "What happens if you get pregnant and go through a whole pregnancy? How will you have a baby without a doctor?" I asked, hoping I would never have to find out.

A baby was the last thing these two people needed.

# CHAPTER TWENTY

Another time, that same year, when I was nine, my mom had run away to her sister's house in Kansas City. My dad had told me she was there, and in my mind, it changed nothing about anyone's lives. I was not hopeful that she would allow Aunt Cathy and Uncle Mark to help her start a new life. Knowing she was there could not even bring me the peace of mind that she was at least temporarily safe. In my mind, when she ran away, she was in even more danger because Frank was a child who was losing a game.

Years later, I would watch movies like *Enough* and *Sleeping with the Enemy* and read books such as Louisa May Alcott's *A Long and Fatal Love Chase*, never having to finish the film or the text to know these stories by heart. "Crazed man thinks of woman as property and is mad that she has the audacity to leave." Someone always gets hurt, usually, fatally.

When I was in my thirties, Frank would tell me about the time my mom ran away to Aunt Cathy's from his perspective. His version was to prove to me that God had His hand on their marriage all along and that they were meant to be together. His version goes, "Your mom had run off again. She was always running off. You know what it was about this time? A car," he began.

My eyes stung. No matter how many years it had been, I still lived in fury, and it manifested in my eyeballs first. "What do you mean a car?!" My stomach could not believe that my mouth wanted confirmation of the atrocity he was about to return.

"She had been wanting a different car, a new car. So she ran away again." He really believed this to be true. To chalk up all of our agony, all of our fear, all of our longing, missing, wanting to be a family again and all of our mother's emotional turmoil, to wanting a car. All to protect his fragile ego from the truth, the truth that he was a putrid person who deserved to rot alone.

He was still talking.

"So, I got my buddy Gary Williams… do you remember him?"

I nodded. He was referring to his friend who was every bit of six foot six and 350 pounds. Together, the pair would've intimidated anyone and everyone.

"I got ol' Gary Williams to come out to the house. We were wondering where your mom could be, and all the sudden he said, "Didn't you say she had a sister down in Kansas City?" So we looked up your Aunt Cathy in the phone book and wouldn't you know it? We drove right smack to her house, and there was your mom's car sitting right out in front. God sent me straight to her. Isn't that a miracle?"

I could not answer that question without violence, so I let him finish his story. "So ol' Gary Williams and I go up to their door and knock, and one of your cousins, a little girl answered it and said, 'Aunt Libby, there are two huge men on the porch.' Ha, ha, so then here comes your mom. She musta know'd it was me. So, we went in and sat down on the couch and talked for a few minutes, and your mom agreed to come back if I got her a new car. Of all the silly things to run away to Kansas City about. Ha ha."

My boundaries didn't exist for Frank. His abundant stupidity and ability to alter reality until it fit his narrative was the only miracle. Scientists should study his brain if he ever dies, but I doubt he will. Someone that ugly will never die.

I remembered that time mom had run away to Aunt Cathy's house. She did not call us while she was there, and we were so distant from her at that time, we did not see her again until she was back home with Frank This time, I was nine, and I was trying to come up with new solutions. I knew my mom needed money for a place to live in a town where he would never find her.

"What happened to the money you got from selling the green house?" I asked on one of our trips to the grocery store.

"I used that to pay off all of Frank's back property tax debt. He owed $80,000 in taxes that he had never paid," she said.

Everywhere I turned, there was a new blockade. Would I ever get my mom back? My hope was fading. Would she ever be safe?

I knew in my heart, she would not.

# CHAPTER TWENTY-ONE

When my mom went back to Frank's after running away to Kansas City, she stopped trying to fight for a say in her own life. She gave in to his will on everything, and he had total control. He had talked and bribed his way into getting her to come home. She would explain to me on our errands that he had changed a lot and had not been physically violent with her anymore. She said that his yelling and temper tantrums had dissipated quite a bit as well.

"You still can't see your children or be who, act, say, or do what you want. You're still a grown woman who is not allowed to make decisions for herself." I pointed out.

She always ignored my point of view, and at the time, I believed that was because I was a child, and no one cared what I thought. Now, I understand that she had completely abandoned all her own wants and desires. She was just happy to no longer be beaten. Now, I realized that she was trying to get pregnant because, in her imagination, if she were carrying his baby, he would be so delighted that he would not hit her. The complete and utter contortion of the mind that she dove into to protect her sanity from the truth is shocking, even twenty-five years later.

One day, when I was ten, Ruby and I were invited to dinner at our mom and Frank's house. "Why are we going to your house?" We hadn't been there in a couple of years.

"He has changed. He isn't as mean," she said, handing me the nail polish remover and cotton balls. A jug of wine brushed my leg on the floorboard.

My sister and I slowly dragged our feet toward the single-wide, neither of us wanting to return to this place. I noticed an enormous stack of hundreds of cinder blocks sitting next to the trailer. "What are those for?" I asked.

"To insulate the house. I'm stacking them under the trailer because winter is coming, and the house has no foundation," she said.

Frank greeted us warmly for the first time ever. We sat in the living room, and he spoke to Ruby and me as though we were friends rather than two pests. My mom sat in the chair she normally sat in to be lectured, and Frank pointed to her and said, "Your mom has something to tell you girls."

My heart fell into my stomach and began to drown in the bile of fear and pain. *"No!"* I thought, *"I can't save a baby, too. I can't save a baby!"* That was, in fact, the news, and Ruby and I exchanged the "try not to cry" look we'd given each other far too many times before.

"Congratulations," I choked out.

We had dinner, and when our mom dropped us back off at home with our dad, I immediately began to pray for the child. From the second I knew he or she was on their way, I prayed. *How could the product of the two most incredibly messed up people in the world turn out to be anything other than messed up?*

I swore to myself that I would help the child in any way I could, but I knew it would be next to impossible. How could I? I was barely allowed to see my mom, let alone see a baby who belonged to the enemy, too. My mom was about seven months pregnant, which is why her husband had us over for dinner. He thought she might be able to keep this one, and he had decided he wanted us to come over more often, be sisters to the new baby, and help our mom.

The next time we went to our mom's house for dinner, I realized that my mom, who was in the very late weeks of her pregnancy, was the one building the foundation of the house by herself while her husband trained dogs. She was picking up heavy concrete blocks, carrying them over to the house, and crawling under it to stack them at seven, eight, and nine months pregnant.

When I realized this I asked her, "Won't that hurt the baby? Shouldn't you be resting?"

"It doesn't work that way, Amelia." It was the answer she gave things that made no sense and were either dangerous or incredibly unfair, but were just how things were, because we were playing by the rules of a controlling child.

I thought, *"What if the next time she miscarries, she dies? She's forty-three now. It could happen."* At the age of ten, my anxiety learned how to build skyscrapers.

When Ruby and I would go to dinner at our mom's house, I would help with as many cinder blocks as I could, but there were hundreds. My mom, true to Libby form, built the entire foundation of their house before winter and the baby arrived. My mom talked about how much she hated her husband, calling him a jackass and the big bad wolf, all the way to and from their house. I knew that, even with her running away so many times, and with it being so late in her pregnancy, his edges had softened somewhat, he was still cruel.

Once, when she came to pick us up, she had a huge, pregnant belly and tears in her eyes.

"What's the matter?" I asked. Ruby was wise. She never asked, and it wasn't because she didn't care. It was because she cared so much.

"We are digging post holes," my mom replied.

"He's making you use a shovel and dig holes right now?" I asked.

"No. That would be fine, but he won't let me do it that way. He's making me use a posthole digger," she said.

"What is that?" I had not seen one used.

"It's this big, heavy thing that shakes you really hard, and I can't hold onto it, so he keeps making fun of me and telling me, 'It's not rocket science,' and that I'm an idiot for not being able to use a post hole digger right now," she explained.

I tried to remember if I had ever seen, read about, or heard a story of anything more cruel, stupid, or mean in my life.

I had read a book about a slave owner in the South who made his slaves who were mothers leave their babies in baskets at the end of the cotton rows, and they could only check on them when they were through picking that row.

When a big rainstorm would blow up, they'd pick and pray as fast and as hard as they could. These women would pray that their babies would still be alive by the time they got there to check. Sometimes, their newborns drowned…. Such a tragic, sad, waste of a beautiful life, and such a horrendous tragedy for the mother who had to listen to her baby scream but was not allowed to run to her child who was merely feet away. Barbaric, unforgivable, and that was the only story I knew that was more cruel.

My mom was this man's slave. "Wasn't Ruby born with her umbilical cord wrapped around her neck?" I asked.

"Yes!" my mom nearly shouted.

"And with as far along as you are now, couldn't something like that or worse happen after being shaken by a post-hole digger?" I asked.

"Yes. That's why I'm so upset," she said.

We were on the same chapter, but not on the same page. When we got to their house, Ruby and I sat inside alone while Mom, nine months pregnant, went outside to fight with a post-hole digger.

Ruby and I sat silently. We never had to speak. We knew what the other one was thinking. We were thinking that our mom had given up fighting for this child before he or she was even born and wondering how many times this child would be put in danger solely because his father must get his way no matter the consequences.

## CHAPTER TWENTY-TWO

The Thanksgiving when I was ten, and Ruby was seven, our mom picked us up to spend the holiday with her and Frank. When we walked out to get into the car, we saw that Frank was driving. Scooting into the backseat, I saw the baby in Mom's arms, a chubby, round-faced, red-headed boy.

"We named him Chad," one of them said as my mind raced.

I had contemplated whether it would be better or worse for her to have a boy or a girl. I had decided that if a girl were to be raised by this man, she would most likely commit suicide before puberty but that a little boy would probably die in an accident when he was a toddler. Neither of these situations was worth consideration.

All I could do was pray.

"When did you have him?" I asked.

"This morning," Mom replied.

I was ten, but I knew she and the baby needed to be hospitalized for more than a few hours. *Watch him expect her to make Thanksgiving dinner when she gets home,* I thought, which was exactly what occurred.

I tried to help with dinner as much as I could and kept asking my mom if she was all right. "I'm okay, but my neck muscles hurt from pushing," she said.

My ability to care about the consequences of her decisions and how badly they hurt her began to wear. I remember feeling that I should have cared more about her being forced to leave the hospital only a couple of hours after giving birth and made to cook a huge holiday dinner for four people from scratch, but I didn't. I started to hyper-focus on the baby.

*"What will his childhood be like? Will he survive?"*

# CHAPTER TWENTY-THREE

When my baby brother was two, the trouble began to arise. Up until then, he had clearly been, even to an idiot of mythical proportions, too young to spank. When he was two, he began to be physically reprimanded for crying, which is something two-year-olds can rarely control.

Rather than spanking Chad on his bottom, my mom's husband would spank him on his leg. He would yank him up by one arm, dangling him, and spank him on the back of his thigh until it was bright red.

"If you spank them on the diaper, they can't feel it," his dad had bragged to me as though he'd uncovered the secret to parenting.

I was thirteen, and I saw this little child, two years old, learn to swallow his tears, his emotions, and his humanity. If he was crying because he wanted our mom, or he was hungry, thirsty, or even just because he was a baby, he was slapped on the leg.

It was also at the age of two that he was taken on weeklong hunting trips with his dad, states away from our mom. She did not want to let him go, and it was obvious he was far too little to be there without her, but it did not matter to Frank. Chad was now his property, his accessory, and he was bringing him to Montana and North Dakota in December–a two-year-old.

Even though I know that it happened because I spent time with my mom while Frank and Chad were gone, and because I have been told by both Frank and my mom multiple times, what I write next seems like it could not be true. I am now a mother, and what I write next is so utterly preposterous, it seems like it must be something that did not actually happen.

When my mom's husband would bring his two-year-old on these hunting trips, he and the group of men he was hunting with would leave my baby brother in the truck with nothing but a puppy and a coat to keep him warm.

When Frank would tell me these stories years later, he would say, "Once, I came back to the truck when Chad was a baby--two or three, couldn't have been any older than that--and he had accidentally locked himself out of the truck. I couldn't find him. The guys I was with, we was lookin' all over for Chad, and I finally found him and the puppy curled up in a culvert fast asleep."

The story, to anyone in their right mind, is of an abandoned toddler falling asleep and nearly dying of hypothermia outside in a North Dakota winter. The idiot telling me the story thoroughly believed it was a cute story about a mischievous boy and puppy taking a nap.

Incredulously, I always asked, "Didn't you worry that he would get kidnapped, lost, hit by a car, die from getting too cold, or at the very least, an authority or game warden would show up, and you would lose him for child endangerment?"

Scoffing, Frank would reply with some such denial, "Wasn't no child endangerment. We was just huntin'."

Nothing could stop Frank from having his way, the exact way he wanted, and he wanted his trophy son, his toy, to be there no matter how much danger he was in.

At three years old, on one of these trips, Chad nearly fell into the Mississippi River while his dad "took a leak." At four years old, my brother was left with a farmer's wife in western Kansas, even though no one on the hunting trip knew her. They knocked on the door and asked her if it was okay to hunt her land and if they could leave Chad with her for the day. They had never before met her, but she said yes, so that was exactly what they did. They left Chad with a stranger for an entire day's hunt. At five, Chad began to wander away from the truck, and once, he was lost for a whole day in the cornfields of Nebraska.

When they were at home with Mom, my baby brother was in just as much danger as when they were on the trips. When he was two, his dad was talking with a customer, and Chad, being a tiny, curious, boy and not understanding consequences, walked up behind his dad and stabbed him in the back of the leg with a screwdriver. Frank turned around and punted his two-year-old son, and Frank told me that story himself.

He was constantly misunderstanding the capacity a toddler had to understand things, and he would severely injure him.

My mom was constantly reacting rather than being proactive. She would get to the point where she could no longer tolerate how her baby was being treated, and she would take him and run away. She ran away with Chad and came back almost every year of his life from ages three to eight.

When Chad was growing up, he was made to work alongside his dad, raising and training hunting dogs. This work is incredibly physically exhausting, and depending on the season, it can be either extremely hot and humid or very, very cold. There was a contraption Frank had made and fixed to the back of his tractor called a "roader." The roader was a system of steel pipes where they could hook up as many as thirty dogs and take them wherever they needed them, all at once.

When Chad was little, his dad would drive the tractor, and he would sit on the roader and ride along, keeping an eye on the dogs to make sure they were all walking and none of them were being dragged. Often, a dog would be stubborn and not want to go where it was being taken and actually hang itself, rather than go with Frank.

I could relate.

Chad was seven, and he was staring off into space rather than paying attention to the new dog, a customer's Brittany Spaniel who was particularly uncooperative. By the time Frank had stopped the tractor at their destination, the Brittany had nearly committed suicide. After helping the dog, screaming at how worthless his son was the entire time, Frank picked up his little boy and threw him as hard as he could onto the gravel driveway.

It wasn't until months later on a hunting trip in another state that anyone would realize the fierce damage that was caused by the throw Chad had endured. Chad started the hunting trip vomiting repeatedly, telling all the grown men in the truck that he didn't feel well and that he couldn't breathe. They continued driving across two states to the hotel.

The first night, Chad threw up so much that when it was time to go hunting the next morning, his dad left his very ill seven-year-old, feverish and vomiting, in the hotel room alone. Chad had nothing to eat all day and had spent the entire day alone. By the time his dad came back to the room, he was still asleep and slept all night that night as well.

The next morning, it was difficult to wake him, so his dad went hunting again. By mid-afternoon, Frank felt guilty and went to check on Chad. Frank told me that when he went to check on him that time, he could tell Chad was dying. He brought him home, driving again across two states to take him to the emergency room.

After many tests and doctors not knowing what was wrong, Chad was flown to a children's hospital in Kansas City. They discovered an enormous abscess in the small child's lung. It was full of liters and liters of puss. Chad was in the hospital for weeks and weeks, having multiple surgeries, and none of us knew if his tiny, weak body would live or die.

Throwing a small child as hard as you can onto the ground, causing internal wounds that nearly kill him, taking a small child who is clearly ill on a hunting trip two states away, and then leaving him in a hotel room just because you want to—I can't begin to fathom.

My younger brother survived his childhood, even if just barely.

My mom ran away with him enough times to completely confuse him. She taught him to trick and lie to his dad just as she had taught us girls. Neither of his parents had the ability to teach him right from wrong, and he ended up making up his own rules for life. He got into a lot of trouble and caused many people a lot of grief as he tried to grow up.

Jordan, Mellissa, and Ruby never really tried to form a relationship with Chad, but I was stupid. I tried desperately. I promised before he was born that I would not leave him. I tried to help him and be his friend when he was a teenager. I understood his self-destruction more than anyone. I had been there for the leg slaps. I had seen the abuse. I did not want to abandon him.

It wasn't until our mom became ill when we were adults that I realized Chad had never thought of any of us as his siblings, and he was not interested in being part of our family. He and I were discussing rehabilitation facilities for our mom with his dad. We were trying to explain to Frank that he was not guaranteed a life longer than Mom's, even though she was sick, and that the financial burden of having her in a facility, even though we all agreed that was the best place for her, might fall on Chad's shoulders one day.

Chad said, "Well, technically it would be Mellissa's problem."

"Why would it be Mellissa's problem?" I asked, although it sickened me that he was referring to our mother's well-being as a problem.

"Because," Chad replied, "she's the oldest."

"Mellissa isn't the oldest. Jordan is the oldest." I was done. In an instant, I was done. This man was twenty-five years old, and he was so far up his own ass that he didn't even know which of his own siblings was the oldest.

The following months revolved around my mother's healthcare, and I was busy doing everything for her because she had become like an infant. She could not shower or feed herself. I worked for Frank at the business Chad would inherit, working for nearly nothing so that it could stay afloat and continue to support our mother. I did everything for her as she could not even use the restroom by herself. I cooked and cleaned for her and Frank and did all of their laundry. At the time, I was also raising a baby and a teenager completely by myself and trying to run my own household.

My brother Chad was never around. He did not help with the family business or his parents even when I called, begging. He eventually wrote me a text listing everything he disliked about me and everything I had ever done wrong in my life. I could not hold onto him any longer. Babies grow up and become men who make choices. They get to choose if the abuse and misdeeds of their childhood make them greater or weaker.

I don't have to worry about trying to save the baby anymore.

# CHAPTER TWENTY-FOUR

When Chad was a baby, Ruby and I spent random weekends at our mom's house but didn't see either of them very often. We heard from our dad that she had taken Chad to our older sister Mellissa's house and lived there for a month, or taken him to her dad's house and lived there for a month, but they were always back before we knew it.

The times that I did see my mom, she seemed to have aged remarkably quickly. She was not allowed to color her hair, and it was almost completely gray. The only times she could color her hair was when she had run away from home or if Frank was on a hunting trip. I saw her color her hair in the sink and then take the box and bottle outside, burning them immediately.

Frank never noticed that my mom would have dark, auburn hair when he would come home from hunting.

My mom's face had far more worry lines. Her face was no longer merely freckled, but now, it was sun-spotted and weathered from working outside, which was all she did. Frank owned a dog kennel, and my mom maintained the health, well-being, hygiene, and overall maintenance of over one hundred and fifty bird dogs. The work was never-ending, filthy, exhausting, and far too much for one person. When Chad was a baby, she wore him in a wrap. When he was a toddler, he followed her around while she worked all day, no matter the weather.

When my mom would pick Ruby and me up, I noticed she cared less and less about how she smelled, looked, and dressed. Rather than changing clothes, brushing her hair, and wearing deodorant, she would come and pick us up, filthy and smelling of sweat and body odor. I knew her self-worth had slipped away entirely. All she was concerned about was surviving the day.

My mom was not allowed friendships with her peers. She couldn't go to lunch with the ladies from church. My mom was not allowed hobbies or interests. She was not allowed to attend her children's sporting or school events. For years, she worked, mothered Chad, and cooked and cleaned for Frank. My mom was a slave to the will of a man who controlled every aspect of her life.

Mom's only freedom and joy was errand day. Once a week, she would run errands, and she would do it leisurely, spending as much time as she could away from her husband. Often, I would go with her, and she talked about how she hated him, how she couldn't do anything or go anywhere.

Another reason she took a long time going to the stores was that she'd go to as many stores as she possibly could to get cash back at the register. She always had two or three secret bank accounts Frank knew nothing about.

Mom would get twenty dollars back from every store and go to five or six different stores each week when running errands. Since her husband thought of balancing the checkbook, errands, taxes, and paperwork as "women's work," he never checked or noticed. She tore up and threw away every receipt as she was walking out of every store. She intercepted every bank statement as it came in the mail every month, for years.

When Ruby and I were junior high school age, Frank would go on hunting trips, taking Chad with him, and Mom would come and pick Ruby and me up, take us to get pizza, and go to the mall. Two or three times a year, for a couple of hours, we would get to be Cinderellas at the ball. I would pretend I had a normal life and a normal mom who could take me shopping anytime she wanted. I would pretend she had not chosen a man over us and that we had always been close. I would pretend that I knew her as well as I would've had she not been stolen away from me.

We would talk, joke, and laugh, and she would spend a ton of money on us to make up for all the motherhood she had given up. Then the spell would break, and we'd have to go home without her. I'd have given all of the shopping bags in the entire world to have kept her. All the secret bank accounts, hiding the evidence and "smuggling money," as she called it, never got her away from him because, no matter how high the funds, she always went back. All that lying and scheming ever got her was sick.

When my mom was older and became ill, I took care of her and worked for Frank at the kennel. He told me a story of a time when he lived with his first wife, Nina. At the time, their baby was still with them, and the baby was very small. Frank had gone out partying, gotten into a bar fight, and had beaten someone nearly to death. He'd gone home to his wife and child, locked the deadbolt, and waited for the police with a shotgun on his lap. When they knocked, he looked out the window, pointed his gun at them, and told them to leave. They left and came back with ten more police cars and Frank's own father.

"Come on out, son," he pleaded.

Frank refused to come out and threatened to kill anyone who tried to make him. Everyone was aware that there was a woman and newborn inside of the house. Frank said that, after about three hours, he released Nina and the baby to the police, and it took him three more hours to surrender to them himself.

"You had a six-hour-long standoff with the police?" I asked, although nothing he said surprised me anymore. I believed him because everything he'd ever done in my presence was either stupid, selfish, or both.

"Yep. Sure did." He always spoke as though the horrible things he had caused were nothing.

"What happened to you that time? How long were you in prison that time?" I asked.

"That time, I didn't have to go to jail. That time, my dad pulled some strings with the judge, and I went to a big nut house out in the middle of nowhere Iowa. Ever heard of Pogalaski?" he asked.

"Yes," I said. "It's a pretty famous psychiatric hospital. Is that where you went?"

"Yeah, it's a really big, scary one. I stayed there for almost a year. I refused to eat any of the pills they gave me, and I wouldn't talk to any of the doctors, so they eventually let me out, let me go home to my dad, and then Nina and my son came and found me again, too," he said.

"So you beat a guy nearly to death and then had a standoff with the police and didn't serve any prison time at all?" I asked.

I always tried to repeat the story he had just told me back to him, but from the perspective of the rest of the world, rather than the narcissist who couldn't see past his own vulture beak. He never answered me, and I'm not sure he even heard me when I would point out the injustices of every story he'd ever told me.

He never had to pay for anything he took from anyone. Frank's dad worked side by side with law enforcement, judges, and politicians and had enough ties or dirt on people to get Frank out of trouble, as long as when he screwed up it was in Iowa.

My mom was only one person Frank had stolen the world out from under, and now her mind was in a prison she could never escape.

# CHAPTER TWENTY-FIVE

Growing up, Ruby and I did not really have a mother. Our mom and her life were so complicated, she was more of a friend we longed for but rarely got to see. She definitely did not play the role of mother in our lives.

Our stepmother did the shopping for groceries, clothes, toiletries, back-to-school needs, and holiday shopping, but other than that, we did not have a maternal parental figure. We searched for mothering in the lives of our good friends and favorite teachers. We had friends with moms who understood our situation, and when we were with them, we felt like we were loved. My three best friends, Morgan, Sam, and Charlotte, had mothers who taught me what I know about motherhood.

Morgan's mom taught me about organization, housekeeping, and looking your best. She taught me about patience and loving your children even when they are going through things we as mothers don't understand. Sam's mom taught me that love is so much more important than anything else and that kind words of encouragement, and letting others know that we are there to listen, is the best way for mutual trust between yourself and your child, or in our case, their friends.

All three of their moms taught me about being present in your family's life and how to remain a caring mother and wife even when you are stretched thin with a career, children who are active with extracurricular activities, and family demands. It was their moms who taught me the most about priorities. All three of their moms showed me Jesus in motherly form.

My sister Ruby had a friend whose mom not only brilliantly mothered her own children but seemed to mother every other child in our community. To this day, she is still my greatest example of Jesus' love in human woman form, and I can still call her right now if I need her. As a teenager, she made me feel loved when I felt like I had no one and nothing left to hold onto.

We had a neighbor across the street growing up who kept an eye out for us and prayed for Ruby and me as well. She made sure we knew she loved us, and she is a wonderful mother to her three boys. She was another role model for us when building the foundation of the mothers we would grow up and become.

When I was a teenager, I felt like there were many holes in me. All of the trauma I had endured as a young child left me unable to create good or happy feelings on my own. It began when I was six and had first moved in with my dad after he had won custody of Ruby and me. Having the comfort of my mom robbed from me, I began to replace that comfort with sweets and food. I did not consciously know it, but my young brain self-soothed me with sugar and junk food. Pizza, cake, cookies, and candy were the only things that brought my brain the same chemicals as the hugs and attention I lacked.

As I grew up, and my hormones began to change because I was addicted to sugar, my body began to produce much more estrogen than it needed and not enough testosterone. At nine years old, I was wearing a bra, and by the time I was twelve, I was wearing a C-cup. I started my period when I was nine and had to deal with that without a mother. It took me years to get the hang of it, and I was always bleeding on myself in public and getting very embarrassed at school.

In junior high, I had horrendous acne, and after a year or two of my face bleeding every day, my dad finally took me to a doctor who gave me a pill that added some testosterone to my body, causing my skin to finally clear up. I have naturally curly hair and had no idea what to do about it, even though my mom has curly hair, but she was not there to help me with any of these things.

My weight gain and naturally curvy body got me all kinds of unwanted attention. Boys my age told me I was fat and acted as though I was repulsive because I did not look like the other girls our age who had not yet developed and because of my acne and frizzy hair. Older teenage boys and grown men would stare at me, which confused me because I thought that I was fat and repulsive, so I thought I must just look old.

I had no mother to help guide me through such confusing times in my life, and I did not know where to begin when asking my dad for help, so I just kept it all inside, struggling with my self-esteem and self-worth.

Our stepmother clearly did not like Ruby and me. She showed her disdain for us in a myriad of ways, but one of the things she would tell us was that our mom did not love us and that if she did, she would not have left us with her to raise. Therefore, asking her to explain my new body or how to handle any of the emotions in my heart was off the table.

So, the table and meals became my favorite place. I self-soothed with food, which was the only drug available to a teenager in a small, rural, Christian community. Fortunately, at the time, my dad insisted that my siblings and I play every sport our school offered. Even though I was overeating, I still played volleyball, basketball, and softball, and I ran track. My body remained healthy and active, but my view of myself and my own body was of sheer hatred.

I began to abuse my body another way in junior high. I decided I needed to lose thirty pounds the summer before seventh grade. Being twelve years old and not knowing the first thing about health or nutrition, I decided to do this by only eating green beans. My stepmother did not live with us that summer, and my dad was busy working multiple jobs and visiting my stepmother, stepbrother, and younger sister in the evenings and on weekends, so Ruby and I were on our own most of the time.

There was always plenty of food in the house, but I refused to eat it, and no one noticed. I did not end up losing thirty pounds. I don't think I lost any weight at all. I made myself sick and completely ruined my metabolism, which has been slovenly ever since.

In junior high school, I was five-foot-six and weighed about 150 pounds. I was a decent athlete, and in basketball, volleyball, and softball, I was good enough to start. However, I was curvier than my mom had ever been in her life and was six inches taller than her. She, too, had always struggled with her own body image.

It was around this time in our lives that Ruby and I began to hear comments and even lectures from our own mom about how being thin was more important than anything. On the way to and from her house for dinner, or the entire time we were running errands with her, our mom would replay 'The Importance of Being Thin,' which was what I called her lectures about how fat people were unlovable, and if we ever wanted to have a husband or a boyfriend, we both needed to be thin.

Ruby was younger, and her face wasn't as round as mine. She had always been thinner than me, so she was not told to lose weight, yet every single time my mom saw me, she would tell me to lose weight. Every single time I got in her car, she would tell me I needed to lose some "chub." Usually, the suggestion would come with a bribe.

"The next time the big bad wolf goes hunting, I will take you to buy a whole new wardrobe if you lose fifty pounds," she would say. Or if it was not hunting season, she'd bribe me with cash. "If you lose fifty pounds, I'll give you a one-hundred-dollar bill," or, "I'll give you one dollar for every pound you lose by the next time I see you," she'd say.

I missed her so much, but sometimes I would dread seeing her because I did not want her to be disappointed in my body. No matter what I did, I could not lose weight.

"If you lost fifty pounds, you'd only weigh one hundred pounds, and you are way too tall and muscular for that," my sister Mellissa would say on the phone when I would call her to ask for advice.

Mellissa was always someone I could call when I had no one else to turn to. She explained that Mom did not know what she was talking about and how Mom had been told by her own stepmom that she was fat when she was my age.

"I went thirty days without eating when I was your age, Amelia," Mellissa said.

"Without eating anything at all?" I asked. I had at least eaten green beans.

"Nothing. I wanted to see if I could get down to the size she wanted me to be, but I never could, either. Everything she's saying to you she said to me too when I was your age, only I had to live with her." Mellissa went on to explain how she struggled as a teenager with anorexia due largely to my mom's issues with her own body image.

When I was an older teenager, I noticed Ruby, who had always been much thinner than me, had her own battle with food, exercise, and body image.

If it had not been for my absolutely wonderful group of friends and their families sticking by my side, helping me grow and develop in my teenage years, I would not have made it. They were my family. My dad was there, and he tried really hard. He was an amazing dad, and he did much more than most, but he was not a mom, and we needed our mom.

# CHAPTER TWENTY-SIX

I realize I have contradictory feelings about both wanting and needing my mom as a teenager and the lessons she taught me and messages she sent me about myself and womanhood. My mom was flawed. She definitely had years of trauma and layers of issues to dig through and heal from. She was never going to be the perfect woman or mother, but who is? I certainly am not. In fact, I have made so many of the exact same mistakes I write about her making.

Without investigating the pain and finding our own personal way of healing, we can never break the cycles that ruin our lives and the lives of our children.

While she gave me body image issues, I still needed her. While she gave me the exact tools I needed to choose for myself a horrible partner, I still needed her. We need our mothers; the good, the bad, the unfair, the sorrowful, the mysterious, and the ugly. If she had been more present in my life, I would've had the power, energy, and love of one of the most important people in a child's life, and without it, I was cheated out of that support.

As imperfect as she was, she was still my mom.

Another form of support Ruby and I were robbed of by Frank was financial. When my dad was awarded custody, he did not ask for child support. He was struggling to get custody of us as it were and only cared about our safety and well-being. In the 1990s, men did not often win custody battles, and he was advised to be amicable and ask simply to raise us in his home, nothing more.

When I grew old enough to understand bills, money, and how much the places I wanted to go to, things I wanted to experience, and clothes I wanted to wear cost my dad, I began to notice my mom had her hidden cash spots. Around her car, dresser, and my grandma's house, my mom, who, by this time had started to refer to herself as a "master smuggler," had the most intricately camouflaged cash hiding places.

Her husband's kennel, with her help, had become one of the most profitable in the country. They were famous in hunting magazines for producing well-trained hunting dogs. They made a very comfortable living and could have afforded to help my dad support Ruby and me.

My dad had six children, four of which were young enough to still be living at home, and it was quite expensive to raise us. He was the claims manager of an insurance company, and he had two side gigs. He played guitar and had always been talented enough to bring home a stack of cash on weekends, and he spent his evenings covering sporting events for the local newspaper of which my older brother was the sport's editor.

However, even though my dad spent his every waking moment working and/or parenting, he could never keep up with raising four kids by himself, and he should not have had to. No matter how many times my dad asked him to contribute financially, Frank always refused.

When I was an adult, after my mom got sick, I went through her keepsake boxes and chests. She had kept so many things from over the years, and among the papers and letters, I found my dad's letters to Frank asking him for child support. Always well written and formal, polite yet firm, there were only about three of them, and I could tell from the letters that my dad had also called Frank to speak with him concerning the issue because they included passages such as, *"In the last phone call regarding the subject, you mentioned that you would only pay child support if God told you to do so. I am now asking you again, has God in some way told you not to contribute to the well-being of your wife's children?"*

My dad was not begging for charity. He was proudly insisting that his children have the best life possible. The communication did not last long because it was not long after my mom married Frank that she was able to build his kennel into something profitable and start taking the cash she'd earned and giving it to my dad for Ruby and me.

My mom gave us county fair and concert money. She took us shopping in the fall when Frank went hunting. She paid for all of our basketball camps, and she was able to buy and smuggle our birthday and Christmas presents to us, but my dad raised us by himself. He kept track of every appointment, ball game, and practice, music lesson, dance, and cheerleading event. He was at every event by himself. He did everything by himself. He paid every bill and bought every grocery item.

When I took care of my sick mother and worked at the kennel, I was around Frank so often that I once asked him, "Why didn't you let her be involved in our lives? What would it have hurt if you had let her go to my basketball games or my choir concerts?"

Difficult questions like this one always brought out the youngest child in him.

"Well, to be perfectly honest with you, Amelia, I don't think she wanted to go. She never really liked going to stuff like that. She never asked," he'd answer.

To someone who is fortunate and doesn't know Frank, it may sound like he just wanted to hurt me by telling me that my mom did not care enough to want to be involved in my life. However, I knew he was not smart enough to have thought of that lie. He did not know my mom well enough, see her, or listen to her well enough to know that she had given up on asking if she could go places, do things, have friendships, see her children grow up, or have her own free will.

My mom had retreated into survival mode very early in their marriage and had stopped asking for what she wanted. She didn't ask to be involved in our lives because he had stolen her voice. Frank Hudson is a thief.

# CHAPTER TWENTY-SEVEN

My mom's days were spent cleaning up dog shit. She woke up at dawn, put on her boots, and cleaned up after over a hundred dogs. She fed, watered, and medicated them, and by that time, it was time to clean up after them again. Next, she would make sure that the brood mommas who were in season got bred to the proper stud, taking diligent notes on the date and time of breeding. She would check on the mommas who were about to have puppies or who had just had puppies and took extra good care of those girls. Then, she would clean up the kennels and water everyone again.

Her afternoons were spent vaccinating puppies and doing kennel maintenance on anything that was broken, checking everyone's collars for comfortability, mowing, gardening, and weed eating. Her evenings were spent cooking, cleaning, and doing laundry until it was time to do AKC registrations and paperwork for customers.

My mom was the one who built the kennel into a successful business and kept it going, and yet, she was not allowed to have money of her own. Frank would allow her to buy household items and groceries, but she had no reason to have bank accounts or cash of her own because he did not allow her to live any sort of life of her own. Even though she worked for every dime she had hidden in her secret bank accounts and then some, every wad of bills she had hidden away and everything she bought Ruby and me, she still referred to as "stealing" and "smuggling."

"You can't steal from yourself," I would try to remind her, but she was brainwashed.

I had seen on every episode of *Oprah* involving domestic violence that the husband would not allow the wife he was controlling and abusing access to the funds. Frank was more masterful at these things than any of Oprah's guests' husbands. Frank had robbed my mom of being able to see any of the contributions she had made, whether good or bad, and her focus was on hiding everything she did and every thought she had from her husband.

Something I am very proud of my mother for is her generosity. She did teach Ruby and me to be empathetic and giving. When my mom would go to town for groceries, she would always buy extra for a family or two in the community that she knew was in need. She would call the school and ask what families needed help, or she would hear about a family in crisis at church and find out where they lived. My mom would buy extra groceries, household supplies, school supplies, and even toys, and if she could find out the children's sizes, she'd leave clothes.

My mom would drop the items on people's porches and drive away unseen or heard. She never bragged about it or told anyone, and the only reason I know is because I was with her. She would even go to the school and pay children's lunch debts and buy books and supplies for teachers. Although my mom was wounded and confused about many things, she still tried to be and do good.

After everything is done and over, and I am an old woman, I know that as complex a woman as my mom was, and as many times as she was literally and/or figuratively shit on, she still tried to be a good lady.

# CHAPTER TWENTY-EIGHT

When you're a child who misses her mother, it is all-encompassing. I had learned early on in my childhood to mask those feelings, but they consumed me. Any story I read or movie I watched where a mother was separated from her child set an ache inside of me ablaze. I had a soft spot for orphans. *The Jungle Book* made me sad. *The Wizard of Oz* made me even sadder.

"Where are her mom and dad?" I asked my older sister.

"She lives with her aunt and uncle. She doesn't have a mom or dad," Mellissa said.

That was the part that always had me worried about Dorothy. I never cared about the witch. Witches could be outwitted, but not having a mother was something we could not fix.

Over the years, my mom and I would have plenty of chances to grow our relationship, but every time, we would be interrupted by our own version of the Wicked Witch. In fact, there were times when that was how she would refer to Frank. She would call him, "the big bad witch," or "the wicked witch," or "the big bad wolf."

She became obsessed with what he thought so that she could predict and trick him. Eventually, her brain began to think of how he would view something first, before she even had her own thoughts.

Eventually, all the lies about where she was going, what she was doing, her secret bank accounts, secret visits with her children, and the secret feelings she had about everything began to take their toll.

I was in my mid-twenties the first time I realized my mom was completely losing touch with reality and in my mid-thirties when it became undeniable. If one is ever curious about their worst nightmare coming true and what it feels like, I can tell you. What's so much worse than wandering around looking for your mother is when you have found her, and she looks you in the eye and doesn't know that it is you. There is a great shock of invisibility, and for the first seconds, you truly believe you have disappeared. It's a tailspin of *"This can't be Earth. I can't be me. That can't be her. Where am I?"* And you land on *"Who am I?"*

When you are speaking with your own mother, and she does not know who she is or who you are, that is so permanently difficult that even in my healing journal I am describing it as though it happened to you instead of me.

# CHAPTER TWENTY-NINE

When I was twelve, until I was fifteen, my stepmother and dad were separated. She and her son (my stepbrother, who is two years younger than me) and my half-sister (who is ten years younger than me) lived in a town a couple of hours away. My dad was incredibly busy spending all of his time either working or driving to see my youngest sister, who was his baby, and far and away, his greatest joy.

It was during those years that Ruby and I were on our own. We took care of ourselves. I took care of the housework and most of the cooking. I made the grocery list, handled permission slips, and made sure Ruby and I had our lunches or lunch money. I took care of reminding Dad about appointments, field trips, and sports schedules. I made sure our uniforms were clean and that we had our basketball shoes and coats on and were ready to go.

The year I was twelve, my dad's mom, his sister, her husband, and their four children came over for a Thanksgiving dinner that I cooked. I was becoming a woman and even kind of a mother, and I was doing it completely by myself. I made decent grades and did well in athletics. I sang well and was active in extracurricular activities, most of which involved music.

There were many, many, opportunities for my mom to support

me, for her to be involved in my life. She could have helped me feel less alone and so much less unloved. Perhaps it should not have been a big deal, and I should have been happy that she was still alive and that she was involved in my life, albeit in a very limited way. Maybe I should have been more grateful for what I did have, but our presence in our children's lives, when they are building themselves and their self-perspective, directly affects how they feel about themselves long-term. The absence directly correlates with the absence of fucks given about themselves in their future. The less my mother showed up for me, the less I showed up for myself.

The energy I spent missing her could have been better spent on academics, art, or sports. Maybe I should have known that, but I was only a kid. All I knew about my adolescence was that my friends were rescuing me. Morgan, Sam, and Charlotte got me through those years and more to come. Not having a mom made me feel insecure and unsafe, but my three best friends always replaced that insecurity. Morgan gave me the confidence to sing in public. Sam and I did such off-the-wall and silly things that we usually did not care what anyone thought of us. Charlotte had always been funny and fun, giving me my self-esteem and my self-worth back after the adults in my life took it from me.

We are still friends, and they are really the only people I can always rely on no matter the situation. Being a teenager is so difficult, and it is even worse when shaken by real life. I'm sure I was not always easy to be friends with, but they always accepted me anyway. I could tell them anything, and they would not judge me. Explaining why my mom was never there or that my stepfather believed sports were evil could have been a challenge in itself, but my friends made it easy for me. They always listened and made fun of Frank to cheer me up. They helped me feel better if I was anxious. Mostly, they replaced the love I did not receive from my mom.

There were also some incredible teachers in my life at that time. My junior high English teacher and I share a birthday, which we bonded over immediately. She and I stayed close even when I grew up. She helped me and encouraged me when I was at my lowest moments.

My high school English teacher encouraged me to excel. He would give me assignments he didn't give other students. "Read this book and write me a paper," he'd say.

If it were not for him, I doubt I would have ever gone to high school at all, and in my adolescence, he was my hero. It was he who planted in my heart the writing seeds. When I did not care about myself, my friends and my teachers cared for me.

# CHAPTER THIRTY

When I was a teenager, unless my mom had run away from home or was running errands, the only way I could see her was to go to her house for dinner on Saturday evening, spend the night, and go to church with her on Sunday morning. I was a young teenager, not yet old enough to drive, have a job, or buy my own clothes. I wore what people bought me or what I liked, and usually that was determined by the color of the garment. I was very young, and my taste and style were still developing.

My stepmother was not living in the home at the time, and my dad was very busy with things that were more important than my wardrobe, so if I wanted new clothes or had outgrown my old ones, I had to wait until the next hunting season to go shopping with my mom while Frank was gone on a hunting trip. No matter what I wore to church, Frank would scoff, make fun of me, and then lecture me. Going to church with someone should never give anyone anxiety. If you invite someone to church, and their only reason for not wanting to go with you is that they know you'll make fun of their outfit, you're doing it wrong.

When I would look through my closet when choosing what to take to my mom's house to wear, I would feel sick and begin to sweat.

I did not own anything that looked like something Laura Ingalls Wilder would wear, and that was what Frank wanted me to wear. When I would go shopping, I would look for something that looked like it belonged to a pioneer woman, but they did not make things like that and sell them in the mall in 2001, so I was open to the attack of a man who mocked me more than the teenage boys at my school... only Frank was doing it in the name of biblical modesty.

I was about fourteen when on one such occasion, I told myself when picking out my outfit that I would not care that he was going to laugh at me and that I would just ignore him. I woke up at their house the next Sunday morning, went to the bathroom, and put on my clothes. I had chosen a lilac sweater that perfectly matched my skirt. The skirt was lilac too, but it had cosmic strips of blues, darker purples, and sparkly silvers throughout. It looked like a microscopic photo of the Milky Way, and I knew my mom would have chosen it for herself when she was Libby. I walked out of the bathroom and into the kitchen for breakfast, and Frank immediately, openly laughed at me, a teenage girl, a guest in his home.

"You know, tighter isn't always better, Amelia." His first insult.

It had not even occurred to me that my clothes were too tight. *Are they too tight?* I thought, trying not to look down at them, fidget, cry, jump out of my skin, or run out the front door and run all twenty miles home. The lecture started with how my clothes were too tight and how sparkles and loud colors like purple were for prostitutes to attract the attention of men, and then, as all Frank Hudson lectures must, ended with how women should have long hair. Modesty and long hair–those were the most important things all women must maintain. Forget health, self-worth, confidence, boundaries, education, autonomy, or anything else a woman must actually attain to help herself or anyone else. No, modesty and long hair. These are the things Jesus cares about, according to Frank Hudson. I went home, took off the outfit, and threw it on the floor in the back of my closet. It was ruined for me now, as were so many things I had once loved but that Frank had ruined.

My mom and her husband met at church, the church I was born

into and baptized in just before my life exploded. The reason they stopped attending there and went to a different church had to do with a pool party. The youth group was having a co-ed pool party for the junior high and high schoolers. Frank, who did not have any children at the time and would not be present at the party anyway, went to the pastor and the head deacon, and in his own words said, "I flat out told them they couldn't do that. I said, 'You can't have a co-ed pool party with teenagers! Are you crazy?!' and they looked at me like I was the weird one."

Frank told me that story twenty-five years later when I was an adult.

"Remember the pastor there?" he asked.

"Yes, he baptized me," I told him.

"Well, you'll never believe it. They tried to tell me I was the crazy one. They said that if I thought of it in a sexual way, I must have problems, and they asked me if I needed to talk about my problems," he said, laughing. "I told them that I remembered being a teenage boy, and they couldn't have a pool party at a church event. We stopped goin' after that."

Any grown man who has problems with children's clothing, children's sports because of the way they are moving or are dressed, or a children's pool party, due to the idea that he believes that they are being immodest, is, in fact, the one with the problem and should absolutely, and immediately, seek help.

Girls' basketball was evil in Frank's opinion for these very reasons. I received lecture after lecture about how unladylike and how un-Christian it was for me to play basketball.

"But you think it's okay for boys to play basketball?" I once asked when I was a teenager being lectured about my favorite thing in the entire world.

"Well, at least the boys aren't bouncing around out there with no bras on for everyone to gawk at," he'd responded.

I had known better than to ask more, because any time I dug deeper into his issues, it would make me physically ill. Having heard him talk about girls' sports enough by now, I knew enough to know that he didn't think any of us were wearing bras.

"The boys are, in fact, the ones out there without bras on bouncing around. The girls, we all wear bras. It would hurt if we didn't." I once offered him a little bit of insight.

"It doesn't look like it," said the forty-something-year-old man.

I had to swallow the vomit in my mouth, *"Why are you looking so closely at children's bodies? They are playing a sport. They are not there to be judged, analyzed, scrutinized, objectified, and certainly not to be sexualized."*

Frank proved nothing but that sports are not evil, but there are men who are evil.

# CHAPTER THIRTY-ONE

Basketball taught me so much more than footwork or ball handling. For one thing, the basketball court was one of the only places I could exist as a kid where I was not in trouble. The game created a safe haven for me where I could focus my attention and energy on something other than the anger boiling in my heart. If I had not been able to leave my emotions out on the court, I believe I may have taken them out on myself.

Even through all of the trauma, loss, insecurity, and disappointment of my young life, I never stopped talking to Jesus. I never stopped asking Him how to handle the issues I was facing. I doubt I would've taken my anger out on anyone else. It was not my style to fight or try to hurt others. I was much more likely to turn the negative energy all the adults in my life had handed me toward myself. Truly, I don't know if I would still be here if it had not been for basketball.

Two of my best friends, Morgan and Chelsea, and I were extremely invested in getting better at the game when we were kids. Our dads were our coaches, and we would play a season lasting from November to March and then we would go to a basketball camp or two every summer. We always went to a week-long camp at a Christian college where our coaches did devotionals with us each night before we went back to our dorms.

One year, I had a coach who asked us what was important to us. I looked around at my teammates, who had been chosen at random out of hundreds of girls. We had only known one another for a couple of days, and in a day or two more, we would part ways again, and yet I already cared about these young women and their answers. Basketball, team unity, and working together had already built a bond between us.

I still pray for those women, though I can't remember their faces or names, all because passing a ball up and down a court had brought us together. The determination to work as one unit to create an outcome had brought us together. Basketball and other team sports create great leaders. I learned how to be a leader on that court. I learned how to communicate without speaking on that court. I learned determination and how to work really hard for the things I want. I learned sportsmanship and kindness there, but most importantly, it is where I found my dignity.

Basketball taught me how to represent myself as a lady who is proud of herself, and therefore, cannot be pushed around. I found my power on that court, not because jocks are supposed to be cooler–that isn't a thing and shouldn't be in movies–but because I knew how hard I had worked and that I could've chosen to put my energy into anything but that I chose to put it into something that brought me strength of character. Basketball helped me walk with my head held high. I wasn't ever the best player, not even close. In fact, I didn't ever make it to the WNBA and I don't hang out with Reggie Miller every day, much to the chagrin of my thirteen-year-old self.

The emotional ties I have to basketball affect me to this day. I have even been known to cry while watching a harmonious play, as odd as that may be. It is not necessarily nostalgia or that my best friend, Morgan, and I had a bond over the sport as kids. It's not even that my dad and I spent a lot of time bonding over the game.

It's that basketball kept me from hurting myself when I was a child who was under attack.

# CHAPTER THIRTY-TWO

Frank owned 20 acres of land with his and my mom's house at one end and the barn at the other. When I was eleven, Frank's dad put a double-wide mobile home by the barn.

At the time, I found this very strange. *"Why would anyone want to live closer to Frank?"* I thought. In every story I had ever heard about Frank's dad, he was a wealthy, womanizing big shot. Not only did Frank's religious beliefs disagree with every aspect of his dad, but I wondered how Jack would feed his addiction to women on Frank's property where nail polish was outlawed. *"How many women will Frank have to run off?"*

It wasn't until I was in my thirties that Frank answered those questions for me, not that I had actually asked. When my mom became ill, I took over all of the work she did at the kennel, where Frank told me enough about his life for me to understand a sliver of his issues. Nothing Frank told me is an excuse. Nothing Frank told me is an explanation. Everything he did to her, everyone he hurt—and there are so many of us—is the direct effect of narcissism meets the inability to empathize or control impulses.

Frank's dad had been married to eight different women. He had done every job from selling insurance to driving a truck from bail bonding to owning a bowling alley in the '70s where Dolly Parton and Porter Wagoner bowled.

When Frank was very young, about ten, he and his older brother were spending the summer with his dad. His dad suspected his wife at the time was cheating with her boss at the furniture store. With his two young, impressionable sons in the car, Jack drove up behind the store after hours where he caught his wife cheating in her boss's car.

He pulled the guy out through his car window and started to badly beat him. The frantic woman jumped out of the car topless and ran around to the other side where her husband was beating up her boss, and Jack backhanded her so hard that she fell unconscious onto the concrete.

Rage and the inability to control one's anger are learned behaviors.

When Frank was a bit older, his dad met a young woman whose dad lived with her. When Jack married the girl, he moved her dad in, too. At some point, the girl began to cheat and vanished one day. I can only assume being in a marriage with someone like Jack might be difficult, and by difficult, I mean intolerable, and so, she vanished.

Jack was left with an elderly man, the girl's dad. Once again. with his two teenage boys in the car, Jack showed them that they were kings and that only their wants mattered. He drove to a cabin in the middle of the woods he knew about and left the elderly man there with no water, food, supplies, or transportation back to civilization.

"I never forgave him for that," Frank admitted about his dad, and I felt like it was a miracle Frank even felt remorse for something his dad had done. That meant he could empathize and feel human emotions.

He just usually chose not to.

I knew Frank's dad had been married to his mother twice, both times cheating vehemently, and that he was never single for very long, but what I could never understand was why any woman would even want to talk to him, much less marry him. I could feel the evil all around him. It must have been charisma, money, and power. He had convinced himself that he and his sons were above everyone else. He had connections with law enforcement and judges. He was the most successful bail bondsman in his area, and he threw parties for police, judges, lawyers, and politicians. Everyone knew him. He could blackmail everyone, and everyone owed him a favor.

In the late 1970s and early 1980s, Frank worked for his dad as a bail bondsman and had seen his dad do horrible things, including having witnesses to crimes killed. Eventually, being heartless caught up to him.

In the 1990s, when Jack was in his late sixties, he married a pretty, much younger nurse. She was a widow who had inherited a lot of money and property when her husband died. All the lakefront properties and resorts she Jack owned were in her name. He had married her, but nothing actually belonged to him. Jack found out she was cheating on him and was going to leave him, so he hired the hitman he had used before to kill her and make it look like an accident so that he could keep all the property and money.

The hitman knew Frank and called him before he took the orders from Jack to make sure Jack wasn't just upset. He asked Frank if he should really kill his dad's wife. Frank, who by this time was married to my mom, called the hit off and called his dad's wife. He told her his dad's plan and told her to get out of town and hide until he could get his dad out of the area. She took that advice and added calling the police and filing for divorce.

So, Jack had to leave the area where he was a big shot with lots of friends, property, money, and resorts to spend the rest of his life in a double-wide trailer on his son's land, hidden away from anyone who had formerly known him.

Many times, Frank would have to drive down the trail through the field in the middle of the night to tell a random woman who was sleeping with his dad to go home. He could not allow any fornication on his property, after all. That would be a sin.

# CHAPTER THIRTY-THREE

Des Moines, Iowa, 1972–Frank's birth date was drawn in the lottery, and he was drafted to go to Vietnam. Every time I heard this story, I was amazed that he made it onto the bus to go get his physical. He was nineteen and had been in and out of prison for three years on a lengthy list of drug-related charges.

Whether he had caused an accident that took lives while on drugs, was caught selling drugs, beat someone up while on drugs, or had destroyed property while he was under the influence, he was always in trouble. He ended up in Iowa selling drugs with a biker gang that controlled most of the pills, cocaine, and meth in the area. Frank was a long-haired, shirtless, druggie biker who had found a shirt and his way onto the bus on time to be taken with all the other men and boys who were unfortunate enough to be called to go to war. He said they made all of them get nude and stand in line for physicals and that it was dehumanizing.

"They did that on our first day of prison, too. Made us all get naked and stand in line together. Made you feel like an animal," he said.

Frank ended up failing his drug test and did not have to go to Vietnam. Anyone who had narcotics in their system did not have to go risk their life in war. Nine percent of Frank's generation was drafted and sent to Vietnam. Those were the good, the clean, the brave, the noble, and the empathetic men of this country, and this information makes me very seriously consider how it would have shaped our culture had it been the dirty, druggie hippie who had been sent to die. Of course, no battles would be won, and all would be lost, but that is often how I feel about what happened anyway. The men who fought bravely in Vietnam won battles, but they also came home brokenhearted.

I was blessed enough to be raised by a man who was slightly too young to go to Vietnam. Had more of us been raised by the men who were courageous enough and mentally and emotionally available enough to go fight, and had those men not either died in action or returned mentally and emotionally, and often physically, maimed, how would society be different today?

Nevertheless, Frank did not have to go to Vietnam. He stayed in Iowa where he was shortly thereafter arrested for a crime and sent to jail. While in a holding cell the first night, he was there with a man who was absolutely drenched in blood. The guy couldn't remember what he had done, but Frank later found out that he was on meth at a party and had stabbed someone to death. That time, Frank was supposed to be in prison for two years for selling drugs to minors, but he was released early for helping with the indictment of a serial killer.

Once in prison, two cells down from Frank's, there was a guy who was constantly arguing with the radio. He sounded like a crazy person, and Frank was bored, so he started paying attention. Every time the news on the radio would talk about a recent murder, the man that Frank could hear, but not see, would argue that the news didn't know what they were talking about and say what had really happened to the victim.

Frank ripped out the title page of his Bible and wrote down what the lunatic was saying. When he handed the paper to the guard, it wasn't more than an hour before Frank was meeting with investigators in the warden's office and signing a paper saying he would testify against the killer and tell the jury everything he had heard. Frank was even able to help them locate some of the victim's bodies. He spent the next two months in the county jail rather than the prison and was able to walk around as he pleased, order food, and have visitors. As long as he didn't leave before testifying in court, he was not treated like a prisoner.

The investigators had enough evidence to charge the serial killer (whose story I looked up as Frank was talking) with multiple murders, and Frank was released. For me, the theme from the stories throughout Frank's life was clear: he would do something terrible, someone would slap him on the wrist, and then not wanting to have to put up with him, they would let him go on his merry way.

# CHAPTER THIRTY-FOUR

When Frank and Nina lived with their little boy in Phoenix, Arizona, in the 1970s, Frank was in a biker gang that dealt drugs and worked with a Mexican drug cartel. He would leave Nina and the baby at home for days while he partied.

After the baby passed away, Nina left and went back to Nebraska to her mom, but Frank went to Vegas to party. He was in a car with three of the Mexican drug cartel guys partying in the desert with enough alcohol, coke, and meth to last them an entire day, but it began to get dark, and they started to run out of liquor.

Frank was in the back seat behind the driver when one of the guys asked his friend, "Why didn't you bring more?" in a jovial tone.

Frank, thinking he was a good enough friend to joke around too, smacked the driver in the head and said, "Yeah, dummy!"

The driver turned around and sunk a buck knife into the space between Frank's left shoulder and his collar bone, yanked it out, and they shoved him out of the car, leaving him for dead.

"It took me a while to even be able to stand up. I was hurt bad. Blood was gushing everywhere. I was lying in a pool of blood." He moved his T-shirt to show me the scar, which was quite visible more than forty years later. "I thought I was going to die that time." He went on, "I laid there thinking about how a coyote was going to come along and eat me soon if I didn't get up. So, I got myself up, and I walked all night. There was blood all over me. I had long hair, and my hair was drenched in blood. My T-shirt was wringing with blood. My jeans and even my boots were full of blood. I really thought I was going to die, then I saw a house light really far away. When I finally got to the house, a lady answered the door, and she just shrieked. I must have looked like the walking dead to her. Her husband took me into town to the hospital. They got me going again, but the doctor told me that if I didn't stop living the way I was living, I was going to die. But that next night, they let me out of the hospital, and I went and partied, stitches and all. I was very stupid back then."

After that incident, Frank kept partying but shortly after decided to go back to Iowa to be closer to family. He was having problems masking his depression even with copious amounts of drugs and alcohol. He was a chef in a kitchen where he and his staff would drink wine the entire shift.

One afternoon, he was sitting on his couch, unable to make himself get up and go to work. He was tired of always being drunk and feeling like he was going to die if he was not drunk. He was staring at his shotgun, deciding whether or not to shoot himself in the head when he started the bargaining with God conversation. He asked God to give him a sign. Should he kill himself or not? Just then, the phone rang. It was his dad just calling to check on him. This was not an ordinary occurrence. His dad said something just told him to check on his son. They talked it over, and Frank's dad decided to come and get him and get him some help. So, Jack checked Frank into a psychiatric hospital.

Frank lived in that hospital for a full year. He started out just as stubborn as he had at Pogalaski Psychiatric Hospital, but eventually, Frank said, he decided to enjoy himself while he was there. He still refused to take any of the medications or speak with any of the professionals, but he did get sober and made some friends. He shot pool every day and became friends with his roommate, whose wife would often come and visit. On one of the visits, she left Frank a

Bible. She simply sat it on his nightstand in case he wanted to read it. He said it sat there for months untouched.

Frank had been raised in a Nazarene church, and his mother was a devout Christian. She prayed for him and made sure he knew it. Every time she called, she told him she was praying for him. He knew he believed God existed, but he didn't think he could give up all the things he knew he would have to in order to have a real relationship with God.

Eventually, he picked up the Bible and began to read it. He read it over and over and began to study and memorize some of it. After a year, he checked himself out of the facility as a self-proclaimed born-again Christian and a completely changed man.

First, he went to live with his mom. There, he continued to read his Bible, go to church with his mom, and even do odd jobs and favors for elders and widows as acts of service. He stayed out of trouble and no longer drank or did drugs. The jobs in that part of the country were scarce, and he was used to drug money and motorcycles, flashy cars, and whatever he wanted to do, eat, or wear. He refused to work as a chef anywhere because he knew that life would cause him to be around drinking and partying, so he went in search of a job that would pay better. He took his few belongings and his car and went to St. Louis, checked into a hotel, and prayed. He needed to find a job before he found drugs. He was very concerned he would relapse, so he went to the first church he saw.

It was a Wednesday evening, and no one had yet arrived for services, but the doors were unlocked, so he went in, sat down, and prayed. Just then, he heard a loud, booming voice behind him and felt the firm clap of a hand on his shoulder.

"Did you come to praise the Lord, tonight, brother?" the man asked.

Frank told him that he was new in town and had come there to pray. The man, whose name was Austin Lyte, asked him if he could pray with him and asked Frank what they were praying about. Frank told him about the psychiatric hospital, his addiction, being born again, and his fear of temptation coming for him in the midst of anxiety due to unemployment.

Austin prayed with him and then said, "So, you need a job? You have a job." And he handed Frank his business card. Austin was the regional manager of the Thunderbird Vacuum Cleaner Sales Group out of St. Louis, Missouri. "Come into my office in the morning. You are now officially a Thunderbird vacuum cleaner salesman."

# CHAPTER THIRTY-FIVE

It turned out that Frank was an incredible door-to-door salesman. Not only could he talk anyone into buying anything, but he was not a family man, so he could take appointments at any time of day. He traveled around the St. Louis area and showed Thunderbird vacuums to wives and families. They bought them, and he made a lot of cash. He did this for years while living out of motel rooms, having no reason to buy or rent a place to live.

At the time, he was still attending church at Austin Lyte's church and still trying to learn from and read as much of the Bible as he could. He read the Bible over and over in his car between appointments and in motel rooms every evening.

When I worked with him at the kennel, he would tell me the same stories over and over. This was due in part to narcissism. He spoke simply to hear himself speak. He was also losing his memory, and he had no idea he had already told me a story dozens of times.

One of the stories he shared with me repeatedly was about, "Ichabod." He wanted me to know what "Ichabod," was so that it did not happen to me. "Do you know what the word, Ichabod means?" he asked.

The first time he asked, I made a *Legend of Sleepy Hollow* joke that flew over his head, and every time after that I said, "Yes. It means, 'the spirit has departed.'"

He always looked shocked and impressed. "Now, how did you know that?"

"You've told me this story a million times," I'd respond, knowing I'd have to hear it again.

"I'd been born again for about three years at that point," he began. "It was the mid-eighties, probably like '84 or '85. I was living in a motel in St. Louis. And one day, this little girl showed up out of nowhere."

The little girl was someone I always worried about even though, by now, she was in her late forties/early fifties or dead. I knew that when he said, "little girl," he did not mean tiny child, but at the same time, I did not know how old she was because he always referred to her as "little girl" when he subjected me to this story.

"She just showed up one day, and we started sleeping together. She'd be there at the motel when I got home, and we'd sleep together. That went on for too long before I started to feel the Holy Spirit telling me something. One day, I went outside to sit on the swing outside the motel, and I felt this horrible feeling of rejection and darkness in my heart. It was the Holy Spirit telling me that if I didn't get rid of the little girl, I would be Ichabod. The Holy Spirit told me that he was going to leave me and never come back, so I went inside and told her she had to leave," he said.

The first few times I heard this story I didn't pry. I was petrified to find out how old "little" meant. I was very scared to find out where the girl had come from and who had been missing her at home.

After a handful of times, I began to ask questions. "What was her reaction to you telling her to leave?"

"Oh, she threw a big, huge fit and started throwing things in the motel room. It was one of those that had a kitchenette, so there were dishes, and she was throwing glass dishes around, screaming at me that I couldn't do that to her. Then she finally left," he said.

"Where did she come from?" I asked. "Why didn't her parents come looking for her?"

"I don't think she had parents. She was on the street when she turned up at the motel. She probably just found somebody else to shack up with," he said.

Finally, one day this story had infuriated me enough that I had to ask her age. He thought he was sharing a story about bravely and nobly fending off temptation before losing God's good graces. The story was actually about a thirty-two-year-old man who was, in his own opinion, at the peak of his relationship with God, seducing a homeless youth, having sex with her, and housing her for months, and then kicking her out with no resources, help, or anywhere to go.

"How old was she?" I was cringing, and he hadn't even answered yet.

"Oh, she was young. Couldn't have been more than fourteen or fifteen. Sixteen maybe," he said.

I knew better than to ask, and I was now left with vomit in my mouth, rage in my hands burning up my arms. *Why aren't you punching him? Tearing off his face?* I asked myself. This poor girl's interactions with Frank had been over for longer than I had been alive, and yet her story still shook me into rage. I was enraged for so many reasons.

He was a man who was never even told that he had a problem with liking girls who were not yet old enough to make decisions about their bodies, future, or whether or not they even liked sex. It was not only joked about by the men of Frank's generation, but they were encouraged to go after girls who were far too young. There are so many songs, especially hair band songs, written in that era about young girls, songs about someone's little sister, or a girl who is far too young to even be talking to, and yet the song's hero is the man who seduces the child. So, the first layer of my rage, the part where Frank's generation was sexualizing and sexually seducing children, was never even frowned upon by any of the men in his life. On the contrary, it was accepted and encouraged.

The second layer of my rage was that, no matter how many times I had the conversation with Frank about how teenagers are too young to give consent--to anyone--even if they like them, because their brains are not yet developed, and they have no experiences to understand consequences or what the weight and magnitude of sex can do to their future, he always disagreed.

"Oh, all the girls were havin' fun back then," he would say as I struggled to refrain from murdering him.

I tried harder to explain. "Okay, so, you know how every child in the world would eat ice cream for every meal if they were allowed? But they can't do that because they'd get sick? The kids don't know that, right? And if they do, they don't care in that moment. They don't understand future consequences, so at the time, they'll want to eat nothing but ice cream."

I was wasting my breath. He already thought what he thought, and explaining new concepts to him was not only impossible because of how closed-minded he was, but also because of how incredibly stupid he was. He couldn't understand metaphors, which was one of the reasons he took the Bible so literally.

Another layer of rage, which still burns vehemently within me, was how could anyone think that they know Jesus at all and then in their mid-thirties have sex with a child? How could he be so completely confused about Jesus and what He stood for to think that that was all right? But for Frank, it was okay. He did it for months before stopping because he had been taught that being a Christian was reading the Bible and picking and choosing the things that didn't, and never would, apply to himself personally and latching onto those things, using them to make himself feel better and using them preach to others.

He represents everything and everyone from his generation that has run my generation out of the pews. It was not Ichabod. Frank never had the Holy Spirit, so he could not have lost It. The darkness he felt on that swing was the wickedness in his own heart boiling over, and for a moment, turning into guilt over having sex with a child.

After that day, Frank vowed never to physically touch a woman ever again, not at all. He was someone who had never respected women, but that was the point when he started to loathe and despise women. If a cashier was handing him change, he made her set it on the counter so he could avoid touching her hand. He would look at the ground when a woman would walk by, and for fifteen years, he avoided all contact with women unless he was selling them a vacuum cleaner, and even then, he demanded her husband be home.

When going through the custody battle over Ruby and me, my dad's lawyers dug up a book that Frank had written during that time in his life in the mid-1980s. It was not published, of course, but the lawyers were able to get their hands on a manuscript that Frank had sent to a publisher.

My dad read it but didn't want to subject me to it, so I never saw the book, but it was all about women. According to Frank, all women were evil seductresses who were only put on Earth with the all-powerful man for one of two reasons—either to be submissive wives and mothers who are obedient to their husbands or as temptations placed here by Satan. No women fell outside of these two categories, and that is still how Frank treats women to this day. He wrote that book thirty years prior, but he would lecture me and other women under those same guidelines for the rest of his life.

No one ever explained to him that the reason he liked young, weak, vulnerable girls who had nowhere else to go and no one else to choose from was because he was unimpressive, emotionally and mentally stunted, and that an adult woman who had her life together would never be interested in even speaking with him, let alone sleeping with him.

If he had worked that out and had been able to improve himself, maybe he would have been able to have a healthy relationship with a grown woman. If he had worked on himself, and still struggled with being attracted enough to young girls for their basketball uniforms and pool parties to bother him, maybe he could have sought professional help with that as well.

Instead, he turned his own sin on everyone else. He made it everyone else's fault that he was sexually aroused by them. He lectured to anyone who was unfortunate enough to be near him about their clothes, nail polish, and eye shadow. He took scripture about women and bent it to make himself feel power over them.

Frank needed to shame women in order to feed his ego layer after layer of evil and wickedness. Word after word of scripture was distorted to fit his own warped mind.

# CHAPTER THIRTY-SIX

At some point in the middle of the 1980s, Frank won so many awards for selling Thunderbird vacuums that he was promoted to manager of his own store and team. They had given him an office in a small town in southeast Iowa where he managed a team that had already been there working under another manager. They remained his team when he took the position. Among these teammates was a gay man.

Anyone who had ever laid eyes on Frank could tell his views on homosexuality. He is a redneck, straight, white man who was born in the 1950s. A wild guess would land you at least somewhere near *"He doesn't like gay people."* And speaking with him for two minutes, one would realize he was a religious fanatic who was too out of touch with humanity to understand anything, and one would know for sure what he thought of gay people.

Many times I tried to show Frank how Jesus really feels about gay people. "You agree," I'd begin, "that we all sin?"

"Of course." At least he was listening.

"And you agree that no sin is greater than any other?"

"All sin is the same. You're right about that," he'd agree.

"So why is it okay for me to be divorced, and you're sitting right here with me, not disgusted at all? Could it be that culture and what you've been told by people about homosexuality is tainting your view? If all sin is the same, how can it bother you so much that you sin in your actions toward them?"

I had lost him. He couldn't grasp it.

When he would display his disgust for gay people, I would be sickened and enraged. When I would feel that way, I could do nothing but try again. I had to do something, or I would kill him, and so I would make an attempt. "Okay, your son Chad is twenty-three years old and has impregnated three different women at this point, correct?" I'd ask.

"Yes," he'd agree.

"And yet, you've accepted him anyway," I'd continue. "He's welcome home and at the dinner table anyway?"

"Chad's an idiot, but he's still my son," Frank would say.

"Exactly my point. Yes, thank you." I would say. "And because he's your son, I'm sure that if the phone rang right now, and it was Chad, and he said, 'Dad, I've made a horrible mistake. I've murdered someone,' you would still love and support him. You'd still go visit him in prison, send him money, get him a good lawyer, and try to get him released. Would you not?"

"Of course. I'd do anything for Chad," Frank said.

"Okay, now, what if Chad came over here right now and said, 'Dad, I need to tell you something. I've been hiding it for years, but I'm gay. I like men.' What would happen?" I asked.

"I'd tell him he was no longer welcome on my property until he repented and got his life right, but I wouldn't ever want to see him again until he got straight," he replied.

"So, is it not safe to admit that your feelings about homosexuality are tainted by culture, human opinion, and what society has embedded in you and that it has nothing to do with sin? Murder is a sin, and you'd love your son anyway, but being gay is the condition to your love?" I'd asked.

Frank could not agree with me, and perhaps he didn't understand my point. I wondered how many people missed the point. Jesus loves us all. We are loved with no conditions, completely covered in His blood, and for me, no one else's life choices are meant for me to consider. Whether it's their sexual preference, which is in no way comparable to murder–I had just used it as an analogy to show someone their error–or whether someone had been married and divorced a thousand times, no one's sex life is any of my business. I know that the love of Jesus is so much bigger than sexuality, it is insulting to Jesus to be so hung up on hating a group of people in His name. Knowing Him for as long and as well as I do, I understand that Jesus hates the hate people are spewing and labeling "Christian" so much more than any sexual preference.

Moreover, I do not believe homosexuality is a sin. For anyone who does, Christian or not, I have two questions. The first: which parts of the Bible are you choosing to ignore? We all pick and choose which parts of the Bible to heed to and which ones are too old or irrelevant. "Oh, that's the Old Testament, so we don't abide by it any longer," I have heard Christians claim.

The same pen who authored the rules that we are not to consume pork or shellfish wrote of homosexuality being a sin, and I wonder why we eat pork and shellfish now but being gay is the wrong of all wrongs. The same guy, Moses, wrote about remembering to keep the sabbath holy and to rest on the seventh day. In fact, back then, the penalty was death.

Moses wrote about a man who was gathering firewood to cook with on the sabbath and they, his own people, killed him. Not only do Christians work on Sundays now, but we even force other people to work when we go to the restaurant immediately after church service is over. Some companies even offer pastors free dinners on Sundays. To me, working on the Lord's day, the day we are supposed to worship and reflect on His glory, is so much more disgusting than anyone loving each other whether they are red, yellow, black, white, or rainbow.

Moses even tells us that we aren't to mix races in the sanctity of marriage, but he had an Ethiopian wife, and up until about twenty years ago, interracial relationships and marriages were so seriously hated in the country I live in that one would consider that before entering into a romance, no matter how strong the love, for fear of one another's safety. Still, today, in the United States, people are attacked for being married to someone outside of their own race, mostly by closed-minded people who claim to be Christians. Why? Because that's what they were taught.

I don't believe that's how they would really feel if Jesus and the Holy Spirit were living in every ounce of their spirit and their heart, because if you live drunk on the love of Jesus in the form of the Holy Spirit, you don't have the capacity to hate. You can't hate anyone when you know Jesus, and I know that was not the question.

The question was, is being gay a sin? And I say, only if it's part of the Bible that you choose to focus on when you think of sin. When I think of sin, I think of hurting people, and love never hurt anybody. Which brings me to the second question: when was it that you chose your own sexuality? If being homosexual is a choice, heterosexuality must be, as well.

I remember exactly when I knew I was attracted to men. I was six years old, and I was sitting on the couch with my mom watching *The Last of the Mohicans*, and it did not take much more than one look at Daniel Day Lewis for me to think, *"Okay, I see why girls want to kiss boys now. I get it."* And then, unfortunately, my raging heterosexuality has bloomed from there. It's unfortunate that I wish I were as attracted to women sexually as I am to men. I would so much rather co-parent my children with a woman who loves me and our family and wants to be my wife than have to fight with trying to even comprehend men.

I have been hurt by so many men, I wish I could just choose women, but I could no more do that than anyone who claims homosexuality is a choice. Sexuality is not a choice. People are born whoever they are. Jesus meets them where they are, and there's one thing about Jesus that I know is true. He loves all of us. Look at the cross where He gave up His very life for ours. He wouldn't have done that if He was worried about whether or not someone eats shellfish, bacon, or ham. He wouldn't die for people if He was worried about whether they were going to interracially love each other or intra-sexually love one another.

There's an ancient Japanese quote. "A man is the room he is in." Meet people where they are as individuals. Love above all.

Frank's story about the gay man who was his employee is probably among the most anger-inducing of his stories. He was the new manager, and the man and his boyfriend had been openly gay and living peacefully in that town for years.

Frank told his employee the first time he brought his boyfriend into the office that he was not allowed there. He explained this to me. "'I'm not gonna fire you now, but if you bring your faggot boyfriend in here again, I will. You won't have a job anymore,' I told him. I guess he didn't believe me because the next morning, I was running a little late, and I came into the office and they were there."

As he continued, my stomach churned. I knew some of this story, but none of the details. "Were they doing something unprofessional? What was your reason for losing your temper?" I asked.

"No they was just standing there in the lobby talking," he said.

"Then why did you have to hurt them?" I wanted him to see how childish and unfair his tantrum was.

"Because I told them he was not allowed to be in there," Frank answered.

"But that was not based on business practices or unprofessionalism. Were the spouses and boyfriends of other employees allowed in the office?" I asked.

"Of course, but nobody else's boyfriend was a flaming queer," he responded.

"So, because you have a problem with gay people, and for no other reason, what did you do?" I knew the answer but wanted him to say the words.

"I beat them both until one of them was so bloody and unconscious that his face was unrecognizable, and the other I threw through the wall. I knew his faggot boyfriend was unconscious, but I just kept hammer-punching him over and over in the face. The secretary girl had called the police, and they came and picked me up," he described.

"So, you beat two men nearly to death in the name of Jesus?" I asked. "Do you think that's something Jesus would have done? Can you imagine Jesus even hitting someone, let alone beating a man unrecognizable?" I asked with so much sorrow in my heart. "What happened to them?"

"The boyfriend was in a coma for a few days. The guy who worked for me would've been okay, but my dad sent someone to take care of both of them so they couldn't talk," he said.

"You mean your dad had them killed so that they couldn't testify against you and press charges?" I asked. "And you never had to go to prison for that? None of the witnesses, police or EMTs went forward?"

I choked back tears as I thought about the injustice–the men, their families, their mothers and fathers, two men losing their lives for simply being in love. I don't know everything about Jesus, I'm not there yet, but I do know that caused Him sorrow and pain. I know He loved those two men. I do know that.

Using scripture to justify one's own sin and condemn others is repugnant. Being a coward who can't fess up to his immature actions, nearly killing people and then having them killed... I can't imagine having to look Jesus in the eye and answering for that sin.

Where and when did the disconnection occur? I'd wondered so many times in my life. At some point in his life, most likely at a young age, Frank's ability to connect and empathize with others was severed. Unless it was himself or his son, whom he viewed as an extension of himself, people were not people. Everyone was a candidate for abuse.

If he disagreed with someone or did not understand them, he would verbally abuse them, and often those incidents escalated into physical violence. If the person was a woman, he would take whatever he wanted from her. Every story he told me about women or girls, the strongest implication was that he did not think of us as human. Gay people he openly referred to as "dogs."

No matter how elementary my message was, trying to relay to Frank that Jesus loves everyone, even people who weren't exactly like him, I got nowhere.

# CHAPTER THIRTY-SEVEN

Frank's story that explains so much, was not shared with me until I was in my thirties. After I had been hurt by this man, after hearing so many stories out of his own mouth about how he'd hurt so many people, he shared with me a story that brought me some clarity.

"Did you know that 911 wasn't even invented until 1968?" he asked. We were taking a break from training dogs, sitting in the shade.

"What? No. That's crazy." I had never even considered it before. "So what did people do?" I asked.

"Sometimes you'd get hurt, and someone would drive you into town to the hospital, but usually, there was nothing they could do for you that your mom hadn't already done," he said. "Back then, moms knew how to do all kinds of stuff. Set broken bones, bandage you up. I was just thinking about a time me and Berry was playing fort and Googled up when 911 was invented–1968," he said.

"What happened when you and Berry were playing fort?" I asked.

The longer we talked, the longer we could rest in the shade rather than working dogs, so I always asked as many questions as possible. Berry was Frank's older brother by two years, and stories involving Berry and their childhood were usually fairly entertaining.

"We was at our dad's house that time. We went there for summers. We was probably seven and nine. The lady my dad was married to that time was a Mexican gal, real pretty, named Christina. They was putting a brick sidewalk in. Had all these stacks and stacks of bricks sitting in the yard. Me an' ol' Bear, nobody was ever payin' any attention to us, and we thought we'd build a fort and have a brick throwin' war. Ol' Bear, he was strong, Man. He reared back and just BAM! Hit me right here with a brick." Frank touched the center of his forehead. "Threw that sucker hard too."

As Frank continued, my brain was exploding. Every question I had ever asked Jesus and myself about this man had been scientifically answered.

"My forehead had this huge, swollen knot on it for months," Frank went on. "My school yearbook picture from that year I even have a knot still."

I had so many more questions now, and this time, I was not just trying to evade working dogs. "So, you were seven? What happened after he hit you with the brick? Did they take you to the hospital?" I asked.

"Yeah, my second grade yearbook picture is embarrassing, man. My forehead has this huge knot. I begged my mom to let me miss picture day, but she wouldn't let me," Frank said.

I was dumbfounded. I had to actually close my jaw. "What happened? Who helped you?" I needed to know.

"I went and sat on the porch and passed out. I guess Christina put me in my bed. I threw up, had a fever, was dizzy for like two weeks," he explained.

"And all those times you were sent to psychiatrists and counselors as a child because you had anger issues and were always in trouble, did your mom tell them about that injury?" I asked gently, knowing the answer.

"No. Why would she?" Frank laughed, honestly ignorant of the correlation.

Everyone he had ever hurt flashed before my eyes—my mother, my sisters, my daughter, his mother, all the little girls, his little boy, my little brother Chad, and all the lives he'd taken because of drugs, alcohol, and anger issues.

He had lived with an undiagnosed frontal lobe injury for sixty years. He had frontal lobe damage. He was sixty-seven years old physically, but mentally, emotionally, and temperamentally, he was a child, a very young child, at that.

His inability to control his impulses, anger, and emotions were all stunted at seven years old. His inability to adapt to social settings and pick up social cues, stunted at seven years old. His impaired moral judgment, every time I had seen him be such a coward, his narcissism, his inability to connect with others and see them as just as human as he is... everything I wanted to understand, went back to this incident that occurred when he was seven--and for a second, I almost felt sorry for him.

It may seem like an oversimplification to blame sixty years of violence, trauma, sorrow, and loss on a brick, but that brick was just a vehicle for poor medical practices, poor parenting, broken and biased judicial systems, and power in the wrong hands paired with no education, self-awareness, or coping mechanisms.

No one ever cared enough about this man to help him, turning him into a monster, and my mom had been married to a seven-year-old for twenty-seven years.

# CHAPTER THIRTY-EIGHT

Often, especially as a teenager, it was difficult to see my friends' moms at our school and athletic events. The more involved their moms, the more jealous I was of my friends. I realized what that jealousy was at the time and shook it off as I didn't want to damage my friendships, but I could not shake off the ache I felt when I saw my friends' moms doing things for and with them.

I had very curly hair, and because I was so young when I went to live with my dad, I didn't have anyone to show me how to take care of it. I would complain to my dad about how much I hated my hair, and he would take me to a salon and try to explain my issues to a stylist. They would try to help me by giving me too much product and not enough instructions, and it would always end in frizz and tears.

Most of my adolescence, I was referred to by my peers as, "the girl with the big, poofy hair." Some of the older girls called me, "Cocoa Puffs." It was something that bothered me more than I think anyone knew. I tried to tell myself that there were more important things in life than one's hair, and I tried to build my self-esteem by reminding myself of my other, better qualities, but these things are difficult when you're thirteen.

Also, I just wanted more manageable hair. It was a frizzy lion's mane mess, or it was in a bun, and that was not fair. I wanted to wear my hair down like the other girls. Eventually, when I was about fifteen, I figured out how to conquer my curls, and people started to compliment them, but if I had had a mother available to me, this would not have been a thing I had shed tears over more than once.

Morgan's mom french braided our hair before our volleyball and basketball games. Back then, I saw this as kind and thought of how generous she was with her time and energy. I also deeply appreciated that, even though my nightmare nest of hair was extra difficult to braid, and it took her twice as long to braid my hair than anyone else's, but she braided it anyway.

I felt bad asking her to braid my hair but loved my hair braided so much because it was finally out of my way, and I would leave it braided for a couple of days afterward, not only because I loved the way it looked, but it felt like a crown of motherly love and affection.

Morgan's mom had spent a mother's love on me. I wanted to be that kind of mom to my children's friends when I grew up. Even still, I hated to ask her to mess with my curls, and I would sit and watch her do everyone else's so I could learn. I wanted to be able to braid my own hair, and sitting and watching Morgan's mom, I did learn.

The Sunday after one of my seventh-grade volleyball games, I went to church with my mom and her husband. My hair was still braided in a french braid, and Frank said that it looked, "nice," so the next time I went to their house, I asked my mom if I could french braid her hair.

This would be the first time in my life that my mom and I had styled each other's hair, something I had seen my friends and their moms do, of which I was so envious. Frank was outside working dogs, and my mom and I were in the house. I remember I braided her hair and put an elastic with a tiny butterfly on it to secure it.

I was so happy and proud. I felt like we were able to be normal for a moment. I knew how to braid, my mom liked it, and it looked pretty!

Later, when Frank came inside the house to get a glass of lemonade, the first thing he did was pull out the butterfly and shove his whole hand into the center of the braid I had put in my mom's hair. I had worried that he might make her take it down, but I was still shocked that he'd done it in the most sophomoric way imaginable. I was shocked that he'd done it the way a bully in an '80s movie about childish teenagers would. Mostly, and probably the main reason that I remember it so clearly, is that I was shocked that I was so good at predicting how he would react to things. Not that his reaction to anything was ever complex, but still, I was a child. I was still learning how social situations and people worked. There was no reason I should've been so good at predicting the reactions of someone I only saw occasionally. He demanded attention the way a child demands attention, but unlike a child, he was dangerous. Any time anyone mentions the movie *Honey, I Blew Up the Baby*, I think of Frank Hudson.

After he messed up Mom's braid, Frank had me sit in the lecture chair so he could read from scripture about what God says about the braiding of hair. In the New Testament, both Peter and Paul mention braids. Within their same individual verse, they mention putting on expensive jewelry. That afternoon, Frank's version of what they meant was that braids were ungodly. Literal braids were ungodly. I knew that he did not have a problem with braids because he had already told me my hair looked nice in one.

Later, when I wore a braid to their house, he complimented it and I said, "But Paul and Peter mention braiding your hair being a sin."

That day, his response was that Paul and Peter meant that spending a ton of time and money on one's appearance was the sin, not the braids themselves. I didn't bother reminding him about the time he'd pulled a braid out of my mother's hair based on those verses. I knew that was not why he'd pulled the butterfly.

He couldn't let us bond. He couldn't allow anyone else access to his wife. She was his and his alone. So, his instant and infantile reaction was to pull her hair, and then he had to justify that action with something and his weapon of choice at that point in his life: fists swapped out with a Bible. He twisted it and used it to manipulate people, especially his wife.

# CHAPTER THIRTY-NINE

My mom didn't know it, but her generation were the first women to be divorced, single, and raising children by themselves, successfully. Divorce was not legal until 1969 unless adultery was proven. In the 1970s and '80s, divorces for other reasons had started occurring, but most women could not make enough money to be able to care for their children alone.

A divorced woman would either need to remarry immediately or ask for welfare. In the late 1980s and early '90s, women started choosing to be single mothers over settling for abusive men and started raising their children themselves, even if it meant working three jobs. State childcare assistance became slightly more accessible, and women became stronger and more independent than they had ever been allowed to believe they could be.

My mother was not allowed to believe. Frank had completely brainwashed her into believing that, no matter what she did, how far away from him she got, or how well she was hidden, she could not make it without him. What's worse, he convinced her that, without him, she could never be happy.

When I was in junior high, the Dixie Chicks song "Goodbye Earl" was played at every school dance. For some reason, the song about

Marianne helping kill and bury her best friend Wanda's abusive husband was a favorite among teenagers. We all knew all the words. It is catchy and clever. It's also a bit odd to be at a school dance in the middle of a circle of your friends who know enough about your trauma to sing, "Goodbye Frank!" at the top of their lungs with you while you cry tears of laughter and sadness.

I was already sad that she hadn't helped me get ready. I was sad that she didn't even know where I was that night but so happy to be blessed enough to have accepting and funny friends who would help make my heart light.

My mom was isolated. She didn't have any friends left. If anyone came near her, he ran them off. If anyone invited her to a lady's lunch, he answered for her with a simple and rude, "No." No explanation.

People felt sorry for her, but there was no one to empower or help encourage her. When she ran away, she had places to go and stay, but she did not have the emotional support of a brainwashed and traumatized victim. She needed friends who had been through some of her trauma with her, the ear of a professional, or a support group for women who had suffered domestic violence. She needed to be told that she could make it without Frank, raise her children, make a living, go back to school, and have friends.

But my mom didn't believe in herself. He'd broken that part of her. She couldn't love herself. He'd stolen that too.

<h1 style="text-align:center">CHAPTER FORTY</h1>

Jordan, my older brother, is thirteen years older than me, and he was eighteen when my mom met Frank. In the beginning, he tried to talk my mom out of ruining her life. He wasn't the only one, of course. People from church, my dad, her friends, and her family all tried, but it was as though she couldn't believe anything anyone said, other than Frank.

Eventually, Jordan accepted that my mom had chosen her path. He lived at our grandma's house, finished raising himself, and put himself through college. My mom missed his graduation.

When my brother got engaged to his wife, her wonderful parents who were friends with my dad knew a little bit about my mom's husband and situation already, so when Jordan expressed his sadness over not having his mom at his wedding, his father-in-law offered to call Frank to try to persuade him to allow my mom to attend.

It took Jordan's father-in-law a few long phone calls with Frank before he finally gave my mom permission to go to her own son's wedding. I can't speak for my brother, but I'm sure it broke his heart that she didn't just stand up for herself and for him saying, "Of course, I'm going to my son's wedding. Try to stop me!"

I was eleven at the time, and it not only broke my heart, but it caused me to stop planning my own future wedding. Like most girly little girls, I had been completely enamored of the whole process of my brother's fiancée's wedding planning. It was so much fun to see what colors, flowers, and music she'd chosen. When I realized my own very far away future wedding would not be important enough for my own mom to attend, a bit of my self-esteem fell away and never came back. These were the important days that we were meant to share with our proud parents, and yet, our mom did not even really know us anymore.

My mom's appearance at Jordan's wedding was one of the first times her lack of self-care caused me to feel that my own life no longer had value. She had shown up, but not really, with wet hair as if she'd still had to fight to the last minute to be allowed to get ready and go. Of course, she had no makeup on, a tear-streaked face, and an ill-fitting dress that looked out of place.

She was not really there. She was not happy to be there. She was tired. Her hair was not styled, she was missing her lilac or light green eye shadow and vibrant lip. There was nothing sparkly about her. My own life lost value because I felt that if the enormously important events in our lives were not important to her, how could we be important to her anymore at all? I am sure Jordan had wished that Libby had been at his wedding.

I know I did. It devastated me to see her there, unhappy.

Before, when she was Libby, Mom and Jordan were good friends. He tried to maintain that, and he loves her so much. Again, I don't want to tell his story, but from my perspective, my brother deserved to keep his mom.

Jordan is the best dad I know. He has two amazing children who grew up without one of their grandmas because that was how Frank preferred it. Jordan deserved to have the support and encouragement of his mom in his life as he grew up, got an education, got married, and raised his children who very much deserved a relationship with their grandma.

As I write about all of the ways her absence broke our hearts, I think of how badly it must have made her feel that she could not be there for Jordan or his family. She internalized all of those feelings of guilt, and they caused her to disassociate more and more because she could not love herself any less.

Every time she let one of us go, she let go of another piece of herself.

# CHAPTER FORTY-ONE

Mellissa is ten years older than me and was sixteen when our mom met her husband. Mellissa finished high school without our mom and went away to college without her. I could not imagine being at college, hours away from home, and not being able to call my mom.

Mellissa is smart, independent, and brave. She did well in college, and I still remember the day Dad drove us all up to see her graduate. I walked into her dorm room expecting to see her beaming with pride. I was only eleven, and I was proud of her, but she was not smiling. Her eyes were full of tears.

"She isn't here." Mellissa sat down on her bed and tried to keep her mascara from running.

Our dad paced the hallway, never knowing what to say when one of us needed our mom, and she was not even in the same universe. It was unfair to all of us. Mellissa deserved to have her mom at her high school and college graduations. She deserved to be able to call home and talk to her mom when she was at college. She deserved to call and ask for motherly advice, come home, and visit her mom. She deserved to have a good mother.

Dad's sister, Aunt Glenna, helped Mellissa plan her bridal shower. She helped Mellissa plan and facilitate her wedding and reception. I was thirteen this time, and again, my mom had to fight and beg to be able to attend her own daughter's wedding.

My mom's dad, who had driven eight hours from Indiana, and my mom's sister, Aunt Cathy, who had driven from Kansas City, a three-hour drive, had shown up early enough to listen to my brother Jordan and me warm up and practice our song before the wedding.

Our mom, who had a twenty-minute drive, got to the wedding five minutes before it began, once again looking unkempt and brave-faced rather than genuinely happy. Of course, she was not allowed to attend the reception, and just like at Jordan's wedding, she had to leave immediately afterward.

This time, I was taking mental notes. My adolescent inner dialogue was shouting, *"Nothing we do matters to her! Why should it matter to us?!"*

Jordan and Mellissa cared enough about themselves that our mother's love was not a necessity. It was a horrendous tragedy that they had to go without it, but go without it, they did. They had lives to live and persevered, but as for me, I still wanted her to love me more than almost anything. More than anything, I wanted to rescue her so she would be allowed to mother all of us again.

Mellissa has two gorgeous girls of her own. She should have been able to call her mom when she was pregnant with her daughters. She deserved to have the love and support of her mom in the hospital when she was giving birth. Mellissa's daughters deserve to have a relationship with their grandma. Just as I said about the guilt of not being able to be there for Jordan and his family, I know my mom carried the weight of not being able to be involved in Mellissa and her daughter's lives.

When I was very small, four and five, Mellissa would take me upstairs to her bedroom in the green house and teach me to sing. She has one of the prettiest singing voices, and she taught me all about how to use the right muscles to sing. When I was five, she taught me the words to "Achy Breaky Heart" in one afternoon because our dad wanted me to sing it with his band that night at the county fair.

Mellissa was always patient with me, and I have always been able to go to her when I have a problem.

The year Ruby and I moved in with our dad and stepmom, I was seven, and Mellissa was a senior in high school. She drove me to school every morning, and even though that year came with so many changes, most of them very confusing and in my opinion, none of them good, Mellissa was one of my constants.

We listened to The Cranberries, REM, and The Spin Doctors in her car on the way to school. I was probably the only seven-year-old who knew all the words to "Linger." If I hadn't had Mellissa, I wouldn't have made it through my childhood or adolescence. I have needed her help my entire life, and she's always been there ready to help me.

Mom and Mellissa were best friends when she was little. Best friends with Libby–I am jealous of that. I often think about my mom in that era of her life, mothering Jordan and Mellissa when they were little. I wish it were like a musical carousel that I could just stop or a Polaroid I could climb inside. I would tell Libby to soak up all Jordan and Mellissa's love and savor it.

I would tell her to love herself like they have always loved her.

CHAPTER FORTY-TWO

My dad's mom was the only grandparent I ever really had. I didn't meet my maternal grandma until I was in my twenties, and I only saw my mom's dad a handful of times growing up. My dad's dad died a month after I was born, so our dad's mom was our only grandparent.

She was the warmest person. Everyone loved her, confided in her, and trusted her. She was my best friend when I was a child. I spent the night at her house every weekend I was allowed to. Some weeks, the thought of spending the night at my grandma's house was the only thing that got me through the week.

I would ask to go see my grandma more often than my own mom. My grandma exuded and radiated Jesus' love. She's the person who taught me to pray, and she prayed for me more than I know.

If I hadn't had my grandma during my childhood, I believe I may have taken my own life. I began contemplating suicide at the age of eight, and without my grandma's warmth, I may have made a terrible mistake. I definitely would not have known enough about Jesus to make it through hard times; she so resembled Him.

My grandma was born with clubbed feet. She spent her childhood, during The Great Depression, in and out of leg surgeries and braces. She couldn't run, skip, or dance. By the time I was born, my grandma was sixty and could barely walk. She had been a wonderful wife, raised two children, was a school teacher, and lived a full life, but she was still too young to be confined to her chair.

However, it did not keep her from being positive. If I couldn't walk to the kitchen without being in incredible pain, I would be a miserable cow. Most days, I am a miserable cow anyway, or I complain that I have to get up and walk to the kitchen. I can't imagine not being able to, and she wasn't complaining in the least.

She was cool. She had amazing stories, and she was absolutely hilarious.

Her name was Imogene, and for some reason, her mother, whose name was Pansy, didn't give her a middle name. Grandma chose her own, and she chose Deloris.

"Why?" we asked her. "Why on earth would you choose Deloris?"

She just liked Deloris, she said.

She hadn't legally added it to anything, but she would just randomly tell people that was her middle name when asked or sign a Christmas card here and there, *Imogene Deloris*, which to me is the funniest part.

Grandma was also incredibly bright. I can't imagine being a young woman in the 1950s, attending college by myself in the city after having grown up in such a rural area, but she did, and she got her teaching degree. She also played guitar and sang.

When we were kids, she would play a game with Madi, my youngest sister, when she was a baby where Madi would sing the line of a song she'd made up and make Grandma sing the line word for word, note for note, no matter how absurd.

Grandma always played our games, listened to our stories and problems, and encouraged us to see life's struggles in a positive light. Grandma complimented us and made us each feel so important. She had ten grandchildren, and I know that even though she's been gone for twenty-three years, if asked, all of my siblings and cousins would say she was the greatest friend any of them ever had.

When I was thirteen, Grandma passed away. It broke all of our hearts. A month after she died, Mellissa had her wedding on the hill behind Grandma's house, just as she had intended to ever since she was a little girl and asked our grandpa to marry her there in that orchard on that hill. It was a beautiful wedding. A carriage brought Mellissa up, and our dad walked her down the aisle. A couple of years later, when that house came up for sale, Mellissa bought Grandma's old house.

Mellissa didn't live in Grandma's old house. She lived in Texas. For a while, our mom used the house to store things. She hid our Christmas presents there and things she'd picked up at garage sales for her future house when she finally ran away from Frank for good.

A couple of times when I was in high school, Mom took Chad and ran away to live with Mellissa in Texas for a couple of months at a time. Mom's intentions always seemed to be to get her life together and move on, and she always seemed to turn out to be telling us she couldn't get divorced again because no one had committed adultery, which was the only biblical reason for divorce, so she, therefore, could not move on.

I would say, "So don't get divorced, just stay away. Stay hidden. Start your lives over somewhere he'll never find you–Georgia, Maine, Alaska–just don't go back! He's rotting your brain! You're not even the same person that you used to be," I would plead.

"I would, but I don't have any money, and I can't take his son away from him," she would say and always go back.

When I was sixteen, living with my dad and stepmother became so intolerable that I threw all of my stuff in my car and I left. I worked in the next town over in a café where I knew the owners had a small, smelly, studio apartment in a building they owned across the parking lot. I asked if I could trade my paycheck for rent there, and since I had already worked at the café for a year and a half and had never missed a shift, and they knew how miserable my home life was, they instantly said that would be a fine idea.

I'd lived in that strange-smelling building for three months when my mom decided she and Chad were going to move into Grandma's old house, which Mellissa had sitting empty in the same town as my job and my small apartment. So, I moved in with my mom and Chad and lived with them for the second half of my junior year of high school.

I was seventeen and hadn't lived with my mom since I was six. I felt loved, secure, normal, and comforted for the first time in eleven years. My mom and I worked separate shifts at the café, and Chad, who was seven, went to school. I picked Chad up from school and watched him on my days off, and my mom worked when I didn't.

It was prom season, and my mom actually got to help me get ready and took me to meet my friends. I was over the moon. I thought we were all happy, but looking back, and especially looking at the photos I took at the time, she looked exhausted.

She was scared. We only lived twenty minutes away from the enemy. The house didn't have a garage, and Frank knew what type of cars we drove. He knew my grandma had lived there, and he knew where the house was. He knew I worked at the café and had already come in while I was working to give me a letter for my mom, which I burned with my lighter in front of him. Mom had applied for a job in the dish room specifically for that reason, so he couldn't see her at the café if he came in to eat.

The three of us were scared, so my mom put props on the front porch to make it look like someone else lived there, a couple of pairs of men's boots and a few empty wine bottles. She and Chad slept in the very back bedroom far away from the doors, which had three locks on each.

One day, when my mom was at work and Chad was at summer school, I was in the bathroom putting on my makeup when I heard a truck in the driveway. I peeked out the window, knowing it was Frank before seeing him. I knew that the bathroom door didn't have a lock on it, and I had left the back door unlocked. I also knew Frank was rude and demanding and would just walk right in.

Frozen in fear, I weighed my options. I could hide in the closet, but he knew I was there because he'd seen my car in the driveway. It was a small house. I knew he would look in every closet. I could wait until he was at the back door and then run to my car through the front door. I was still frozen when he walked straight into the bathroom without knocking. I was stunned. Even for him, walking into someone else's house and then straight into the bathroom without knocking?

He laughed at my terrified expression, "Where's Chad?" he asked.

"I'm not telling you, and you need to leave right now," I said, thinking about what to do next considering what happened to women when they tried to call 911 or run away from this man. The bathroom closet connected to the bedroom, so I ran through the closet, grabbed my keys off my dresser, and ran out the front door.

Frank caught up to me at my car, "Just tell me where Chad is!" he screamed.

"I'm not telling you shit, you psychopath!" I yelled back.

"I know he's here. Where are you hiding him?"

I was in my car backing out, "He's obviously not here since I'm leaving. He's a child. You think I would leave him here with you?" I shouted out the window.

"I don't know what you'd do." He was mocking me, implying I had bad judgment, even though he knew nothing about me. I had been taking care of his son who was finally starting to heal and enjoy his life.

I drove to the café and ran straight to my mom. "He's here! He's at our house! What do I do?" I was frantic.

My mom was calm, "What? Oh, I told him he could go and pick Chad up. He came in here and asked me, and I told him he could," she replied.

"Chad is at summer school, and you could have called me and warned me," I said, not in the least bit surprised that she'd forgotten about me and had not considered that I might be scared of the enemy we were all losing sleep worrying over. For the second time, he had walked straight through a bathroom door that I had closed.

"Oh, he's at summer school. I forgot. Well, go pick him up and take him home, and let Frank take him for the day," she said as though she were telling me about the weather.

So, I picked Chad up and took him home, and handed him over to the big bad wolf. Later that week, my mom told me that she and Chad were going back to live with Frank. Mellissa didn't think that I was old enough to live in Grandma's house alone, and she was right. I was seventeen. I would've turned it into a party house.

I couldn't go back to the apartment in the café parking lot because one of my friends had already moved in. My mom wanted me to live in the double-wide by the barn that Frank's dad had put there and lived in for a few years. His dad had passed away, and the house was sitting empty.

Instead, I chose to move in with Mellissa in Texas.

## CHAPTER FORTY-THREE

My plan was to spend my senior year of high school living with my sister and her husband in a Dallas suburb. At first, I was excited, and all of my friends back home were cheering me on via MSN messenger every day that summer while I waited for school to start. I knew it would be culture shock to go from a high school of only two hundred people total to having five hundred people in my graduating class alone and about two thousand in the whole school.

*"There aren't even two thousand people in my whole town,"* I kept thinking. Before I left, that concept seemed exciting. When I got there, it turned out to be lonely.

I've never had trouble talking with people, speaking up, trying to be disarming and approachable, so I didn't have any problem making friends. In each of my classes, I had a couple of friends I was excited to see each day.

The problem was, I was overwhelmed and exhausted. Trying to keep up with where everything was located inside the huge school building, and where everything was in town, was causing me anxiety. I worked at Subway, but not always at the same location, and this was before I even had a cell phone, let alone a phone with GPS. I drove a tiny '94 Ford Aspire, and it was having trouble helping me find

Subways in a new, and to me, humongous place. I needed a real friend, not just someone I had met in geometry class.

So, I used some of my savings to buy a Greyhound ticket home for the weekend of our county fair. I stayed the weekend with my friend Melody and rode the Greyhound back on Sunday, which took twelve hours one way, and I was lonely. I was sad that I had a mom who didn't even know where I was and a dad who no longer seemed to care.

I was still seventeen, but I felt like an adult now. I had been on my own, making my own decisions, whether good or bad, for a year. The most important lesson I was beginning to learn was that adulthood was just as sad and lonely as childhood but with battles and choices that determined one's future. I had only scratched the surface of this lesson, and the weight of it was too heavy to carry, so I looked for relief. I looked for fun. Isn't that what young adults tend to do?

Melody and I went to the county fair, and I saw all of my friends that I had not seen in months. By the end of the weekend, everyone was begging me to come back home, so on the Greyhound on the way back to Texas, there were really only a couple of things on my heart. How was I going to break it to my sister Mellissa that I wanted to go back, and where would I live? Would I move into the double-wide on Mom and Frank's property and tough out living next to Frank so that I could spend my senior year at my own school with all my friends, or would I live with Melody or another friend?

I could not go back home to my dad and stepmother's house. I had burned that bridge for a reason. I loved my dad and wished for our relationship's sake that my teenage years had been different, but I would rather be homeless or dead than ever live with my stepmother again. My dad still loved me, and we were still friends, but it was not until much later in my life that he and I would have a conversation about how his wife had treated my younger sister Ruby and me. For now, that was a topic we hurdled over and danced around.

When I got back to Mellissa's from my trip back to Iowa to the fair, my dad was the first person I called. He agreed that I should come home and that he wanted me to be closer to him, even if it wasn't under the same roof. He also thought it was important for me to have my senior year with my friends, teachers, and counselors who knew me. We talked about what it would mean for me to live in Frank's house on his land.

"How far away are those houses on his land?" my dad asked me.

"The double-wide that Frank's dad lived in is down by the barn about a quarter of a mile away from Mom and Frank's house," I said.

"So you wouldn't be in the same house as him. Would he be trying to tell you what to wear and do again?" My dad was hopeful that I would come back, but he was also a realist who wanted me to think things through.

He told me he had a bad habit of being impulsive when he was my age, and one of his favorite pieces of advice for his children was to be still and rest, waiting for God to show them the direction in which to move.

"I doubt he cares what I wear or do anymore. I doubt he'll have any rules for me other than no people can come over, and Mom's not going to be allowed to help me with anything like groceries or buying me stuff with his money," I answered.

"You know what I'm gonna say. Be still, and ask God for the answer. Talk to your mom, and see if she thinks you'll be happy there," my dad said.

After hanging up the phone, I emailed my mom. For the last few years since Frank had gotten himself a desktop computer for making his kennel a website, my mom had an email address that she would check once a day to see if any of her children needed her to call them while he was outside training dogs.

So, I typed up an email to momescaped at Yahoo because that was what she'd chosen for herself. She'd run away so many times now, that that was what her mind revolved around—when and how she would get away from him next, in fight or flight mode. And I was about to invite all of that into my life, not because it was what was best for me or because I would feel loved, safe, or happy there, but because that was what I knew and what I was used to.

I did not have the self-worth or self-esteem to try something new.

I did not value myself enough to stay in Texas. I did not love myself enough to give myself the strength I needed to survive without my friends and their families.

A few hours after emailing momescaped, she found time away from Frank to call me. She was overjoyed to have me move into the house by the barn. She had been waiting for years for me to be old enough to live there by myself so she wouldn't feel so lonely.

I told her the only way I would be able to live there is if Frank didn't hassle me about what I wore, what sports I played, or anything else I chose to do. My mom agreed and said that since she and Chad had just come back from running away, Frank was not going to bother me, and he would actually be happy because, if I were there, she wouldn't run away again unless he did something to me and it caused me to leave.

"I'll just tell him if you leave, Chad and I will go with you, and he won't bother you," she said. "I'll talk to him about it when he comes in the house."

When I hung up with my mom, I started to think of all the times I had been mid-phone conversation, and she'd hung up on me because Frank was coming in the house, and she wasn't allowed to talk to me. I thought about all of the times I had been hurt by both of them.

I thought, *I only have one year left, and then I'll go to college and have my own life.*

That evening, Frank called me to speak with me about living in his dad's old house. His only rules were that I didn't have any friends over, no parties, and he would pay the utilities, but I would have to put gas in my own car and buy my own groceries.

This was the exact arrangement I already had with my sister in Texas, only if I went and lived next to my mom, I would have my own three-bedroom house and get to graduate with my friends.

So, I packed up my stuff and went back to Iowa.

# CHAPTER FORTY-FOUR

Living alone in the double-wide on Frank's property during my senior year of high school had pros and cons. One of the pros was that I almost never saw Frank. The only time I ever saw him was if he was taking care of his horses, and we'd wave to one another as I walked to or from my car.

I silently appreciated him allowing me to live rent- and utility-free in a house that he owned, and he just as much appreciated me being the only reason his wife was not going to take his child and run away from him that year. Another pro was that my mom sneakily stocked my fridge and pantry and left gift cards and gas money under my mattress every week. This was wonderful because I was allowed to concentrate on my last year of high school, scholarship essays, and cheerleading rather than having an after-school job.

Mom would often leave a sparkly pair of earrings or a new top in my closet while I was at school. Once, I came home to find six new pairs of shoes she'd bought and a note that said, *"A woman can never have enough shoes."*

The con of this arrangement was that she was still hiding. She still had to sneak around to buy me these things. She bought me a cell phone so we could coordinate a meeting at the corner of our road so I could get my stuff out of her car just in case Frank was at the barn when she got back from running errands. She could not let him know she was helping me. She couldn't let him know that she had put anyone before him or his wishes. By the end of the year, I was amazing at pushing the con away and focusing on the pros.

*"At least I get to do cheerleading,"* or *"at least I kind of have a mom now." "At least I get to live alone." "At least..."*

I had accepted too much of the least amount of effort the most important people in my life could give me for so long that it had broken my expectations meter. I never demanded any more of anyone. I never demanded any more respect, kindness, or patience from anyone. I became a target for abusive people, and I remained that way for far too long.

Being that target caused me a lot of pain and regret.

Another con to having my mom so close by was her infatuation with me being thin and encouraging me to lose weight. One day, in the spring of my senior year, my friend Nicole came home with me after school so we could get ready to go out later that night, and there was a Snickers wrapper and a note on my kitchen table.

In my mom's hand, the note read: *'I found this in the trash can, and I just wanted to tell you that if you stop eating this junk, you could be really skinny and cute. Love, Mom. P.S. Don't tell Frank that the umbrella I bought you came from me.'*

Any time my mom bought me something, she went out of her way to remind me not to tell Frank where it came from.

Nicole looked up at me with tears in her eyes. "Oh my God, Amelia. I'm so sorry," she said.

"I know it's weird that my mom goes through my trash. She does it every single day," I said making light of it. "But hey, at least I don't have to take the trash out!"

I would always try to make jokes about the odd circumstances and situations my mom and Frank put me in and downplay the trauma so as not to overwhelm my friends with too much. If someone asked me why my mom was never at our school events, or if I had come to school crying, ever since childhood, I hid the darkest parts of my pain from my friends, and for their sake, made jokes. That was why we sang "Goodbye Frank" instead of "Goodbye Earl." That's why my friends knew about 'momescaped' at Yahoo, because that stuff was so insane it was funny. I had to explain to Sam why the porch where I had lived with Mom and Chad had men's boots and empty wine bottles all over.

When Nicole was upset over my mom's note that day, I genuinely, initially thought it was that she was upset over my mom's judgment of me eating a candy bar. Nicole and I had been friends since fourth grade, and one of the things we had bonded over was our very curvy bodies and our struggles with junk food. I knew she'd been listening when I talked about my mom's hypercriticism of my weight, but what she said next proved to me that Nicole was an even better listener and friend than I had ever even realized.

"No, I mean that she's still having to sneak around and that he hasn't changed. I thought that would be different now that you live here, that she was getting to be your mom. I am so sorry you have to deal with that," Nicole said.

I turned away from her quickly so that I wouldn't cry and headed to my bedroom where we'd been going before we saw the note when she stopped to hug me. She was showing me I needed to love myself better. She was showing me that she was listening and that she cared. Nicole was showing me that I should not have to accept being treated that way and that I deserved better.

Unfortunately, I didn't listen. I had been shown and told much more often that I was an afterthought. I was just one of those people who was no one's favorite or most special person. I was on the back burner, and that's how I treated myself.

Shortly after that, we had our high school graduation, and it was Nicole who turned around to ask me why I was sobbing after we walked to our seats before the ceremony.

"She isn't here," I said, trying to catch my tears before they left foundationless streaks down my cheeks.

"I'm so sorry," Nicole said, turning back around. Graduation was starting.

It was happening, the day I had known I would have to beg for her to be at since I was a little girl, and she'd missed Jordan's college and Mellissa's high school and college graduations. Every time I had asked my mom to go to my graduation in the weeks leading up to it, she'd say, "I really don't think he's gonna let me go."

The night before graduation, my mom had called me back so I could ask her, and she said, "I'm pretty sure I won't get to go, but if I do, I'll have to leave right after. Here he comes, gotta go," and she hung up on me.

Even though I lived there now, I still had to email my mom. Frank had told me I could not just call to talk with my mom unless there was an emergency. "If there's a fire, call. Other than that, you don't need to be bothering your mom. She's got work to do," he said.

What he actually meant was, "This is my toy! You can't borrow it!"

I went up on stage to sing the song Morgan and I had written about our classmates and our futures. When I looked out into the audience, I saw my mom, Frank, and Chad. Frank had come to my graduation, too, not to be supportive and to show me that he cared too, but because my mom had begged him so much that he gave in, but only if he could be there to babysit her.

It was on that stage singing that song that I had previously felt proud of, but now, I felt judged under his scowl. I felt stupid, embarrassed, and like I was not human enough to be up there on that stage. It was on that stage that I knew I would never be able to have a wedding because I refused to have one without my mom there, but Frank's presence on the most important day of my life would be so much worse.

It was on that stage that I decided my future, my heart, my self didn't matter. He had attacked and attacked and attacked, and I was vulnerable. I was a child. I always lost. I was defeated.

They left right after the ceremony, and I didn't even get to hug her or have my photo taken with her. As I write this, I realize I have no photos of my mom and me taken after the age of six years old. If I felt that horrible about Frank being there without even having to deal with him or live with him on a daily basis, I can't even imagine my mom's lack of self-worth.

She must have not even felt like she was human. She was now fifty years old, and she had either been running away or treated like shit for twelve years straight, all of which were exhausting. She and I both tried to make that year happy and stress-free for one another, and I have a couple of fond memories of my mom from that time, but most of what I remember is the fear that I could not matter to her because she did not belong to herself any longer was confirmed to be true.

I was now a legal adult who had been raised in an environment where caring about myself was something I was never taught, and I had to simply try not to self-destruct. Not harming myself was the daily goal, and beyond that, I could do nothing more. Big goals were not for people like me.

Forget about dreams. I was just trying to survive.

# CHAPTER FORTY-FIVE

Filling out a FAFSA, taking the ACT, applying to colleges, and picking one to go to are things that most high school kids do with the help and guidance of their parents. I did all of those things alone. I took care of myself and made my way through the last year of high school parent-free.

The independence I learned benefited me, but the loneliness I felt scarred me. I spent my seventeenth Christmas alone. I drove myself to the ACT, no pep talk. I decided on a college and was accepted. I had won so many scholarship essay contests that I paid for my own books and had money left over. Being on my own, I qualified for free tuition and had even auditioned and been accepted into the university choir. I should've been excited, but I honestly did not care about myself. I still lived in Frank's double-wide trailer and planned to drive myself to college from there each day.

My friends and I did not drink or party yet, and the only drop of alcohol I had ever drank was the wine Frank had given me when I was six. The summer before our freshmen year of college my friends and I spent trying to savor the twilight of our childhood. My friend Julie and I had heard that they were having American Idol auditions in the theater of the college I would be attending. We went to the auditions, and while we were there, my friend Zac called me.

"Hey, are you in a band right now?" Zac asked.

"I'm not, but I can be. Why?" I asked.

"My band is playing two weeks from today at the Wolf Theater, and we need a band to open for us," he said.

"Consider it done. We'll be there." I said.

I didn't win the American Idol audition, but I now had more important things to do. I called Morgan, who played guitar and sang. We had written a handful of songs together, and Morgan was immediately able to find a drummer and bassist. We started meeting at Morgan's church to practice every evening since we only had a couple of weeks to learn fifteen to twenty songs. We sounded great for teenagers. The guy playing drums was also a very talented guitar player. I'm very happy we were able to play music with them that summer. It was a lot of fun.

The night of our gig at the Wolf Theater, I was very excited. I let my friends dress me in a teal Pink Floyd shirt with matching eye shadow and my "all cute and punk," jeans. For 2005 in rural Iowa, I was looking pretty fierce.

Our band, which we'd never even given a name, opened for Zac's band, and we sounded pretty good. There wasn't much of an audience, comprised mostly of our friends and some band members' parents, but we all had a great time anyway. As after any and every event we had ever been to, the after-party took place at the café I had worked at in high school. That was where I had met Zac. That was where everyone went after everything. Sometimes, the café was the main event as it was the only twenty-four-hour restaurant in the area.

There was a guy at our gig I'd seen a few times before at Zac's other shows. I didn't know him very well, but everyone else knew him by name, so when he said he didn't have a ride to the café, I told him he could ride with Morgan and me. The kid was about six-foot-five-inches tall, so he sat in the front seat of Morgan's Beetle, and I sat in the back seat. When we got to the café, Morgan pulled me to the side and said, "I wish you hadn't invited him. Now, I have to drive him back to his house instead of taking you back to your car at my house."

I didn't blame Morgan. It had been a long day, and my car was in a different city than the café and a completely different city still than where this kid lived.

"Oh, shit, I hadn't thought of that," I said. I wasn't thinking about logistics. I was just riding the high of having sung for an audience. Music, pancakes, and my emo eyeliner were all I was thinking about. "Just take us back to my car, and I'll take him back home," I said.

So, after the café, Morgan drove the kid and me back to my car, and then I drove him forty minutes back home where I found out, much to my surprise, that he was only fifteen. He was a lot bigger and taller than me, and his mohawk stood an extra six inches on top of his head. When we got to his town, I asked him for directions to his house, and first he gave me directions to a park.

"Don't you want to go swing or something? I don't want to go home yet," he said, getting out of the car.

"Not really. It's already midnight, and I have a long drive home after I drop you off. Please get back in the car." I said. "Where do you live?"

He started to give me directions again. By now, I'd had a very long day, and my energy was spent. I wasn't familiar with his town, and it was dark. This time, he directed me to a dark and silent train yard. I realized the road we were on was a dead end, and there was nothing but empty trains in front of me.

I stopped the car and turned to him to scold him. I was going to say that if he didn't tell me where to take him, I was going to leave him there, but I didn't have a chance. Before I could open my mouth he was on top of me, his right hand over my nose and mouth and his left hand pulling down my jeans. He had already taken his belt off, and now I realized that was what he had done when he got out of my car at the park. He pulled my jeans down as far as he needed to in order to take my virginity away from me in one minute. One minute and it was gone, taking any shred of dignity or self-worth that I had with it.

*"Goodbye, Virginity. Goodbye, Innocence."*

He was only there for one minute when I got his hand off my face and started to shriek and kick. He opened my car door and jumped over me and out, turning back to say, "You know what a plan B pill is, right?"

I was reeling. "What?" I was trying to close and lock my door and pull my pants up at the same time.

"Plan B. Go to the pharmacy and get one. You might need it," he said.

I left him in the train yard and sped away bleeding and feeling more filthy than I ever had in my life. Now, on top of being worthless, I was also disgusting. Someone had taken the last thing I had. My virginity was something I was holding onto, something I was going to choose what to do with, and it was gone, ripped away in one second while I watched.

When I got home, I fell asleep in a chair, crying. The next day was Sunday, and that Monday was my first day of college. I had twenty-four hours to get over this, put on a brave face, and go to my first day of classes. I had twenty-four hours to figure out what to do about whether or not I was pregnant or had an STD.

I called Mellissa, and it took me a long time and discussing other topics before I got the nerve to tell her what had happened. She was horrified and apologetic. She helped me find the courage to schedule an appointment with the school nurse the next day at my university. Mellissa called our dad to tell him what had happened to me and then called me back to tell me he said he was sorry. He was going to give me space, and I could come to him if I needed him.

I needed him. I needed an army. I needed people to help me fight and figure out how to go on living. I needed my mom. Instead, I sucked it up and went to classes the next day.

The next afternoon, I looked at two school nurses and said, "I was raped two nights ago. I need a plan B pill and STD tests." They gave me what I needed and asked me if I was going to press charges and asked me if I wanted a rape kit.

"No, I was alone with him at night. It will just be my word against his," I said, and the nurses knew that to be true too.

For a full week, I wanted to tell my mom what had happened to me so that I could have a hug, love, some comfort–a mother. The following Saturday night, I couldn't take the pain by myself anymore, so I broke Frank's rule and called my mom. I still lived in the house they owned by the barn.

"Can you drive down here?" I asked her on the phone. "I really need to talk to you."

"You know he won't let me," she said.

"It's a really big deal. I really, really need you to choose me for once, and just come down here," I begged.

We played that game back and forth for a few minutes before she said, "Fine. I'll be down in a minute."

When I told her, she scolded me. "I have told you and told you to never be alone with a boy." She lectured me, and I felt worse when she left.

My freshmen year of college was spent hanging out with the boys I went to high school with who had gone to the same college as me. We were seeing who could get the most drunk every night of the week. I didn't show up to most of my classes. I stayed drunk so that I didn't have to remember that I was a piece of trash.

I wanted to die, but I didn't have the guts to kill myself, so I just drank.

# CHAPTER FORTY-SIX

For some reason, every time my mother showed me that I was not important to her, rather than giving up on our relationship, it made me fight harder. When she didn't want to come and talk to me the night that I was struggling with having been sexually assaulted, I called her from less than a quarter of a mile away and asked her to come and speak with me in person about something horrible.

I had never begged her for help before, yet I could tell when she said her husband wouldn't let her come and talk with me, she was using that as an excuse. The older I got, the better I was at recognizing when he was keeping her from things and when she was using that as a way to not have to do something she just did not want to do. After an entire childhood and adolescence of letting me down and giving me heaping doses of low self-esteem, now, I not only felt like I had to rescue her, but I also felt that I had to earn her love. I told myself that I was unlovable and that my own mother didn't love me, so no one should ever have to try.

In my freshman year of college, I stayed drunk so I didn't have to think about how lonely I was and how lonely I would be. I couldn't admit that my mother was flawed, that her judgment and opinions of me were no longer loving because she was no longer capable of love.

Her spirit had been so broken that she could no longer love her children or even herself fully and with the selflessness that we and she deserved. Someone had robbed her of the energy for that, and she had been stuck in survival mode for too long.

By the end of my first semester of college, I had mostly B's and C's, but I was losing interest in everything, including choir. By the end of my second semester, I had failed everything including choir, which is pretty difficult to fail. In order to fail, I had to just simply not be there, and I wasn't.

I wasn't anywhere. I was on a dirt road getting drunk with some boys I had known since I was nine whom I knew would never hurt me. They didn't want to go to prison for killing the guy who had made me miserable, so they held my hair when it was time to puke instead. Morgan and I started out not being able to share a six-pack without getting tipsy, and by the end of the school year, we each needed our own and to split another.

One night, I was too sick from being drunk too many nights in a row to go out, and I stayed in and felt lonely enough to see who was on MySpace. That was the night I met Tyler. Wide Awake and Dreaming was the name of his punk rock band. I was nineteen, and it was 2006 so to me, that was spectacular. Their page said they sounded like The Used, which was a band I didn't like but pretended to love so that I could talk to boys. And, so, I did. I talked to a boy on MySpace about bands I didn't like and many other topics all night.

He was tall with pretty blue eyes and dark hair. He was too good-looking for me, but he was in Kentucky, so he didn't know that. He had only seen pictures of my face and not the body I so loathed and despised. In the beginning, I hoped we would just be friends and that he would maybe let me sing a song with him one day, but the chatting on MySpace turned into phone calls and by May, we were staying up all night to talk on the phone, which was keeping me from caring about school. But it was also keeping me from drinking.

I should have been more responsible. I should have reached out to a professional and found ways to cope with my pain, but I had no idea how to do that or what I was doing. I had no parental guidance, and I didn't want to bother my family with my problems, so I made terrible decisions.

If I had ever been taught to love myself, I would have chosen better for myself. Instead, I chose long phone calls well into the night with a guitarist from Kentucky whose band was on tour. Tyler would call me from the tour van, and the other guys in the band would say, "Hello!" He would get done with a show and call me instead of talking to the girls who were actually at the show. I felt special and cared about for the first time in my entire life.

Tyler and I talked for months, and we were both smitten. At the time, I had two-part time jobs. I was my brother Jordan's receptionist at his insurance office in the afternoon and worked at Walmart from 6:00 to 11:00 PM.

One day when I was the only one left in the insurance office waiting for five o'clock, I checked my MySpace messages and found one from a girl I didn't know named Ashley. In her message, she explained that the guy I was talking to was not really in a band. She said Tyler was her boyfriend David's friend and that they wished they were in a band, but they were just two nineteen-year-old kids from a small town in Kentucky and that neither of them even played instruments. Ashley said they didn't have jobs. They weren't in college yet, and they kind of just messed around all day. She had heard that I might want to come and meet Tyler in person, so she just wanted me to know before I came all the way from Iowa.

*"Also, he's been using David's pictures,"* she wrote. *"You need to ask him for a real picture of himself."*

I read that last line, and my stomach dropped. It felt like everything I knew about this boy and everything I felt for him was a total lie. I was devastated. His southern accent and charm and those pretty eyes didn't help.

I was too young to realize that he was my coping mechanism. I had convinced myself that we were friends, and that at the very least, we were musicians who would collaborate one day. He had told me he wanted more. He had told me he cared about me and wanted to meet me so we could start something. He told me he wanted the same things I wanted, "A family in the Appalachian Mountains," as he put it.

Tyler talked about his mom, aunts, and cousins as though living in Kentucky would finally give me the love and support I needed. He told me everyone in his family would adore me, and he couldn't wait to meet me and then introduce me to them. We talked about all those things for hours, and while I knew it was all fantasy, and we had never even met, I at least believed he was the kid in the pictures. I at least believed he was who he said he was even if I might never get to meet him in person.

Tears burned my eyes as I packed up my things and locked the office door. As I pulled out of my parking spot my phone rang.

"Hello?" I answered.

"You probably don't want to talk to me anymore," he said.

# CHAPTER FORTY-SEVEN

In my senior year of high school and first year of college, I lived in the double-wide on my mom and her husband's property. I assumed that my mom felt the same way about this as I did. In the beginning, I felt we were finally getting all those years of separation back. We would get to be mother and daughter again.

Day by day, this proved to be a fairy tale I had been telling myself. She was just as absent from my life from across the field as she was when we lived in different towns and worlds. Still, I foolishly assumed that I would be able to live there until I was ready to move on and that no one would be telling me at nineteen to find a place to rent.

"Why not allow me to save my money so I can buy a place of my own in a couple of years?" I asked when my mom told me I was going to have to move out. "You are seriously not going to let me live here anymore?" I asked, shocked.

My mom was trying to convince me that I wanted to move. "You will like living in the city better. It's closer to school and work," she said.

"I failed out of college, and I'm not going back next year, and I'm not going to live in a trailer park in the gross part of the city!" I was getting mad.

"Frank needs this house for the people who are moving here to train dogs with him, and you're moving into your new trailer by July first. We're going to come and move all of your stuff for you, so just deal with it, okay?" She said it as though she was telling me to tuck in my shirt.

The trailer and the trailer park were dingy. There were oh, so many cats. Naked babies walked around outside. A shirtless man yelled at me to stop driving so fast through the driveway, and he was right, but I was a nineteen-year-old girl. How was I supposed to think about anyone other than myself, much less anyone's cats or naked babies?

Sam and Morgan came by a couple of times to help ease my even deeper loneliness. "Trailer Hair," was what Sam affectionately named the new casa. After a couple of weeks of Trailer Hair, I threw a few bags into the back seat of my car, buckled my Care Bear into the passenger seat, and drove thirteen hours to Tyler's house in Kentucky.

# CHAPTER FORTY-EIGHT

I will be the first to admit how childish and pathetically irresponsible I was at the age of nineteen, twenty, and probably well into my twenties. Even now, sometimes I make childish and irresponsible decisions. I blame my decisions in early adulthood on my enormous lack of self-esteem and self-worth. When I really dig into it, I feel that I was stunted in my trauma from the age of six, trying to put together a puzzle that I stubbornly needed to get right before anything else could happen, but because time after time, I could not find the puzzle pieces or the pieces rejected me when I did find them, I fell and failed over and over.

I never learned to love myself enough to grow up, but life did not wait for me to grow up. Life kept happening to me, and I never had time to process my feelings, mistakes, or trauma. I never gave myself a chance to grow up. I turned my experiences into guilt, anxiety, and sadness, and self-medicated with alcohol and food. My self-esteem was so low at nineteen that, even though he had lied to me about what he looked like, and about being in a band that was on tour, Tyler was still better than nothing.

The comments my stepmother had made my entire childhood about multiple different aspects of my personality being intolerable paired with my mom constantly disappointing me and choosing her husband over me, and her infatuation with reminding me that men like thin women, had completely convinced me that no one would ever like me. They had convinced me that I would be alone forever.

My self-perception was so bad that I believed any man in the world would be embarrassed to be seen with me. In every photo from my high school senior trip in my friend's old photo albums, I'm covering my face with my hands. I thought that I was roadkill ugly and mortifyingly fat at a size fourteen, two sizes bigger than the average woman at that time. So, I drove across most of Iowa and most of Kentucky in a straight shot with no breaks. Thirteen hours. I had thirteen hours to wonder if he would like me or if he would think I was too fat or too ugly. I had time to think about how I would be able to start my life over and have a family.

I had always wanted to be a mom, but I didn't think I would ever be able to have a husband. My stepmother and mother had convinced me that I would never be able to find a man willing to marry me. So, as I drove, I imagined Tyler as my husband, with a couple of little kids in a small house in the Kentucky mountains.

I didn't make it to his house until 1:00 in the morning. I called Tyler as I was turning onto his road. He was at home by himself because his mom was at her boyfriend's house for the night, which was where she usually stayed. He had the porch light on, and when I pulled into the driveway, he came out to meet me.

"Well hello, sweetheart," he said, giving me a big hug.

He looked like the pictures he had sent me after he admitted (only because I found out he was using photos of his friend) to using fake photos–sandy brown hair, scrawny, and my height rather than tall, dark, and handsome as I had once been led to believe. I had decided not to care what he looked like or even that he had started our friendship off with a lie. I was just happy there was a guy interested in me. I never believed that could happen. So, in love with the idea of even being able to have a family, I hadn't considered that he may not be a good father.

*"I'll be strong enough to teach him how to be a good father,"* I thought.

It hadn't occurred to me that I might not have the energy and patience to be a good mother if I were also trying to teach him how to be a good father. At the time, I was not yet a mom, and I was young and had so much energy I could not imagine being tired. Neither could Tyler. We spent the summer exploring the mountains, caves, lakes, and waterfalls of Kentucky. Sometimes, his friends David and Ashley would join us. Sometimes, it would be just the two of us. We became best friends and had some amazing fun.

We also had a good deal of problems. I had foolishly, selfishly, and irresponsibly abandoned both of my jobs. I behaved like a small child and went off and left my brother without a receptionist and just stopped going to my job at Walmart, too. I acted like a brat who thought she could do whatever she wanted, and Tyler and I were running out of money. He had never had a job or any money, and I had only about $1000 when I started my trip. Tyler's mom lived with her boyfriend and left Tyler and me in her heavily rat-infested hoarder house, which was crumbling around us.

There were dozens of rats living in the basement, and there were holes in the floor and walls where these huge rats would run through the house. Anytime we came in the back door, three or four rats would be in the trash can, and there was filth and trash everywhere. I am absolutely terrified of rodents of any kind, yet I stayed. Rodents are my greatest phobia, and I stayed. I loved my future children enough and thought this guy was the only way I would be able to have babies, so, I stayed.

I started with Tyler's mom's kitchen. I scrubbed it from top to bottom. It took two full days. I moved to the living room and then the bathroom that didn't have a hole in the floor of the shower. We couldn't use the showers in either bathroom because they were both in shambles and had to go to a nearby town to Tyler's aunt's house to shower. I cleaned Tyler's mom's entire house, and then I got to the laundry room, where it looked like years' worth of laundry lived in piles on the floor. It wasn't until I opened the washing machine to find a dead rat lying on top of the load of laundry that I had just washed that my guts rolled over, and my heart told my brain, *"We are far too tired for this project. It's useless. We are done."*

So, I asked Tyler how we would go about getting rid of the rats, and he said, "Well, we can't until my mom pays the trash bill, and she's like, a year behind on it."

"What do you mean?" I was completely confused. He had always taken out the trash.

"You know that huge mountain of junk behind the house? That's about a year's worth of trash. Mom stopped paying them to come and get it, so I just threw it back there. Down in the basement is full of trash too."

That was the first time he had watched me do a ton of work without offering to help me or even telling me that what I was doing was useless because he wasn't holding up his end of the bargain and never would, and I still stayed. I stayed with him, but I could never live like that, so I decided we were going back to Trailer Hair where maybe there was a herd of cats, an army of naked babies, and an unidentifiable hair in the sink, but there were no rats.

# CHAPTER FORTY-NINE

We told Tyler's mom that we were going to try our luck in Iowa, and she was devastated. When I had left for Kentucky, my mom gave me a couple hundred bucks and a map. She told me she would make sure the rent got paid for a couple of months at my trailer park spot in case we wanted to come back, and other than that, she had nothing to say, certainly no emotions, so I was shocked to see Tyler's mom crying. I felt horrible and wondered if we should stay. Maybe she did care about him more than someone who leaves their son in a rat-infested nightmare with no job, transportation, money, resources, or food. Maybe I was wrong about her. I began to second-guess myself.

Tyler started out the drive to Iowa, and about an hour into the journey, he said he was having a panic attack, pulled over, and asked me to drive. After a few minutes of driving, I asked him what was wrong. He told me he had never been anywhere without his family. He'd never left the area he had grown up in, and the only other states he had been to were Virginia and Ohio, which border the part of Kentucky he was from. He started to cry, and I felt even worse. I had three guesses.

*Maybe we should just pack up my stuff and go back to Kentucky?* I thought. *"Maybe I'll lose him if we live away from his family? Maybe he'll leave and go back home, so I should just go back with him now?"*

I thought that, for the sake of my future children, I might have to be the stronger one and the more sacrificial one in the relationship. I thought that, because I was unattractive, and he was doing me a favor by even being with me, the least I could do was live where he wanted to live. We spent the rest of our long drive talking about how we were going to pack up my furniture and store it in my grandma's old house, the one my sister Mellissa owned in Iowa, get my clothes, and go back to Kentucky.

When we got back to Trailer Hair, I felt safe, clean, and at home for the first time since I had left.

"Are you sure you don't want to just stay here?" I asked him. "Isn't it clean, and there are no rats?! We could both get jobs, and my college is a couple of blocks away. I could re-enroll, and you could even enroll. We could walk there."

I was starting to get excited about the idea when I looked at him, and he was sobbing. A few days later, we were on our way back to Kentucky with plans of living in Tyler's mom's house, getting jobs, saving our money, and getting our own place as soon as possible.

When we got back, I got dressed up in my most professional attire, made a resume, printed copies at the library, and drove around handing them out. I did not give up until all fifty were gone. A couple of days later, I was working in the office as a receptionist for the Human Resources Representative of a large Kmart. I liked my job and my boss. I enjoyed what I was doing, but every day when I got home from work, Tyler would talk about how miserable and bored he was staying home without me all day. There was no way he could get a job and go to work because he didn't have a car, and I had to take my car to work. So, he dragged my mood into the gutter every night.

With the amount of money I was making, we figured that it would take us at least a year before we would have enough money to move out. The thought of staying in that rat-infested house for a full year was so depressing that we started to fight. In September, we had been together for four months, and we were fighting so often that I started to think about driving back to Iowa and leaving him.

He didn't fight fair, I had noticed. I would tell him I was upset about whatever problem I was feeling most defeated about at the time, and he would respond by calling me a name or bringing up something I did that he didn't like. I would be trying to solve a problem, and he would be trying to be right, but neither of us were right, and that would make him mad, so he would attack my personality.

We were two hurt children who were trauma bonding over our horribly traumatic childhoods. Tyler's dad had been a drunk who beat him constantly until he was eight, and then he only stopped beating him because he drank himself into the grave. His mom was left with an eight-year-old, a three-year-old, and nothing else. They were very poor. It was rough.

My childhood was full of trauma, too, and neither of us had any self-esteem. He was self-conscious because he was always too small, and I was self-conscious because I was always too big. We thought we were one another's only hope, and we bonded over that unconsciously. Two stupid kids who would fight and make up, and fight and make up, and by November, I had noticed that all of that making up we were doing had caused me to miss two periods. We took a test, and I had him look at it first.

"You're going to have a baby, baby!" he said.

I was too happy about having a baby to realize that I was going to have a baby.

# CHAPTER FIFTY

The second I found out I was pregnant, I changed. I started to care about myself through the eyes of my baby. He or she had to have a good, healthy, happy, clean, well-educated, and fun life. I had to make sure of this, and now Tyler was going to have to stay with me because I was pregnant with his baby.

So, I demanded we move back to Iowa. We needed to be around my family, who had a few more dollars in the bank and resources at hand and a few fewer rats than Tyler's family. We didn't have a place to live when we first came back to Iowa, so we slept on an air mattress on Sam's floor for the first ten weeks.

I found an OBGYN, and they told us I was about ten weeks pregnant when we first got back to Iowa. I got a job at a clothing store, and Tyler would drop me off at work so he could use my car to look for a job. After a couple of times of having to walk home after a long shift on my tired, pregnant, feet, I started to wonder if he would ever grow up.

When I would get to Sam's, who worked evenings and wasn't home, after walking twenty blocks from work to find Tyler asleep on the couch, I started to become irritated. It was 8:00 PM, and instead of making his pregnant girlfriend a snack and picking her up on time, he'd fallen asleep, mouth open and drooling on the couch. It was actually scary, even terrifying. I was having a baby with someone who was showing absolutely no signs of maturing.

When I was twelve weeks pregnant, Tyler, Sam, our friend Tonya, and I were having a game night when I went to pee and found blood in my underwear. I couldn't catch my breath.

"My baby! My baby!" was all I could think or say. I loved my baby even before conception. I had named her when I was sixteen. I was petrified.

I came out of the bathroom and told everyone I was bleeding and scared and needed to call my mom. It was a Saturday night, so my doctor would not be available. I didn't want to go to the emergency room because I wasn't in any pain and thought maybe if I didn't move, if I laid still and prayed, I would be okay, and my baby would be okay. I still desperately needed to ask my mom what to do, so Tyler handed me my phone, and I broke Frank's rule and called my mom.

"Hello?" she answered.

"Mom, I know I'm not supposed to call, but I need help. I'm bleeding. What do I do?!"

My mom knew I was pregnant. She loves babies and was so excited when I told her we were coming back to Iowa and I was three months pregnant. I'd emailed momescaped@yahoo, though it just so happened she was not "escaped" at the time. She was living with Frank, and Chad was ten. She got my e-mail and called me back when Frank wasn't in the house. We were able to talk about the baby and how happy we were. She told me she went to town to run errands on Mondays now, so we started to meet and shop together for baby clothes and furniture every Monday once I was back in Iowa.

Now, Frank was in the house, so my mom's response to her terrified nineteen-year-old daughter who was possibly having a miscarriage was, "Uh... I think you have the wrong number."

"No, Mom, please not this time—don't hang up." I was rushing to blurt it out when she hung up. My friends and boyfriend were gawking.

We called the emergency room, and they said it sounded like I had torn my placenta but that if I was not in any pain or bleeding heavily, I was not having a miscarriage. They said to be still and call my doctor on Monday morning. I laid still on Sam's couch and prayed my baby was okay.

Around midnight, my phone rang, and my mom was whispering, "You know you can't call like that." Her scolding cut into me. A sliver of comfort or apology would have carried me to forgiveness, but I would have to trudge up that hill again without her help.

"Now, what's going on?" she asked.

I told her again. She said the emergency room sounded right and before getting off the phone, told me to e-mail her next time.

Monday morning, we did an ultrasound, and while the baby was still too small to tell the gender, it was healthy with a strong heartbeat. My placenta had torn slightly but would mend itself if I was careful, and my baby was going to be all right.

# CHAPTER FIFTY-ONE

When I needed my mom the most, she was never there for me, and in those moments, I was always too busy surviving and getting through them on my own while carrying the added burden of how bad it hurt to be told what sounded like, "You are not my daughter. You have no mother."

I could not listen carefully to what she was really saying. In every, "E-mail me next time. You know not to call. You know I can't go," and every, "Don't tell Frank," what she was really saying was, "I am obsessed with what every single second will or could do to set him off. His reactions to things that most people consider normal are so violent that I have dedicated every brain cell I have to making sure he is not upset by anything. I think about him before I think about you so he doesn't kill me, and I can still be around to help you in the ways that I still can even if I can't be there or answer your phone call."

When she chose him over me I heard, "You are not important. His rules are more important than you, even though I hate him because you are valueless, and even a man I don't like has more worth than you." And because of the way my dad's wife had treated me confirmed that I was worthless, I fully believed my interpretation of my mom's actions.

It was not until I myself had to spend a lot of time around Frank as an adult that my brain began to immediately go to, "What will Frank think or do? How will he react?" before anything else, that I fully understood what a narcissist with anger and control issues can do to change and shape someone's brain. He had fully depressed me and put me in survival mode, and my initial thought of everything was him and his reaction first above all else. My mom was in survival mode. She would never have hung up on me or been away from me in the first place when she was Libby.

My baby was okay, and so was I, so I went back to work at the clothing store. But the longer Tyler and I lived on Sam's floor, the more apparent it was that we would not be able to save enough money to rent our own place before the baby came if we were relying on my income alone. I made about $150.00 a week, and with having to buy food, gas, and a pack of cigarettes a day for Tyler, which was about $30 a week, we were only able to save a month's rent and no deposit in the two months we had been back in Iowa.

I never wanted to be a nagging wife. It seemed horrible to have to nag your husband to do something and much easier to just do it yourself, but what I didn't realize until Tyler was my boyfriend was that some things you can't do for someone else. I couldn't get a job for him, so I complained to my mom rather than nag him. On Mondays when we would meet at the store, I would complain not only about how he wouldn't get a job, smoked and wouldn't quit, and talked to me like I was garbage, he blamed it on being homesick and depressed, but those were things he did not have to take out on me.

My mom gave me the money for a deposit on a small, one-bedroom house, and I had saved the money for the first month's rent. Something happened when we moved into our first tiny house together that inspired Tyler to get a job at a nearby factory. He was even making decent money. The baby was due the first week of July, and although we were still fighting a lot, and both of us were anxious about becoming parents, things started to seem like they might work out. I started to get excited about having my baby, and Tyler stopped calling home to cry to his mom that he missed her as often.

My mom never got to go with me to an ultrasound appointment. Even though my sister Mellissa and I were pregnant at the same time, both with our first babies, Mom missed our "sisters" baby shower.

By the time we were having baby showers, Mom didn't even seem to care that she was missing our life events. She lacked the spirit it took to be sad. Mellissa and I were sad that she wasn't there, and I once again took note that I would not ever be able to have my dream wedding because my mom wouldn't be there. Then, I realized she was the only one I wanted in the delivery room with me, and she wouldn't be there, either.

# CHAPTER FIFTY-TWO

On Friday, July 6, I went to my last baby doctor's appointment before my due date. My doctor could tell I was miserable as it was a very hot summer, so he asked if I wanted to be induced on Monday. Tyler was able to go with me to that appointment. We both excitedly agreed we wanted to meet our new baby on Monday.

Monday I was too nervous to allow myself to think about how sad I was that my mom was not going to be there. I was twenty years old and having a baby. I was a grown woman who didn't need her mother, I kept reminding myself. Before I knew it, I was in too much pain to even think about my mom's absence.

There's a time for every woman, I believe, in the middle of labor where she says to herself, *"How can I get out of this? I can't do it. There's no way! I can't do it. I'm not doing it. I'm leaving! How can I leave?"*

We still had no idea if we were having a boy or a girl because our baby would never cooperate during ultrasounds. No matter what the ultrasound techs tried, the little feet were always curled up and in the way. Everyone's guess was boy, so that was what everyone was saying. The doctor and nurses kept referring to our baby as "he."

I labored for twelve hours, and then there was my baby. I started to cry when they showed me the baby's face and not tears of joy and relief, rather, tears of disappointment. "He looks just like me. He's gonna look like a girl!" I cried.

"She does look just like you, and she is a girl!" Tyler said.

It occurred to me how out of it I must have been to have been so confused and cared about something so silly. My baby was here, and she was beautiful, healthy, and perfect. They cleaned her off, and as they rolled her cart away to do her checkup, I heard my mom's voice in the hallway.

"Oh, is that my granddaughter?! Yes, that is my granddaughter. I can tell. She looks just like my daughter!"

At first, I thought I must be dreaming, but then she was there. My mom was standing there in the room with me.

"How are you here?" I asked.

"It's Monday. I went to run errands, and you weren't there, so I figured you were having your baby," she said.

"Did you get to see her?" I asked.

"Uh-huh. Just for a second. They're going to clean her off, but they'll bring her right back," she said. "Are you okay?" she asked.

Just moments ago, I thought she didn't care, and now she was here. I told her I was okay and that I was still under an epidural. We spoke for a few more moments before she had to go.

I believe that Jesus knew that for my mom and me, Ella needed to be born on a Monday.

# CHAPTER FIFTY-THREE

I cried the entire way home from the hospital, convinced that I was a terrible mother because I'd neglected to buy a newborn neck positioner for her car seat. I had not even realized that that was a thing that existed or would be necessary. As we drove away, her head started to wobble all over the car seat because she was so tiny and new. I held her little head still and cried big tears all over her white dress with yellow ducks.

*"How many other things do I not know about and will I mess up? I thought I would be good at this, and I'm terrible."* I thought.

I laugh about it now. I was twenty, Ella was three days old, and I was shocked that I was messing up motherhood. Now, after having messed up motherhood nearly every day for seventeen years, it seems funny that I ever thought I would be good at it.

No one is good at it. Some are better than others in different aspects, and some try harder than others, but even on a mother's best leave-it-all-out-on-the-field-day, she screws up something or someone. Motherhood is impossible because it asks us to be fully pouring into our own cups and fully pouring into the cups of our children simultaneously and without dripping a drop, usually while everyone from every seat in a sold-out house screams. So, on the way home from the hospital, that was when I believe I first felt postpartum depression.

Tyler and I lived in a small house inside of a park, and one of the stipulations of our lease was that we keep our yard mowed. Otherwise, the city would fine our landlord, and she would then fine us. All summer, even though I was pregnant, I push-mowed our yard, which was about an acre. We didn't have the extra money for a fine, Tyler said he was too tired after work to mow, and I liked the way it looked matching the park and didn't want it to look trashy.

If I could do something myself rather than nag, I always did. When Ella was five days old, our landlord came by to see our baby and to tell us she got a warning from the city that our yard needed to be mowed. I hadn't mowed in a week because I was either planning to give birth or in the hospital. We told the landlord Tyler would have it mowed by the end of the day.

The day was getting away from us, and I started to nag. He kept putting it off. By evening, I was considering doing it myself. I didn't want to be that woman. I didn't want to be the woman who couldn't just do it all.

"If you'll just start it for me so I don't hurt myself, I'll do it," I said.

I had just nursed the baby, and she was asleep.

*"Maybe I could mow really fast before she wakes up to eat again."* I thought.

Ruby had come by to bring us lasagna, and I trusted her to watch the baby while she slept, but I realized I didn't trust Tyler to watch her.

He started the mower for me, and I mowed the yard in the July heat five days after having a baby while my boyfriend sat inside watching TV. I started to cry a couple of minutes into mowing the yard because I knew that I had chosen so wrong for myself and for my baby. I had made such a horrendous choice.

By the time I was done, I was so hot, red, and out of energy. I dragged my body into the shower, and even though my sister was there, I began to scream, "I want my mom! I want my mom!" like a small helpless child.

Postpartum depression, exhaustion, disappointment, and physical pain had broken me. I had torn my episiotomy stitches and had to go to the hospital and be cauterized.

I wish it were as easy to heal emotionally as it is physically.

# CHAPTER FIFTY-FOUR

By the time Ella was three months old, I had plunged deeply into postpartum depression and loneliness. Tyler was working long hours at the factory. At the time, I was very grateful that it seemed like he was going to support his family. I should have been more appreciative. I should have known that we were blessed. I should have been in worship and prayer at the potential we had to prosper. I should have known that my baby would not always have her days and nights mixed up and that she would grow out of that phase and I could rejoin society at some point.

I should have realized, at some point, I would see another person who wasn't a screaming baby or a miserable boyfriend. Tyler's depression got worse because he was always homesick. Every chance he got, he was on the phone with his mother, and I was still alone even when he was home.

Still, I should have been happy he was working, and I could stay home with my baby. I should have used that time to plan our next step in the right direction. Instead, I let loneliness and depression exhaust me. There was no one to call and talk with about it because Mellissa had just had a baby, too, and she was exhausted, too. My friends were all still in college and able to party and take naps, so they wouldn't have understood.

On Mondays, Ella and I ran errands with my mom, and I vented to her about the way I was feeling. Mom suggested we move to my hometown, which was about thirty minutes from where Tyler, Ella, and I lived.

"There's a house for rent about a block away from your dad's house. I saw it the other day when I was in town dropping stuff off at Jordan's house," she said.

My brother, Jordan, lived a block away from my dad, stepmom, and younger sisters, Ruby who was seventeen, and Madi, who was eleven.

"You could be closer to everyone and have help." My mom could see I was running out of energy.

I convinced Tyler to move to a trailer house a block away from my dad's house in the town where I grew up. At first, he didn't want to go.

"You make no sense!" he said. "If you want to live closer to family that will actually help, we need to move back to Kentucky. Your family has never helped you and never will."

"My mom already paid the first month's rent, the deposit, and, by the way, she's also bought every diaper and outfit your baby has ever worn. She bought her baby bed, her swing, her bouncer, and her car seat. What has your mom done?"

He had no response. The only thing his mom had done was drive to see her new granddaughter, bringing her teenage daughter and loud, toddler boy with her who woke my newborn up every time she fell asleep. Tyler's mom could not afford a hotel room, so they were trying to stay in our one-bedroom house with us and our newborn.

I begged them to take Tyler's little brother, who was only three, somewhere for a couple of hours and then bring me back something to eat. Tyler took his family somewhere, they forgot to bring me back food, and then they made so much noise when they all got back that I drove to my dad's house with my newborn and spent the rest of their trip at my dad's house.

Tyler was furious, and his mom was heartbroken that she didn't get to see her granddaughter enough. I was constantly shocked by how nothing Tyler's mom ever did was her own fault. Being rude and not giving a weeks-old baby time to sleep–not her fault. Never working so never having any money–not her fault. Her son having to move away from her in order to find the resources it took to survive–not her fault.

We moved to my hometown and only lived there for a couple of weeks before chaos struck. Tyler was even more miserable than before. Now, he had a thirty-minute drive to work at what was already an early shift. He had an hour less every day to rest and call his mom, and he started to yell at me even more often and call me names even more. He even started to yell at our infant.

One Sunday evening in late September when Ella was almost three months old, she was in her swing crying while I tried to scarf down dinner before picking her back up, and Tyler screamed, "Shut up!" at her.

Then he threw a baby blanket at her face. The next day, I told my mom what had happened because I always told her everything he said and did to me. She was the only person to whom I could vent. After dropping Ella and me off that day, she must have gone to my dad's office and told him about Tyler's tantrum.

That evening, while I was rocking Ella and Tyler was in our bedroom on the phone with his mom, my dad burst through the front door without knocking, his eyes on fire with anger.

"Where is he?!" he demanded.

"What?" I was shocked and dumbfounded.

My stepmom, Debbie was following close behind my dad, a look of horror on her face. My dad was already in the bedroom dragging Tyler by his collar out the front door.

"Are you okay?" My stepmom looked concerned about me for the first time in my entire life, and my dad was in Tyler's face screaming at him. "What is happening? Your mom said he doesn't treat you right, and he throws stuff at the baby?" Debbie touched Ella's hand, and I saw that she truly did care about my daughter.

I didn't know what to say, so I just looked out the window. Now, my dad was on the phone yelling at Tyler's mom, asking her if she knew how her son treated his daughter and granddaughter. I could hear him telling her about me having to mow five days after having my baby.

Dad calmed down a little bit and came in the house. "You're coming home with us. Get your stuff. Come on." He wasn't asking me, he was telling me, and I didn't like it.

I didn't understand it. I had made my bed. I had, insanely, accepted the way I was being treated. Being called a bitch and told to shut up. The time when I was pregnant that Tyler yelled "Fuck you, you little whore!" at me because I didn't want him to call his mom that night. The times when I was pregnant, and he forgot to pick me up from work. Mowing while pregnant and five days postpartum, not fully healed. Him yelling at the baby. I had chosen this, and this was what I thought I had to do.

"No, I can't go with you," I said. "He will leave me if I go to your house tonight. He'll take his stuff and go to Kentucky, and Ella won't have a daddy anymore."

"So you're going to let him hurt her? What if next time he throws a glass at her or picks her up and throws her?" My dad was getting mad again.

"He won't do that… it was a blanket." I couldn't imagine Tyler actually hurting Ella, but throwing a blanket at her tiny face rather than picking her up so I could finish my dinner was something I could never unsee. It was the beginning of me giving up on him, even though it took years, because now he wasn't just hurting me anymore.

Dad and Debbie left, shocked and furious that Ella and I weren't going with them. Tyler was sitting in our car on the phone with his mom.

At dark, he came in and said, "I'm going home to Kentucky. You can either go with me or stay here with your fucked up family, but I will never, ever set foot in this town or anywhere near your fucking family ever again."

As we drove back to Kentucky, tears rolled down my cheeks. This was why he was so against living so close to my family. He knew my

family would see what he was like and force me to see how unacceptable his treatment of me was.

Tyler was just like Frank in that he knew he hated himself and that
he had nothing to offer the world, so he took great lengths to keep the
world out of his business. He had no friends, and his circle consisted
of his mom, his girlfriend, and his newborn.

Still, I didn't want Ella to be away from her daddy, and I could
never take anyone's baby away from him, so, we drove thirteen hours
that night, stopping every couple of hours to nurse and change our
newborn.

# CHAPTER FIFTY-FIVE

At some point in the year we were in Iowa, Tyler's mom had cleaned her house, ended the rat infestation, and was fixing her crumbling fireplace and bathrooms. Otherwise, I would have never gotten in the car with Tyler and let him take Ella and me back to Kentucky. Still, the entire drive there, I needed to be reassured that his mom's house did not have any rats living in it.

"I won't be able to sleep if there are rats," I said. "I will have to stay awake guarding her all the time. I won't stay if there are rats."

Tyler reassured me the house was cleaned out. His uncles had hauled off all the trash and cleaned the basement. They had gotten rid of all the rats and the trash. When we got to Kentucky, Tyler's mom's house was fairly clean. There were no rats.

The sleeping arrangements she had planned for us were not going to work because she had gotten a cat, which she kept locked in her bedroom where she was going to have Tyler, Ella, and me sleep. The cat had peed on everything. The bedding had been washed, but the furniture and carpet had been soaked with cat urine to the point that it made my eyes burn to be in the room. I told Tyler we would have to sleep in the living room on the couch and loveseat with the baby in her swing.

The first time Ella woke up to nurse that night, there was a roach crawling on her. As I sat on the couch nursing Ella in the dim living room lamp light glow, I started to see the roach infestation. The walls, the furniture–they were everywhere. I was too tired for this shit.

*"I've been through enough. Why in the fuck can't this bitch just keep her house clean?"* I thought.

In the morning, I told Tyler about the roaches, and he promised me we would be able to move out soon.

"No. We can't move out soon. We were in this exact same position last year at this time trying to move out of here, and we couldn't do it, and now we have a baby, so we definitely can't do it." I said, starting to cry.

This was too much. I was reeling from the anxiety of feeling I was never a good enough mom and never an understanding enough wife. My hormones were everywhere, and my baby was still so young that she needed me every second of every day. I couldn't remember who I used to be and had no idea who I was. How could I possibly make a healthy decision if I was going with my unhealthy gut?

Tyler started to get mad and then said, "No. You know what? I'm not going to let you make me lose my shit today. I'm finally home, and I'm going to go find David and go see my family. I'm going to have an awesome day." And then he left and went to play like a child with his friend for the rest of the day.

Tyler did that every day for a week and didn't even look for a job. I refused to stay in the nasty, roach-infested house, so I begged one of his aunts to let us stay in her basement, which had heat and an air mattress. Ella slept in her swing, something I didn't even know was incredibly dangerous. There is no way Ella and I were alone. We had guardians or we would not have survived. I was in survival mode.

After a week in Kentucky, I was asking him when he was going to get a job. My family was calling me on a cycle, and I was ignoring their calls. I didn't want to tell them about the horrible decisions I was making.

"We just got back. Don't worry, I'll get a job." Tyler would say.

I knew better, but I also didn't have the energy to fight. Nothing I said could matter anyway. He was home where everyone enabled him to continue to be lazy and childish.

By day nine, mid-afternoon, he finally brought me my car back, and I had all of Ella's and my things sitting in the driveway ready to go.

"You're just going to leave then? You're not even going to give me a chance?" he asked.

"When people have a baby, they line up a job before they move to another state. They don't move on a whim and then spend nine entire days wasting time before even putting in applications. We have a baby, and you are still a baby. I'm not leaving you. I am leaving Kentucky. You can stay here and take some time and decide if you want to be your mother's son or your daughter's dad, and then you can either stay or figure out a way to come and be Ella's dad. I won't date anyone else. I will be taking care of our daughter and praying that you show up for her too."

I got in the car and drove away, stopping at gas stations to nurse Ella. A quarter of the way home I called my stepmom to ask her and my dad to come and meet me at my halfway point so Debbie could drive my car while I slept next to my baby's car seat in the back seat.

Debbie drove while I sobbed over Ella's dress, this time Peter Rabbit on blue corduroy.

# CHAPTER FIFTY-SIX

Twenty years old with an infant, no money, no job, and no husband. How did I live through that? Ella and I lived with my dad, stepmom, and younger sisters until we found a low-income apartment in the same town. We lived there alone for a couple of months with the help of my mom and food stamps. I didn't know what to do.

*"Should I put her in daycare and find a job or go back to school?*

I didn't want to leave her and add separation anxiety to my already overwhelmed heart or hers. I knew for Ella's future and mine I had to do something, so I found a babysitter and enrolled in cosmetology school. That was when Tyler started to call.

He was going to find a way to get to Iowa after spending two months in Kentucky doing absolutely nothing but hanging out with David. Tyler had no money or job, so he decided to sell his guitar and buy a Greyhound ticket. Tyler came back, and we started over. He got a job, and with my tax refund, he got a Jeep.

Ella went to the babysitter, and I went to cosmetology school. Tyler was still angry with me that he had to give up his childhood. He still did things without thinking about us or considering how it would affect us, like buying a canoe with our last $100 or trading his new Jeep straight across for a pickup truck that was older than us and broke down on the way home. He still burned fifty dollars' worth of our money on cigarettes each week. However, even with doing all of the baby work, all of the errands, being in school, and being the one to make all of the difficult decisions, I still thought we were going to make it. I still thought we were going to grow into adults with a healthy, happy family.

We moved to the city to be closer to his job and my cosmetology school. Our apartment was really nice, and Ella was a happy baby. While leaving her all day to go to school killed me, and I missed a lot of school simply because I could not stand the thought of leaving her, slowly but surely, I made it through cosmetology school.

In Iowa, it's supposed to take about twelve months to get through school if you go full-time. It took me eighteen months. They calculated hours spent, and when you had enough hours, you graduated. It was fun, and although I was terrible at every aspect of it, could not get the hang of any of it, I made some friends, and it gave me the social life I was craving.

I started school at the same time as a woman named Angie who immediately latched on to me. Her laugh was loud, and her whole face glowed when she smiled.

"You're actually really funny," she said when I made fun of the orientation video under my breath on the first day.

Angie and I were both twenty-one. She was married and had two little boys at home. We commiserated over motherhood, relationships, and being annoyed with the other girls in our classes. By the time both of us went out onto the floor to start doing hair on paying customers, we had spent time together with one another's families outside of school and considered each other good friends. When Angie's cousin Bertha came in to get her hair done, Angie said, "You should be Amelia's client! She'll do a better job on you than me. She's good at crazy cuts and colors like you want!"

Bertha was seventeen and liked to play with fun hair colors. She stayed my client the whole time I was in cosmetology school. My school was in a town called Russellville, where Angie and her family, including her cousin Bertha, lived. The salon where I hoped to be a stylist when I graduated was also in Russellville.

A few months before graduation, I asked Tyler what he thought of moving to Russellville. He agreed that it would be better than living in the city we lived in and was still close enough for him to easily get to work each day, so we started to look for a place. There was a tiny town right outside of Russellville with nothing but a couple of houses, a couple of old churches, a Civil War battlefield, and a post office. In this town, Rockford, we found for rent a trailer that was owned by a really nice married couple who were not much older than us, and they had a little boy. They had a farm and lived in a house on one end of town and owned the rental trailer and three acres that it sat on on the other side of town.

The woman thought Ella was adorable and was already talking about me coloring her hair. We moved to the tiny town of Rockford, Ella turned two, and I graduated from cosmetology school and got the job at the salon in Russellville that I wanted. Tyler had a job he didn't mind, and we had friends. Things seemed to be going so well that we started to talk about actually having a wedding.

# CHAPTER FIFTY-SEVEN

Tyler and I had been talking about getting married since before we met in person. When we were still talking on the phone every night before I drove to Kentucky to meet him for the first time, we talked about getting married and having a family. The first week we were together in Kentucky, he took the plastic string from the wrapper of a pack of cigarettes and half-heartedly said, "Do you still want this?" It was supposed to be a proposal and a ring. For me, it was what I thought I deserved.

When we moved to Iowa and into our first house, the one we lived in when Ella was born, he bought us matching wedding rings from Walmart and spent months paying off their total cost of about $300. I was very impressed by that gesture, not because the rings were expensive or attractive but because it meant he was finally thinking for himself but not entirely about himself. The wedding ring was the first thing he had bought me.

Two years later, we still were not married. Our relationship bumps and my belief that no one I knew wanted to see me marry him, paired with the fact that my mom wouldn't be able to attend, prevented us from tying the knot.

Now that Ella was two, we were starting to sort our lives out and keep up with groceries and bills, and I asked Tyler if he wanted to elope.

"Why don't we just go to that wedding chapel in Des Moines?" I asked.

"Just tell me the day before and what time," was Tyler's unromantic response.

I called and booked our ceremony at Vern's Wedding Chapel a couple of Saturdays in advance, and then I remembered my childhood friend Charlotte was getting married that day, too, and we were planning to go to her wedding.

*"Oh, I better change the date of our wedding,"* I thought. *"It will be depressing to see Charlotte have a real wedding and a real gown with a real man and her friends and family around her happy and proud, and I won't be anything but sour and jealous of her on her big day if I have to marry this kid wearing khaki shorts at Vern's the same day.*

But I didn't change the date. I kept my wedding on the same morning as Charlotte's to further punish myself. I wanted to hurt as much as I could for being such a fat, ugly ogre and not deserving the same love and support as Charlotte, who was beautiful and thin.

The week leading up to our wedding, I bought a simple, white dress from a place with the word 'Barn' in the name and yes, I felt like a cow.

I asked Tyler to buy me flowers. "Roses if you can find them. I would like to have a bouquet."

The night before our wedding, I went over the details of the next day with Tyler so that we weren't late to either wedding we were attending the next day. "Could you please watch the baby while I get ready? I want to be able to take my time putting on my makeup so she doesn't end up getting any of it on my dress."

Tyler agreed that he would watch her while I got ready the next morning.

"Where are the flowers?" I asked.

"Oh, fuck. I forgot. We'll have to stop and get some on the way there," he said.

The next morning, Tyler got dressed in a white button-down shirt and khaki shorts. Then he invited his friend Kent, the neighbor, over to play video games while I got Ella and myself ready. I didn't want to start an argument the day of our wedding, but my two-year-old was getting into everything, and I was trying to enjoy the morning.

"I thought you said you would watch her while I got ready today," I said, walking into the living room.

"I did say that," Tyler said without looking up from the screen.

"I just don't wanna be late, and she's getting into my makeup," I stammered.

"Send her in here! It'll be fine," he said.

"Are you guys going somewhere? Because I can go," the neighbor, who was a considerate man, said with apology in his eyes.

"We're getting married today," I said.

Our neighbor, Kent, looked horrified. "Oh, my God, dude what the fuck are you doing? You invited me over to play games on your wedding day? What is wrong with you?" He scolded Tyler and apologized to me, leaving and shaking his head in disgust at Tyler, who was now embarrassed and infuriated.

The entire way to Walmart to get my flowers, Tyler called me every cuss word and name he could think of for embarrassing him in front of his friend. I tried to explain that I didn't mean to embarrass him or make him mad and that it's just hard to get ready with the baby in the room. I even told him to forget about buying me flowers because, at that point, I had cried my makeup off and did not feel the slightest bit pretty anyway.

"Shut up, bitch!" he said, slamming the car door to go into Walmart. He bought me a bouquet of red roses and threw them at me. "Here! These good enough?" he asked. "I'd hate to have you call your family and tell them I didn't remember to get you flowers or some shit, you over-dramatic whore."

I sat silently in the car on the way to the chapel, which was run by Vern, a woman from a small town in Iowa. One can likely picture and smell the room, so I won't describe the chapel. The only person attending our wedding was a gorgeous, curly headed, bright blue-eyed girl in a white dress. I kept looking at her, reminding myself that she needed a daddy and that no one else would ever want me.

I sucked it up and did what I thought was right for Ella.

Later that evening at Charlotte's wedding, I plastered the smile of a happy and proud friend on my face and tried not to think about her gown, flowers, music, and champagne, or her mom and dad and her groom being so much better than mine in every way. I felt a bit of pride in myself as well.

After all, I was getting extremely good at faking that smile, and at least I was good at something.

# CHAPTER FIFTY-EIGHT

Despite the fact that Tyler did not keep a job for longer than a couple of weeks at a time, I was still able to keep up with our bills, groceries, household necessities, his gas and cigarettes, my gas, and the cost of daycare.

We were now married, still living in our little trailer on a big lot in Rockford, and I was working at the salon in Russellville. We were settling into what was not such a horrible life, and I thought that, if I could keep up with the baby, the bills, the housework, work, still make dinner, and bring him his plate every night, we would be all right.

I thought, if I could serve him and our family every waking moment, he would eventually stop calling me names, yelling at me, and telling me to shut up. I thought that he would eventually find a job he could be happy enough to keep.

Six months into our marriage, my two-and-a-half-year-old daughter had stopped calling me "Mommy" and had started calling me, "Shut-Up-Bitch." She wasn't yelling those words or even saying them angrily. Ella genuinely thought that was my name.

One evening, while I was watching her play, she looked up at me, held up her sippy cup, and asked for, "More juice, Shut-Up-Bitch?" and I started to sob.

"Can't you see that what you say and how you treat me is going to affect how she believes she should be treated by men in her future?" I asked Tyler.

Any conversation with Tyler where he could be shown examples of his own behavior ended in tears for me, but I was already crying. My question and pleading with him that he stop calling me names for Ella's sake was met with enough insults and attacks on me that Ella and I had to leave the room. We usually spent our time in a room Tyler was not in so that he couldn't be mean to either one of us.

Still, I worked, I mothered, and I prayed that he would be happier. After putting Ella to bed one night, I was cleaning the kitchen and asked him if he could restock the diaper bag for the next day, to which he responded, "Here in a minute."

He always responded with, "Here in a minute," because he knew I didn't have a minute and that I would just do the task myself. I was so tired that night from a day that had started at 6:00 AM and didn't end or have any breaks to breathe until well after 10:00 PM, that when I picked up the diaper bag I dropped it, and the entire thing spilled on the floor. I sat on the floor and cried. He watched me.

"I just need some help. I can't take her to daycare, go to work, pick her up from daycare, come home, cook, clean, and do all of the baby stuff by myself every single day. I am so tired." I cried.

He said nothing. He didn't pick up the bag, the diapers, or the fruit snacks. He didn't pick up his wife. He ignored me entirely.

That spring, there was a knock at the door. My mom and Chad, who was now twelve, stood on my porch. I was elated, shocked, and astonished. They had run away from Frank, and it was now my turn to host them. I was so proud I was finally going to be the one who could keep her from returning to her abuser. Chad and my mom took their things to Ella's room, and I brought her toddler bed into mine.

Over the next few months, Chad went to school, and Mom worked. She got a job at a nursing home, and she and I took turns taking care of Ella, cooking, and cleaning. We took turns paying for things and running errands, and I regained some of the strength, energy, and endorphins I had lost over the last three years. Having a partner who contributed taught me that it was not my fault that Tyler didn't help me and that it was not my responsibility to inspire him to help.

My mom lived with us for three or four months until she saved her money and rented a double-wide three blocks away. I was still able to see her, and she was still free, but I was sad to see her go even if it was not very far. Mom still watched Ella, who had just turned three, every chance she got. My mom was absolutely enamored with Ella. If my mom wasn't at work, she was picking her up to go play.

While my mom lived with us, Tyler didn't yell at me or call me names. He knew that, if he did, she would call my dad or someone even scarier, and they would put an end to it, and possibly him, in the process, so he kept his mouth shut.

Around our first wedding anniversary, my mom unexpectedly came to pick Ella up, and as she was walking up to our porch, she could hear Tyler yelling at me. All those months of holding it in must have nearly killed him because the yelling erupted like a volcano when my mom moved out. Tyler's yelling and hurtful words caused me to develop a bleeding ulcer in my stomach.

"You have to eliminate the stress from your life," the doctor had told me.

"I'd have to eliminate my husband," I joked.

"You do what you need to do. I'm that serious," was his medical advice.

"You are coming with me," my mom said to Ella and me both, "and I'm not taking no for an answer, Amelia. It's enough! Your daughter thinks your name is Bitch! Get a few bags, and come on."

This was the second time one of my parents had demanded I leave this man, along with a doctor who had said it too. It was beginning to sway me. I stared at the ceiling lying in bed most nights thinking, *"You're already doing it all anyway. You're already doing all of it alone. You're already a single mom. Just leave."*

"Take Ella to your house, and I will be over in a few minutes," I told my mom.

"Oh, so you're gonna take our baby and move out!" Tyler yelled.

I gave him an ultimatum. I told him how much I loved him and our family, "But you have to contribute something, and I believe in you. I really do. You can either get a job and keep it for two months or pick a college and go to school for at least two months, or you can decide to be a stay-at-home dad and do most of the baby chores, including watching her while I'm at work, but I can't keep paying for daycare while you sit on the couch. I can't keep doing everything while you sit on the couch, and you have to figure out how to stop yelling at me and calling me names. I still want to be your wife. I still love you, and I still want to see you. I want you to see your daughter every single day." I said as I packed our things. "I'll be three blocks away. Please, Tyler, please do this for us. Will you please pick something, and do it for our family?" I asked.

He promised he would, and I promised myself that I would give him two months to prove to me he could be a husband and a dad.

# CHAPTER FIFTY-NINE

I had promised myself that I would not give up and move back in with Tyler unless he had kept up his end of the bargain and kept a job or went to school for at least two months. It only took me two weeks to realize he was going to need longer than that to even begin the process of proving to me that he wanted to be a good dad because, in those two weeks, every time I called him to come over and pick up his daughter for quality time with her, he was at Pecan Grove, a creek where he liked to go to wade and canoe.

Every phone call ended in me crying and throwing my phone because I knew he wasn't going to do any of the things I had asked him to do. He was not going to be a good dad to his daughter, or get a job, or even pay rent while I was gone. He had managed to sign himself up for Phoenix Online, but every time I asked him when he started or what classes he was taking, he didn't know the answers. He took his leftover student loan money and went to visit his mom in Kentucky.

I was not surprised Tyler was still acting like a child. I went to our landlord's house, apologetically. The man who owned our trailer answered and invited me inside. We sat in his living room. His wife had just left him with his son to raise by himself, he explained. I explained what was happening to my marriage, that we were moving out, and not to let Tyler back into our trailer when he got back from Kentucky unless he didn't really need the rent or utilities to be paid.

Unfortunately for him, he understood too well, and as I turned to leave, I felt like hugging the poor guy. He was always more than kind and accommodating. He was a good dad and a hard worker. I wondered how she could leave a man like that, but knowing them for a year, I knew she was just as selfish as Tyler. They were in Kentucky and Rhode Island while their babies were in Iowa.

A couple of weeks went by, and Tyler came back to Iowa. He gave me a glass rose he'd bought in Kentucky. He said he was sorry and told me all he needed was to be around his family back home for a little while and that he felt better now. Now, he was going to go to college online, go to work, and see Ella every day. He was ecstatic, and so was I. I believed him, and I believed *in* him. Ella was taking a nap in her bedroom, my mom and Chad were at work and school, so, when Tyler came back so happy, we celebrated our love, and we were intimate.

"Where are you going to live though?" I asked as he was getting back in the truck.

"I already talked to our landlord. It's all squared away. He's going to let me live there in our trailer until I can pay everything back up. Just give me a little bit of time, baby," he promised, and I cried tears of joy. He was going to grow up and finally be the man Ella and I deserved.

I went to work the next day so happy, telling my friends the good news. Most of them were skeptical, but I was sure he had changed.

The weeks following proved my friends right. Every time I called Tyler to see his daughter, he was at Pecan Grove. One day, after telling Ella who missed her daddy that he was on his way to get her and him not showing up, she and I drove to Pecan Grove. Tyler's truck was parked where it always was, so I got out and walked to the truck to see if he was inside or down by the water. He was inside the truck, and my heart hit my feet when I saw he wasn't alone.

Bertha, the nineteen-year-old girl whose hair I had been doing for years, was in my husband's truck with him. He rolled down the window and looked at me, eyes dancing with laughter that he was trying to fight back. His lips were curling up in a smile he was trying to fight down.

"What is this?!" I asked. I was holding our baby and trying not to lie on the ground in a puddle of heartache and pain.

"We're just talking," he said.

"What are you doing with my husband?" I asked Bertha.

"We're just talking. He was upset with everything that's been going on, and we were just talking about everything." She was so quiet I could barely hear her.

"He is my husband, and we are working on our marriage, and you are going to never, ever speak to him again!" I said.

"You aren't going to talk to her like that or be telling anybody what to do, Amelia. Take Ella, and go home," Tyler said.

"What are you talking about? You are my husband!" I said, bewildered and hurt that he had stood up for Bertha against me. He had never stood up for me before, and now he was standing up for a stranger against me and our baby? I was enraged. "If you want to stay married, you need to not touch her and take her home, and you," I said, looking at Bertha, "need to never speak to my husband again."

Tyler laughed, said, "Go home, Amelia," and rolled up his window.

Just days ago, he and I were in bed together, and now I was walking back to my car with another woman, girl rather, in his truck. When I got home, I called my friend Angie. "Why is your cousin hanging out with my husband alone at Pecan Grove?" I asked.

"I don't know," she said with a tone in her voice that I had heard before. She had always been incredibly two-faced with the girls in cosmetology school that she didn't like. She would talk to them with condescension in her voice and tell them one thing while sounding like she meant another.

"I think they're just talking," Angie said.

*"But I told them to talk, and I hope they destroy your marriage because*

*I'm a sad, bored, lonely, woman with nothing better to do,"* is what she meant.

"We are still married, and we're working on our marriage," I told her.

"Well, I don't think they're sleeping together yet," she said as though my marriage and her cousin's life were her puppet show.

"Tell her to leave my husband alone!" I told her.

"I can't really stop them, but I'll try," she said, meaning the opposite. She found my pain entertaining.

The next night, I asked my younger brother Chad to watch Ella while I drove three blocks over to our trailer to see if Bertha was there. I walked in on my husband cheating on me on our couch with the pictures of our daughter on the wall above them.

"Put your clothes on. I want to talk to you," I said to Bertha.

I was completely done with Tyler, but I had something to say to the girl who destroyed my marriage, my daughter's relationship with her dad, and her own life, that night.

After she was dressed, I said, "You know we're still married, right?" I took off my wedding ring and set it on the counter.

"Yes." She was always meek.

"And that means you are sleeping with a man who thinks that it's okay to have sex with another woman while he's married," I said. "He will yell at you. He will call you names. He will not support you or himself. He will not work, and I really need you to listen to this part, Bertha, because you are too young to settle for him like I did, and you are too young to ruin your life. He will get you pregnant, and he will not help you. You will struggle forever if you settle for him."

Tyler sat silently, listening to my speech about how he was a pile of vomit.

"Why? Why my husband?" I asked her.

"I'm just not very good at this," she said, quiet as a mouse. That was the only answer I ever got from her. She just wasn't very good at this, meaning finding someone to date was too difficult and the reason she had to sleep with my husband.

My marriage was over, and I was crushed. My heart was broken. I sat in my car wailing gutturally until midnight before coming inside and falling asleep next to my tiny, sleeping, daughter. Now, it was just the two of us.

# CHAPTER SIXTY

I'm sure my relationship with Tyler may sound like I was chasing after a guy who never liked me or wanted me, and then I got pregnant, so he tried but couldn't make it work because I was intolerable. In reality, that might even be true. Maybe he never liked me. Maybe he tried his best, and I demanded too much of him.

He did not have to treat me the way that he did even if he didn't like me. He didn't have to treat Ella the way he did, even if he didn't like me. He could have lived his life and I mine and co-parented his daughter with me with little to no contact. We could have found someone to be the middleman, to set up times for him to pick her up and see her.

Tyler and Bertha are still together. He and I got divorced three years after he cheated on me with Bertha, when Ella was six. I begged him to see his daughter, but he was rarely without an excuse. He had to work, car trouble, a cold, allergies–it was always something. When I would call to invite him to her ballet recitals, T-ball, or birthday parties, he would use the excuse that he did not want to be around my family.

"But you are missing her childhood," I would plead.

Tyler and Bertha had a little boy when Ella was five. Now, she had a brother that she barely got to see, so, I reached out to Bertha mother to mother. "Ella needs to be involved in your lives and be part of your family. Her dad's absence is causing her self-esteem issues, and she acts up, is in trouble because she misses her dad, and doesn't understand why he doesn't pick her up."

I would explain to Bertha that I suffered from the same type of situation in my mom's absence as a child. Bertha told me she understood completely because her dad didn't pay any attention to her, and he was absent from her childhood when she was little.

The first few times I spoke with Bertha about Tyler seeing Ella more often I would feel optimistic because, at least, Bertha understood.

*"Maybe she will insist he go see his daughter. Maybe they will start to invite Ella to their house, and Ella will finally have a daddy,"* I would think.

Eventually, by the time Ella was around seven years old, it occurred to me that the reason Tyler had chosen Bertha over me was because she did not point out what he was not doing that he ought to be doing. She was not going to bat for Ella because she could get hit with the ball, and it would hurt. She was too cowardly to even try.

She was without opinion. Everything Tyler said was how it was, no matter how wrong. Bertha was meek and quiet, and that was what Tyler had always wanted, someone to push around who wasn't going to try to make him grow up or be a better person.

Tyler and Bertha bounced from apartment to apartment in the surrounding area where Ella and I lived until they had been evicted so many times that they had to move in with Bertha's mom. When they moved in with her, Tyler's new excuse for not being able to take Ella on his court-ordered Wednesday evenings and every other weekend was that there was no room for her at his mother-in-law's house.

"So, take her to the park or to get ice cream. Please take her anywhere," I would beg.

He was always too busy.

When Ella was nine, we called to invite him to her basketball game and found out he, Bertha, and their son had been living in Kentucky for six months without telling Ella. That was when Ella really started to show signs of absence abuse. To neglect your child, to make them wonder and worry where and how you are and what they have done wrong to become abandoned, is abuse.

Ella started to throw herself down on the floor, scream, cry, and have tantrums. When she was asked to do something as simple as take out the trash, she'd collapse and cry. She was already overwhelmed with an adult-sized heaping load of grief, and anything on top of that, no matter how seemingly mild, was too much.

Even though I had been through it myself as a child, I did not know how to help her. I did not know what to say, so I tried to keep her busy so she couldn't remember he even existed. Moving to a completely different state without so much as hugging her goodbye or telling her they were gone, was sick, even for Tyler.

Cheerleading, basketball, gymnastics, violin, piano, and trumpet–I realize now as I write this that I did exactly what my dad did for us when Ruby and I missed our mom. My dad would pep talk us through it, reminding us that we were Boyds, we were bulldogs, and that we were amazing. Then he'd make us get ready for ball practice so that we could go be a kid.

Without knowing it at the time, I took the same approach with Ella, but unfortunately, childhood abandonment cannot be fixed with a pair of knee pads and a volleyball, especially because the child wants the absent parent at their games.

I could not meet a man to replace Ella's dad because he was not doing his share of the parenting, so I did not have time to date. I could not make enough money to stay afloat because, when you parent alone, every time your child is sick, hurt, or needs to be picked up from school early, that responsibility falls on one set of shoulders.

So, I had to work part-time jobs with flexible hours and put Ella before my career goals, dreams, aspirations, free time, and my own romantic life, which I was happy to do, and I love my daughter, but it would have worked out much better for everyone if I had been allowed to make more money or have a significant other in my life. If Tyler had helped ever, even for one year, maybe I could have accomplished something other than motherhood.

When Ella was eight, and Tyler still lived an hour away from us, I had to have surgery. My surgery caused me to be in bed, feverish, and unable to speak or do much of anything else for two weeks. I texted Tyler explaining all that and begging him to come and get her for just one of the fourteen days that I was down.

He told me he was too busy.

After trying it in Kentucky for a year or two, Tyler and Bertha moved back in with her mom an hour away from Ella and me. They came over a few times to see Ella at our house, which at first brought me great joy. I felt like he was finally going to be her dad.

But visit after visit, he would yell at me in my own home, critiquing my parenting after not having been involved in her life for nearly a decade. So, I told him he could come and pick her up or stay outside and they could play, but I wasn't going to listen to him berate me in front of my daughter in my own house.

He never came back. He blamed me from then on saying, "You don't make it very easy," when I asked why he wouldn't come and see his daughter.

By the time she was eleven, she had her own phone. He never texted or called, and it made her very sad. When she was eleven, I had a baby. Her little brother took up most of my time, energy, and attention. He was still an infant when one cold, January day Ella fell on the ice, hurting herself badly.

I called her dad, asking him to take her to the doctor, "My baby screams and cries everywhere we go. I can't take him to a doctor's appointment for Ella. I have no one else to watch him," I begged.

"Sounds like a *you* problem," Tyler said, hanging up on me.

I told Ella, who had overheard the conversation, to ice her back and tell me if it still hurt in the morning, and we would go to the doctor. Six months later, that summer, she came inside the house with tears streaming down her cheeks. I asked her what was wrong.

"I sat too long on the porch. That made my tailbone hurt," she said.

I was confused, I didn't realize her tailbone had been hurting for six months. We went to the chiropractor, and it had been broken and healed wrong. The chiropractor adjusted her, and she felt better, but she will have permanent, mild pain and damage for the rest of her life, both physically and emotionally.

She had sucked it up and dealt with a broken tailbone at eleven years old because she knew her mom was overwhelmed with a new baby, and her dad was too selfish to take her to the doctor. So, all of that pain and all of that sorrow that I went through as a child in my mother's absence by choosing the wrong man, I myself created the same pain and sorrow for my child. I chose the wrong person to create a baby with, and I dragged my daughter through the same misery I endured. I never got help for my trauma, and I didn't make good life choices so that my child didn't have to go through it, too.

I hope that anyone who hears our story and can relate will end the cycle. Break the curse. Ella is almost seventeen now, and she's wise beyond her years. She sees people in situations for what they truly are rather than what she hopes they will be or thinks they should be. She's in therapy, and she's healing and learning. Her children, if she has them, will not watch their mother suffer or struggle like she watched me. The people in her life will not be abandoned. She is too selfless and too kind for that. Her heart is empathy incarnate.

Recently, Tyler treated Ella and me so badly that we had to block him from our phones. He cursed the two of us out for the last time, calling us, "sons of bitches" and "little shits." We are trying to heal and can't give him any more chances. She actually realized that and ended it before I did. Sad—I feel just pure sorrow.

My daughter is lovely, so intelligent, well-read, can sing, and is a good writer, friend, sister, cousin, and niece. She is stand-up comedian level funny, and she's beautiful too. I can't imagine not seeing her every day, and if I could not see her every day, I'd be calling her, texting her, begging her to be my friend. Not the other way around.

When I met Tyler, I had a suspicion that he wouldn't always be around, and I should have left right, then but I wanted to see it through. And then I had a baby with him, and I thought I had to see it through, but if a man speaks to the mother of his child the way Tyler spoke to me even once, give up, sister, and move on. He's not your problem anymore, and he's certainly not your baby's problem.

It took me thirteen years to give up on someone I should have walked away from and never looked back that day at Pecan Grove.

# CHAPTER SIXTY-ONE

The morning after walking in on my husband cheating on me, the show had to go on, so I got my three-year-old daughter ready for her day with my mom, and I got ready for work. I was the stylist who opened the salon every morning at eight o'clock. But we almost never had a customer until at least 9:00, so I went to the backroom that we used to mix color to call my dad. I was incredibly upset and needed a pep talk. My dad was my biggest cheerleader, and he hated Tyler, so I thought I needed his words to get myself through the day.

"Dad," I said, trying not to cry. "Tyler cheated on me."

My dad sighed before saying, "Amelia, if you will just lose a little bit of weight, you could have any guy you want."

I knew he had not thought about what he was saying before he had said it. I knew that he knew a long time ago that Tyler would eventually cheat on me, and he was already thinking well into my future. I had travelled on the same train of thought he had arrived there on.

*"Well, she's smart, kind, pretty, and a good mom, but she's going to have to lose some weight before she can find any decent man."*

And yet, I also knew that I was too tired to respond with everything I wanted to scream.

Actually, I wanted to lie down on the floor of the salon and roll my body out the door and into my car, drive off a bridge, and never have anyone see my fat body ever again while yelling, "My body didn't do this particular thing! In fact, the bitch he cheated on me with is fatter than me! You are stuck in 1975 where they tricked you into thinking you should be mean to fat people or see them as less than human, but I don't see anyone as more than anything but a pile of crap! Whether they're short, tall, fat or thin, you jerk!"

I had called my dad for support, and he handed me shame and a new problem to worry about for the day. Instead of screaming those words, I started to cry. He realized he should have said something different and told me something cliche about it all being okay and at least I have my mom and Ella, and everyone loves me. He meant he loved me, and my siblings, mom, and daughter loved me. I went back to work, but I really never forgave him for saying that until just this second.

Living with my mom was wonderful. She was like the husband every good woman deserves. She thought of ways to make my life and Ella's life easier. Since I worked during the day, she switched to working evenings, so we no longer had to pay for daycare. She made breakfast, and I made dinner. We both cleaned, and Chad did the yard work. Life was so easy that, when my manager put in his two weeks' notice, the regional manager of the salon chain I worked for began training me to be manager of the salon.

I began to go see my friends from before Tyler, and because my mom was home from work by nine o'clock every night, I was able to have a social life again. I was making great money at the salon, and I was so happy I lost fifty pounds without even trying.

A year flew by, and just before Ella's fourth birthday, our perfect lives came to a sudden halt when I came home from work one day and Frank, who wasn't supposed to even know where we lived, was loading our furniture into a trailer that was hooked to the hitch of his truck.

As I pulled into the driveway, he half smiled and half waved at me. Chad was helping him load our things, and inside the house, my mom was packing. Without telling me, she had taken my four-year-old to see the enemy and had agreed to move back in with Frank.

Apparently, without even asking me, they had also decided that Ella and I were going to live in the trailer, on their property, the one I had lived in when I was a senior in high school. The one they had kicked me out of just before I went to meet Tyler.

I knew that nothing I said was going to change anything. My mom had already told the landlord that we were moving out. I couldn't afford daycare, rent, and the bills by myself. I couldn't take Ella away from my mom, and I had become accustomed to having a co-parent that actually helped me. So, I put Ella in my car and followed my mom, Frank, and Chad home.

# CHAPTER SIXTY-TWO

My daughter Ella has always been what you'd call 'an old soul.' She was born into trauma to two twenty-year-old children who had no idea who they were or how adult life worked, and neither of them had ever seen a healthy marriage or healthy parental relationship.

Her dad's dad was an alcoholic who beat him until he suddenly died when Tyler was eight years old. Tyler's mom raised three children by herself with very little income, chronic stress, and no education. Her mom's dad tried his best but was essentially raising six children on his own by the time I was eight years old.

I had an absent mother, a chronically depressed stepmother, and a stepfather who was off-the-charts-level crazy. Tyler and I had no idea how to love each other, stay together, or parent Ella. We had never seen any of it done.

When Ella and I moved in with my mom, I thought she would have a better life. There was no more yelling or arguing, and everyone was working together to make Ella's life better. Then my mom changed her mind, and without discussing it with me, took my four-year-old to go meet Frank.

I don't want to tell too much of Ella's story for many reasons, including my not doing it justice and her being a wonderful writer herself. She'll tell her story when it's time, but she did tell me about the first time she met Frank, and our first impressions of him are similar. She was four; I was six. We both used the words, "goblin," "intimidating," "revolting," and "scary." We both remember looking up at my mom, her grandma, for reassurance that it was even safe to be near him and wondering why she could not see how terrifying a beast he was.

If I had it to do over again, I would have never trusted my mother. I look back and wonder why I did and how I couldn't see. Taking my daughter to meet Frank was completely against my wishes, and she did not have permission, and yet I was helpless. When he came to get our things and moved us into his extra house, I should have gone anywhere else, but I didn't.

I wanted my mom to be able to help raise Ella because she didn't get to help raise me. I thought Frank had changed. So, we stayed, and I thought I was watching. I thought I knew how Ella was being treated when I wasn't around. I thought she would tell me if anything was amiss or if she felt negatively in any way about going down the trail, through the bird dog field, to her grandma's house.

When she was four, while I was doing housework, Ella would play outside in our fenced in yard. Ten minutes later, I would go to check on her, and she would either be in the middle of throwing her tricycle over the fence and then climbing the gate to ride her trike to my mom's house or she would have already been halfway down the trail. She had to be supervised more closely for a couple of years after that because she'd sneak off to her grandma's house, that's how good of buddies they were.

My mom took care of Ella while I managed the salon that was now a forty-five minute drive away because I had to move without being considered or even confided in beforehand. Yet, the relation-ship my mother and daughter had, and the fact that I didn't have to leave her with a stranger or someone that did not love her, was worth it. My only rule for my mom was that Ella was not to go anywhere with Frank alone, be left alone with him, or be lectured by him on any subject, and I asked them both every day about these topics when I came home from work.

My beautiful, innocent, four-year-old was being taught to lie, 'nail polish remover and take your earrings out before you get home' style. 'Secret bank account, get cash back at the store' style.

I knew that would happen, and I thought if I talked to Ella every day about how wrong that was and how Gram was not doing the right thing, she would understand. I thought that, if I asked her, "Did you go anywhere with Frank today?" she would know not to lie to me, but she was four. They were telling her to lie to me and exactly what to say, and she liked going places with Frank. She called him Grandpa, and he always took her to McDonald's or to get candy after the errand to the lumber yard or the tool store. She wanted to lie to me so that she could keep going places with him. He taught her to clean a quail and a fish. He taught her how to ride a horse and how to fix a car. He also ruined her self-esteem with his lectures about how worthless women are and how most of them are whores.

The only time Ella ever did tell me about something Frank said to her, she was eight. "I can't wear this dress to church anymore," she said after riding with my mom and Frank from a Wednesday night service.

"Why is that?" I asked.

"Frank called me a 'whore' when I got in the car and said this is the dress of a prostitute." She sniffled.

We had to have a discussion about how that simply was not true. About how Frank's ideas were archaic and how he didn't even deserve to be in the presence of women. I explained to her that there was nothing wrong with prostitutes and whores, either, and that we love those people, and Jesus loves those people too. We talked about what the word "hypocrite" meant and how anyone talking about others negatively based on biblical teachings must be forgetting the two most important parts of the Bible: Jesus and love.

Ella and I had discussions like that one daily for years, and I wanted to leave, but I was afraid I couldn't make it on my own. Every time I talked about leaving, my mom would either tell me I couldn't afford to live on my own with Ella and that I would lose her, or she would pay for a new class or lesson for Ella. By the time she was nine, Ella was taking violin, piano, ballet, tap, cheer, hip hop dance, and gymnastics. My mom bought every instrument and costume, and what was even more miraculous to me, she went to Ella's recitals! She got to go and didn't take no for an answer from Frank.

I thought perhaps he was finally getting old enough that his zealot-meets-control-freak attitude was softening. He treated Ella like a granddaughter when I was around, and my mom was allowed so much more freedom to grandmother my daughter than she had received to mother me. I didn't want to take that away from Ella or my mom.

My mom had one dress for each day of the school week as a teenager and only a couple of outfits when she was a small child, so she filled Ella's closet to the brim. Every week when she and Ella would get home from shopping, they would have new dresses, outfits, and shoes. Every Christmas, my mom would stack dozens and dozens of toys in my closet to wrap for Ella.

She was being cared for during the day by her doting grandma, and then when I was home in the early evening, I'd take her to a different, fun, lesson each night. She got to live on a puppy dog farm with puppies to play with every day, and Frank even bought her her own miniature horse to ride. There were five other horses, a four-wheeler, and outdoor adventures.

I thought she was living the dream. We had to discuss Frank's insane ideas far too often, but other than that, I thought Ella was a happy little girl. Then, when she was nine, she started to throw fits, tantrums, and act out. I honestly thought in the beginning that she had just become spoiled. It took me way too long to realize her dad's absence, and Frank's constant berating of her, my mom, and women in general had eroded her self-esteem, and she was becoming old enough now to understand that her dad had moved to Kentucky without telling her, showing her just how little he cared or even thought about her. She was becoming old enough to understand what Frank was saying when he made her recite like a parrot, in front of customers, "What's the fastest way to a man's heart, Ellabug?"

"Good cooking and no whining," was the answer, which was something that I didn't know about that makes my stomach roll over even now.

One might think these aren't horrible tragedies. She wasn't physically abused. There was no violence. However, when someone, especially an impressionable, young child whose opinion of themself is rapidly forming, is told something over and over, it is traumatic. It's traumatic to be told you matter so much less than you thought, and her dad was telling her in every ticking second of his absence that he cared more about himself and less about her. Frank was telling her in every lecture, comment, story, biblical reading and/or tale that men, men, men, were more important than she was.

Her spirit was collapsing, and I misread it as bad behavior, just like my dad had done when I was her age and I missed my mom. After so many tantrums, I would realize what was happening and try to console her and try to explain that her dad ignoring her was not her fault. I would try to explain to her that Frank was an idiot of mythical proportions and that she shouldn't ever be listening to him when he is talking, no matter what he was talking about. I would leave her feeling better, and she would act better for a while, but my words could not heal wounds.

I would weigh the pros and cons of staying or leaving, and life, work, and single motherhood would swallow me whole. I would talk myself out of leaving because I had no savings and nowhere to go. My relationship with Jesus was in shambles over something I have not even brought myself to write about yet, and I was mentally and emotionally paralyzed.

So, I stayed where we were at least physically safe because I could not add potential homelessness and starvation to my list of woes. I owe Ella a thousand apologies. My mom and I both do because we tried to patch Ella's wounds with Christmas presents and ballet shaped band aids. We threw Disney World, Chick-fil-A, and new outfits at emotional turmoil. We expected her to understand things far too complex for a child, no matter how mature or intelligent, to process.

I am so sorry, Ella. She is almost seventeen now. She is so wise. She is dealing with the trauma in her own way and on her own terms, and I will let her tell you the rest of her story.

# CHAPTER SIXTY-THREE

One night when I was twenty-four, and Ella was four, I was awoken to a phone call from my mom in the middle of the night.

"Have you seen Chad? Is he down there?" She was worried.

"No. What are you talking about?" I asked.

Chad had taken his dad's debit card and truck and vanished in the middle of the night with his girlfriend. By the time I got off the phone with my mom, Tyler was calling me telling me that I needed to talk my little brother, who was only fourteen at the time, into going home because he had shown up at Tyler's apartment with his eighth-grade girlfriend.

I talked Chad and his girlfriend, Fannie, into coming home because everyone was worried about them. The next day, I went to have a serious discussion with my mom and Frank about leaving their debit card and keys where their fourteen-year-old had access to them, and about how Chad and Fannie had been allowed to spend the spring horseback riding alone and were now sneaking off in the middle of the night.

When I said, "You might want to start thinking about what you're going to do if she got pregnant last night," Frank snorted, laughing.

My mom said, "Oh, Amelia, they are only fourteen!"

That was May and my gorgeous little niece was born in February. Fannie's pregnancy was extremely stressful for her and everyone who knew her. First, she did not know what she was going to do, and who could blame her? She was fourteen and pregnant. How terrifying, how devastating. Her pregnancy was challenging because she bounced back and forth between keeping her baby, giving her baby to my mom to raise, and placing her baby with a family in Lansing, Michigan for adoption.

For the months that my mom believed Fannie was going to give her the baby to raise, my mom was ecstatic. She bought baby clothes, a swing, and a crib. Frank added an extra room to their house and began the legal process of adopting Chad and Fannie's baby.

My mom was by Fannie's side at every sonogram and doctor appointment, which, I will be honest, made me incredibly jealous. This was Chad's baby, so my mom was allowed to go and be supportive of the mother, unlike my pregnancy where I was hung up on and told not to even call.

About halfway through her pregnancy, Fannie decided to put her baby up for adoption. Personally, I supported this decision and told Fannie she was doing the right thing. My mom and Frank did not need to try to raise another child. Their home was not a stable environment, and their fourteen-year-old had just ran off and gotten someone pregnant.

When Frank and my mom found out Fannie was talking to a married couple in Michigan, and they were going to adopt the baby, my mom changed. I had seen her sad all of my life, but this was a new wave of sadness. She had been shifting with the tides of tragedy for nearly twenty years, and now I saw in her eyes she was injured, beached. I had never seen her that sad.

Frank gave their lawyer $10,000 to try to stop the adoption and get Chad paternal rights, or himself grandparent rights, to the baby. Stress and chaos ensued for months, and then Fannie decided to keep Alexis and raise her herself.

It took a few months before Fannie was comfortable leaving Alexis with my mom, but once she did, the two were inseparable.

When Fannie was at school, volleyball, or cheerleading, Alexis was with my mom. If Fannie wanted to go to a dance or on a date, Alexis was with my mom.

My mom was finally beginning to be happy again. She was watching Alexis and Ella, her two little girls, all day while their moms were at school and work. My mom's life regained purpose. She made the girls breakfast and lunch. She put them in pretty outfits and did their hair. She taught them both to read, write, and do math before kindergarten. Even though she didn't get to raise her own little girls, Fannie and I had given her the gift of helping with ours. My mom was the best grandma any parent or child could ask for when it came to everything except Frank.

Even though she lived a quarter of a mile away from me, she may as well have been on another planet. If I was taking Alexis and Ella to the zoo, I had to ask Frank if my mom could go with us rather than just asking her if she wanted to go. If we were going to visit Ruby or to see Christmas lights, to the carnival, or trick-or-treating, I couldn't just tell my mom the plan and what time I was picking her up. I had to ask her husband first.

"You are fifty-seven years old. Why can't you just do, go, be your own person, and how long am I going to have to ask him permission for you to get to go trick-or-treating with us?" I would ask.

More often than not, Frank would tell me no, Mom couldn't go with us. When it was something she really wanted to do badly enough she would spend hours or days ahead of time begging him to let her go and then threatening him with leaving and taking every one of us with her.

When she was out with us at events or get togethers, she was never fully present. This is one of the things my daughter and niece remember the most about their gram.

"She would immediately start talking about how we couldn't stay gone very long and how we'd have to start heading back the second she got in the car," Ella said when we looked back on these trips.

They were trips that should have been fun, but my mom was still in fight-or-flight mode. Everything she thought about revolved around Frank and his violent reactions and controlling rules. When she went with us to see Ruby and her children, an hour and a half away, she talked about leaving and how Frank was going to kill her for being gone so long the entire time. She was anxiously manic, and she could not enjoy her daughters or her grandchildren. She was supposed to be watching my kids and Ruby's kids play and instead she was worried about how her husband was going to knock her teeth out when she got home—not for cheating on him or for spending their last dime (not that those would be acceptable reasons to hit your wife either)--but for simply trying to be a grandmother and mother.

My mom's nerves were wearing thin, and she was starting to make less and less sense. When I was twenty-eight, I had to have surgery and wasn't allowed to drive myself home afterward. I begged her to drive me to and from the hospital, which was only twenty minutes away, and she said Frank would not let her.

The lines blurred between what he was not allowing her to do and what she thought, if she asked, she'd get lectured for even asking about and not having the energy for even one more damn lecture on the topic of not helping her own children. It devastated me to have to lie to nurses and drive myself to and from that procedure. Waking up from surgery alone and walking into the pharmacy to get my prescription, alone, when my mom was so close but so far away, was more painful than my physical wounds. The scarring from that surgery is gone, but the scars from being alone for it remain.

Ella and I began to feel the effects of being around Frank too much, as well as the effects of being worried about my mom. We began to worry that Frank was going to hurt my mom. If it was late at night, and we heard the kennel dogs barking like crazy, we would instantly think, *"I hope she's okay. I hope he didn't lose his temper and kill her this time. That might be why the dogs are freaking out."*

Every time we heard the four-wheeler heading toward our house, Ella and I would become anxious. My stomach would become upset. The four-wheeler meant Frank was coming down the trail, and that meant he was going to demand one or both of us come and help him with something terrifying, dangerous, and asinine like asking my small child to help him move six rowdy horses from one pasture to another or asking her to climb up on the roof and hand him nails.

I would either have to argue with him or be bullied into letting her help him, worrying about her the entire time. If it was something too dangerous for her, I would have to drop what I was busy doing and go help him myself.

Ella and I were in fight-or-flight mode, too. Frank was in charge of all three of us, our emotions, thought processes, and therefore, our lives. We all three struggled with wanting to leave but not wanting to leave Alexis.

"If we leave now, we'll never see the baby again," my mom would say.

"You can still see the baby. Fannie will still let you see her." I would argue.

"It won't be like it is now. I won't be able to watch Ella and Alexis all day. I'll have to get a job. You will have to send Ella to daycare. We will only get to see Alexis once in a while, and Fannie needs me. The baby needs me." She had a point.

If we left, everything would change, so, we got better at being strong. We struggled through every day in survival mode. Even Ella was in survival mode, and she and I coped with ice cream and pizza. We both started to gain weight. We would try to get healthy, but we were so oppressed by Frank's presence and the all-encompassing fear, hurt, unfairness, anxiety, and depression.

# CHAPTER SIXTY-FOUR

Everyone has those moments where they walk into a room and can't remember what brought them in there, or they go to the store without a list and forget a couple of things they came for. The busier I am, or the more stressed I am, the worse my memory suffers.

My mom was having more and more of those types of experiences, and I thought she was just getting a little older and a little more forgetful. It was astounding to me how she could live with all of her life trauma and pain and function at all, so, when she would wake up every morning and take care of 150 bird dogs, her husband, Chad, Ella, and Alexis every day, it was understandable when she would forget I had asked her to pick up laundry detergent when she went into town.

As Chad got older, he caused my mom even more grief. Shortly after his daughter Alexis was born, Chad ran away again. He was depressed because Fannie had broken up with him, so once again, in the middle of the night, he took his dad's debit card and truck, and this time, he was headed to Mexico. To this day, I still don't understand why he chose Mexico, but he was fifteen and clearly very stupid.

He picked up another fifteen-year-old boy along the way, and by the time they got from Iowa to Kansas the next morning, they figured the police would be looking for them in Frank's truck, so they decided to switch vehicles. In a small town, they stopped outside of a post office and started to get into a lady's SUV. When they noticed a baby in the back seat and a terrified lady running out of the post office screaming at them, they jumped back into Frank's truck, and, just their luck, the lady was the chief of police's wife. A full-speed chase through town and out the other side, Chad driving through a field with police cars following him, jumping out and running away on foot with a loaded shotgun in his hands, and he landed himself in a jail cell.

Once again, white male privilege and money thrown at a problem won, and much like Frank at that age, Chad did not do any real time at all. He was in a jail cell for less than twenty-four hours, and Frank had paid for him to only have to take anger management classes.

My mom worried about Chad constantly. He was always doing the most incredibly stupid things a teenage boy could do. When he was sixteen, he was in trouble with the law again because he shot a neighbor's dog, and when he did that, he shot across a road, which is illegal. Again, his dad paid for him not to be in any real trouble.

When he was seventeen, he started dating my friend's little sister. I grew up in the town this little girl lived in, and I knew her mom, so I knocked on their door. Maybe it's just me, but if someone's own sister gets in her car and drives thirty miles to knock on my door to tell me not to let my daughter date her brother because he's bad news, I'm going to listen, but this lady didn't listen to me. Chad and his new girlfriend were allowed to go on dates, and I once again found myself sitting in the lecture chair across from Frank.

"How are you allowing him to date her? Don't you see that he has already ruined a teenage girl's innocence and childhood? Don't you see that there's already a young girl getting up in the middle of the night to hush a fussy baby, and we are just going to allow this to happen again? I came home from work the other day and Chad's belt was in my bed!" I was infuriated.

Frank laughed his mocking laugh at me, and just like himself, Chad could do no wrong.

I turned to my mom. "Are you wanting to use the same lawyer with this baby as you did the first one or…?"

"Watch your mouth, Amelia!" was her response, and I gave up.

A few months later, I was singing at Chad's wedding because they were seventeen and pregnant. The poor girl was too meek and scared of life to walk down the aisle, so they got legally married that day after everyone had left. She was too childlike to stand in front of her own guests.

Chad and his wife's relationship deteriorated when my nephew was still too little to walk or talk. They stayed legally married, but the girl moved back in with her family and gave up on Chad before the baby turned one.

Losing all these babies was so difficult for my mom. She lost her little girls, had multiple miscarriages, thought she was going to raise Alexis herself, and then having that ripped away, having her grandson around for only a year before having him taken away, caused my mom so much sorrow. I believe it was all too heavy to bear. She started to forget more often. She started to say things, and even do things, that made absolutely no sense.

She was always stubborn, so when I asked her to go get Ella a softball helmet and she came back with a bicycle helmet, I said, "She can't use a bicycle helmet for softball," laughing.

We got into a tiff, and we would just get into little arguments about things like that. I didn't have the time or the energy to argue with her and thought, *She just wasn't thinking when she was at the store and is now too stubborn to admit how silly Ella would look with a bike helmet on up to bat at her ball game,* because that is such a hysterical notion. I laughed about it and moved on.

When my mom went to the wrong dentist office, we just thought she wasn't paying attention. She was going to the city one day, so I told her she should stop at a store called Plato's Closet on the way home to see if they had any jeans in Ella's size.

When she got home, she said, "I looked all over the place for that

Juliet's Closet you were talking about and couldn't find it," which made me laugh until… well, I still laugh about that. Life is a jigsaw of shockingly funny pain.

My mom loved singing at church. She, Ella, and I would blend familial three-part harmony, and it was so fun to sing with people who knew what they were doing. When they asked my mom to be the star of the church play, she had over 100 lines to memorize. She worked so hard on that play. All the time for months, she worked on memorizing her lines. She was amazing in that play. It wasn't a sad play, but it made me cry with pride.

My mom helped people every week when she went to the store. She didn't just go for herself and her family, but she always went for someone in the community, too. The good, kind, selfless and thoughtful sides of my mom and her talent for music and acting, and taking care of everyone but herself, is what I will try to remember about her as long as I can keep my memory.

# CHAPTER SIXTY-FIVE

Ella was two months shy of five years old, and she and I were excited for a busy weekend. Late Friday afternoon, we went to Des Moines to see Ruby graduate with her master's degree and then we ended the day with Ella's very first dress rehearsal.

It was the day before her first ballet recital, and the whole way to Des Moines, to watch Ruby graduate, I was calling my dad. I knew he would be headed to the graduation too, and Ella and I wanted to sit with him. He was always forgetting to bring his cell phone with him, so when he didn't respond, I figured he'd forgotten his phone, and I must have just missed him in the crowd. Still, I needed to talk to him and remind him of Ella's recital the next day. I knew if I didn't call him the day before, he would forget.

I tried calling his cell phone and his house before I went to bed that night, but no one answered. The next morning, after putting Ella's makeup on her and slicking her hair into a bun, I called my dad's house. My stepmom answered and said he wasn't home.

"Do you know where he is?" I asked.

"No." She was annoyed.

"Is he up at the ball field maybe?" I asked. He coached Little League and was usually doing something having to do with sports.

"I don't know." Debbie was even more irritated.

"Well, did his band play last night?" I was starting to get worried. I was not worried about my dad, but I was worried that he would be late to Ella's recital.

"I don't know, Amelia." She said it like it hurt her to speak to me. I wondered how someone could not know where their husband was and not even seem to care.

My mom, Ella, and I had a wonderful time at the recital. Ella looked adorable, and we had a lot of fun. I was a little disappointed that my dad had forgotten to be there, but I understood. He was one of the busiest people I knew.

*"He was probably painting bleachers at the ball field or coaching a practice."* I thought.

The last time I had seen him, he was running the bases with my four-year-old daughter at her T-ball game. Ella refused to run the bases without her Papaw.

After the recital, my mom took us to Applebee's for lunch, and just as we sat down, my brother Jordan called my mom's cell phone. My heart dropped onto the table. There would be no reason for Jordan to be calling my mom unless it was important.

The conversation was short. All my mom said was "Oh, okay. I'll tell her. Bye."

"Tell me what? Tell me what? Tell me what?" I said.

"Oh, your grandpa, Matthew died." she said.

"My grandpa died?" I asked.

"Yes, Matthew. Your grandpa. He died," she said.

"My grandpa Matthew died when I was a month old. Do you mean my dad died?!" I was having an out-of-body experience at this point.

"Oh, yes. I guess that… that's right. He is your dad and your grandpa," she said pointing first at me and then to Ella. She delivered the news like she was reading the menu. Ella was still too little to understand exactly what was happening. I had to call Ruby, or I was going to die too.

"You call Mellissa and do not tell her the way you just told me. Please tell her more gently and say, 'your dad,'" I told my mom.

"Ruby, are you sitting down?" I had only heard that phrase on TV and always found it to be cheesy, but I honestly did not want her to faint. "I have to tell you something, and it's bad. I mean really, really bad."

I could hear my mom fucking up the instructions I'd just given her as I told Ruby, "Dad died."

Sobbing.

My mom saying, "Mellissa? Uh… Matthew died."

Screaming.

*"We have to get the fuck out of this Applebee's,"* I thought.

Now, it's kind of funny. In fact, it sounds like I'm making it up. How could the news have been explained any worse? There's no way. We didn't order. We got up and left. I told my mom she did a horrible job. She started to defend herself rather than comfort me.

Looking back, I can see how much that news broke her when Jordan told her. She didn't butcher that moment because she was heartless or not thinking. She messed it up because it made her sad too. It broke her heart too. She wasn't thinking clearly because her ex-husband, whom she had once loved enough to marry twice and make four children with, had suddenly died incredibly young. He was only fifty-five, and she was only fifty-seven.

My mom met her own mortality in that moment. How do we prepare for that moment? For the moment we have to tell our children their dad has died? We expect too much of our mothers. We expect them to flawlessly execute things no one should ever have to do.

I drove Ella and myself to my brother's house. Ella played Barbies with Jordan's daughter while we waited for our little sisters, Ruby who was only twenty-two and Madi, who was only seventeen. Madi had to drive all the way from a track meet four hours away with the news that her daddy had died.

A police officer had seen our dad's truck out by the pit he liked to fish in early Saturday morning and went down to the water to check and see who was fishing. He found my dad's body face down in the water. We still don't know how he ended up there. He had a weak heart, born with two holes in it. He was diabetic and could have fallen in, having a seizure. He had been drinking and could have fallen in and drowned. Or, he could have just given up on life. We don't know, and for me, how he died doesn't really matter. How he lived was powerful enough to make a person forget he was gone.

Passionate, animated, funny, kind, hardworking, great musician—all words used to describe my dad. The funeral was so crowded, there were people standing outside of the building.

My dad had written a song before I was born about salvation. It was a time in his life when he was giving up his ego and giving in to Jesus. He remarried my mom shortly after writing the song that begins with the line, "I lost my way because I tried to go alone," and ends with the line, "but I'm safe here in His arms and it's a miracle."

Days before the funeral, people were reciting that song and writing it on Facebook. People had remembered lines from "Miracle" not having heard the song in twenty years. "I was down and broken hearted couldn't finish what I'd started." At the visitation, my siblings and cousins, who loved my dad like he was their own, were talking about how it needed to be read at the funeral.

"I'll sing it," I said

"You can't sing it." Jordan looked so sad.

I said, "I have sung that song a million times. We used to travel to different churches, and I would sing, and he would play guitar."

"I know that, but you won't be able to sing. You'll be crying the day of the funeral. Trust me. You might get partway through it and…." Jordan was trying to spare me the pain. "You can read the lyrics. How about that?"

Later, my cousin Asher, who was a pastor and loved my dad, said, "I heard you're going to sing the song."

"I will probably just read it. Jordan is probably right. He thinks I'll cry," I said.

Asher referred to my uncle, his own dad, who loved and cherished mine. "My dad says you've never really sang unless you've cried during a song."

That's the only thing I really ever got to do for my dad. If he taught me anything, it was how to do things you absolutely did not want to do. So, I put on my Boyd face and I walked up to the microphone and I sang his song to the people who loved him. After I was done, I fell apart into the arms of my dad's best friend and drummer. I'm so grateful he was there to catch me and remind me that there are pieces of my dad in all of us.

After we buried him, I started crying most of the day. I had read somewhere that a mother shouldn't cry in front of her children, so I would try to hide it from Ella. I would try to wait until she went to bed, then I would stay up all night crying. If I did fall asleep, by some miracle, I would have nightmares about him. He was a teenage boy standing in a field. There was a huge bull in the field. He yelled for me to help him, but I couldn't make it in time. The bull attacked and killed him, and then there he was right by my side, walking next to the field.

"Why didn't you save me?" he asked. "Why did you just let me die?"

How ridiculous a dream, and yet, it was all I could think about. *"How could I just let him die? How could I not check on him more? He was constantly calling me, checking on me."*

My dad was the only person who ever called me to tell me I was a good mom. He was my biggest and only supporter. After he died, I gave up on life completely. Grief is the most exhausting emotion, and sudden permanent change is the most difficult thing for a human to deal with.

I was furious with God. I took my dad's death as a direct attack from God on me. I took it personally. I completely stopped praying, singing, and going to school. I was enrolled full-time at Iowa State University. I failed my classes because I missed my finals, then I stopped going to work and lost my job.

For a full year, I did nothing but what it took to keep Ella healthy, educated, and on time to her lessons and appointments, but if it wasn't something for Ella, I simply did not do it. I even stopped brushing my teeth and lost half a tooth. It just cracked, and that's how I felt. I felt like a cement block that someone had thrown off the Empire State Building and like the world was asking me to put myself back together without any cracks. I was in too many pieces, and I didn't care to put myself back together. I slept all day while Ella was at school. I took care of her all evening, and I stayed up all night crying and smoking weed. My mom paid my bills that year and bought our groceries. Otherwise, I don't know how we would have survived, and I almost didn't survive.

I almost took my own life too many times to remember. Suicide was almost all I thought about. If I wasn't mid-daydream about a time my dad had taught me something on the basketball court or a time he shared a microphone with me singing with his band, I was thinking about killing myself. I was so done with God, people, and life. All of the tragedy that had attacked me in my life and all of the horrible things that had happened to me, and nothing hurt as badly as losing my dad. At that time, I couldn't have imagined a time when I could talk or even think about it without sobbing.

Jesus used my daughter and my dad to teach me how to get back up after that attack. Eventually, I stopped crying as long or as often and started to sleep more at night. I started to write songs about him, and that felt better than crying. I found a job at a beauty supply store, and I picked myself up and started to put myself back together. There were still cracks–there will always be–but they got smaller.

As I was starting the long process of giving up on the agony and giving in to the healing, I had a dream that my dad was walking up my driveway, and Ruby and I were standing on my porch watching him and asking each other if he was really there.

"Is that him? Is he really there?"

And as he opened the gate to come into my yard, we ran to him. When we got to him, we turned into little girls–Amelia and Ruby, his little girls, the girls that had run out of that barn right next to that porch that day so long ago when he was coming to get us for Christmas, and Frank was hiding us in the barn.

In my dream, our dad hugged us and said, "If there's ever a storm, you get to that church."

That's when I woke up. My church was nearby, and we always went there if there was a tornado warning because it had a basement, and Ella and I lived in a trailer, but that's not the kind of storm my dream meant. My dad didn't mean church either. He meant Jesus. No one taught me more about Jesus than my dad and his mom, my grandma.

It took three or four more years for me to really feel like I was going to be okay after that, with a lot of setbacks in life due to the depression that my dad's death caused. My self-worth suffered in that misery, and because I didn't want to live, I certainly didn't want to work or do anything else.

I just did not care about anyone or anything except Ella. She was and is my best friend, and she's the true hero of the story because she got me through it all and inspired me to keep going if only for her and not for myself. My dad taught me many things. In fact, most of what I know and most of my talents come from him. He raised me by himself, and two of the most valuable lessons I learned from him are not to ever let anyone disrespect me and to do the things I absolutely do not want to do, working to get myself where I want to end up.

# CHAPTER SIXTY-SIX

When Ella was little and I would go to work, if she wasn't at school, she was with my mom. My younger brother Chad is ten years older than Ella and was homeschooled, so he was always around too. They were more like brother and sister than uncle and niece because he did things to torture Ella rather than to help her grow up happy and safe.

Even though by the time she was five, Chad was already a father himself, he did things like lock her in the quail building with 3,000 quail. She couldn't get out and was terrified. Once when she was seven, he caught a baby mouse, put it inside her pony's mouth, and when the pony chewed up the dead mouse and spat it back out into Chad's hand, he threw it into Ella's hair. Bullshit like that turned into even more serious abuse.

When Chad was seventeen and had a second teenage wife, and a second newborn, he must have been stressed out and sleep deprived because when my seven-year-old Ella wouldn't do whatever chore he was trying to bully her into doing for him, he took a vacuum cleaner hose and beat her with it until she had welts all over the backs of her arms, legs, and bottom.

My mom and Frank had completely trained Ella not to show or tell me about any of these events. This one, someone from our church even asked Frank about but no one came to me, and no one told me until Ella did, eight years later.

I didn't know about any of Ella's stories of how she was abused by Chad until we were safe away from those people. If I had known, I would have immediately rescued her. I would have thrown our stuff in the car and driven away right then and there, no matter what, but I didn't know, and it was not because I did not ask. I asked Ella all the time. I knew Frank and Chad were cruel, stupid, and not the best people to leave my daughter with, but I thought I was leaving her with my mom, and I had clear rules about Ella's time around Frank and Chad.

My mom was the one who was lying to me, and she had taught Ella to lie so well and to overlook her own comfort so well that Ella learned to expect to be treated that way by Chad. She thought it was normal. She was so little when it started, she did not know it was abuse. If she had not had outside influences like school, her friends, media, and other family members, she would have accepted it forever and she would have grown up to make terrible choices for herself. She had no self-esteem as a child, none. My brother Chad, his dad Frank, and her own dad, Tyler, are the people to thank for her lack of self-love.

I really do not know what to say or do about making sure our children are not having experiences we as parents are not even aware of other than this: if I, as a child, had not been expected to accept Frank's abusive nature, I would not have ever allowed my daughter to be around him. If my boundaries had not been broken and moved repeatedly, especially regarding Frank, and if I had not been asked, as a child, adolescent, and young adult to overlook and allow him to mistreat me and people around me, I would have never even let Ella meet those people, including my mom.

Ella has wonderful memories of her Gram. My mom took really good care of Ella as far as nutrition, education, extracurriculars, and helping me pay bills and buy groceries, toys, and clothes. We couldn't have asked for a better Gram and yet if I had it all to do over again, I would have said, "You can meet my daughter when you have left the toxic waste dump you live in with monsters. I don't want even a droplet of that to get on my beautiful, precious, daughter."

And that's what it is, too, an accumulation of droplets. The drops say, "This is what you deserve," and we accept what we think we deserve. We learn to live with poison because we don't think or even know that there is better out there or that we are drinking poison.

The trailer we lived in that Frank owned was getting old, and things would break every year. The nearby kennel drew in and fed all of the mice in Iowa, and they lived comfortably in the walls of my trailer no matter how clean I kept my house or how much rat poison I used. We constantly heard the mice scratching inside the walls, and at least once a day I would catch a mouse in my house on a glue board or trap.

Every summer, a swarm of wasps lived inside the space between the roof and the ceiling in Ella's bedroom, and we had problems walking past that part of the house to the car without getting stung. Every summer, our air conditioning would break and every winter our furnace would break. Frank would get around to calling the cheapest handyman who was an elderly man, and he took two weeks to fix whatever it was that was broken. It would hold until the next hot or cold season but inevitably, every single winter, we would go two or three weeks without heat and have to use space heaters, stay in one room, and hang blankets over the doors and windows.

One might ask why I did not have someone fix it myself or just completely replace the air conditioner or furnace. It was a trailer from the 1990s that I not only did not own but was hoping I would not have to live in for too much longer. Spending thousands of dollars to fix or replace something in that house was also a great risk because I had already been kicked out of that house at a month's notice once before, and I was constantly living with the fear that Ella and I would be asked to leave again. I also never had the money to make expensive repairs because even though my mom helped me a ton, I was still a single mom with no help. Ella's dad's monthly child support was so little that it would pay one bill and be gone the day it was loaded onto the card. In fact, it is still that way.

So, I did not replace the furnace or the air conditioner, and I would have severe anxiety all winter every year until the furnace broke. Ella and I would be reminded just how little Frank thought of us and his inability to just take care of getting a furnace in a house he owned fixed so the little girl and single mom who lived there did not have to freeze to death.

It is true, we did live there rent free. He did not have to let us live there at all. He did not have to let us live there for free. I should have taken advantage of those years of not having to pay rent and saved my money, then put a down payment on a house of my own. I have no good excuse as to why I did not try to do that. I dreamed about it, and every time I would mention it to my mom, I was told I could not make it on my own. Every time I brought it up, my mom would tell me my electric bill was $800 last month and ask how I would pay that and the mortgage when money was already tight as it were without those bills.

I believed her. I had no faith in myself. I thought as often as I had lost in life, losing my mom when I was little, losing Ella's dad, losing my dad, losing my job, losing academically, I believed that if I ever tried to do something for myself and Ella, I would lose. I believed that if I tried to move out, I would lose my home and possibly even my daughter. I believed I could not take care of her without my mom, so we stayed.

We took abuse and we made it normal. I did not show Ella my pain, and she did not show me hers unless it was in the form of a tantrum that was directed at me for something I had done. She would throw herself down on the floor and scream if I asked her to do something as simple as put her shoes away, and I didn't know until years later that it was because of the way Chad was treating her, Frank was lecturing her, and her own dad was neglecting her into believing she was worthless.

All of that in a Gram rapped bow of, "Don't tell your mom."

# CHAPTER SIXTY-SEVEN

I owned eight cars between the ages of sixteen and twenty-eight and that was not due to upgrading. When you're poor and have never had any credit, you buy a $2000 car, and it lasts you a year or two if you're lucky. When you're a single mom, you pray your shitty car last till tax season and then you decide if you're going to use your entire tax refund to buy a new piece of shit car or fix the one you have.

When Ella was eight, we had a particularly rough time of it with cars. The one I bought with my tax refund had a bad transmission. Frank insisted he be the one to pick out all of my cars, and he picked a Chevy Impala with a transmission that lasted three months. It took my entire savings account and help from my mom to replace the transmission, and then I finally had some peace of mind while driving for the first time since I had started owning vehicles, twelve years prior. I knew this car's transmission was not going to go out because it already had. What a relief.

Then one dark night, coming home from ballet lessons on a back road, we hit something hard and metal. My car flipped it into the other lane and then a semi-truck hit it too. I pulled the car over. It was a mess, but we were not hurt. The truck driver came to check on us and told me it was a piece of farm equipment. The Red Tractor in the next town over had dropped something in the road, and it totaled my car when I hit it. The Red Tractor owner showed up after the police took our statements. He accepted it was his fault and the police wrote that in their report.

The Red Tractor's insurance was horrible. They would not pay for a rental car, so I had to go two weeks without driving anywhere. We missed lessons and appointments, and we were running out of groceries. I called the man who owned the Red Tractor, and he said he was in Florida on vacation and his insurance should take care of it all. The insurance told me to take out a loan to buy a new car and then pay it off when they gave me my check. I had never had any credit so I said, "One, I shouldn't have to pay interest on a loan. I've never taken out a loan for anything in my life. I paid cash for my car. Two, I don't think I even have the credit for that."

The insurance agent said, "Whose fault is that?" as though a young, single mom should have good credit just in case someone else totals her car and she has to take out a loan for a new one. Wouldn't having insurance be pointless if we all had to do that?

So, I lost my job because I couldn't get to work and because we couldn't go get groceries, I sent Ella down to my mom's house for every meal and went two weeks without eating. It was a full month before I got a hold of the Red Tractor's owner's wife. I got their receptionist at their business to give me the wife's phone number so I could explain to her that I lived twenty miles from the nearest town, her insurance wouldn't pay for a rental car, I had lost my job because of all of it, and I was about to starve. She was so apologetic she immediately rented me a car with her own money and got her insurance company to send me a check for a new car.

The insurance company gave me a check for the amount the ten-year-old car was worth, minus the amount I had just paid to have the transmission replaced. So, when Frank took the $2500 they gave me to buy yet another Chevy Impala, same year even, it only took two weeks this time for the transmission to go out. No money, no savings, no job, no transmission.

The loser effect. The winner effect. These are real things. Our brains adapt and calculate the risks we will and will not take based on how often we win and lose. Our brains rewire themselves based on how often we win and lose. One of the reasons people get stuck in abusive situations is because they feel like they do not deserve any better. Another reason is because they do not know any better. My brain was physically re-wired to never try to leave.

No matter how many times Charlotte, Ruby, Sam, or Morgan would tell me that I was not doing well, or Ella was not doing well out there at Frank and my mom's house, I stayed because I was so scared that if I left, I would fail. I knew I would fail, and the ways of failing out there with absolutely no one to help me, not even the "bad guys," were scarier than staying.

# CHAPTER SIXTY-EIGHT

*"How could I leave for good and try to make it on my own if I couldn't even make it into town for groceries? I am a failure as a mother. Someone should just take Ella away from me."*

These were thoughts I had those months I was without a car. We had gotten the transmission replaced because our neighbor worked on cars and agreed to take payments but even after replacing the transmission, the car still did not run well. It was old and constantly having issues. At this point, my brother Chad was nineteen and because Frank made $250,000 a year and let him have his own debit card, Chad had bought and paid off a truck and had amazing credit.

"Why don't you just let me go buy a car, put it in my name, but you make the payments? It will be brand new, have a warranty on it, and Mom will help you pay it off?" Chad was very convincing.

I had never had a new car before, and it would feel really good to know when you got in your car that it wasn't going to break down on the side of the road, which was something I had never experienced.

My stipulations were simple. "Four hundred dollars a month for four years is all I will do. Do not go over four or four." He promised me he would abide by my rules since it was my money.

Chad brought me back a little blue car. It was ten thousand dollars and nothing fancy. It didn't even have power windows, but I didn't care. It was brand new. It had a warranty, and finally, I could get somewhere. Chad told me it was five hundred dollars a month for four years and I thought, *"Okay, I can focus and make sacrifices, and I can do that,"* and since I had not signed anything, and since I had stupidly trusted Chad, I agreed.

I trusted Chad way too much. I had not realized brothers would lie to their sisters like this, but it happens. It turns out the car was five hundred dollars a month for seven years, not four (which by the way, I think should be criminal. Loan companies should not be able to do that). However, I did not find any of that out until years later when I thought I had one more year left to pay on the car but actually had three years left to pay on it.

But at the moment, I was excited that I had wheels again. Next, I needed a job. My mom was getting older, and there were more and more dogs at the kennel every year. The work was physically taxing, outside for hours no matter the weather, and I did not want her to have to be out in the harsh cold or swelteringly heat by herself all day any longer than absolutely necessary. So, when she asked me to start working with her, the pros seemed to outweigh the cons. Best of all, I wouldn't have to work with Frank. He had his own assistant. I wouldn't have to drive to work, so I could save on gas. If Ella needed to be picked up early from school or she was sick, I would be right there.

My mom said that each week she'd be the one to write my checks, so she would either write it for more than Frank had agreed on, which was $200 a week, or she'd give me two checks. She also said she'd make sure my car payment got paid every month if I was short. Part of me just wanted to help my mom. Part of me just wanted to be around my mommy.

So, I started working at the kennel.

# CHAPTER SIXTY-NINE

My very first day at the kennel, I almost quit. Not because it was physically excruciating labor but because of how absolutely asinine everything was set up. I almost can't tolerate knowing there's a more efficient way of doing something and doing it the hard way.

The one hundred and fifty dogs were spread out over ten acres. Had they all been together, caring for them would have been much easier, but Frank wasn't the one who had to take care of them, so he spread everything out. The dog food was in one building near one of the kennels. If there had been food near every set of kennels, feeding all of the dogs would have taken twenty minutes, but it took an hour and a half because we had to walk across ten acres. I had helped my mom before over the years, but I was just washing kennels and watering the dogs, so I had not realized how ridiculous the feeding system was.

They could have easily built automatic feeders twenty-seven years into the business. Frank welded all of the kennels himself, so why not store food near each of them and weld up some automatic feeders? If all of the dogs had been on concrete instead of just half of them, my mom and I would not have had to go inside of "muddy" (and I use that word loosely) pens to feed dogs who jumped on us, and we would not have ended up covered in literal dog shit an hour into our day.

The dogs on the dirt and in the pens were the ones Frank and his assistant, Travis, had not gotten around to training yet. They were a year old or older and had rarely ever even been touched. Other than my mom feeding them each day, they had not had any human interaction.

When she was younger, one of her jobs was to do something called, "Whoa Break," these dogs. Back then, she was whoa breaking thirty pound, four-month-old puppies who could absorb what she was teaching them and not seventy-five pound, year old, full grown, dogs that had grown "Kennel Dumb," a term used to describe a dog that sat in a kennel too long with no human contact and therefore knew nothing.

Mom had gone so long without whoa breaking any of the dogs that we were now going to have to mess with seventy-five pound maniacs who took off, tangled us up in the check cord, acted crazy, and knocked us down. So, that's why I almost quit my first day.

I told my mom I was quitting, and she was furious. Mom needed me to whoa break those dogs because it had hurt her knees and her hands doing it the last twenty-five years. She couldn't do it anymore, they needed me, and I was letting them down. How dare I give up on my first day?

As much as I hated coming into a mess that I didn't care enough about to clean up, I cared about my mom. Whoa breaking is teaching a dog to stand still. You use a rope, and it is really, really hard on your hands. The dogs slam into your legs and knees the entire time, and it's just very physically demanding on your whole body.

My mom was in her sixties. I cared about helping her. I also cared about my brother Chad, still, at that time. I didn't yet know about him torturing Ella or that he had lied to me about the price of my car or any of the other malicious things I know about him now. I still cared very much about him and his future, and he was to inherit the kennel one day. His dad did not believe in life insurance and the kennel was all Chad had.

So, my mom and I were outside right at daylight every morning cleaning kennels, feeding, watering, medicating dogs, and making sure the right brood momma got bred to the right stud. When it was time to take Ella to school, my mom would take a break to run her into town and I would continue working. Mom would bring me back a coffee and donut holes and then I would spend the rest of the day whoa breaking the cable dogs.

One afternoon, Mom and I were taking a break, sitting on buckets under a shade tree, when she nonchalantly mentioned Frank had cancer.

"What kind of cancer? How long has he had it? Maybe he'll die! Do you think he'll die?" I was unapologetically happy that someone had cancer.

"I think it's colon cancer. I think he's had it for a couple of months… like six months? I don't know. I don't know if he'll die or not, but he will be gone a lot, so you'll have to help Travis," she said.

Travis was Frank's assistant, but helping him was the least of my concerns. "Wait, why don't you know what kind of cancer your husband has or anything else about it? He's your husband. You live with him."

My mom showed no emotions the entire time Frank had cancer. Whenever he became weak, he had to start doing all of the cooking. She stopped cooking and cleaning other than the laundry, which she had to do because he was getting sick every night all over their bedding and he ruined at least a pair of jeans a day, if not two.

I was a bit proud of her at first. I thought, *"Yes. This is what someone who makes her leave the hospital four hours after giving birth so she can go home and make Thanksgiving dinner deserves! This is exactly how he deserves to be treated. He deserves to be shown how little his wife cares about him. He deserves to be shown he is unloved!"*

It turns out it was colon cancer, so, that first year at the kennel I worked as my mom's assistant half the time and Travis's assistant when Frank was gone having surgery or chemo, the other half of the time. Frank paid me $200 a week, but my mom gave me more than one check a week sometimes because no one could possibly raise a child on that little amount of money. I kept my car payment current, and things started to seem like they might be okay.

I even met a guy I kind of liked. Ella was in fifth grade, and other than sudden outbursts that I didn't understand at the time and chalked up to her being a preteen girl, life was tolerable. I started to make plans for when we'd leave and what we would do after I paid the car off.

Working with my mom every day went well at first. In the beginning, I felt like we were healing very old wounds, spending quality time we were robbed of. I was able to learn things from her that I never would have if I hadn't worked at the kennel. If something was broken, she'd fix it. If a dog was sick, she healed them. If a new brood momma couldn't figure out how to nurse or care for her babies, my mom showed her how and showed me how to run the kennel in the process.

We whoa broke all eighteen of those banshee dogs, which is teaching them how to stand perfectly still when we say the word "whoa." Mom taught me how to worm and vaccinate the puppies, which when we did together as a team, only took a few minutes. About a year into working with my mom, vaccinating turned into an argument.

"You just gave that puppy wormer! No, no, no, no! Don't! No, Mom, you can't give that puppy two doses of wormer! He was ready for the vaccine." Giving a puppy two doses of wormer could kill the poor thing.

"You don't know what you are talking about! I've been doing this for twenty-five years! I've done it a million times!" She would get very defensive if I pointed out a mistake, but she always had been like that. Too much wormer could have killed the puppy.

Luckily, he threw it back up, but we were argued every month during vaccinations and worming. Mom was always about to give a puppy an extra shot or an extra dose of medication and refused to let me do anything except for hand her the puppies. I could not figure out why it was so hard for her to concentrate, but I was too busy with everything else at the kennel, helping Travis train dogs in the field when Frank was gone, and when I was at home, Ella took up the of the rest of my energy.

I had bigger troubles and concerns, so worrying about my mom and why she was forgetting very simple things would slip my mind.

# CHAPTER SEVENTY

I had been working at the kennel for about a year when Chad, who had returned to dating Fannie, his first girlfriend with whom he had his first baby, moved into a tiny house near my trailer. For years, Frank and Travis had spent their mornings training dogs and their afternoons building Chad an enormous house next to the barn, and when he and Fannie got back together, they decided to put one of those shed-like tiny houses behind their future mansion in anticipation of it being finished. Their daughter Alexis, my niece, who was now six, spent so much of her time with my mom and me at the kennel that it was convenient for her parents to live on the property.

Chad had never helped Frank and Travis with building the house, but often Frank's brother would come over, and by the time they thought they were almost done and ready to start insulating and doing the inside of the house, Frank said he had already spent well over $200,000 on the house, and he hadn't even done the math on how much he had spent paying Travis in labor.

I understood when over the years, Chad would yell at me for living in his parents' extra house, rent free. I'm sure all of my siblings have had the same thoughts. I should have grown up. I should not have lived there for as long as I did. I should have had to pay my own electric bill or my rent. I was lazy and immature and using our mom. I have had all of these thoughts myself many more times than all of my siblings put together.

I have absolutely no excuses. I stayed because I wanted my mom to have the sliver of joy she got from having her granddaughter nearby and being able to watch her grow up and because I was too terrified to move. I did not offer to pay rent in a house that was already paid for and falling down around me because if I had paid rent, I would not have been able to afford gas, groceries, or my car payment.

I thought when Chad moved into his tiny house that his selfishness had ended, and he was doing the same as I was doing, trying to be near Mom to help her and bring her happiness. I thought he was there so our mom could watch his daughter grow up, so he could help his dad who had cancer with things like training dogs and building the massive house he was about to move into.

However, I rarely saw Chad or Fannie. They worked multiple jobs and were usually not home. It seemed to me that Fannie found out Chad's five-bedroom, two-story house was almost done, and she had started dating him again so that she could be taken care of. She broke up Chad's marriage with the mother of his son and had just shown back up in our lives again, laughing about how Chad was still legally married.

To me, it appeared to be a guilty laugh, like she knew she'd done something wrong, but she couldn't help it, and since she was so unfortunate looking, I did not judge her too harshly past that. Who knows what I would have done in her shoes having been a mom for six years at only twenty years old. She was most likely already exhausted. I would have probably wanted to move into the enormous house, too. However, even then, I knew that that was what Fannie was up to and that she and Chad would not last very long their second try.

I had met a guy and had been dating him off and on. It was never very serious because I had a ten-year-old daughter whose dad had abruptly abandoned her, so I had only ever introduced her to one guy.

In the six years that I had been single, only one guy had ever been worth introducing her to, and he's still one of my very best friends.

Ella didn't need to see me go on date after date. I kept my romantic life private, and I hadn't introduced her to my new guy. He wanted to spend more time with me, and I didn't want to sacrifice my time with her in order to do that, so I told him I wasn't ready for him to meet her yet. One evening, he showed up at my house unannounced. He lived forty minutes away and had plenty of time to tell me he was coming over and didn't tell me.

Luckily, Ella was not home. She was at church with my mom when he showed up. I explained again that I was not ready for him to meet her, and he told me he was in love with me. I could see in his eyes he meant what he said, or at least he thought he did. Over the next months, I tried to keep feeding the relationship and getting to know him better. I let him meet my friends. I gave Ella the teddy bear he got her and told her about him, but I still could not fathom a scenario where he could fit into our lives.

Honestly, I did not think he was emotionally mature enough for me to explain the rules we had to put up with in order to live where we lived. I was not allowed to have men over at my house under any circumstances after dark. Even if it was 5:00 PM and dark because it was winter, according to Frank Law, I was not allowed to have male guests. I don't think the man I was dating was emotionally mature enough to understand that I was made out of trauma and damage, so I pushed him away a few times. I wanted to be his girlfriend, but I knew it would take someone deeper than him to handle me. So, if we were intimate, we were always careful. We were unbelievably careful.

Christmas Eve that year I found myself staring into my bathroom mirror, hand over mouth, tears streaming down my cheeks in disbelief. I had felt odd for a couple of weeks, so I decided to take a pregnancy test, never thinking in a million years that I would be pregnant. But here I held positive test, thanking God as I cried tears of joy. I had been praying for the chance to have another baby since Ella was two, and now she was ten, and my prayers were answered.

I'd have thought there was no way for me to ever be able to have another baby because I was always single. Protecting myself and my daughter from heartache and more abandonment, my mind immediately began to race with thoughts about what we would do, where we would live, if my baby's father would want us to move in with him, and how Ella would feel.

The first person I told was the baby's dad. He made my decision about whether or not we were going to live with him or not very easy when he first said, "It's not mine! I know that much!" followed by, "Never contact me again!"

Unfortunately, thanks to Facebook, when my baby was two months old, I was scrolling one sleepless night while nursing my baby and saw that his dad had gotten married a couple of weeks after my baby was born. Other than that, I know nothing about him anymore, and he has never contacted me.

The second person I told was my mom. She was elated. She loved babies, and she had wanted me to have another baby one day as well. We both had hoped and prayed that I would be married by then but as we know, life does not happen exactly how we hope and pray.

Being a single mom with no help, struggling to make ends meet as it were, it's very difficult to pick up the phone and tell your married, successful, educated, amazing parents to their own children, siblings that you are pregnant. They all gave it a real college try to seem happy for me, but they didn't want me to have to raise another child with no help, around Frank and Mom. I didn't either. The days ticked by, and while I never considered abortion, I did spend every waking moment in continuous prayer.

"What do I do?" was the main theme of my prayers. The only thing I could do–I had to tell Frank I was pregnant. He was going to explode in anger and rage because I was a whore who had "gotten herself pregnant," as he loved referring to single moms. Even though Chad was living with a woman whom he was not married to (while he was still legally married to a different woman) on Frank's property, I was not even allowed male guests on the property.

I asked my mom, who was the master of lying to Frank, what to say when I told him.

"Just don't tell him," was her response.

She was getting lazier and less creative with her lies lately, and I didn't know if that meant she was so sick of his shit that she didn't care anymore or if she was just too tired to keep fighting him, and she was giving up. I had bigger things to worry about. I came up with my own lie.

I told Frank, Travis, and anyone who knew Frank that I had been single for so long that I decided I wouldn't be able to have another baby unless I did it by myself, so I went to a sperm bank in Kansas City and was artificially inseminated. I don't know if anyone believed me or not. Frank at least pretended to believe me.

He was gentle, understanding and kind and told me to, "Hang in there. We'll figure it out," and I went back to whoa breaking dogs with a little bit of hope and joy.

*"Maybe things would be all right after all. Maybe God is going to bless me now."*

# CHAPTER SEVENTY-ONE

Making a list of all the baby stuff I would need, trying to figure out how to afford it, and making an OBGYN appointment, paired with having to sit down due to lightheadedness and nausea while in the middle of washing kennels, made time fly, and before I knew it, my first trimester was over.

There is nowhere more lonely than pregnant and alone. In all of my darkest, scariest, loneliest, moments, there was and has been nowhere more lonely than pregnant and alone.

The second trimester was where my postpartum depression and anxiety began. I was already having doubts that I would be a good enough mother.

*"How could I do all of the newborn phase alone? With an eleven-year-old and work?"*

I began to panic all day every day, and I began to sleep worse and worse. I had an incredibly active and large baby who would move around all night, keeping me awake. I was due in August, and by March, I had realized I wouldn't be able to pay my car payment or buy groceries in August or September if I wasn't working. I had to have six weeks off. My job was too physically demanding to work after giving birth, and I was thirty-one now. I was too old to be invincible like I thought I was after I had Ella.

Chad and Fannie had been asking me how much I would charge them to clean their tiny, shed-like house. They were both slobs who didn't like cleaning, and it was always filthy. I don't mean, someone left their shoes out and dishes in the sink, I mean disgustingly smelly and filthy. I told them I would clean it for twenty-five dollars a week if they would put that money toward my car payment, which was still in Chad's name, and they took care of paying each month. I always gave them cash, they would deposit it into their account, and they would pay my car payment so that Chad's credit wouldn't suffer and so my car wouldn't be repossessed.

So, all spring and summer, I worked outside often in ninety to one hundred degree weather, and then I hauled my huge, pregnant, belly over to Chad and Fannie's house to clean up what could only be described as a frat party sized mess, every day.

I don't even know how they made such an incredible mess in just one evening. I went every day because if I skipped a day, the mess was too great for me to clean by myself. The first time I cleaned their house, I had to enlist the help of my eleven-year-old. It took Ella and me three hours to clean a tiny house. There was used, poopy, toilet paper on the bathroom floor. There was food stuck to all the dishes, which hadn't been washed in weeks and had mold growing on them. There was a used tampon on the floor in the living room, and Ella and I to this day remark on how could that even possibly be. There was blood on their bedding and piles of trash and drinking glasses and bottles everywhere. I almost gave up after walking into the scary mess the first day, but I needed the money. With an extra twenty-five dollars a week, I could put $100 a month away for bills when the baby came.

I was not surprised when my mom told me she couldn't go to any of my doctor appointments with me. She seemed to be getting less and less interested in everything she once enjoyed. Her spirit had slowly extinguished over the years. I had seen her deepest passions and desires turn into things she didn't even remember she liked.

I was a little upset that she was allowed to go to Fannie's doctor's appointments when they thought my niece Alexis was going to be their child, but now that I was having a baby, completely alone, she was not interested in being there for me. Since I was living there and working there, I had always imagined that if I had ever been blessed enough to have another baby, I would have my mom by my side in the delivery room. At the beginning of my third trimester, I started to panic.

*"Would I have to deliver this baby alone?"*

# CHAPTER SEVENTY-TWO

Six months into my pregnancy, I was working at the kennel with my mom, and she called Ella, who was ten and at school at the time, a bitch. My mom was upset about something Ella had said or done or forgotten to do and called her a bitch. It hurt my feelings so badly because I was pregnant, and I was going to be raising another child completely alone, and my mom was the only person I had left to gain support from. And if she didn't like my daughter and was looking down on my parenting, how could I have another baby?

All the doubts and horrible feelings I had about having a baby, bringing him home to be raised alone by me while I struggled to be around Frank and my mom, came to a violent explosion that day. I started frantically texting Ruby and Mellissa a nonsensical mess about selling my baby, giving him up for adoption, how badly that would hurt, and how I would have to kill myself if I gave my baby up. How that would mean Ella would need a place to live.

My mind was spinning out of control. I needed professional help. I needed to be rescued. Ella needed to be rescued and baby Henry needed to be rescued. We needed to go somewhere safe, to live some-where safe where people didn't make us feel unwanted.

Instead, I ended up making my sisters upset and "sick of my shit," as one of them put it. I don't blame either of them. They were right. They had their own families, their own children, their own problems, and I was not their responsibility. It was me who put myself and my children in these predicaments. I was the one who got pregnant with two babies with two different dads who did not want to help me. That was none of my siblings', my parents', my friends', or anyone else's fault, story, problem, or issue. My sisters had every right to be sick of my shit. My kids had every right to be sick of my shit.

Also, I should have learned when I was a child how to express my emotions and ask for help in a healthy manner, rather than waiting for my problems and emotions to exploded into suicidal thoughts. But I didn't; I never learned. I want to learn, and I'm trying to make better choices for myself and my kids so that I don't have such extreme life issues that I feel depressed and lost enough to want to end my life, but I'm not there yet. It's my journey, not my sisters'.

So, by the time I was ready to have my baby, my mom was really the only person I was talking to, in order to have a partner in the room with me. I waited until my induction was scheduled to ask Frank if my mom could go with me to have my baby.

"It depends on what we have going on that day," was his initial response.

My mind was racing with, *"I'm not asking if she can go get ice cream. I'm telling you that I'm going to go do something that's so difficult that, sometimes, women die during it. Sometimes babies die during it. I don't wanna go alone. I'm scared."*

When your mind has to process a thought like that where you're being told to your face that you do not matter, it can only land on one conclusion: *"You are a piece of shit person who does not deserve to have anyone with you ever. You are a big, fat, piece of steaming shit."*

I caught my breath and choked on my tears just enough to crack out, "It's just that I don't think you're allowed to drive home after you have a baby, and I don't want to be exhausted and stranded at the hospital with my baby."

Travis, who was listening and thought he was funny, said, "Hey man, if you're ever exhausted at a hospital with a baby, call me. I'll give you a ride."

They both laughed. Frank told me to get back to work, and I had my answer.

Frank said, "It depends on what we have going on that day," and he meant, *"Nothing about you matters to us. Not your life, not your death, not your giving life, not your health, not your safety, not the health or safety of your children. Even though you pour your life into helping the business I own and helping my wife, she's my wife. She's not your mom. She's mine. She's mine. She's mine."*

It probably seems hypocritical to be happy Frank had cancer but not understand why he wasn't supportive of my having a baby… to be happy it's a possibility that he might die, but be upset he won't let my mom come with me to have my baby.

I struggled with that hypocrisy, and the conclusion I come to when I ask myself what Jesus would say about it all is that Jesus would not have let someone like Frank be involved or be around Him enough to let Frank have enough control to dictate His emotions. Evil, controlling, narcissists do not get to be in my life anymore, and that way, I don't have to struggle with having negative feelings about those people.

# CHAPTER SEVENTY-THREE

It was mid-August. I was thirty-nine weeks pregnant, my baby weighed ten pounds, and my doctor was worried that if we didn't induce labor, the baby would be too large to deliver, and I would have to have a C-section. I scheduled my induction for August 13, and I was told to be there at 4:45 AM.

I talked Chad into driving me by bribing him with donuts. He promised to pick me up at 3:30 in the morning so we could drive the hour to the hospital for my appointment to go give birth by myself. I dropped Ella off with my mom and Frank the evening before so that she could get ready for her school day with my mom, and my mom could take her to school while I was in labor the next morning.

I tried to sleep, but I could not. I was going to wake up at three o'clock in the morning to get ready by myself to go do something alone that could kill me. I could die tomorrow, and I could die alone. I had lived such a lonely life that I did not feel comfortable asking anyone I knew to come and sit with me, in case the medical staff told me that me or my baby could have complications or die. Out of nowhere, in the middle of childbirth, especially with large babies and obese mothers, people die.

The feelings and thoughts, *"How could I be such a miserable sack of shit to not have anyone with me? Why can't my mom go with me? Why am I so undateable and unlovable that my baby's father isn't going with me? Will I die? Will I die and leave Ella and a baby? Will my baby die?"* moved through me until they were a tangled mess. So, I could not sleep, and before I knew it, it was 3:00 in the morning, I had not slept yet at all, and the hospital was calling me.

The hospital called to tell me not to leave yet because they had so many women in labor, they didn't have a bed for me. I tried to explain to them that I was being dropped off. "I won't have a ride if my induction is after 7:00 AM," I told the maternity ward receptionist, but she didn't seem to understand and told me they would call me back when they had more information.

I texted Chad not to pick me up and tried to go to sleep, but now I was even more worried. Now, I was worried that my induction would be postponed, and I would have to swim through the thoughts and feelings I had last night all over again. I was afraid I would go into labor and have to drive myself in labor, to the hospital, an hour away.

Around 7:00 AM, I called the hospital to see if I was still going to be able to have my baby that day. They acted as though I was bothering them and had no information for me.

I called my mom and explained the situation to her. I told her Chad was going to take me, but now that it was postponed and he was at work, he would not be able to drive me. I asked if she was allowed to drive me. She put the phone down and asked Frank. He said my mom couldn't drive me to the hospital, but he wouldn't mind taking me. I knew that the only reason he didn't want her to take me was because he didn't want her to pay more attention to me than him. He didn't ever want me to be the center of her attention, not even on the day I was giving birth to her grandson.

"I don't want to ride to the hospital with Frank to go have my baby. I'm already nervous enough." I told her.

"That will really hurt his feelings," she said.

That comment made me feel like I was the only person on some faraway planet. My mom was more worried about the feelings of her husband, whose to-do list for the day consisted of drinking coffee, than her daughter who was having a difficult time finding a ride to her labor induction. I hung up the phone and decided to drive myself to the hospital.

At nine o' clock that morning, my OBGYN office opened, and I called them to ask if they knew of my situation. I felt like crying. I was not trying to see if I could still get my hair cut today or if I could get my oil changed. I was trying to see if I was going to have a baby! In a much more polite fashion, I relayed my concerns. My doctor's receptionist was much more apologetic than the maternity ward receptionist had been. She said she would call the hospital, find out, and call me right back.

When she called me back a few moments later, she asked if I could be there by noon to have my baby. My doctor's office knew that I lived an hour away from the hospital and that my family was not going to be there for my baby's birth. I had even made sure to mention in my registration that I did not want my labor and delivery nurse to ask me, "Where is your partner?"

I drove myself to the hospital and lugged my suitcase and my baby's bag through the sticky-hot parking lot with my huge, pregnant belly. It made me feel ashamed and like I stuck out like a sore thumb, although I'm sure no one even noticed me. I felt like people must have thought, "What is wrong with this bitch that no one's with her today?"

I took the elevator alone and felt like sobbing or maybe even screaming, "How did I get here?! I am way too kind for this!!!"

When I went to check in, they told me they still did not have a bed for me and that I'd have to sit in the waiting room. They told me someone would come and get me when a bed opened up. Looking around the waiting room at the family members who had come to sit and wait while their daughter-in-law or their granddaughter had her baby, I could tell from the look in their eyes they were very confused by me. Their eyes translated, "Why is she alone?"

I was alone because I was told as a child that I was dramatic every time I needed my mom and did not have her. Every time I was sad that my mom was not around, or I was worried about her safety, I would be called dramatic or over the top.

"Woe is me," my dad would say. "You always have a 'woe is me' attitude."

I remembered my dad saying that when I was a child, when I was crying about whatever my mom was missing. While I tried to outgrow needing my mother, some days, you just want your mom. I never learned how to ask for help from anyone or tell anyone when I was feeling too alone because, when I was growing up, every time I voiced those feelings, I was told I was too much.

Now, I had no idea how to ask for help or from whom to seek help. I had alienated myself from the two or three people who had offered to be there that day because I didn't think they should have to sit with me for twelve sweaty hours.

When I was finally called back to labor and delivery, the first thing my nurse asked me was, "Where's your partner?"

I briefly explained to her why I was alone as I changed into my gown. She took my vitals, and my blood pressure was too high for her liking. I didn't tell her that I hadn't slept, my personal life was in shambles, I had never felt more alone and unloved, I had no idea how I was going to bring a newborn home and raise him with two crazy, elderly people who didn't really even like me and an eleven-year-old that I was already raising by myself. I told her it was probably just nerves and would go back down once we began.

By some miracle, she bought it and started my induction. I was relieved because there was no way in hell I was going to be able to go through that morning ever again.

This was my second baby, so we expected labor to be six to nine hours long. Around the five-and-a-half-hour mark, I told my nurse I needed to push. She told me to hold still and not to do that because she had just checked me, and I was nowhere near pushing time yet. I told her to check again, and thankfully, she listened to me. She checked me again, her eyes grew wide, and she told me not to move and ran to get my doctor.

Delivering my ten-pound son was nothing like delivering my six-pound daughter. I needed more people helping with my son. My nurse, who I had known for six hours, was on my left leg and another nurse, someone I had just met five seconds prior, was on my right leg, and she was telling me not to yell.

I was not expecting that. I was pushing out a ten-pound baby, and my very experienced doctor was even visibly nervous, and this stranger was still telling me not to yell?

My doctor looked me in the eye and said, "Okay, this next one you have to push as hard as you can. This is it. You have to do it now." And he meant it, or Henry was going to be stuck where he couldn't breathe. I went for it, we got him out, they handed him to me, and I instantly knew something was wrong. The crying sound he was making sounded like Ella's name.

"Ella! Ella! Ella!" he cried.

I wanted to laugh at the coincidence, but I immediately panicked. I could tell he needed his lungs cleared.

"He can't breathe!" I told my nurse.

The rest of the crowd was clearing out of the room. Henry and I were having our skin-to-skin contact moment, and my nurse turned around when she noticed his breathing too. She hurried him to the nursery, telling me he was most likely okay and that they would check him. She came right back to clean me up and move me to the room we would be sleeping in that night.

"I'm sure he'll be fine. They will bring him to your room as soon as he's checked out," she reassured me.

I sat in my room praying for my son and waiting for them to bring him to me. About an hour later, a very young nurse who looked like she had not yet even experienced prom, let alone childbirth, came to explain to me that my baby could not spend the first twenty-four hours of his life in my room with me because his blood sugar was too low, and he had amniotic fluid in his lungs. He would have to be given a formula with sugar in it and be hooked up to oxygen for at least twenty-four hours while they monitored him, and I would have to walk to the nursery to see him.

"Can you feel your legs yet?" she asked.

This was so much and not nearly enough information, and I was still reeling from the day I had just had. "Wait, how serious is this?" I had no idea whether she was telling me my baby had a Band-Aid level boo-boo or if she was telling me I might leave this hospital alone.

"It's pretty serious," was her response, which led me nowhere.

"I can feel my legs. Can I see him?"

"Yes, you can, but after this visit with him, you'll have to call down to the nursery and ask if it's too busy for you to be in there. They might tell you to wait until it clears out," she said, and I was flabbergasted.

She was acting as though I had asked her if I could see my goldfish, not asking to see the baby I had stitched together for thirty-nine weeks with my own cells. He was mine, and I was being told I could not take him into my dark, warm, lair to nurse his blood sugar up and breathe the oxygen of prayer and mother's love into him.

The nursery had far too many loud noises, a couple of new dads, way too many beeping machines, bright lights, and loud monitors for my baby to be in there alone. I looked at him, and my first reaction was to forbid myself to love him. I tried not to love him because I had no idea if he was about to be ripped away from me.

I was in my most vulnerable state. My body had just contracted to the point that a ten-pound, twenty-four-inch long beast had been torn from it, and now they were looking at me like I had done something to hurt the beast. He was my blue-eyed twin! My daughter's carbon copy! I reached out and touched his back and fell in love with him.

"When can I nurse him?" I asked the nearest nurse.

"Don't stroke his back like that. They don't like that. They just wanna be touched and not stroked."

I started to think at this point that maybe some of these nurses wanted punched in the mouth.

"When can I nurse him?" I asked again.

The nurse retrieved one of her office chairs. Having been hooked up to an IV for six hours, the fluid in my body was starting to pool in my feet and they were swollen to four times their normal size. I wished that I could nurse him in my bed with pillows around me and my feet up, but instead, I had to do it in an office chair with no privacy, monitors beeping, and other people's husbands in the room.

That first evening, the day he was born, I struggled with whether I should have Chad and Fannie bring Ella to see her brother. I knew she was excited to see him and that if I told her she couldn't because he was in the nursery, she would be worried about why he had to stay in the nursery. I decided to call Chad and tell him the baby had complications but to go ahead and bring Fannie and Ella to the hospital so that Fannie could drive my car home.

I knew someone would have to come and get the baby and me in my car when we were released because I refused to drive myself home without sitting in the back seat holding his tiny, newborn head. I told Chad that I didn't want Ella to worry but that it was serious, and I didn't know what was going to happen or what to do.

When Chad, Fannie, and Ella got to the hospital, they were able to see the baby through the nursery window. Once in my room, Chad asked me what was going on with the baby, and I tried to explain it in a way that let the two adults know that I was panicking and exhausted, scared and alone, but also not let my eleven-year-old daughter see anything of the sort. Either it went right over Chad's head or he was a bigger asshole than I thought, because all he said was, "I was told there would be donuts?" referring to the donuts I promised him if he drove me to the hospital at 3:30 that morning, which seemed like a lifetime ago at that point.

After they left, I nursed my son once more and returned to an empty hospital room to cry myself to sleep. All day Saturday, day two of Henry's life, I called the nursery and asked a stranger if I could come and see my baby. I felt like a prisoner, a criminal, someone who had done harm to the baby. To utter the words, "Can I come and see my baby?" felt and sounded so insane to me. It began to put me in a strange daze. Returning to the empty room with a blood stain on the sheet was devastating. I began to pray harder than I ever had in my life. I felt Jesus in the room with me.

Saturday afternoon and evening, Henry did what the nurses called, "honeymooning," which was where all his symptoms went away, and his blood sugar, heartbeat, and oxygen levels were normal. They let me have him in my room, and my older brother Jordan, his wife, and daughter all came to see my gorgeous, fat, red little boy. I was starting to feel better and not to worry so much about him. My mom brought Ella to see him, and I felt so proud and even loved.

*"This is what it's supposed to be like,"* I thought.

Then after taking him to the nursery for tests that evening, I was told he would have to stay in the nursery again, and separation anxiety started to kill me. I wanted my baby! I wanted him more than anything!

I was up every two hours, calling the nursery and asking if I could see my baby and then walking to the nursery to nurse him for as long as a two-day old baby will nurse before falling asleep. I prayed over him and nursed him in the nurse's office chair in a bright room with loud babies, far louder nurses, and beeping machines.

Sunday morning, I was in the bathroom peeing, and I forgot to pat dry. I was on my way back to the nursery and I just wiped like normal. I forgot I had episiotomy stitches and wiped right up them. Fire thrown on my most sensitive parts is the only way that feeling could be described, and that is what happens to mothers who do not have any help or adequate rest. We start to forget obvious things and become unhealthfully overwhelmed.

*"He is first. Until he's okay, I don't have time to pat dry,"* I thought, and I shook it off.

The whole day Sunday, I walked back and forth to nurse and hold my baby, even though there was a tornado warning, a cherry on top of all the stress.

*"This is going to kill me,"* I thought as I would walk back into an empty hospital room.

They still had not changed the sheets, and that blood stain stared at me every time I re-entered the room, reminding me that there was no one there to help me ask for new sheets or bring me more water or a snack.

That empty room is where Jesus undeniably showed up in my life. That empty room is where my relationship with Jesus went from, *"I'm pretty sure He loves me,"* to *"Jesus loves me more than anyone in my whole life."* If I had not felt His presence in my room, I would not have left that hospital alive. Every time I would walk past the nurse's station to go nurse my baby, I would think, *"I am trying really hard not to kill myself. My hormones are making me think I am worthless. The fact that I am completely alone is making me feel worthless. The fact that my baby is not doing well is making me feel like I am a loser who cannot win and is destined for pain. I'm too tired to endure it alone, and I want to die. I'm trying not to kill myself."*

The nurses were not aware, and they went back to their typing and their tuna sandwiches, but Jesus… He heard me, and as He always does when I'm in trouble, He sent Morgan.

Morgan showed up. He came to check on me Sunday when I was at the point where I thought I might actually tell a doctor or a nurse that I was having suicidal thoughts. He calmed me down, took my mind off of my anxiety and worry for a couple of hours, and gave me the will to hold on for a little longer. I love him and do not know what I would do without him.

I told the doctor that was filling in for my doctor Sunday night that I was not doing very well, and the separation anxiety was really getting to me.

His response was, "You can go to the nursery and see your baby anytime," and once again, I felt like a drama queen.

"At least he's just in the nursery and not in the NICU," my doctor said to me when he arrived the next morning, which also made me feel like I was overreacting and feeling too emotional.

I was nursing Henry in the nursery when one of the older, more empathetic nurses who could tell I was miserable, leaned over and said, "Do you need some money? Are you out of money?"

I was too tired, overwhelmed, and frustrated to be offended.

"No, I have money. I'm running out of clean clothes, pads, I have an eleven-year-old at home, and I just wanna take my baby home!" I choked back tears.

Sunday night, I couldn't sleep either. I stayed up all night nursing and praying that we would be released the next morning because

Monday morning, day four of his life, I would be kicked out of my room because my insurance only covered four nights, and I would either have to sleep in the cafeteria (which I fully planned on doing if they had kicked me out) or left the building without my son (something I would never have been able to do).

Monday morning, Henry's pediatrician said he was perfectly fine and that we could go home. I was elated! I got my baby dressed in his outfit and called my mom to come and pick us up. I had been calling her off and on throughout the entire process, and she knew how exhausted and traumatized I was by the entire situation, but she asked me if it would be okay if before she picked us up, she washed the puppy room.

Henry and I cuddled and nursed in the rocking chair for another hour and a half while my mom washed the puppy room and drove to pick us up, and all the while, I was not thinking, *"I should be put first here. I should not have had to wait for anyone to pick me up. There should have been someone already here."* Or even, *"I should not have had to wait for her to wash the puppy room first. I am more important than washing dog shit down a drain. I am sitting here with her grandson...."*

Instead, I thought about how great Jesus is for saving my son and keeping me from hurting myself. In the beginning and in the end, Jesus is the only One any of us can ever truly count on.

# CHAPTER SEVENTY-FOUR

Frank reluctantly gave me a six-week maternity break without pay. I had sacrificed everything I wanted for my entire pregnancy in order to save the bill money for the month and a half I would not be able to work and still come up with everything the baby and Ella needed– alone. My mom was more and more distant. She didn't want to see the baby as often as I thought she would, and she kept saying and doing odd things.

One morning, she needed to use my car to take Ella and Alexis to school because her car was in the shop. She had been taking my daughter and niece to school every morning because I had a newborn, and my mom loved mornings with the girls. Ella and Alexis got into my car, ready for school, and a minute later, my mom came back inside the house, loudly telling me my windshield was fogged up and that I would have to take the girls to school.

"Shh. I just got the baby to sleep," I whispered. "I can't take the girls to school. I have to sleep now while he's sleeping, or I won't get to at all. Plus, it will wake him up if I put him in the car." I said, nearly falling asleep as I said it. Henry was about a month old, and I had only slept in twenty-minute increments since his birth.

My mom looked confused. "What? Who is asleep?" she asked.

The look on her face told me she'd forgotten about my baby. I was sleep deprived, and that hurt my feelings and made me mad at her. She was allowing Frank to consume so much of her mind, time, energy, and thoughts now that she had only the capacity to keep up with his narcissistic, controlling, demands. My mom couldn't take time for even a thought about anyone else.

I rolled my eyes and stomped out to my car to show her how the defrost worked, "Every car is the same," I said.

By the time Henry was one month old, it was clear that I would need help. I was going to get into a car accident or fall asleep holding the baby. Sleep deprived beyond human abilities, I had no help other than Ella. There was no one else to ask, so I sat her down one evening to ask her if she wanted to be homeschooled.

Homeschooling was something we had discussed ever since she was seven or eight years old. She was gifted, always far above her grade level and the public school she attended, which was the only option in our area, was not doing her justice or getting her ready for college, which was my main concern. I never removed her from public school prior to having her brother, because she had friends there. However, her education, we both agreed, would be more powerful and useful if it were catered to her with hand-picked curriculum chosen by someone who had her best interest at heart.

She was eleven and in the sixth grade. I explained to her that this was a very important decision. I explained the pros and cons of being homeschooled and the pros and cons of staying in her current school. The only problem she had with homeschooling was the social aspect of her life being less busy. Academically and otherwise, she had always wanted to homeschool too. We decided that since she still took dance, violin, and piano, and went to church twice a week, she would like to try homeschooling for a year.

For the remainder of my time off work recovering from giving birth, I would stay up all night with the baby, sleeping for the fifteen to twenty-minute increments that he would sleep and beg for the clock to turn to 8:00 AM so that I could go to bed. At eight o' clock each morning, Ella would watch her newborn brother in his rock and play while I slept for as long as I possibly could. Sometimes, the baby would go forty-five minutes without screaming to be fed or changed and sometimes I would get two hours of sleep. By eleven o'clock each morning, Ella was sick of watching him, and I would need to get up to make lunch, clean the house, do laundry, run errands, nurse the baby every couple of hours, and rock him to sleep.

Newborns have far, far, too many doctors' appointments, all of which the mother and baby have to travel to rather than having a physician come to them. Ella was my angel in the back seat holding my tiny angel's head. I don't know what I would have done without Ella. She sacrificed so much and grew up so fast. I called her dad a couple of times asking him to come and pick her up to take her somewhere, anywhere, just so she could get away from the screaming baby for a couple of hours, and he couldn't do it. Her dad was too busy, and the baby continued to scream.

The baby screamed at piano and violin lessons, which were in another city so I couldn't just drop her off, take the baby home, and then come back and get her. The town we lived closest to did not offer any type of lessons, so it was a one-hour drive. Before telling Ella we would have to postpone piano and violin until her brother was old enough to go without screaming, I called her dad to ask if he could take her to music lessons. Tyler cursed me out and hung up on me. I was stupid and desperate, so I called back.

"The lessons are in the same town you work in–" Click, he hung up again.

My mom couldn't take Ella to her lessons because Frank would not let her. Everyone in Ella's life let her down, including me.

Henry was four months old, and I had been waking up at five o'clock in the morning to nurse him, give him to his eleven-year-old sister to watch while I went to work at the kennel a quarter of a mile away for six hours (running home every two hours to nurse my baby), and then I would get home at noon and take over with the baby.

Ella would do her schoolwork, help with the baby and the house-work in the evenings, and then I would be on my own, usually up all night. I had not slept for longer than a couple of hours at a time in four months, averaging about two hours a night but usually in twenty to forty-five-minute increments. My brain had started skipping levels of sleep, going straight to the REM cycle within minutes of closing my eyes. I was starting to do things like back into other people's cars and run red lights. I was completely out of it, struggling so greatly that even my mom noticed.

One evening, my mom drove down the trail on the four-wheeler. "Ella's gonna come and work with me at the kennel in the mornings until the baby is sleeping more at night okay, El?" she asked Ella, who knew it would help everyone out if she agreed.

She had already done every job there was to do at the kennel, most things better than the adults. So, for four months, from November to February, my eleven-year-old made sure our bills got paid. Ella woke up at five o'clock every morning, and my mom picked her up and drove her to the kennel, where together they took care of one hundred and fifty dogs. Sometimes it would rain or snow, so Frank, his assistant Travis, my mom, and Ella would go inside the house and eat pancakes and bacon. On those days, she would get to come home early, but usually, she worked for six hours alongside my mom.

Everything was hard, everything was exhausting, and nothing was fair. I may never stop feeling like a terrible mother for handling that situation the way that I did. My daughter should not have had to do any of that. She was still a baby, and I was forcing her to help me raise mine. It's the worst thing I have ever done, and I hope Ella knows that I know that and that I am sorry.

In mid-February, Ella was washing a kennel and slipped and fell on the ice, landing on her tailbone on an iron bar. She didn't want Frank to yell at her for not working, so she sucked it up and kept going. I didn't even know about the injury for a few days as she was trying not to bother me because she knew I was overwhelmed with her infant brother. I asked her dad to take her to the doctor. He said he couldn't. I didn't know how badly she was hurt, so I told Ella if it wasn't better in a day or two, I would call the doctor. She didn't mention it again for six months.

We didn't know her tailbone was broken for six months.

When your entire life revolves around the wants of a narcissist, you start to unconsciously do whatever they want without even realizing it.

My mom should have said, "No, Frank is not more important than my daughter and being there when she needs me."

I should have said, "No, Frank and his kennel are not more important than my daughter."

But I didn't because I was brainwashed into thinking I had to live there, had to work there, and had to do what he said because I couldn't make it on my own. I was vulnerable and exhausted enough to believe it, and he was washing our brains.

How could I be upset that my mom did not go with me when I had my baby, but I asked my daughter to go to work for me at my job when she was only eleven years old? Sure, I worked at the kennel in the summertime when I was eleven, and it was a family-owned business where she worked with her grandmother, but those are just excuses. Those are just things I told myself so that I could keep putting Frank and what he wanted above all else.

He had started to rot my brain to where I was focused on nothing but keeping him from yelling at us and lashing out at us. How could I be upset that my mom wanted to wash the puppy room before picking the baby and me up from the hospital when I asked an eleven-year-old Ella to watch her infant brother so that I could go clean that very same puppy room every morning?

I never would have done any of that before Frank convinced me that he and his demands were more important than anyone else's health, safety, or well-being.

# CHAPTER SEVENTY-FIVE

In November when Henry was three months old, Chad and Fannie, who still lived together in their tiny house at the end of the property with my trailer, the barn, and their enormous, unfinished house, ended their relationship. They had never been married to each other, but both of their names were still on my car loan. I was still paying them five hundred dollars every month in cash, so they would pay my car payment.

Before she left, a teary-eyed Fannie came to tell me she and Chad had not paid my car payment in three months, and she was working on trying to pay it back up so that it didn't get repossessed. While I was busy having a baby alone, while I was struggling to make ends meet with two children and no help from their fathers, my own brother had taken my car payment and spent it without telling me, for three months. My stomach went into my throat and was about to explode through the top of my head.

"What?! What did he even spend the money on?!" I was devastated.

"He got a tattoo, and he got some girl he's been sleeping with a tattoo. I don't know what he did with the rest of it. It shouldn't get repossessed. I'm working on it," Fannie said.

I told her I wanted the login information to the online account so

I could pay it myself from then on, and she gave it to me before she left. Forgiving Chad for that was something I didn't have the energy for, and now, I had to come up with three months' worth of car payments–fifteen hundred dollars–which was more than I earned at the kennel in a month.

It took me months to realize that that whole summer that I had cleaned Chad and Fannie's house (in order to have enough money to have a maternity leave) in the summer heat after working dogs all day outside, while seven, eight, and nine months pregnant, had been for free since they were stealing instead of paying my car payment.

When I logged into the car loan online account, I found that Chad had also lied about the loan itself. I didn't have a five hundred dollar a month car payment for four years. I had a five hundred dollar a month car payment for seven years, and I was nowhere near done paying it off.

*"Without a car, I can never leave. There is no way I will ever be able to leave this place. I have to pay my car off before I can leave, and now the baby is crying again."*

In March, the baby started sleeping two or three hours at a time, and I felt refreshed enough to go back to work at the kennel. I felt terrible that Ella had to work there for four months, so I let her stay home to do homeschooling and have free time without the baby. I started having my mom watch Henry inside her house while I took care of the kennel maintenance right outside her back door. I came inside every hour to check on them and nurse Henry.

One day, when he was seven months old, I looked up from my work to see Frank take off on the four-wheeler with my baby sitting in front of him. Frank was not even holding on to Henry.

My entire body froze. *"I have to actually watch my precious little son die,"* I thought.

Even writing about it now, the blood drains from my face. I thought I was going to watch Henry fall to his death. Frank did not understand babies, developmental phases, or that my son was too young and too small to know that he could get hurt. Henry was too little to even understand what getting hurt was or about gravity and falling. He was too little to understand holding on to make sure he didn't fall. Frank honestly thought my baby, who was becoming more and more overwhelmed, was having fun.

He drove over to me where I was still frozen.

"Say, hi, Mom," Frank said as I rushed to them, taking Henry off the four-wheeler. "Why can't he ride?" Frank asked.

I walked quickly with my son through the backyard to the front to see what in God's name my mom was thinking letting my seven-month-old on a four-wheeler with an imbecile like Frank. I don't remember what I said because it's all a blur. My mom's excuse was that Frank insisted. He took the baby out of her arms and took off with him.

"Yes, I know that Mom, but you have to say no. You have to protect the baby. You can't let Frank hurt him. He backed over his own child! Do you want me to lose my son?!"

I stopped to really look at her. She had fought battle after battle with this monster idiot she called her husband. She had saved her daughters, her son, and her granddaughters from getting hurt time after time and didn't have it in her to fight anymore. So, I started trying to do the kennel maintenance with the baby, which was a three to four-person job, all by myself. My mom seemed to have given up on everything. She, Ella, and I were all three dead tired and running out of options.

*I can't leave my baby with her anymore. Now what am I gonna do?"*

## CHAPTER SEVENTY-SIX

My mom loved Henry enough to fight for him after all and promised me she'd protect him no matter what Frank said.

"Then I need to talk to Frank freely about what a baby can and can't do," I demanded.

I sat down with Frank and my mom and laid out all the boundaries I had for my son, along with having to point out what could hurt him in their house.

"You mean to tell me a baby that size doesn't know not to touch a hot stove?" He was serious, and I had to answer him respectfully without losing my temper. "How could anyone not know a stove is hot, Amelia?"

I truly wondered how anyone was safe around this person. "You're just not going to be able to hold him or be in charge of him even for a second," I told Frank, and I made my mom swear she would abide by that rule.

I had not yet known and would not find out until years later about all the times Ella had been injured as a small child under Frank's supervision, or the lack thereof. I had forbidden him to be in charge of her and had still foolishly believed they had respected the rules I had with my child. So, I let my mom watch my baby while I worked outside, and Ella stayed home down the road and did her schoolwork. Finally, I was starting to catch my breath. It started to feel like maybe we could do this. Maybe we could live here and not die of suffocation under the smoke veil of Frank's narcissism.

My son was eight months old and I was rocking him to sleep when Frank knocked on my door. "You've noticed your mom acting goofier and goofier lately?" he asked.

I honestly had not noticed. I was giving one hundred million percent of my physical, mental, and emotional energy to my baby. I was working a physically demanding job and killing myself with guilt over not spending enough energy or attention on my daughter. I was only sleeping three or four hours a night, and that was broken up into forty-five-minute intervals. I had barely looked at my mom or even in a mirror in eight months.

"Yes?" I half asked.

"I took her to see Doctor Spiva today, and he said she's got something called advanced phase dementia. Ever heard of that?" he asked.

I was too tired to be sad about my mom's diagnosis because, unfortunately, I knew exactly how her entire illness and the remainder of her life would go, down to the details.

In that second, I let the weight of it all brush past me and land in the hands of Jesus. I didn't let it knock me down or crush me. I knew that this was what I had been training for my entire life with this piece of shit asshole. I knew that I would have to advocate for my mom. I knew that I would have to fight for her. I knew that I had been studying this moron's every minute mannerism, word, reaction, and idiotic move since I was six years old, and that this was the reason. Those were the skirmishes, and this was Gettysburg.

My mom needed a specialist and a checkup every six weeks. She needed medication that was closely monitored by someone other than herself, the person with advanced phase dementia. She needed nutrition, rest, peace and quiet, and joy. I knew she needed lists, notes, reminders, no stress, no responsibilities, and no one mad or upset with her.

I knew she would receive none of that, and in most cases, she would receive the exact opposite. I knew now that I had to get her out of there. I had been trying my entire life to rescue her from him, and now my time was up. Her brain had given up.

When Frank left, I immediately started to pray about what to do first.

# CHAPTER SEVENTY-SEVEN

Frank did not educate himself on advanced phased dementia or understand what the disease consisted of for the first three years after my mom's diagnosis. The first year, after we found out, he was in such deep denial that he treated my mom exactly the same as he always had. Their phone would ring, and he would scream from the other room where he was playing solitaire on their desktop computer, "Answer the phone!"

Ella and I would be at their house for dinner or inside the house because it was raining during work, and we witnessed Frank screaming from the other room for my mom to answer the phone hundreds of times. She had forgotten what to say on the phone. She had forgotten how to hold conversations. She had forgotten how to write down messages for Frank when he wasn't in the house, which would really piss him off, and he would rant and rave, making my mom cry, for hours.

It didn't take her very long to completely forget what the word "phone" meant, and still, Frank would scream at her and call her names the way he did when I was a young child, the way he did when Ella was a young child. Only now, Mom, too, was a young child. My mom did not understand and began to stop listening to everyone, completely disassociating herself from the present. Frank would be screaming as loud as he could at my mom, and I could tell from looking at her that she was not even mentally in the room. If she had been taken care of and loved, she would not have done that, and her decline may not have been so rapid.

"She doesn't understand," Ella and I would try to tell Frank. "You can't yell at someone who doesn't understand."

"Oh, she understands. She's just stubborn and doesn't want to answer the phone anymore," he'd say. "She doesn't want to run the vacuum sweeper or cook dinner or even do the dishes anymore, Amelia. She's just gotten lazy."

"Have you looked dementia up yet? Those are all things that pertain to her disease." I would try to start the dialogue and be shut down by a seven-year-old in denial.

"Being lazy is side effects of a disease? Okay!" he would mock me.

I had a baby and a child, my mom, and his business to take care of, and I was too tired to fight him sometimes. He was in complete control of my mom, and in most ways, he was in control of my children and me as well.

I felt helpless.

When I tried to get him to let me administer her medication, it was the same response. "She'll get lazier and lazier if you do everything for her."

"She has high blood pressure medication, too, and if she doesn't take that, or she takes too much of it, she could die. She can't keep track of anything. I'm here every morning anyway, so please let me do her medicine," I would beg, and he would refuse.

My mom started putting the dishes away dirty, and he started screaming at her about that on a daily basis. I tried to bring my kids to eat dinner at their house as often as I could just to make sure Frank didn't beat my mom for something she did by accident. Ella and I started doing the dishes while Mom played with the baby. It was not a good situation for my children to be in, but it was worse for my mom to be alone with Frank.

In late spring, Chad introduced us to his new girlfriend, who had a baby younger than mine with a man who was not Chad. Karen wore a sapphire necklace that looked exactly like the only valuable thing my mom ever owned. Considering Chad had stolen all of my necklaces when he was dating Megan, a girl who was two girlfriends ago–a girl he was still legally married to–and considering that he had just stolen fifteen hundred dollars from me, I told my mom to look closely at the necklace Karen was wearing and see if it belonged to her.

Sometimes, because my mom's disease was so new to me, I was so distracted with my children, and because Frank was trying to down-play every symptom, ironically, I would forget my mom had demen-tia. I should not have told her to look at the necklace. Before dementia, my mom would have simply looked at the necklace and told me later whether or not it belonged to her.

With dementia, my mom walked up to Karen and started yelling at her to give her her necklace back because, "Amelia said it's mine!"

Chad, Karen, and Karen's infant stormed into my living room so that Chad could chew out his sister in front of his new girlfriend, both infants, and Ella. He listed, as though he had a pre-written speech, everything he disliked about me. His lecture was something only someone who had hated someone for a very long time would have been able to spew. Every mistake I had ever made, and every-thing I had ever done wrong, he laid out in disgust.

I was still struggling every second of every day with postpartum depression, sleep deprivation, trying to work, do motherhood alone with two kids, and I had just started looking after my mom who had dementia and an abusive husband.

I simply let Chad rant. I didn't ask his new girlfriend if she knew he was married. I didn't ask if she knew he had a little boy he hadn't seen in years. I didn't ask if she knew that he had cheated on his wife, who was his second baby mama, with his first baby mama and then cheated on her with a random girl whom he had bought a tattoo for with his sister's car payment. I didn't even ask her if she knew that even though she had a four-month-old baby, he was going to waste no time getting her pregnant again, even though he was still legally married to someone else.

After Chad was done with his lecture, I said, "Did you know Mom has dementia?"

"What?! No." He was shocked. Mom had been diagnosed at least three months prior, but Chad was so selfish and into his own life that he did not even know.

I turned to Chad's latest hobby. "She has dementia, Karen, advanced phase dementia, so just ignore whatever she says about your jewelry." And turning to Chad, I said, "Mom is sick, and I have my hands full with my kids, Mom, your dad, the kennel, and everything else. I didn't know you felt that way about me, but I don't really have the energy to care right now, so please leave."

They left, and I shook with emotion for hours. I prayed and then swallowed my feelings so I could get up at 5:00 the next morning and take care of everyone all over again.

# CHAPTER SEVENTY-EIGHT

The tax refund I got that year almost completely went to catching up my car payment after Chad had caused it to be behind and buying things like clothes and shoes my children had needed all year. Ella's dad's $341 a month in child support paid for our phone bill, about half a week's groceries, and one tank of gas and was gone.

Henry's dad did not only never contribute financially, but he never even texted to see if my pregnancy was successful or if I had had a boy or a girl. Shortly after my tax refund came, it went back out, and I was living from paycheck to paycheck again.

Frank no longer allowed my mom to write my checks because she had dementia, and it could get messed up, but he was still fine with letting her administer her own medication. By Friday each week, my kids and I were out of everything.

Frank had raised my paycheck $50 a week, but the $250 a week Frank paid me turned into $125 the second it was in my hands because my car payment was $500 a month or $125 a week, leaving me with only $125 a week to feed and clothe my children and pay my other bills.

Usually, as I pulled up to the bank drive-through on Friday to deposit my paycheck, I was relieved. Although I would be broke again by the end of the day, we could at least get diapers, groceries, and gas. If we were frugal for the next six and a half days, we could make it.

One summer Friday, the bank teller handed me my receipt, and it showed my balance was a negative eight hundred and fifty dollars, even after depositing my check. I pulled my car with my kids into the parking lot to take deep breaths, trying to figure out what could have happened. I went inside the bank in my sweatpants with baby puke on them and asked them to pull up my last few transactions, assuming my identity had been stolen.

"It looks like you have about eleven hundred dollars' worth of Apple and iTunes charges," the teller said.

I was so confused. I had never and would never buy anything so frivolous. "You'll have to call Apple," the teller explained.

I went to my car and talked to my almost twelve-year-old, who had her own phone for a year because, often, she had to watch her baby brother while I worked outside a quarter of a mile away. I asked her if she knew anything about the charges. Ella said she did not know anything about them, and then the baby woke up and started to scream. I had to nurse him from my car while I was on the phone with Apple, finding out that Ella had in fact spent $1100 on iTunes.

It took me a week and a half on the phone with Apple and my bank every day getting all of that money back. It made me even more exhausted and traumatized than I already was, and it kicked me in the teeth even more. There should have been someone else helping me raise my baby so that my eleven-year-old didn't feel like she needed to seek revenge on me. There should be someone else helping me raise my twelve-year-old so that they could be on the phone getting our money back, or maybe she would have not even have had the chance to spend all of that money in the first place, had I had some help.

There was not. There was no one.

The only person helping me was my mom, and she had dementia, so her help usually caused more problems than it did good. I explained to Ella that if she ever did that again, they would not only not give the money back, and that I would have to come up with the money on my own, and that we did not have it, and we were even having trouble affording food.

She said she understood, but when I said I would need to take her phone away from her at night, she stood outside my bedroom door screaming, "Give me back my phone! Give me back my phone!" until the baby was shrieking so loud, I had no other choice but to give it back to her.

Again, I needed help, and there was no help.

I put an app that AT&T recommended on Ella's phone that prevented her from spending money or using Apple or iTunes. She immediately deleted the app and made a new Apple ID saying she was eighteen years old so that she would have access to anything she wanted. I didn't find this out until six months later when she did all of this again.

She stole my new debit card number while I was asleep and put it in her new Apple ID, making me overdrawn $600 before I found out that time. That time, Apple did not understand and did not give me the money back. The bank told me I could do what was called a Fresh Start Loan, where I could pay the money Ella had spent back $50.00 a week until it was paid off. That left me with $75.00 a week to pay my bills and raise two children, and it was Christmastime.

Everyone I knew blamed Ella and said things like, "Well, I guess she doesn't need Christmas presents."

But they did not understand the full story or what she had been asked to do to help her family. She was being treated like an adult most of the time, she was secluded with a bunch of terribly unhealthy adults and a screaming baby, and no one was reaching out to her or helping her, or even being her friend. She was only twelve. As depressed as she was at the time, I am tremendously happy that all she did was steal money from me and not end her own life, as she has told me she thought about many times during that awful time in our lives.

Ella was back in public school, in seventh grade, and I was trying to do everything I could to show her that I loved her and that she was important to me, but my main focus should have been my baby while

Ella's dad focused more on her for that short time that babies are babies. I could not have a conversation with Tyler that didn't end in him calling me names so that he did not have to help.

During that time, Ella was not my main focus, and Henry was not either. My main focus was trying to get Frank to understand how sick my mom really was and that I could not continue to let her watch Henry because I was afraid he was going to get hurt or worse.

"What will you do if you're not going to let your mom watch him anymore?" Frank asked.

"I guess I'll have to take Henry to daycare and get a different job in town so that I can pay for daycare and the rest of my bills," I said.

"Well, that won't work," was his reply, and we both knew it wouldn't work.

It wouldn't work because no one would clean up after, feed, water, medicate, maintain the kennel, watch over the breeding, take care of mothers and puppies and whoa break at a kennel with one hundred and fifty dogs for $250 a week, except for me, and that was only because I lived there, and I was trapped.

I tried to explain to Frank that my baby's health and well-being was more important than the kennel and that we would leave if we had to. He clearly did not care. He paid his assistant Travis $600 a week to help him train the dogs in the field and gave Travis a bonus every time they sold a dog. Sometimes, Travis's paycheck and my paycheck would bounce. Frank could not manage money the way my mom had. He had lost the person who ran his business, not with him, but for him, and he was in denial that she was even sick.

Frank still yelled at my mom every time she made a mistake. She'd forgotten how to drive the four-wheeler, something she had no business being near much less trying to drive by herself, but Frank insisted she remain as active as she always was, and he would become furious with her and scream at her when she could not figure out how to start the four-wheeler.

One day, I tried to make Frank understand by comparing his side effects from colon cancer to my mom's dementia. "You know how you have trouble holding your bowels, and it just comes out whenever it wants? You have no control over it?" I asked Frank, who had been shitting himself a couple of times a day for a year and a half.

Even while standing there talking to Travis and me, Frank would shit his pants. Standing there talking to a customer, he would shit his pants. He refused to wear any type of protection, so he just literally shit his pants.

He knew what I was referring to, so I continued, "Just because we can't see Mom's disease doesn't mean it isn't real. Just because she isn't bleeding or pooping her pants or bruised, doesn't mean she isn't very, very sick. Didn't she help you when you were sick?" My mom had been shit on in the middle of the night and had to get up, change clothes, change the sheets and wash their bedding, for years.

"Your mom is a very patient lady. She's cleaned up a lot of messes," he said.

"So why can't we help her with her disease? Why can't I give her her medicine and we could be more understanding with her instead of yelling at her and calling her names?" I begged.

He never treated her better after my pleading. His abuse got worse, the more furious he became that her disease was happening to him. The more he yelled at her, the worse her mind worked. I knew he didn't quite understand the comparison between him being sick and her being sick the first few times I brought it to his attention in that way.

"What is the difference between cancer and dementia? Why can't you treat her with the same kindness?"

He didn't understand, and it didn't open his eyes as I had hoped and prayed. It would take me another year and a half to figure out why he did not understand.

# CHAPTER SEVENTY-NINE

Travis had a wife and two children, so he could not afford to live on $600 a week, and sometimes when our paychecks would bounce, nothing at all. So, in October, he quit working for Frank. My baby was one, my daughter was twelve and in seventh grade, and I was going to have to somehow figure out not just how to do all of the kennel maintenance and care for the dogs but also start training the dogs side by side with Frank in the field.

It was long hours of physical work in every kind of weather, and that was not the worst part. Working with a vulture who tore me down and called me names, tried to make me feel bad about how terrible I was at working dogs all day–that was not the worst part. The worst part was that I was not comfortable leaving my son with my mom. Sure, she could still feed him, change his diaper, and keep him from swallowing and choking on small objects, but too many times for my comfort, I would come inside to check on them and she would be doing something odd like turning all the gas burners on on the stove for no reason.

She could not remember that too much cow's milk hurt his tummy and made him sick, so I needed her to give him only a cup of milk each morning and then water for the rest of the time he was with her. I even pre-made cups and left her notes, but she just kept refilling the same cup with cow's milk all day.

I nursed him when I was home with him in the afternoons and evenings. I only wanted him to have one cup of whole milk in the morning while he was with my mom because more than one cup caused him to become constipated. She could not tell me if he had had enough diapers or if he had a dirty diaper, which is important for a one-year-old but especially for one who was chronically constipated because someone gave him too much milk by accident, repeatedly.

Then one day, she used spoiled milk. Each time something like that happened, I would sit across from Frank, crying and begging for there to be another way, telling him it was not working, and she could not watch Henry anymore.

Frank could not see past himself far enough to care about the very real problems that lie ahead of us.

"How can you of all people not understand?" I tried to get him to use the molecule of empathy he possessed if he had even one.

"What do you mean me of all people?" he asked.

"You lost your little boy. There was an accident, and now your son is gone forever. Do you really think that I should have to lose my son so that you can keep your business?" I asked, and that was when he told me all of the gruesome details about the death of his little boy.

Even after that conversation, he still did not understand or accept my concerns. "Your mom will miss the baby if she can't watch him," he said.

"Everyone will miss him if he dies!" I said, and while he let me take more breaks to run the one hundred yards to the house and check on Henry and my mom, he didn't hire anyone to work dogs or hire anyone to watch my son.

Every time I threatened to quit or to move away, he would tell me there was no way I could afford rent, my car payment, car insurance, daycare, groceries, and utilities.

"You know how much your electric bill was last month?" he asked.

"No," I would say, ashamed that he paid my utilities.

"It was $750. Now, how are you going to pay that if you're cutting hair or working at McDonald's?" he asked.

Although I thought $750 was high for a trailer house, it had been nine years since I had an electric bill in my name, so I had only heard that prices were increasing all the time but did not know by how much. Plus, all of those other bills and the fear of leaving and starting over on my own when all I had ever done in my life was lose terrified me.

I was petrified that I would try it on my own, and I would lose my children. So, I woke up an hour before dawn every day and sat on my couch in the dark silence with my eyes closed, begging Jesus to help me with the day. I could not have gotten up and gone to work every day with Frank if I had not spent time with Jesus like that.

The sound of my alarm going off, no matter the time of year, would cause me to start to sweat and have anxiety that would rattle me and make me physically nauseated and shake. I would sit and ask Jesus to help me to help those feelings subside and to help me not pick up the shotgun Frank used to train the dogs with and shoot him at close range in the face.

Every day, I'd ask Jesus to make Frank not yell at my mom or me or call us idiots. I begged Jesus not to let Frank call her stupid. I would pray for my children. I'd pray for my mom. I'd pray for at least an hour before starting my day.

Having grown up around the kennel, living near it for a decade, and working at it for two years, I knew that Frank did what he called "culling" the dogs, which was just a way to say it so that you don't feel bad for shooting a perfectly healthy dog in the head. I knew he put dogs down when they were, as he called it, "untrainable," but until I was training dogs with him, I had no idea how many he killed.

He killed over fifty dogs in front of me. Some of them, I had become friends with. Some of them, I had to hold while they died. Once, he had me hold a black and white male that had simply just not had enough time spent with him yet on a check cord while Frank shot him in the head. Unfortunately for the puppy, he missed and just nicked the dog's scalp so that blood was spraying all over me. Frank was too stupid to make sure he had more than one bullet in the gun, so he had to walk all the way back to the supply room for another bullet to finish the poor puppy off, far too long after the initial wound.

I was not good at training dogs with Frank. I don't think anyone ever has been. He told me story after story about times assistants would just stomp off and quit because he wouldn't do something their way, and in every story, the helper's way was exactly how I thought we should be working and how I suggested we train.

When the kennel was doing well and was productive and popular, it was because my mom or I were whoa and here breaking the dogs first before Frank and his assistant took them out to the field and put them on birds to finish their training. The way Frank and I were doing it now, the dogs knew nothing at all when we took them out to the field. They didn't know "here" meant to come when they were called. They didn't know "whoa" meant to stop and not move.

My job was basically to chase them around and catch them and then get yelled at and called names when the dogs, who had never been taught anything, inevitably knew nothing. When pleading with Frank to allow me time to whoa and here break the dogs first, I compared it to putting four-year-olds on the basketball court, handing them the ball for the first time, and expecting them to play like Michael Jordan. He didn't understand the analogy.

"Bottom line, we need more help!" was my point. "We need someone to help you work dogs while I whoa and here break puppies and watch Henry myself."

But he never listened to me, ever. I was not only a woman, but I was an "interferer," as he called me often. "How can I interfere in my own life? All of this directly affects my life, my children's lives, and my mother's health."

"Just don't worry about it," he'd say, laughing with an implication that I was just a silly woman who was acting "all weird," as he called my emotions.

Frank shooting the dogs wasn't the only senseless and stupid way he killed them. He always weaned and sold them at six weeks even though they would have been more healthy if he waited until they were eight weeks old.

One of the ways he got them to wean so early was by giving them calf milk replacer, which is powdered cow milk that tastes and smells sweet. He kept it in its original paper bag in the dog food room, which had, at any given time, one to two tons of dog food inside, and as one can imagine, about a zillion mice. I kept telling Frank we could not keep giving puppies the calf milk replacer unless he got a container that was mouse-proof to store it in.

Every day, there would be more mouse excrement in the milk, and every day, I would tell him, "I don't even want to put my gloved hand in that bag, let alone make it into milk for puppies to drink."

I kept thinking, *"You need to remember to get a container next time you're at the store,"* and yet I couldn't remember. It would slip my mind. For one thing, I had two kids to worry about, and my brain and wallet were at capacity. Frank only had himself to worry about. Why couldn't he grab the container? Finally, I remembered and put the milk replacer in a container, but it was too late. Customers had started calling and saying their puppies were sick or dying. For weeks, Frank had noticed that the puppies were sick. He had asked me over and over why they were sick.

I kept saying, "The mouse poop in the milk?"

"Dog stomachs can handle a little bit of mouse poop, Amelia," he'd say, or he'd pretend like I hadn't answered him at all.

There was one puppy in particular, a very chubby, white female who had pretty, dark ticking all over her. She walked around with a swollen head and acted like she didn't have any brain cells at all. We assumed her head had been injured in an accident with a whelping box and her mother lying on her. Puppies got injured overnight all the time from having their mom lay on them by accident. Frank had been cleaning her head wound and was aware of her injury.

A customer, who had bought a puppy from that same litter as the little female with the head wound, called to complain that their puppy had died and that their vet said there was leptospirosis in the puppy's stool.

"I told you," I said after I looked that word up.

"You told me what?" he asked.

"Leptospirosis is a bacterial infection found in mice stool," I replied. "One of the side effects is that their brains will swell up. Their kidneys are failing, and they are vomiting and having diarrhea because of the mouse poop."

Frank had to walk all the way up to the house to his own computer and look it up before finally agreeing that I had been right the entire time. If my mom had still been running things, none of that would have ever happened. The first time she bought the milk replacer, she would have put it in a container, but I was trying to use logic.

I thought if I said something like, "Not only can a newborn animal's kidneys not handle any type of other animal's feces or urine, but is it even right to feed puppies mouse poop?"

I thought something easy and simple would be done about it, but not with Frank. With Frank, everything had to be his idea, or it was not right or even true.

# CHAPTER EIGHTY

Saturdays, the kennel was extra busy because that was usually the day of the week when people would come and pick up their dogs that were there for training or pick out puppies to buy. Ella and I would clean the kennels and puppy room and feed and water the dogs while my mom watched the baby inside the house or in the front yard nearby.

Then customers would start to show up, I would usually take the baby home, and Ella would help Frank with customers. Usually, while Ella and I were doing the chores, Frank would sit in the house and drink coffee, but one morning he came outside, not to help but to follow us around and tell us how we were doing each and every very basic task incorrectly.

I walked up on him screaming in the face of my twelve-year-old daughter as she was feeding the dogs, who were on cables in the dirt. Those dogs had big barrels with the tops cut off for their water buckets, and I didn't have to water them but once a week because of how big their water buckets were. Ella had been crying for long enough that her face was swollen and red, and her eyes were bright red and full of tears. Frank had been yelling at her because a dog that was loose three nights prior (with one hundred and fifty dogs that was a very common occurrence; there was usually a dog loose every night), and he had put the pup on a random cable instead of back on her own cable without telling me.

With all of my abundant daily duties and responsibilities, I had not noticed when I had fed those dogs and checked their collars every morning that he had put her on a cable that was missing a water barrel bucket. He had put her there and not told anyone. He had not told anyone she didn't have a water barrel and didn't go check on his own animal and property within the last three days to make sure she and all of the other dogs had everything they needed.

Now, he was yelling at my twelve-year-old because as he said, "This was a really nice pup. She's already sold, and she hasn't had a drink in three days!"

I stepped in and pointed out all of the ways it could not possibly be Ella's fault as she had been in school all week and not even there. I pointed out how he was yelling at her because she was a child, and he was a coward who didn't like yelling at me as much because I didn't mind pointing out how wrong he was, and that if he sold a dog and that dog was important to him, maybe he could simply walk past them on a day-to-day basis.

"Even managers at Pizza Hut can walk around and check their employee's work, Frank!"

He kept screaming at us. We finished the chores, and when we walked into the front yard where my mom was pushing Henry on his tree swing, my mom could tell we had both been crying. I needed to be able to tell someone who understood, and once in a while, at times, she still was lucid and understood. That day, she understood when I told her what had happened.

Frank heard me tell her, and the next Monday, rather than working dogs, he tried to lecture me. Instead, we argued all morning. I was done being lectured. He could kill me for talking back. I did not care anymore.

I asked him what he would think of a farmer with $200,000 worth of corn in a field who couldn't be bothered to check on it once every other day even though it's six feet away from his back door, and it's his only income.

Frank asked, "Then what do I pay you for?"

"I am trying to help you with Mom,, your housework, your laundry, cooking, and cleaning, and my household, raising my one-year-old and my twelve-year-old by myself, run my own errands, work dogs with you all day, and take care of all of the dogs every morning. Everyone else you worked with either took care of the dogs or helped you train them, not both. I'm doing both. Everyone else I know who runs errands, does the cooking, cleaning, and laundry for a household, does it for one, not two. I do it for mine and yours. Everyone else I know who is a single mom has another parent who helps and takes the kids every once in a while, and I do not. I parent all alone. I'm asking you to simply check my work." I tried to explain, but he had stopped listening in the middle of it and never did agree to help check on the dogs.

Every time Frank was too lazy to make our lives run smoothly enough that he did not have a reason to throw a tantrum, a new chore or responsibility would fall on my twelve-year-old's shoulders due to the fact that mine were already full. I started having Ella walk down the trail to the kennel every evening to check on every dog and make sure everyone had food and water so that we didn't get yelled at as often. We still got yelled at all the time anyway because we had an impossible amount of work, I was one person, and she was a little girl.

Frank also owned four horses that he had Ella care for. I had not realized how incredibly lazy, unmotivated, and disorganized he was until Mom stopped doing everything for him, and Ella and I had to start.

Ella had braces, and every six weeks she had to go and get them adjusted. I always made the appointments around 3:00 PM so that I didn't have to miss work at the kennel because Frank did not allow me to have any time off work, no matter the reason. If I asked, he threw a huge fit and lectured me about making my appointments for after we were done working dogs. Once a year, Ella's orthodontist wanted to talk about progress and next steps, and he only did those consultations in the morning, so I had to take off work. It was the only day I took off the entire five years I worked there except for Sundays, which Frank insisted that we not work because of the Sabbath.

On the one day I took off, Frank had to do all of the kennel chores alone that day, and it was winter. The temperatures were below freezing. The dogs' water was frozen, and I had been carrying buckets of water to the dogs three or four times a day so they could get a drink before their water froze again. I assumed that since I had taken the day off and was not home most of the day that Frank was going to do water rounds. Saturday, I did it, but Sunday Ella and I had off, and we took full advantage of the rest on Sundays.

Frank did not give the dogs enough water, and when I got back Monday morning, I could see that all of them were severely dehydrated. They had blood in their stools, and one of them, a black and white female named Annie who was already sold, was a goner. We tried putting her in the puppy room under heat lamps, but Tuesday, Frank asked me to take her to the vet.

The vet didn't like Frank, and Frank knew it. Since he was constantly having to bring dogs in for senseless human errors that often resulted in the death of beautiful animals, the vet loathed Frank. I drove Annie to the vet and dropped her off knowing I'd never see her again and decided it was time for me to start doing the kennel chores on Sundays too. The rest of my workday, after taking Annie to the vet, was spent being screamed at for losing the four thousand dollars that dog was worth and me screaming back, "I was gone two days! All the dogs were dying, and one was dead when I came back!" I suggested, once again, maybe it was time we got some more help.

Frank admitted that he didn't want to have to hire anyone else because he didn't think he could pay anyone a living wage. I asked why we didn't cut our overhead and just raise puppies.

"No more birds. No more ammunition. No more bird medication. No more training. No more feeding one hundred and fifty full-grown dogs. Just mamas, studs, and puppies. Why can't we do that?"

Frank said he wasn't a puppy mill, and I silently disagreed. He went to get feed one afternoon, and I asked my mom if she still had any secret bank accounts. She was understanding me enough that day, thank goodness, that we quickly accomplished closing her last accounts. There was only about $60 in them. She hadn't been remembering to get cash back or save any more, and Frank had stopped allowing her to drive when the doctor told us she had dementia.

Toward the end of Ella's seventh grade school year, the world was going crazy because the Covid pandemic had just begun, but we were all more worried about my mom. Ella could see that I was sick with anxiety that Henry was going to get hurt or sick if my mom kept watching him. Also, it wasn't good for my mom to be watching the baby. She needed peace and no responsibility. Ella decided to be homeschooled again for eighth grade to stay home with her little brother while I was at the kennel, and although I felt guilty that she had to sacrifice going to school with her friends, I was relieved my baby would be safe.

Everyone's world had to revolve around Frank and what he wanted us to do. I was sitting on my porch with Henry on my lap when Frank rode up on the four-wheeler. He had come to explain to me that none of the registrations or paperwork for any of the dogs had been done since mom started "acting goofy." He told me that customers had started to call wanting their American Kennel Club registrations.

"Do you mean that two years' worth of paperwork hasn't been done? That is like, two or three hundred dogs." I was shocked.

Frank said, yes that's what he meant, and he'd come to ask me if for fifty extra dollars a week, would I catch it all up and start doing the paperwork. What could I say? This was not actually a question. I needed the money, and if I said no, terrible things would happen for the kennel. Also, I was trying to help. I was always just trying to help.

# CHAPTER EIGHTY-ONE

Frank was more like a helpless toddler than my actual toddler. When I went to start doing the paperwork for the kennel, most of the files and records he had kept written down on stacks and stacks of copier paper. Some were written in notebooks, and a few things were written on napkins and paper towels.

It took me hours and hours for weeks to organize and get caught back up while my twelve-year-old watched my toddler. Not only was Frank never appreciative of what we were sacrificing, our entire day now from dawn until dusk, but he still did not help with any of it or stop yelling at us. He would play solitaire on the computer while I sat in his kitchen doing paperwork. I could not bring the baby to his house because babies get fussy in the evenings, and Frank would yell at Henry for crying. Ella had to keep the baby at home so he would not be yelled at by the man whose paperwork I was catching back up. While I did the paperwork, I did laundry for Frank and my mom, cleaned their house, and often brought a meal with me so Frank didn't have to cook.

Frank still did the grocery shopping with my mom who would go up to people in the store and tell them Frank was her dad. He told me one time she started taking things out of a stranger's cart while he was paying, and the guy yelled at her.

"Why aren't you watching her more closely and stopping her before she does some of these things?" I asked.

He said one time she wandered off, and he couldn't find her.

"She's like a baby." I tried to tell him. "She can't remember how old she is, where she is, or anything sometimes... like a baby.... She's mentally the same age as Henry." I was so concerned that she would get hurt while she was on an errand with Frank.

"Oh, she's just being a goof. She's just being goofy," he would say, and fire would shoot through my guts.

*"How am I going to trick him into thinking he thought of this? How do I get him out of denial to where he believes she needs to be looked after more closely?"*

Around my son's second birthday, I had been sick with Covid for three weeks, and because I was not allowed to have sick days, I could not recover. One day, I was coughing very hard, I had 103 degree fever, and it was August, so I did not think I should be out in the 100 degree weather. I tried to stay home, and Frank came into my house to get me out of bed.

That day, we ended up doing nothing but sitting there while I coughed and struggled to breathe, and he told stories about his childhood until we put the dogs away and put the birds back. I was not only physically sick, but I had never fully recovered from postpartum depression and anxiety because I had felt my baby was in potential danger nearly his entire life at that point. I thought that with everything else I had on my shoulders, I was beginning to lose my mind.

After calling a few times to ask for his help and being told no or cussed out, I reached out to Ella's dad again while I had Covid. I asked him to take Ella to go do something fun when I got better, and we were sure she couldn't spread the virus around.

He said he'd call me back in a couple of weeks, and when he did, I couldn't believe it. He had never called me. This was the first time in an entire decade that he had called first.

*"Maybe things are changing, and I'm going to get some help!"*

However, Tyler's call was to inform me that he had been in touch with a lawyer to not only have full custody of Ella switched to him but to have me psychologically evaluated and possibly have my son removed from the home.

"Sorry to mess up your whole deal that you have with your son there, but uh, you are calling me and asking for help so much you know… I just feel like you aren't really right, mentally," he said, and I could tell from over the phone that he was chewing gum and smiling.

I started to cry, which I knew was exactly what he wanted, but I couldn't help it at that time. I was dying. I was drowning. She was his child, and I was her sole caregiver. Why would he want to hurt me so badly? That doesn't even make sense, I thought, because even if you hate me with everything you are, if I'm the only person taking care of your daughter, wouldn't you want me to be healthy? It seemed like since before he was born, my son had been balancing on the cliff of being ripped out of my arms.

So, for a minute, I fell for it. I was at my most vulnerable, and for a cheap and easy thrill, Tyler took advantage of my emotions.

After I got off the phone with Tyler, I texted all of my friends while shaking and crying. I was imagining my little baby son in foster care. My friends calmed me down. They reminded me of how good of a mom I am. They reminded me of how my kids have everything they need and want and that Tyler not only did not want custody of Ella, but that he couldn't afford a lawyer even if he did. It was September, and I had stopped getting child support in March because, according to Tyler, he didn't have a job.

Of course, my friends were right, and nothing came of Tyler's false threats. We didn't even hear from Tyler again for another year after that phone conversation, but it still hurts that someone went out of their way to pretend they were going to call the law on me while I was trying so hard to take care of my children by myself with Covid, postpartum depression, and the exhaustion of not sleeping well or having a chance to rest in years.

Kennel paperwork started to take a lot of my evenings, and it gave me access to Frank's desk and important papers and bills. I happened to glance at the stack of electric bills. My so-called $800 and $700 electric bills were either being read wrong or being used to make me think my household was more expensive than it actually was. The bills had Frank's house, the small house Chad had lived in, my house, the barn with the freezers, the puppy room with lights and heaters, the dog food room, the bird building with lights and heaters, the fly pen, the brooder rooms, and incubation room on the bill. My portion of it ran about $75 a month, not $800.

*Why would anyone want to brainwash someone into thinking they had to stick around? Wouldn't it take just as much energy to do that as it would to just be kind so they wanted to stay?*

<h1 style="text-align:center">CHAPTER EIGHTY-TWO</h1>

I threw myself both into church and routine. I told myself that if I could make it to Sunday morning, I could make it to Wednesday night. The only joy I received in my life were my children and my church, just like my mom before Frank tore her spirit completely out of her body. We even went to the same church as my mom and Frank because when my mom was well, Ella and I would sing specials with her.

Ella had friends at church, and I started leading hymn singing on Sunday mornings, teaching Sunday school for Henry's age group, and I even started my own children's choir. On Wednesday nights, I got to church early and made a meal for the youth group, helped lead worship, and then taught a Bible study class. I thought that if I could focus on projects and my kids, sharing what I knew and what I felt about Jesus with them and their church friends, I could make it through the week without letting Frank rot my brain the way he had done my mom.

Ironically, the teachings and life of Jesus was Frank's favorite topic too. Telling everyone he knew that Jesus was God's son and not God spread into every day of our lives.

We would be standing in the dog training field with the dog on point and Frank would say, "You know another reason you can tell Jesus isn't God..." and start off on a lecture that would take the rest of the day.

Every twisted thought he had in his head, he thought was put there by Jesus. I had seen him take the check cord attached to a white and ticked female named Dixie, who must have been a good judge of character because she was always terrified of Frank and would never go to him when he called. He was furious with her for not going to him, and he pulled her so hard she slammed into the tractor, cutting a gash in her face. The entire time he was sewing her face up, he preached to me about how he knew Jesus.

During the year 2020, an avid watcher of a specific news channel, Frank came outside in the mornings ready to talk to me about racism, which he did not think black people actually had to deal with anymore at all and that they were making it all up. He had told me stories about how when he was a little boy growing up, black people had to go to the back door if they wanted to knock on a white person's door. People had signs on their front doors that said, "Coloreds go to the back," and yet he was arguing with me about critical race theory.

"You don't think people that have to, within your lifetime, go to a different door, have had less opportunities than you? It's a literal separate door!" I was passionate about such a topic.

He was infuriating. He would always disagree. "They could have worked harder," he'd say.

"How do you work harder if you aren't allowed in that position at your company? Or even allowed in that part of town?" I'd ask, enraged. "What if because your grandpa was a slave and your dad had to work since he was a child just to keep a roof over your family's head, you didn't have a car to drive to that part of town where the jobs were?"

He had already stopped listening to me.

His position was always that black people didn't want to work. They wanted handouts, and now they were wanting compensation for slavery.

"Every time I see a black guy in a gas station or someplace, it makes me sick. I just wanna stomp him. It makes me sick when those black people go to our church. You know the ones who live over there by the church? It's not that I don't think they should be allowed to exist. It's just that, number one, they can't have white wives, and white men can't have black wives. You know Garth and Petunia... they have a half-black granddaughter?! Their daughter took up with a black guy! And number two, they need to go live in their own communities, especially those black-black like really dark, big lipped, blue gum black people. It's scientifically proven that we are made differently than them."

When he'd say these things, I would feel lightheaded and nauseated.

I would almost fall off the force-breaking table I was sitting on when he would say such vile things. How could anyone be so disgusting? How could anyone be able to convince themselves that they knew my brother Jesus and then feel this way about His brothers?

When I would tell people about Frank, they often wouldn't believe me. As active as I had become in the church, Garth and Petunia, our pastor and his wife, would sometimes come to visit my kids and me at my house. I thought they would believe me, and I would need their help someday both with prayer and understanding what I was dealing with when it came to Frank and his denial of my mom's illness. With each visit, I would tell them more about his inability to manage his anger issues. I told them about how he controlled everyone who lived there and how he had physically harmed my mom, other people, and the animals. I told them about how he screamed at Ella and me and how he belittled us. Pastor Garth and Petunia listened, and we would pray.

Now, based on their later actions, I don't know if they really ever believed me or if anyone I ever shared any of my story with believed me, and that made it more difficult to leave too. If no one believed me, how could I get help when I needed to leave?

During one afternoon trip down memory lane, as Frank droned on and on about his past life to me while I sat on the force-breaking table, half listening and thanking God I wasn't out in the training field being yelled at instead, Frank told me a story about a time he and his friend test drove a truck.

"It must have been the early 70s back when they didn't do none of that stuff where they hold on to your driver's license while you test drive," he said. "You could just go in and ask for the keys and take a truck out. So, we pull into this place in Tulsa and leave my car there. We took this truck out all day." He was laughing hysterically. "We got drunk and took it mudding. Brought it back with the fender hanging off, absolutely covered in mud. You should have seen them salesman faces." He laughed.

"What happened? Did you get arrested?" I asked.

"No. We just got in my car and drove away." He was still chuckling.

"Wow. Can you imagine if it had been two black guys?" I asked.

"What do you mean?" Frank asked.

"Well, if it had been two black guys, first of all they wouldn't have been allowed to test drive a truck unless they had cash and driver's license given to the salespeople. Even then, depending on the business, they still might not have been allowed. And if they had brought a truck back in that condition they would have been lynched, would they not? In 1970, or whatever you're talking about?" I asked.

"Yeah... I mean–" He started to stammer. He had no good response.

"I'm just saying that black people have different experiences than us, and they don't have the same opportunities as us," I said as I noticed that he had already stopped listening.

# CHAPTER EIGHTY-THREE

After I had done all of the kennel maintenance, which I started at dawn and took about two hours, I helped Frank with the dogs. My job when assisting Frank with the training was, first, to help him hook the dogs up to the roader. The roader was a series of iron pipes hooked to the back of the tractor with thirty places to hook dogs by their collars. We would drive thirty dogs to the bird field where we would park them under shade, and then Frank would sit on the bench, drink coffee, and talk for hours, while I sat on the force-breaking table in front of his bench.

Unfortunately, sometimes we would have to get up and actually go work dogs because they were already sold and people would have specific dates they wanted their dogs finished by, so they could come and pick them up and take their dogs hunting, mostly for ground foul. To train the dogs, we would start them out on a check cord, which is a rope that's about thirty yards long. I would walk out into the field first to distract the dogs while Frank planted the live quail in a thicket of prairie grass.

Next, I was supposed to catch up to the dog and step on their rope or pick it up after they smelled the bird but before they ran up to it, causing it to flush or fly. I am a mid-thirties mom of two who is overweight and hasn't worked out, other than walking and lifting heavy feed bags and buckets, in eighteen years. I'm never, ever going be as fast as a healthy, six-month-old bird dog puppy who has two more legs than I have. If we had taught the puppies the word, "whoa," which means, "even though you smell the bird you're not allowed to move no matter what," before we put them in the field with the live birds–birds they were bred to love, birds their ancestors for generations had been bred to smell and find–we would have been much more successful. Frank would not have to yell at me the entire time, calling me everything from idiot to stupid and saying everything we did out there in the field was a circus. He would not have had to complain every day that the dogs weren't learning anything.

I agreed. They weren't learning anything. We needed to stop drinking coffee and start taking them out and teaching them how to whoa before taking them out in the field.

After the dog would find the bird, I would pick up the dog's rope and hold on to it while Frank walked over to the bird, telling the dog "whoa," repeatedly so that the dog would connect the dots. The hope was that the dog would think, *"I get to find the bird, but he gets to kill it. I don't get to kill it. I have to stand here until it's in the air."*

Then, Frank would kick up the bird, it would fly, I would let go of the rope, the dog would chase the bird, Frank would shoot the bird, and it would fall to the ground. Usually, the dogs had no problem finding the birds as we yelled, "Dead bird! Dead bird!" But new puppies, when we first started them out, would not immediately understand the birds were not for them. I would have to get to them and step on their rope before they found the bird and took off for the forest to eat their prize. Some of them would just lay down right where they had found it to eat the bird. More often than not, a dog's reaction to finding the dead bird was to run over to the twenty-nine other dogs on the roader and do a victory lap, showing off their bird.

These dead birds would sometimes land on the other side of the field a quarter of a mile away, and I was expected to get to the dead bird at the same time as the dog. If I didn't, I was yelled at and called names. I would cry openly without even trying to hide it from him every day. He would tell me I just needed to get better at being his assistant. I would tell him I didn't want to. I didn't sign up for that job. I had no interest in that job. I wasn't built for that, and I didn't have the energy for it. He didn't see the other things I did every day or understand and see how many things I did each day, even just for him. He would tell me that I needed to get in better shape. He asked me if it would help if he made me a track to jog on.

My self-esteem was at the lowest it had ever been in my entire life. Every once in a while, I would post on Facebook, "What do you do if your boss calls you stupid and an idiot?" just out of sheer desperation. I thought maybe someone had dealt with something similar or at the very least someone would remind me that I'm not an idiot. I was beginning to wonder if I was even still alive. I felt so tired, I didn't know how to feel alive anymore.

I wore the same exact black T-shirt and black sweatpants every day because I was covered head to toe in wet dog shit by six o'clock every morning. Dogs would jump in their shit and then jump on me as I fed them, watered them, and cleaned up their poop. Even if only half of them jumped on me that morning, there was still seventy-five shitty paw prints on my shirt and pants by the time I was done with the chores.

The dogs on the roader would step in their shit and then jump on me every time I would go get a new dog to work. Once a month, I would have to worm each and every dog, and those days I would even have shit in my hair. When you accept that your life is that of someone who wears dog shit on their clothing, head to toe every day, and your boss screams at you and calls you names, you start to question your humanity.

You start to feel like you are dog shit.

After we would get done working dogs each midday, we'd have a pile of dead birds and a small cage with the remaining live birds we had not used. Frank would drive the tractor with the dogs back up to the kennel, and I would carry the dead and live birds up to the bird building. I let the living birds go back into the fly pen to live at least one more day, and then I would give the puppies on the cables the dead birds as a treat and a way to introduce them to their love of quail.

When Ella started watching Henry while I was at work, that freed up my mom to follow me around all day while I was working. Although I said she should be resting, Frank disagreed. He was constantly giving her tasks to do. He started having her take the dead birds to the cable puppies, and sometimes she would remember what that meant, what to do, and where to go, and sometimes we would see her off in a tree line dumping the birds out in it pile so she wouldn't get in trouble for not remembering where to take them.

One time, she brought the dead birds inside the house. One time, she was gone for far too long, and Frank was already inside the house playing solitaire on his computer, so I went to go find her. My mom was wandering around the backyard with an empty bird bag mumbling to herself with tears in her eyes.

"What's the matter?" I asked.

She looked up at me with the eyes of a little kid. "I don't have my lunch money," she said, pulling her pockets out to show me.

I reassured her that she would be okay and brought her into the house.

I told Frank what had happened and that we needed to keep a closer eye on her. He said something dismissive and filled with denial, and I went home to my babies to worry about my mom. When I was with my mom, I would worry about my kids because they were thirteen and two and alone. Even though they were only a quarter of a mile away, they still needed my help.

When I was with my kids, I worried about my mom. I was always stressed out and worried about what odd thing my mom would start doing next or need and not be able to receive. I was always worried that she was thirsty or hungry and not able to remember what those things meant and how to get her own food. Frank was certainly not going to help her. So, I started going in her house to make her breakfast between the kennel chores and working dogs, and that's when I realized she had somehow gotten it in her mind that she was supposed to be drinking salt water.

My mom had been putting spoonfuls of salt in her water glass because she thought it helped with leg cramps. That particular episode took me having to call my younger brother Chad and his newest girlfriend Karen to come over and tell Frank that Mom would die if she kept drinking salt water. Frank didn't believe all three of us and called my mom's doctor to ask a nurse.

When he got off the phone he said, "Well, I guess that's a really good way to have a stroke. Who'da thunk it?"

Frank promised to keep her from salting her water, but I still had to beg him to let me administer her medication. He didn't want her to drive because he knew that that could mess up his car. He didn't want her to do the kennel paperwork or the taxes anymore because that could mess up his business, but letting her give herself her own medicine and letting her watch my baby were things that didn't matter to him, so he wanted to hold on to those as long as he could.

Occasionally, a dog would just refuse to retrieve. They were stubborn, and they thought that bird should be theirs. We had trained a big, pretty male named Gunner who was black with white ticking. His coloring was called Silver Roan, and he was very beautiful and very smart, but we had a hard time getting him to retrieve. First, he wanted to keep his birds and not give them to us, so after a few times of seeing he was having that issue, Frank lost his temper and hit him in the nose with the butt of his rifle. These outbursts would often cause us new problems because now Gunner didn't even want the bird in his mouth at all. The injury and shock that someone would hit him in the face confused the poor fella. So, he'd pick up a dead bird, carry it a few steps and then drop it. Gunner repeated that until losing interest and running away, never retrieving the bird.

With each of Frank's tantrums, dogs would start having a new issue, and we would have to tell the owner of the dog that we needed a few more weeks. We also needed time for the dog's injuries to heal after Frank was violent with them.

Somehow, we put a temporary fix on Gunner's retrieving skills, and he looked good when his owners came to get him. A few months later, Gunner was back for a retrieving tune up. His owner needed

Frank to help him stop dropping his bird mid-retrieve. Unfortunately, and probably unbeknownst to Gunner's owners, this meant using the force breaking table.

I had been sitting on that table every day for a year and had never seen it used. I had worked at the kennel for four years and had never seen it used. Frank and his previous assistant Travis did not use it in front of people, so if I was walking that way, they would stop. Before we started, Frank apologized to me for what I was about to see. He told me I didn't have to do anything but hand him stuff and that it was going to be ugly.

He said, "This table will be covered in piss and blood when we're done."

Frank put Gunner on the table and gave him about six inches of chain from his collar to a wire above his head. He put another collar on a chain and hooked it to the post that came up from the table to the ceiling. Gunner could barely move his head. Frank put a shock collar around Gunner's neck and another shock collar around Gunner's waist with the electric prongs on the dog's testicles.

Writing this takes so much energy, and I wasn't allowed to scream, cry or yell. I wanted to scream, "You fucking sadistic fucking freak! I'm getting my entire family and all of these dogs away from you! You fucked up, piece of shit, psychopath from hell! You invented hell! You! That was you!" and then shoot him in the face with his own gun.

I wanted to tell everyone, but who would believe me? Where would I start? I've filled seven notebooks so far. Seven notebooks worth of shit he has done and never gotten in trouble for. So why would anyone do anything about this now?

All I could muster was, "I don't know how you can do this to another living creature," and Frank ignored me.

He put a retrieving block, which is a piece of wood six to eight inches long with a block of wood on either end, in Gunner's mouth. Gunner didn't want to hold it and dropped it, so he was simultaneously beaten in the face with it and shocked in his most sensitive areas. He peed all over himself every time.

I sat on the bench with my eyes closed, my mouth filled with vomit, and I had to lean over and puke. Frank laughed and said I would have to get tougher if I wanted to be a bird dog trainer.

"You're not tough, and I don't want to be a or a dog trainer if this is what it means," I said.

He did that to Gunner repeatedly until there was dog piss and blood all over the table and then told me to go put Gunner away for the day. When I got back, he told me a story about a time there was a very stubborn dog named Bob who lost all his teeth being there for force breaking.

"You beat him so hard in the face you broke all of his teeth?" I was sick again.

"Most of them. He didn't have many left by the time we was done." Frank was proud of himself.

"His owner never asked why he had no teeth when he came to get him?" I asked, knowing the answer.

No one ever questioned Frank or tried to correct him. No one thought his level of stupidity was worth arguing with and no one could figure out how to argue with him. How do you argue with someone who thinks humans can drink salt water and that the best way to get a beautiful animal to obey you is to bash their face in?

You cannot argue with that person or connect with them, so you have to just get away from them.

# CHAPTER EIGHTY-FOUR

I will forever, absolutely love snow and rain, snow and a hard enough rain that the dogs can't smell the birds. While it would make kennel chores much messier, colder and difficult, I at least would not have to work dogs with Frank. Training dogs with Frank was at best excruciatingly boring and at worst completely traumatizing.

If it was snowing, he and my mom would sit in the house drinking coffee, while I took care of the dogs, and then he'd come out and ask me if I thought my kids would want to come down for pancakes.

I'd say, "Yes," and go home and retrieve my kids.

The first few times, I would drive home elated because all we'd have to do is eat breakfast with them, and then I would be able to go home and get warm. I could maybe even sit down for a minute, and it would add hours to my usually jam-packed day. Ella would be happy too. She liked homemade pancakes and bacon and not having to be in charge of the baby hours earlier in the day.

However, as time went on, the more time we spent with Frank, the more we saw him beat animals, yell at his wife who had dementia (to do things she was not only incapable of but sometimes she had no idea what he was even screaming), how he treated us and even how he treated the baby, caused Ella to stop wanting to go to breakfast.

When Henry, who was two, was at Frank's house, if Frank was talking on the phone, we would have to somehow get Henry to be quiet. Often, quieting a two-year-old is impossible. After a couple of times of Frank yelling at my toddler, I had started taking Henry outside no matter the weather, right when the phone would ring.

I have stood barefoot in the deep snow on Frank's porch, holding my screaming, cold baby because it was easier than listening to the tantrum of a sixty-eight-year-old man. Frank didn't even have the courtesy to cut his phone call short, and I would be out there for as long as I could before I considered walking barefoot to the car to warm my son. Sometimes, I didn't have time to put my boots on before the baby started fussing during Frank's call.

So, because of the way Frank treated people, Ella had started to throw fits when I would come home and tell her it was a pancake day. She started trying to refuse to go, and I knew that if my kids did not go to breakfast, Frank would come down the trail to my house and try to make them.

Frank didn't take no for an answer, and I knew that if Ella back talked to Frank and tried to refuse his invitation to breakfast, he would look at me with his pouting, hurt little boy feelings, and say, "Well, I guess we'll go hook dogs up if Ella doesn't want to eat breakfast," and I wouldn't get my snow day after all. I'd have to sit out in the cold while Frank sat on a bench, bad mouthing my daughter.

One snow morning, when Ella was refusing to go to breakfast, and I was explaining to her that I needed that morning off, it was -19 degrees, and I was already too tired from watering one hundred and fifty dogs by hand with water buckets because the hose was frozen, feeding them and shoveling up all of their frozen poop.

I asked if she could just, "Please go eat breakfast?"

She said no, and I walked into my bedroom and threw myself on the floor. I kicked, screamed, cried, and beat the floor with my fists so hard I hurt myself, just like a toddler. I threw a toddler fit. I exploded. The pressure, trauma, exhausting responsibilities, and anxiety had all gone too far. I was now so vulnerable, I was infantile.

My daughter mocked me from the living room about how I was

acting younger than my son, and she was right. I had just thrown a toddler fit in front of my toddler. How good of a mom am I for that? Just amazing example after amazing example.

I got up and took my wet-from-snow and dog shit clothes off and got into clean clothes. Ella and I took Henry to breakfast at Mom and Frank's house. I don't remember that particular morning, but I'm sure it was not pleasant. No aspect of life was pleasant anymore. The pandemic was still raging and scaring everyone. No one had any money. I was still doing everything for far too many dogs and four people. I needed a break. I didn't get any breaks, but eventually the seasons changed and brought with them new and unexpected problems.

In the spring and summer, Frank had to mow the bird field with the tractor. Mom didn't know what to do with herself anymore and would just wander off or follow Frank around the field for hours in direct sunlight and heat—on foot. I hadn't realized that was going on because I was busy with my kids until one spring afternoon, Frank came to ask me if I could babysit my mom in the afternoons while he mowed. So, every afternoon he would bring her over, and she'd nervously pace through my house because she was afraid she would be in trouble for being there.

"He's gonna kill me! He's gonna kill me!" she'd repeat while looking out the front door.

Ella and I would try to reassure her that Frank said it was okay for her to be there, but because for the last thirty years of their marriage it was not okay for her to be with us, she could not understand. She was so far into fight-or-flight mode that she had lost touch with reality.

Sometimes, I would be so busy with the baby I wouldn't be able to keep her in the house, and Ella would have to chase her down and try to get her to come back. Sometimes, my mom would make it back to the tractor before Ella could catch her, and that would result in Frank stopping the tractor, getting off of it, and following Mom, who was running back toward my house thinking she was in trouble, yelling and screaming, "He's going to kill me! He's gonna kill me!" while Ella and Frank walked behind her.

My mom would burst through my front door, panting, with huge eyes saying, "He's trying to kill me! He's trying to kill me!"

All of this was confusing for Henry and traumatizing for Ella and me. We were seeing those moments when she had first met Frank, and he was really trying to beat her to death, relived through her eyes. Her mind was so confused, she was living on pure adrenaline. She didn't know if she was in trouble or what for.

In her mind, all she knew was he was, *That guy we are all afraid of—he's telling me to do something, and I can't do it. RUN!"*

Ella and I tried to explain that to Frank. Ella said, "She's trapped in the past in those moments. She thinks you're going to hurt her."

"Oh, pfft, but I've never hurt her," he'd say.

"We aren't going to do that," I stepped in. "We have bigger problems than pretending you never hurt her. She's also scared to be at my house because anytime she's ever been allowed to be anywhere with me, Ella, Alexis, or Ruby, you'd yell at her for being gone too long until she didn't ever want to go or even want to even *ask* to go anymore. The last time she saw Ruby, she started saying you were going to kill her if she didn't leave soon, the second we got to Ruby's house," I said.

"Pfft. You're talking crazy talk." He tried to deny it, but Ella was there too, and we both had numerous detailed stories of times we had to calm my mom down and tell her we couldn't leave places like ballet recitals and the zoo because Frank was going to yell at her when she got home, even before she had dementia.

Many of the reasons behind Frank being in denial of my mom's condition was that it meant facing that he was to blame for putting her there. So, his solution for what Mom should do while he mowed was to put her on a riding lawn mower to have her mow their front yard. She tore the lawnmower up the first time she tried. After he fixed it, she started going way too fast. The entire time she was mowing, she had a terrified look on her face, and it scared Ella and me too. My mom could have gotten severely injured, and I kept trying to explain to Frank that if she got hurt or lost or anything happened to her, it would be his fault, and he would be in trouble for elder abuse and neglect.

I thought that if I scared him into realizing his ass was on the line, maybe he'd care enough to hire someone to look after my mom, or he would, at the very least, start doing a better job of it himself.

Now, I wonder if I ever did the right thing in any of those moments or the ones to shortly follow. Anyone outside looking in would say, "Get out of there! Why are you still there?" But now my mom was his property, and she could not think for herself. I couldn't leave her. I also had nowhere to go to take my children. I reached out for help from Chad multiple times because he could have been talking to his dad but did not want to be bothered with any of the mess.

If all of my siblings and I had gotten together to fight for my mom to have proper care, we would have probably had to get a lawyer and fight Frank in court and prove his abuse and neglect while I still lived there somehow. And how would any of that work? I could not leave while we fought it out in court because my mom could have gotten hurt or died in my absence, but I also could not live there while fighting Frank in a court battle.

My siblings love my mom, but they knew she had made her bed and continued to go back to it over and over, for years, no matter what we did or tried. They knew it was not their life, it was her life, and she chose it.

I didn't and don't blame them. In fact, I know they did the right thing and wish I had chosen my own path rather than my mother's path, all those years, for my children's sake.

## CHAPTER EIGHTY-FIVE

Although watching dogs be shot in the head or beaten by Frank was horrendous, when a female dog would get accidentally pregnant, it was even worse. I worked for Frank for five years, and two of those were helping him train dogs. In those two years, he let five different female dogs get accidentally pregnant.

I was constantly suggesting we build more kennels so that every dog had their own, which would have been more comfortable for the dogs and prevent accidental pregnancies, but Frank barely wanted to work dogs. He was never going to build more kennels.

We had to put a male dog in with a female because bird dogs are very territorial. While a male and a female can usually get along without fighting, two females will kill each other and two males in one kennel together would kill each other. That was why we docked their tails when they're puppies, so they wouldn't get torn off through the fence in a fight.

It's not always easy to tell when a female is in heat, especially if there are dozens and dozens of dogs. One of the females, Aspen, who was not even born at our kennel but was a training dog dropped off for summer camp, got pregnant while she was at our kennel. Frank was a coward, and he didn't even tell her owners, who drove from

Colorado to pick her up after paying eighteen hundred dollars to get her tuned up for quail season. They were faced with the options of either sitting this season out because she would have just had puppies, having a litter with a dog whose owners lived in Kansas City, or having her litter aborted.

Aspen's owners chose to go ahead and have her puppies, but that not only meant her owner couldn't go quail hunt with her that season but that her body would have completely changed for hunting forever, and she'd never be as good as she was before she had nursed a litter of pups.

Another time, a family from Houston had picked out a small liver roan female and named her Sassy. We were supposed to have her trained by a certain date, and Frank let her accidentally get bred. At that time, she was such a small dog, neither of us noticed she was pregnant until I walked outside one morning at dawn to start my chores and saw her having her puppies, and the male she was in with was eating them.

She had just started having her babies, so I picked her up and put her in a whelping box in the puppy room to finish having her litter and went inside the house to tell Frank. After we got done working dogs that afternoon, he told me to go see if she was done having her puppies and if she was done, to put them in a bucket and bring them to him. I thought he was going to inspect them to see which stud had bred her so that we could put it on her paperwork, but instead he threw the puppies in the dog shit pond. He wanted Sassy to dry up so he could still finish her on time. Without her puppies, she went crazy, and I don't blame her. We never did finish training her because she would do nothing but howl, whine, and lie down, and we ended up giving the people in Houston a different female and using Sassy for a brood mama after all. So, Frank threw about ten gorgeous puppies away for no reason.

Misty was her owner's pride and joy, and I'll never forget the day she got bred on the roading machine to a dog whose dad was her grandpa. Frank didn't tell that family that their dog had accidentally been bred either, and Frank's friend Clark and I sat listening to that poor man have to call and explain to his wife that their family fur baby was bred.

In this case, that was not joyous news. A female bird dog will never be the same for hunting after having a litter of puppies, so usually a hunter will save breeding his female for after she has hunted a few seasons. Misty's owner had not even hunted her one season, and she was a fantastic little dog. He was excited to hunt with her. Now, he was faced with having her puppies aborted, which also meant she would never be able to have puppies or missing a season. The subsequent hunting seasons, she would not be as quick and agile as she would have been had she never nursed a litter.

Frank was telling him his options were to either leave her there to have and raise her puppies and therefore miss hunting that season, have the puppies aborted, or take her home and let her have her puppies at home but bring them back when they were born. This man had paid $4000 for this dog and an extra $1800 for us to tune her up over the summer, and now he was devastated and so was his wife.

Clark and I were horrified and embarrassed. Frank was acting like a complete jerk toward the customer, who was bewildered and asking questions, trying to make an informed decision. Frank was a defensive little boy.

He didn't want to talk about it and kept telling the customer, "Look, man, it's no big deal."

"Do I get to keep the puppies if I let her have them?" the man asked.

Frank laughed in his face. "Ha, ha, no. That's not how it works."

I would have lost my temper and let Frank have it. I would have yelled, "I leave my dog here, and you let her get bred, and I don't even get to keep her puppies?!"

I would have been livid, but the man kept his composure. I kept reminding Frank, not in front of the customer, of course, that Misty was Griffin's granddaughter and that the stud that bred her was Griffon's son, but he ignored me. All eleven puppies came out with birth defects, and Frank kept and sold them anyway.

A black roan female, who was already sold, started to show puppy, and Frank had no idea who she was bred to, but we did know she was a superstar bird dog and her going home date was quickly approaching.

"You're gonna have to take that dog to the vet and have her fixed," he said. "If they remove her uterus, she won't have those puppies and won't get ruined."

The vet did the procedure, and two days later, I picked up the dog. The vet said, "Tell Frank he's not welcome here, and we won't do business with him anymore. Those puppies were fully gestated. She was about to have those puppies. I refuse to help Frank do things like that…." He trailed off. Then the vet shook his head and looked at me. "Listen, you just work for the guy, and I know it's not your fault, but just tell him we won't do business with him anymore."

"Unfortunately, I'm his stepdaughter, and my mom has dementia, so I have to help him now, but I'll tell him," I said.

"Oh, I see. This would have never happened when your mom was in charge," the vet said, and then told me he was sorry about what I must be dealing with.

Everyone was sorry. Everyone felt sorry for me, felt sorry for my mom, and felt sorry for the dogs, but no one knew how to stop Frank from being an evil, narcissistic control freak who only considered himself with every decision he made.

Occasionally , I would complain to my friends about the way Frank treated me, and my friend Avery would remind me that she had a fully furnished, empty house in a nearby town. Every time she would offer for my children and me to move into her house, I would refuse her offer because I just knew something would go wrong. It would be an almost sure thing, but as many times as I had lost over the years, I would lose that too. I could not bring myself to even think about leaving my mom with Frank in her current condition.

During the time I trained dogs with him, I was lectured more about women and our incompetence, manipulation, and weaknesses than any other topic. Frank absolutely hates women. He preaches more about the way women dress and wear their hair, jewelry, and makeup than anything else, but once in a while, he'd say something so asinine, I would have to find out more. Believing he was a prophet and that he knew everything about Jesus, he would tell me things like, the only people who will be allowed in Heaven were those who were born to a married, Christian couple.

"So why are we even witnessing? Why are we doing mission work with people who don't fit that very specific profile? Why even spread the Gospel?" I asked.

"Because we're supposed to tell everyone about Jesus, but the only people that are truly chosen are those who were born to married Christians under the covenant of marriage. God didn't even create people who were conceived out of the covenant of Christian marriage." This was his response.

"Wait, I thought God created everyone?" I asked.

"No. Sex created those people. God created the people who were conceived under a blessed marriage," he explained.

"So, Chad's kids, your grandkids–they weren't created by God? And neither of my kids were created by God?" I asked.

He raised his hands up and said, "I don't make the rules."

After the political media began the abortion discussion again, Frank couldn't shut up about it, and he always referred to a pregnant woman as someone who had, "gotten herself pregnant." Once, after listening to hours of his opinions on pregnancy, I finally had to know.

"Why do you always say someone 'got herself pregnant'? You know no one can impregnate herself. It takes a man too." I assumed this was a figure of speech. I assumed, "She got herself pregnant," had come from the men of his generation not wanting to take the responsibility for accidental pregnancies, but his answer was even more shockingly ignorant.

He said, "Well, a woman knows when she can get pregnant or not, Amelia. And if you're so loose with your morals and your decision making that you go out and get pregnant anyway, you got yourself pregnant."

I had to rub my eyes and shake my head around to make sure I was really there for that and not in some *Saturday Night Live* skit where they make fun of men from the 1950s. "Hold on a minute. Are you telling me you think women know when we can get pregnant?" I asked.

"Well, yeah."

"You mean like our knees turn purple or our left ear stops working for that week, or what do you think happens that we know exactly when we are ovulating?" I asked.

"Women have always been able to tell when they can get pregnant," he said.

"We can vaguely, kind of get an idea if we keep track of the days of the cycle on a calendar, but we can't tell exactly when we are ovulating." I gave up. Why would I begin to try to explain ovulation to him?

He had all of these opinions on women and their behaviors and what their rights should be, but I don't think he ever had the privilege in his entire life of having a real conversation with a woman. I don't mean to compare female humans and female dogs, but historically, and due to men like Frank, have we not been treated the same as creatures who are unable to make decisions for ourselves and yet blamed for every consequence of those withheld decisions?

I could look into the eyes of a female bird dog who didn't want her babies taken away and feel her heart break. I could look into the eyes of a twenty-year-old Nina Hudson, who had to leave her baby in the NICU for three months without being allowed to go see him or even call and check on him, and feel her heartbreak.

Men have no place in deciding what we do with our babies or our bodies when they can't even run their businesses. If women had been allowed to rule the world, there would have been no wars. We know how much effort, pain, discomfort, anxiety, trauma, and stress goes into creating life, and therefore, why would we give it away in exchange for money, power, or land?

We know better.

# CHAPTER EIGHTY-SIX

My entire life, people have told me things they had never told anyone else. I noticed it the first time when I was in high school when Charlotte and I were in the middle of a big fight that had been going on for months. Even though we were fighting, she told me her deepest, darkest, secret at the time.

Then she teared up and said, "I don't know why I told you that. I always tell you things I wasn't going to tell anyone."

I'm not prying when this happens. I'm not asking the right questions or even asking any questions at all. I'm just listening, and strangers I've never met before, or someone who doesn't even like me will tell me a secret or a difficult thing to say. Something along the lines of, "Wow. I've never told anyone that before!" or, "I wasn't going to say all of that. I never talk about that."

People open up to me, and that is not always a blessing. The longer I sat across from Frank, listening to his life stories, the more he forgot I was a woman. He definitely did not consider me a man because then he'd have to treat me with an ounce of respect, but he very clearly forgot I was a woman.

The time he very incorrectly explained ovulation to me, I could see, to him, I'd lost my femininity altogether. He constantly talked about his obsession with thin, small women. He was constantly reminding me when telling the story of how he met my mom that she was not ever his type and that losing fifty pounds would not hurt her. Every time he would tell me a story about his partying, hippie, motorcycle, and rodeo days, he reminded me that he liked thin women. Every time a customer would bring their wife, if she was thin, he would talk to me after they left about how, "She was a pretty lady, wasn't she?"

His filter was completely gone with me. The more stories he told me, the more genderless I became. I wasn't a woman anymore, and the locker room talk came out occasionally, making me feel the sickest I felt about anything he'd said so far. He had insulted every race of human being in front of me. Black people, he called the N word and never held back on his disapproval of them. "Chinamen," was what he called every Asian person or Asian American person. Embarrassingly, he would share views of how the "Chinamen are taking over" to every single customer who entered the premises. He would sit and bad mouth Native Americans, who, in his opinion, were filthy drunks, and every European country had its own reason for being disgusting to him. He loathed people from the Middle East. Everyone was hated by him.

I had been listening to his racism and his hatred of women in small doses since I was a little girl, but it was not until he forgot that I was a woman that he started to say things that made me go home and vomit.

Frank's obsession with a little girl at church, my thirteen-year-old daughter's age, who was in Ella's youth group, became very obvious, very quickly. The little girl had a younger sister and a mom who was known around town for her drug use and irresponsibility. She sent her daughters to church but didn't go with them, and I'm sure it was because she felt judged by the people there who knew she struggled with addiction.

I wanted her at church anyway. I prayed for her anyway. I struggled with addiction. I eat my trauma and smoke weed. Just because her vice is different, doesn't mean it's worse. In fact, she was a beautiful woman, and she had very bright, creative daughters who were inquisitive and wanted to learn about Jesus. I taught them both in different classes at church.

On Monday mornings, after seeing the girls at church the day before, Frank would start talking about how one of them didn't have underwear on under her yoga pants.

"Don't they know you can tell they don't have underwear on when their pants are so tight like that?" he would ask.

The conversation would start with a question like that, which was not actually a question but an accusation and an implication. At first, it sounded to me like he wanted a real answer or a solution to the problem. It sounded like he wanted me to dress them properly for church in more modest clothing.

He would lecture me for an hour or two about the way little girls dressed in the 1950s when he was a kid. He would pepper in comments about how immodest many of the little girls at our church dressed, focusing particularly on the older of the two sisters. Many times, this conversation was him talking and me silently trying not to throw up or even call everyone in this little girl's life, putting him on speakerphone so they would know who to protect her from.

His rambling would eventually rabbit trail to, "You know Candice has seen her mom have sex, right?" he'd ask me.

The first time he asked, I still thought he was shaming their mom and her behavior. But by the sixth or tenth time he asked, I realized he was sexually attracted to thin, small girls, and now that he was comfortable speaking about this with me because I was no long a woman to him, he would ask me every time we would have this conversation, "You know that Candice has seen her mom have sex, right?" This question turned into, "You know that little Candice girl is having sex, right?"

The first time he asked me that, I jumped out of my skin, "What!?" I asked, even though I didn't want to know what he was thinking.

My brain had tried to ignore all of this all these years—when Ruby and I were very small and were not allowed to go barefoot in front of him; the constant lectures about modesty, especially regarding to little girls; his hatred of little girls wearing shorts, bathing suits, or anything even remotely resembling something a woman would wear like yoga pants; his awkward complementing of small women or talking about them after they were gone; his obsession with Candice and her relationship with her body or sex, even though she was only thirteen or fourteen at the time. Frank even bought Candice a few gifts and would give them to her in front of his own granddaughters whom he was not buying anything for.

When he would talk about the women of his past being thin, small, and very submissive, doing exactly what he said like obedient children, the "little girl," as he called her from the Ichabod story, I tried not to let it add up, but there was always the question, even when I was a child, about his fascination with little girls and modesty.

When my mom met Frank, he had a friend named Wayne. Wayne was the type of guy who, even as a seven-year-old girl, I knew not to be alone with him. He gave off an evil spirit, and I don't even like to say things like that about people, but this guy's son is currently in prison for raping a twelve-year-old girl, and that was after his son had spent his adolescence in juvenile detention for molesting a five-year-old girl when he was twelve.

So, I knew that I should never be alone with Wayne even when I was a child, based on a feeling, and I knew that Frank was very good friends with this person, such a friend that when Wayne's son's verdict came back guilty, Frank's reaction was, "Oh, no. I was hoping he wouldn't have to go to prison."

Wayne's wife, Devyn, had no teeth, and I put the puzzle pieces of her life together from things my mom and Frank said about her over the years. Devyn had a relationship with meth, and I can only assume that was to kill the trauma of having been forced to sleep with her brothers and her dad her entire childhood. Then, she grew up and married Wayne. So, all of these lectures about immodesty, Candice and her mom, lewd women and sex, always included poor Devyn.

During one of these disgusting ramblings of a pervert, Frank said, "I used to feel sorry for ol' Devyn because of what her dad and brothers did to her, but the Holy Spirit told me not to. You know why?" he asked me.

I was terrified. Every time this piece of shit had a disturbing thought, he blamed it on the Holy Spirit. The more perverse the thought, the more he was sure it was the Holy Spirit who had given it to him. I didn't have to ask, and I didn't want to know, but he was telling me anyway.

"She liked it," he said.

"What?!" I had hoped I'd misunderstood, but my face and ears were already red and radiating rage.

"She liked it, or she wouldn't have kept letting them," he said.

I tried. For what reason, I have no idea, but I took a deep breath and tried. "If a little kid was allowed to eat ice cream for every meal, would they?" I asked.

"Well, sure." he agreed.

"But kids can't eat ice cream for every meal because they'll get sick and eventually, they'll stop growing, their organs will shut down, they'll die, right? But if you told a child all of that was going to happen, would they stop eating ice cream for every meal or keep doing it anyway?" I asked.

"They'd probably keep eating ice cream," he said.

"That's why children are not old enough to make their own decisions. That's why they can't consent to sex. They don't understand the consequences. They don't understand their bodies. Her dad and brothers may have made her feel loved and special, and she was too little to know that was wrong, or maybe it was violent, and she hated it. Either way, why in the fuck would the Holy Spirit be talking to you about someone else's sexual trauma and telling you to judge her?" I was trying, but I was mad, so I lost him at the word, "fuck."

Frank hated that word. He would always tell me to, "Watch my mouth," and stop listening when I used the word, "fuck." That word made him uncomfortable. Any curse word did because that's what society had told him was wrong. Society had told him cussing was wrong, being gay was wrong, wearing immodest clothing was wrong, a woman with short hair who dressed too masculine was wrong. He could cling to those things because society had taught him those things, but he could not look at himself and see his flaws or work on them and improve himself.

The comments he made throughout the years made me uncomfortable enough to remember them all in detail but not enough for me to jump to the conclusion that Frank was attracted to young girls until the morning where I was sitting through the "Newlyweds in the Bible," lecture for the billionth time. The lecture begins, "In the Bible, when a young couple would get married, they'd be able to take a year off from work, military, or any responsibilities to get to know each other."

The gist of the lecture was usually to explain to me how much stronger relationships and marriages would be if we still practiced this ritual. Then it would turn into him talking about how they probably spent that entire year having sex. The time Frank said, "All young men wanted to get married back then because they knew what awaited them for that first year. Playing with little girls is fun, let me tell you."

Verbatim, in my ears.

That sentence went into my ears and killed some of my brain cells. Some of my soul died. I did not inquire as to what he meant. I did not want him to explain. I was just glad my daughter had never been thin and was always too round and outspoken for him just like I myself was when I was a little girl. Fortunately, my daughter and I were too curvaceous and Rubenesque to ever draw reactions from him like Candice or her sister.

I have thoroughly thought about this conversation just recently because I want to get it out of me. I don't want to know anything at all about Frank Hudson, but this is the thing I wanted to know the least. I don't want to know it. I don't want to have even heard it. I don't want to have noticed any of this. I hope I am wrong. I hope that it is just a bunch of unrelated things that I should have ignored, but that is how people get hurt, ignoring things like these comments and obsessions.

This was a man who had never been intelligent, so of course he was going to choose a partner who had less experience than him. He's never been impressive in any capacity, so he was going to choose someone who he was in control of and who couldn't leave. He had very little to offer anyone, so he was going to want someone who had no one to compare him to and who didn't talk back. A young girl would be his choice, not a powerful woman. He absolutely hates women, especially if they have even a hint of confidence or power. He would want a powerless, self-esteem lacking girl.

After finding out Frank had been emotionally and mentally stunted at seven years old by a brick to his frontal lobe, I understood even more. He made jokes the way children do, and his sense of humor was that of an immature little boy no older than ten or twelve. He was attracted to, I believe, who he saw as a reflection of himself. To be clear, I don't think that after the Ichabod incident that Frank ever touched any underage girls. However, I write about this for two reasons. One of them is that I don't think Frank ever even knew he dealt with this demon. I think he tried to run from it by becoming infatuated with feminine modesty so he could keep his arousal away. I think he stamped it down by trying to convince himself that he hated women and anything that reminded him of sex.

He needed therapy. Anyone who has these thoughts, either sexual thoughts of minors or absolute one-track minded obsession with young girls and their clothing, even if it's presenting it as the opposite of being attracted to them, needs to be investigated. These issues need to be talked about with a trusted professional. I'm not saying it's even Frank's fault. He got hit in the face with a brick, and no one did anything but honor him and allow him to make horrible decisions, which ruined and took people's lives for decades to the point that he actually believed that he could do no wrong and that the Holy Spirit was speaking to him about other people's sex lives.

The other reason I write about this is because I ignored this behavior, those comments and lectures. I accepted them because I was introduced to accepting everything this toxic waste dump of a person said and did. If myself, my sister, or my daughter had not been being protected by angels, we could have been molested. We were brought into a situation where we were not to question very questionable behavior from this man. He was always doing and saying horrible things, and we were always just supposed to live with it.

This is how children get hurt. We cannot ask our children to overlook being put down, insulted, spoken to or about negatively, or having their moms or grandmothers or anyone be spoken down to or about in front of them. We can't ask our kids to just accept everything because that's when the cycle of trauma continues and that's how, pretty soon, the child doesn't know what is wrong or right anymore.

We all must have healthy boundaries, and if my parents had said, "Being around this man is not acceptable for my children," when I was a kid, I wouldn't have accepted that for my daughter. I'm thankful that my daughter was not hurt, and I will never accept anyone like Frank in my life again, and neither will Ella.

# CHAPTER EIGHTY-SEVEN

Dementia is nothing like what TV and movies portray. In *Christmas Vacation*, Aunt Bethany hilariously sings "The Star-Spangled Banner" when they all see Santa Claus and she recites the Pledge of Allegiance when asked to say the prayer. I wish that had been my experience with my mom and her condition.

She was sixty-three when diagnosed, but if I would have really been paying attention, I would say I noticed signs of her personality change, more confusion, memory loss, and mental fatigue ten years before that when I lived with her in Rockford before she went back to Frank for the final time.

Dementia is not just memory loss. I'm no doctor, but to me, dementia is such mental and emotional strain, stress, and exhaustion that a person's brain starts to protect itself by cutting ties with reality. My mom, when faced with any issue back then in Rockford, would say, "I'm so tired of this shit." No matter the situation, she said it every time anything arose that was an extra thing on her plate. She had been in fight-or-flight mode and panic mode for so long that she was running out of gas–permanently. She was too old, worn out, and tired to continue to be resilient and too isolated to gain energy or motivation from the support of her friends or family. She started to completely shut down, turn her brain off, and give up on life.

After her diagnosis, I started paying more attention to her behavior, something that is not natural in humans. It's not as natural to notice your parent's needs as it is to notice the needs of your children. I had been overlooking her behavior and her health for years because she was my mom, not my child. I thought of her as a capable adult who could handle her own healthcare. I had children of my own, and a really healthy mom who worked outside, walking and lifting for hours every day. I had not been paying attention to her mental or physical health because our entire lives, my siblings and I had been choking down the fact that our mother was involved in an unhealthy and unhappy marriage where she was treated like a slave and had no control over where she went or what she did, who she saw, what she wore, or how she lived.

We knew those things, so thinking about her mental and emotional health was something we steered clear of thinking about so as not to ruin our own. I, however, foolishly took it upon myself to chase her around my whole life trying to bring her some semblance of temporary happiness in having me as a friend and Ella as a distraction. I wish I had been more like my siblings and avoided that. How I did not realize what I was doing, or that it would not work, or save her, or end well for anyone, I do not know.

Each day, my mom walked by herself the quarter mile to the barn to clean, which was really just throwing away my belongings. I had stored keepsakes and decorations in the barn because they didn't fit in my house. First, she threw away my Christmas tree and decorations. I was a little sad because some of those had been things Ella had made when she was little, and some of them had sentimental value but at the time, I didn't understand what was happening to her brain. I was still trying to help her.

"Why did you throw away my Christmas tree?" I asked.

She did not remember doing it at all.

"You have to try harder, Mom, to remember things. Do you know that you have a disease?" It was the first time I had asked her. I didn't know if Frank had even explained it to her yet.

"No, I don't!" She was acting like a teenager that day.

Frank insisted Mom help me while I took care of the kennel chores in the mornings, and she was more work than the actual job. It would have been easier to let my two-year-old son help me. Mom would wash the dog excrement the wrong way, wash it all over the area we had to walk or wash it into the grass. Frank would come out of the house and scream at her every day that she was an idiot and try to teach her the right way.

"Don't you think that since she can't understand that there's a drain over there, and that's where we're washing everything, that she just doesn't remember?" I would ask on Monday.

"How could she not understand? She's just being stupid." He'd say to me, and to her, "Did you eat your 'stupid pills' this morning, dear?"

He would ask her repeatedly throughout the day if she was "eating stupid pills." He was not referring to her actual medication. He was asking her if she was taking pills that were making her stupid.

I could not wash the kennel for her because I was washing the other one, so my armpits would burn with stress-sweat and rage as I would have to wash dog shit down a drain listening to my mother, whom I knew had the mental capacity of a toddler, be screamed at and belittled. When we would get to where we worked dogs, I would ask Frank if Mom remembered to take her medicine.

"I'm sure she did, but that's not really any of your business, is it?" he'd ask.

"I live here, I work here, and she's my mom. How is it not my business?" I'd ask.

"Quit interfering!" he would yell in my face.

I would cry the rest of the six hours we worked dogs.

When she would pour the dog food down the drain instead of into the dog's buckets, he would scream at her that she was an idiot.

On Tuesday, I would start to yell across from the kennel I was washing to where he was screaming at her, "She has a disease! She doesn't know any better!"

By Wednesday, I was trying to explain to him with the metaphor that, just because she's not pooping her pants like he is, that doesn't mean that she isn't sick just like he is, and what if I screamed at him that he was an idiot and asked him if he'd taken his 'stupid pills' every time he pooped his pants?

It took me a full year of Wednesday's strategy to realize that he did not understand the metaphor and thought that I was simply making fun of him for shitting himself. I would say it much more gently to him. I knew I was dealing with a narcissistic seven-year-old and that everything had to be delicate for him.

When my mom followed me around, and we were alone, I would try to get her to focus on how I was doing things and try to get her to remember the correct way to do things, and for that, I am ashamed of myself. I didn't realize until about two and a half years in that she was too far gone for things like that or the necklace I made her, reminding her of the day of the week. I would flip it to the right day every morning. It was made out of post-it notes and paper clips, and it reminded her of the day of the week and what she did each day. It reminded her to brush her teeth, take her medicine, eat her breakfast, etc.

It worked very briefly, but she was being screamed at by her husband every day, and her daughter and only friend was not helping her rest but trying to encourage her to get better. She couldn't get better. She could only either stay the same or get worse, and the stress we were putting on her made her much worse.

By Thursday, I was losing my shit. My mom was constantly letting dogs out by accident, which meant spending hours trying to chase down a dog that hated Frank with him on the four-wheeler, speeding after the dog until it was exhausted, laid down, and gave up. When my mom would let a dog out, my initial reaction was always to throw my head back and say, "Goddamnit!" Not at her but at the universe, at the dog, the dog shit, the dementia, and Frank. I didn't even think that she knew that I was upset when I would do something like that, but one day it made her cry.

"You don't have to say it like that," she said, sniffling, and it broke my heart.

"I'm not mad at you," I told her. "I'm just mad."

I knew she cried when Frank yelled at her and that she understood he was calling her names, but I thought my sighs and under-my-breath curses she had missed because she was not paying attention and never all there, but she *felt* more than I realized. For all the times I lost my temper on her disease, near enough to her for her to feel that negativity, I am so ashamed. She needed peace, love, support, rest, comfort, nutrition, hydration, and for someone to give her her damn medicine. I couldn't do any of that for her, and by Friday, I was walking up to Frank and yelling at him that I needed one day.

"One day! I need one day this week where you are not screaming at your wife! Just one day! Would you be yelling at your wife if our pastor was standing here? If your friends were standing here watching? If Jesus was standing here watching?" I didn't care if he hit me. I wanted him to lose his temper and hit me.

We would usually spend our entire Friday not working any dogs but arguing all morning over whether or not it was okay for him to yell and call my mom names.

"You shouldn't be calling your wife an idiot or stupid even if she doesn't have a disease, but your wife has a disease. Why can't you control yourself and the way you speak to people?"

"So what am I supposed to do, just always be so sweet and nice and say oh, lovey and deary and snuggle poo or act like a faggot?" he said, using his impression of someone with developmental delays while hitting himself in the chest, the universal immature person signal that they are calling you slow.

I got up and walked to my car. He was the most disgusting, pathetic waste of time I'd ever spent years trying to change into something resembling a human. He was insinuating that treating my mother and me with respect and acknowledging that we should not be yelled at and called names every day was the equivalent of all of us being homosexual mentally handicapped people. Insulting people with mental disabilities and gay people and my mom and myself all at once made the alarm go off in my head that said, *"If you don't walk to your car, you're going to walk over to that rifle and do something you didn't come here to do today, so you better leave."* And that was the first time I threatened to leave and walked away.

Later that evening, I heard the four-wheeler and Frank was in my yard. He came to ask me if I was really going to leave. I told him I never wanted to leave my mom here with him, not the first time when I was six or the second time when I was eighteen and not now. He was offended that I was implying that she wasn't safe with him. I just wanted to end the conversation. I'd had enough of him that day.

"Did you ever think that maybe you just can't be happy, Amelia?" he asked.

I remembered the first person who ever asked me that question, my stepmom—people who hurt you want you to think you are broken and that it isn't that they're abusing you but that you are either asking for too much, your standards for happiness are too high, or that you are just incapable of happiness. I remembered the second person who asked me that question, Ella's dad. He, too, tried to make me think that I was not capable of happiness.

Had this been the first time I'd been asked, I might have been shocked. Had it been the second time, I might have started to believe it, but since it was the third time, and no one who was not abusing me had ever asked, my answer was simple.

"It's not my job to be happy. It's my job to exist and help and serve the people around me. I can't do that as well if one of them is screaming at me or calling me names or screaming at my mom and calling her names. It's as easy as that," I said, and I went inside to finish cooking dinner.

Frank did not give up on yelling at us or belittling us, and my mom's crying turned into tantrums where she would throw down whatever she was supposed to be doing and walk off and go in the house. I praised Jesus for that because soon, Frank stopped trying to force her to work, which made my job so much easier. My mom's condition was worsening, and Frank was still in denial.

## CHAPTER EIGHTY-EIGHT

After months of being forced to help me with the kennel maintenance and being screamed at by Frank for doing it wrong, my mom had gone inside the house crying enough times that Frank could no longer get her to go outside and help me.

I would wake up every morning an hour before daylight and ask Jesus to be with us that day and to not let my mom, whom I was thinking of as more of a little sister at that point, get into trouble. I would ask Jesus to provide her, my children, and myself a way out so we could be free of the misery that was being in the presence of Frank Hudson.

At dawn, I would go into my mom's house to make sure she had breakfast, which he would let me make for her, but he would still not let me administer her medication or let me help her with it at all at that time. She would eat breakfast and then sit in her chair, the chair where she had been lectured for hours and hours on useless topics about how women should not wear pants, makeup, or earrings. The chair where she was lectured about why she couldn't go out to lunch with the ladies from church. Lectured about how she couldn't participate in her children's lives, and now she couldn't remember some of her children.

He had sucked every bit of her spirit and personality out of her.

After sitting in her chair for a couple of hours, she would walk past us working dogs through the field to my house, where Frank would make my mom be my thirteen-year old's responsibility. Ella was already watching my two-year-old, and when my mom would show up at our house, she would be too much for Ella to handle. Ella would make Henry a tray of snacks every morning, and if she went to the bathroom or into the other room, my mom would dump the baby's tray in the trash.

My mom would pace and wander around, not remembering where she was and thinking she was in trouble for being there. She would go into the barn where there were things that she could hurt herself with, but Ella couldn't follow her with the baby. Ella could only text me that she was scared and worried that her grandma was going to get hurt. The more I told Frank that Ella couldn't watch my mom and my baby and that we desperately needed another person to help us and that my mom needed a full-time chaperone or nurse, the deeper into anger-filled denial he became. Ella was just lazy, he would say. My mom couldn't be causing that much trauma to Ella, he'd say.

"You can't watch Mom and keep her from wandering off in the evenings, and you're a full-grown man who isn't even watching a two-year-old," I would point out.

"What do you want me to do?" he'd ask.

"I don't know what you should do, but my thirteen-year-old and I cannot pick up every bit of slack and do every single thing you need done for five people and hundreds of animals. We need help!"

But there was no help. Their son Chad, no matter how much I texted and called begging him, would not help. No one at church could be inconvenienced enough to even visit, and finding a nurse for my mom would require effort from Frank. I knew from the beginning that the only way Frank would do the right thing in this mess was when my mom's illness started to affect him so greatly and negatively that he had to begin to make steps to find her long-term care.

One morning, Ella texted me that I'd better take a break from working dogs because it looked like my mom was throwing away important things from the barn into the dumpster. I told Frank I'd be right back and took the four-wheeler down to the barn next to my house to investigate. When I got there, my mom was throwing away things from a tub of my keepsake belongings from high school.

"Mom, why are you throwing those away? Those are important to me." Even though I knew it was dementia, at this moment, dementia looked exactly like my mom.

"We don't need these. We haven't used this stuff in years," she said, tossing more in the dumpster.

I stood up on the four-wheeler and peeked into the dumpster. My letterman's jacket was in a pile of dirty diapers. She was about to throw my choir medals in when I caught them.

"These are mine. Stop," I said.

She was mad. "Those are mine! They're not yours! They're mine, and I don't want them anymore!" She sounded drunk, and I wondered if she was dehydrated.

"Look, Mom, this says Amelia Boyd. That's me. These are mine." And as I said it, I felt as helpless as the fourteen-year-old Amelia had when she placed the medal in the box, knowing her mom was not there to hear her earn it.

I had taken solos to districts and received ones so that I could go on to state all four years of high school, even during the years that I was living alone and raising myself. My mom had not been there for me then, and now there was no chance of ever winning her or having her be there for me. She was still trying to throw away my things. I grabbed my yearbook with my name engraved on the cover out of her hand.

"See, Mom? This is mine. That says Amelia Boyd."

"I'm Amelia Boyd! My name is Amelia Boyd! They're mine!" she yelled.

"Who are you? What's your name?" I asked gently. She had not yet forgotten her own name until that day.

"Amelia Boyd. That's me!" she yelled.

I just gave up. I let her throw all my things away. She was suffering and struggling so badly, and no one was coming to help. I was arguing with a person who was losing her mind and then arguing about her with a person who never had a mind to lose.

"She's down there throwing all my stuff away and telling me she's me," I said when I got back down to the force breaking table, wiping tears off my cheeks.

"Do what?" Frank asked.

"She says she's Amelia Boyd, and those are her choir medals, her graduation cap and gown. She's throwing it all away," I said.

I wasn't sad that my belongings were gone. I was devastated that he'd fully broken my mom to unrepairable heights. He responded by saying we better get busy working dogs.

I could feel the weight of simply being around Frank putting a strain on my mental health. I could feel parts of my brain and personality being too tired to shine and their lights turning off and going black, even in the five years I had to work with him, being around him far too often.

My mom had been married to him for thirty years, and I thought about that in terms of if I had to live with him, how much of him could my brain take? I thought she probably had started to lose her mind within the first year of their marriage. He steals a person's spirit through many different avenues–telling them they're worthless, never letting them speak, making them listen to his lecture for hours, controlling their every decision and move because they don't want him to yell at them for how they did or did not do something, yelling at them and calling them names, never listening to their needs for something to change, never compromising, and involving them in doing things that are so ridiculously, unimaginably stupid and dangerous that they forget who they are in order to simply survive.

In my everyday life, even when I was not around him, I found myself thinking what he would be thinking or what he would think, rather than my own thoughts. The barista would be pouring my coffee, and I would think, *"She wouldn't be wearing that low-cut top if she didn't want everyone to look at her."*

A thought like that one would pop into my mind when the

previous me would not have been thinking about another woman's clothing choices at all, ever.

*"That little girl needs to wear a longer dress,"* would pop into my mind, and I would feel queasy because I knew I was trying to protect her from men like Frank, but how long before I was thinking that little girl wants men to look at her in that dress like I knew Frank was thinking?

It sickened me. I judged everyone now because I had been exposed to his judgment of everyone other than himself.

The Covid vaccine had just come out, and he was so convinced that it was turning us all into robots that he spoke in depth, to customers, while I sat embarrassed, trying to figure out how crazy these people must think he was, but none of them wanted to argue with someone who was obviously unhinged. He thought the Covid vaccine was putting lead, metal, and other ingredients inside of human bodies so that eventually we would all be robots. He was saying this out loud. He thought he had proof and would tell customers all about it.

It's unfathomable to me how anyone could ever trust him enough after five minutes of being around him to leave their dog with him.

If someone dropped their dog off at the kennel while I was there, I would think diligently about where to house the new dog so it would be safe under our care. German dogs are incredibly territorial, and a new one that had been a pet inside of a house most of his life would not usually be a competitor in a fight with a dog who had been in a kennel and in many fights.

Frank's dogs started scrapping when they were puppies, and by the time they were six months old, they'd had an ear ripped or a tender paw from a battle that got too rough. Frank had been raising and training these animals for thirty years, and yet he still lackadaisically tossed dogs in with whomever was closest or whichever kennel had only one dog in it, without thinking about the personality of the dog, without checking with me or thinking about whether a dog had been in a fight before.

If I had left the kennel for the day, a new dog could end up tossed in with anyone. It really worried me when he would tell me a customer was bringing a dog later in the evening after I was home for the night, but I had too many other things to worry about.

I had worried every evening of my life since he entered my life that he was going to lose his temper badly enough, and my mom wouldn't be able to run away in time, and he would kill her, but now I knew she was helpless and unable to run away in time. Every night, when the dogs would start to howl, I would ask myself, *"Is it a coyote that they are barking at, or is it my mom's screaming in pain that has them riled up? Should I go down there and see, or will he hurt me too?"* Now, I had the new worry of, *"What if he fell asleep watching a movie and she got up and walked out the door and got lost, or are the dogs barking because she's hurt and he's asleep? What if she's cold, hungry, thirsty?"*

A few times, I had noticed she had gone outside and tried to do chores in the evenings because she had left hoses where the dogs could tear them up. Even as a child, I knew the number one rule of the kennel was to keep the hoses away from the dogs because if they tore them up, they could get pieces of hose stuck in their intestines and die. I triple checked my hose placement every time I walked away from a hose, and still somehow, some mornings, there would be hose everywhere. Sometimes when I walked out to do chores in the morning, the water had been left on all night.

One night, I heard a dog screaming and shrieking for hours. I tried to sit and have my prayers that morning before dawn, but the way the dogs had been going on and on for so long down there, right behind my mom and Frank's house, I couldn't stop worrying long enough to even pray. I grabbed my flashlight and skipped going inside the house to feed my mom breakfast and went straight out to where the screaming was coming from. Shining my light on the big kennel, I could see blood everywhere. There was so much blood it had pooled in four of the twelve kennels and was running down into the washout. The dogs got louder as they always did when something was wrong.

In the second kennel, Frank had put the new dog who had arrived the previous evening, in with a male who was not only incredibly violent but extremely unintelligent. I opened the door and grabbed the new dog's collar, pulled him out of the kennel and shut the door. I hooked the dog up to the roader and just as the sun started to rise, I inspected his wounds. The poor thing was a male who had been raped all night long. Frank had put him in with a male and they were right next to a female who was in heat.

I ran into the house to tell Frank I needed help. "You've got a new dog out here injured really badly," I said.

He took a sip of his coffee and kept sitting at his desk.

"No, I mean you need to get out here right now," I said.

He slowly stood up and put on his boots. I had time to process that he knew there was a new dog out there, not even thirty yards away from his front door, that had been screaming all night and that it was a living, breathing animal whom people loved, and he did not get up and go check on the pup. This dog was much smaller than normal bird dogs. I had hooked up the new dog and Frank told me his name was Truman.

Frank nonchalantly unhooked the dog and flipped him over on his back.

I looked at the dog's wounds more carefully and because of their appearance, I said, "That's not a male. That's a female."

Then Frank and I looked at each other and realized that was just how this dog looked now. We both sadly shook our heads. The dog's testicles had been sawed open, and because Frank was too cheap to ever call the vet and the vet was no longer working with Frank anyway, we were carrying Truman over to the force breaking table so that Frank could crudely sew Truman up while I held him down.

This pathetic excuse for a man can't even take care of animals, and every night I had to leave my childlike mother in his care.

# CHAPTER EIGHTY-NINE

Every day, there was a new episode proving to Frank that my mom needed someone taking care of her, and everyday Frank would either tell me to flat-out shut up and get off his back about it or tell me there was no one to help us.

"I noticed her hair looks like it hasn't been washed in a long time, and she doesn't smell like she's been showering," I told him.

"You think I don't notice that? I have to live with the nasty thing. I have to sit in the truck with that awful smelling woman," he'd say.

"Don't you think it's because she can't remember how to take a shower?" I asked.

For that entire summer, three full months, I would beg Frank to let me help my mom take a shower, and he would tell me that she knew how to shower but that she just didn't want to because she was lazy and difficult. He had this entire scenario in his mind where she was getting her hair wet to trick him but not actually showering.

I blatantly pointed out his stupidity. "So you think she's going in there and getting her hair wet to avoid showering so that she can get yelled at and make you mad?" I asked. "A woman who had no problems showering before but now has dementia and is now, coincidentally, choosing to lie to you and get yelled at over simply showering?"

Even he knew how stupid he sounded.

It was a hot, sweaty August, and my mom and other women in my family were prone to urinary tract infections. Now it was time for me to bring the words like "neglect" and "elder abuse" into the conversation again. The first few times I mentioned that if my mom wasn't getting herself clean in the shower, she could end up with a UTI, and that those hurt like fire and drive people crazy, and that she'd need medicine for it if she had one, he told me that he was not going to discuss, "nasty woman's issues," with me.

I told him that if she got sick and died because she had an infection or because she wandered off and hurt herself that he would be held liable and could even go to prison. He continued to ignore me.

One Sunday afternoon, Frank called me and said, "Uh, could you come down here please, Amelia?"

I handed my daughter my baby and drove down to see what he needed. I was in panic mode because he never called me on a Sunday. I had already done the kennel maintenance before church, and he wanted me to remember the rest of the Sabbath and keep it Holy, so if he was asking for help, it must be bad.

My mom was sitting on the couch in a daze when I walked in their door. "She fell," he said from his desk chair.

"Fell where and how?" I asked.

"She'd gone out to clean kennels. I thought it was good for her, but I went out to check on her a couple of hours later, and she was just sitting on the trailer, covered in dog crap. It's all in her hair and all over her back. I saw where she'd slipped and fallen in the washout. There was a big smear of dog crap. I'm guessing she fell and smacked her head. Her glasses were lying there in the wash out." He was talking, and I was looking at my tiny mom, who had lost sixty pounds over the last few months, forgetting to eat. She looked like a little kid.

He'd fallen asleep on the couch, and she'd wandered outside. His wife, whom the Bible he thumped straight into our noses told him to cherish and respect, had slipped and fallen in dog shit because he'd robbed her of every mental faculty. She did not know what to do when that had happened, and my heart broke. Knowing she'd gotten hurt when I was so close but so far away, all of my childhood fears were happening before my eyes.

"Anyway, she's being stubborn." He was still talking. "Maybe you can get her to shower and get some clean clothes on her."

"Come on, Mom," I said, helping her off the couch.

It was the first time I had to give my own mom a shower. She had no humility. She had no idea she wasn't supposed to be nude in front of me. I helped her take her clothes off, and I asked her to try to turn the water on. She did it, and it was way too hot.

"See? It gets too hot, so you just dip your head in like this."

She couldn't remember how to set the temperature, and that was one of the reasons she couldn't shower herself. I set the temperature and washed her hair twice, first to get the dog shit out and again to try to scrub the months and months' worth of dead skin off of her scalp.

I showed her how to wash her body, but when I said, "Don't forget your feet," she didn't know what I meant.

I dried her off and got her dressed, and while I brushed her hair, I knew that I would now be the person who attended to my mom's hygiene and that I was going to have to put my foot down so firmly on Frank's throat that he had to let that be.

I dressed my mom, sat her down at the kitchen table, and made her a sandwich. I got her a glass of water and a glass of milk, and I sat across from Frank and told him she had absolutely no idea how to take a shower. I told him that I was going to give her a shower every other day. I could see in his eyes that he had overheard me in the bathroom giving her instructions, having to say, "No that's not the shampoo," or, "No, your foot. We're washing your foot—no, your feet. Here, here, Mom. I'll do it."

"She also had on two pairs of underwear," I said. "Do you know why?"

There were tears in his eyes. This was all starting to become real to him, and he was a child. I had to remember they were both children.

"She had on the most filthy, poopy, underwear I've seen on an adult and a cleaner pair over them. She is totally confused. I told you months ago that she was not remembering to flush the toilet and that I knew she wasn't remembering to wipe because there was no toilet paper in the toilet and now, she's wearing multiple pairs of filthy underwear. Your wife is sick. She needs help. She cannot give herself a shower, or medicate herself, or dress herself, or brush her own teeth or hair, and you are just going to have to admit that and let me do those things for her," I said firmly.

He was crying, and I knew he was finally allowing himself to be vulnerable enough that I could stand up and walk into the kitchen and see what her medication situation looked like. I opened the bottles, and Frank was still crying, so he didn't stop me.

"Look," I said, showing him the contents of her three medications, one of which was for high blood pressure and the other two were supposed to be for preventing her dementia from getting worse. They were all mixed up. "There are blue pills in the white pill bottle and gray pills are in the blue pill bottle." I put the lids on them and put them back where they belonged.

"Mom, can you come over here and show me how you take your medicine, please?" I asked.

My mom came over to the counter and tried to open the pill bottle but could not remember how the childproof caps worked and kept spinning the lid around and around then instead of giving up like I'm sure she did most days and just not taking her pills, because Frank was watching, she got a steak knife out of the drawer and tried to saw into the lid. I took it out of her hand and walked her over to the couch where she started to doze off.

Frank and I had a conversation about how, with this disease, I tried to tell him, it would get worse. "She will not be able to feed herself next," I said. "Then she will need to wear diapers, and eventually, she'll forget how to walk, talk, and eat. Eventually, she'll forget how to swallow, and that is how she will die."

He didn't believe anything he had not seen. He was still talking about how Jesus was going to make her better, how she was going to make a full recovery and be her old self again when I left, but he did agree to let me take care of her hygiene every morning and every night, shower her every other day, and administer her medication.

From then on, most of our conversations were concerning my mom's health and how thin taking care of two households, the kennel, both of my children, and my mom was spreading me, and how we needed help. Frank and I were both in agreement for the first and one of only two times.

We were in agreement this time that Chad should be helping. He should be the one working dogs. He should be helping with the kennel paperwork, and his wife should be sitting with my mom during the day so that my thirteen-year-old did not have to. The other thing Frank and I agreed on was that Chad and his latest wife were selfish.

As Frank worded it, "Chad's an idiot, Amelia. That's all there is to it."

His own dad was saying this about him. I tried to imagine my dad bad-mouthing me in that manner, and I could not even imagine it.

"Chad is an opportunist. He goes where he sees an opportunity. He's selfish, and he's always been an idiot," Frank said.

Chad had a nearly finished, gigantic house on the property, twenty-five acres, and a lucrative business that he and he alone would inherit, and he couldn't come to help with his mom who was dying of dementia and being mistreated at the hand of his dad.

If Chad had been there, everything would have been different. He could have told his dad that our mom needed proper care, or showers, or fed more often, or more than one check up at the doctor each year. He could have been out there washing that kennel so that she hadn't been. His new wife could have taken her turn sitting with her mother-in-law so that my mom hadn't wandered off. So many things would have been different had we had the help of two more adults.

So, I would text Chad or call him when something would happen and I needed his help, and he'd either ignore me or tell me he was going to work on the issue but never did.

Daily, I would mention needing his help to his dad, and he would remind me, "Chad is an idiot."

After feeding my children dinner and getting the baby ready for bed every night, Ella would lay down with Henry so I could go get my mom ready for bed. She'd forgotten which clothes were pajamas, and she tried to sleep in her jeans. She'd forgotten how to brush her teeth. One evening while I was brushing her teeth, I noticed a green bruise on her forehead in the shape of a thumb and fingerprints.

"What happened to your face?" I stood behind her and looked at her face in the mirror.

"He squeezed my face like this." She started to do it herself, flinched, winced, and stopped herself.

The rage of a league of soldiers raced through every cell in my body. I was standing in the same bathroom where a six-year-old me had been helpless against this tormentor. I wasn't six anymore.

"Why does she have a bruise on her face?" I was in his face.

He could have hit me with his entire six foot five, two-hundred-and-eighty-pound body, and I wouldn't have felt it.

"Now, calm down a minute." He sounded like a teenage boy in trouble.

"Why does she have green fingerprint bruises on her face?!" I was screaming.

I stood in his living room, listening to him tell me a story about how she had gotten stung by a wasp, and he had to restrain her because she was screaming and flailing around.

The shift in energy and my extreme outburst had caused my mom to be lucid for a moment, long enough to explain to me that she had put on her shoe and there was a wasp in it, and it stung her foot. She dumped it out of her shoe, and it flew up and got stuck in her hair. She was screaming trying to get it out of her hair, and that's when Frank started trying to kill her.

"He was trying to kill me!" she said.

I sat down. I was so tired of all of this shit, and I had no idea why Jesus had chosen me to solve it and figure it out. It was clear to me that He picked me a long time ago, and I thought in the very bottom of my heart that the Lord knew these experiences were the only way to show me true selflessness, kindness, patience, faith, and love, but in these moments I would have to call on Him to speak for me. He took over so that I didn't kill Frank Hudson that night.

"She's always screaming that I'm gonna kill her." He was whining.

"Do me a favor, Frank, and point to the place in your house where you held her still and subdued her so that she stopped screaming and flailing around," I said.

Frank pointed to the area in front of their front door. "Okay, and do me a favor, Frank, and point to the place in your house where you grabbed her by the back of the head and body slammed her by her hair the first time she ever tried to leave you. It's the same spot. The front door. She's been running away from you causing of her bodily harm for thirty years, so how can you not fucking see that?!"

"Hey!" he yelled because I had said the word, "fucking."

"No, you are going to sit there and listen. Someone squeezes my mom's face hard enough to leave fingerprints, they just sit there and listen. This woman has two sons. Both of them will happily kill you if you ever lay another finger on her again. Both of them. Happily."

He knew it was true.

I went on, "And one of those sons is a Boyd. I am a Boyd, and I can tell you but you already know, that means something around here. My brother Jordan is friends with everyone—sheriffs, police officers, judges, and probably most of the jury in this part of the state. You will never, ever touch her again."

I tried to explain to Frank that he had caused her to think he was going to kill her their entire marriage and that everyone who knew her thought he was going to kill her. He completely ignored and dismissed me on that facet of the problem, but he did agree to never be physical with her again. I knew he could not make that promise because he was too immature to control his temper.

"How do we get her to stop screaming and yelling all the time?" he asked.

I tried again. "Imagine all day every day, your urethra feels like it's on fire. She has a UTI. She needs an antibiotic to kill an infection she's had for months in an area of her body that has a lot of nerve endings and is very sensitive. She needs medical attention."

Again, he told me he wasn't going to discuss "woman's issues," and I went home and worried about my mom.

# CHAPTER NINETY

I'm sure I could not have been a very good or pleasant friend during most of my life, but certainly not during those years when I was taking care of so many people and animals and never myself. I took a ten-minute shower every day when I got home from the kennel in order to wash the dog shit off myself before taking my youngest baby from my oldest baby. I got up an hour before daylight to pray and other than that, I did not have a moment to myself or for my friends.

I was able to text but never had the time, money, or energy to hang out in person. I texted the wonderful friends I had left often about how stressed out and miserable I was. They all had the same reactions to the way I was being treated by Frank.

"It's like you're a slave."

"You talk about yourself like you are mud."

"I wish there was a way for you to leave."

"Does he not understand basic, human bodily functions?"

Frank did not. He didn't understand anything about human anatomy. Ever since he had colon cancer and the surgeons removed multiple inches of his intestine, every time he ate, he instantly needed the restroom.

He would ask me at least once a week, "How does eating make me have to immediately go to the bathroom? I mean, how does it know?"

I would start out with words like "digestive system," and "mastication," but he'd stop listening so that we could almost have that conversation again next week, and that's what we did about every important topic. We would almost have the conversation, and he would get overwhelmed, confused, or think that because I was a woman, I could not possibly know what I was talking about. I started to pray that a man would intervene and tell him what he needed to understand.

We were showing a few dogs to three potential customers one morning in the bird field when my mom wandered out of her house to walk through the field to my house. These three men and Frank ignored my mom, and Frank ignored my plea to help her down to my house so she didn't get hurt with the chaos of multiple people, multiple dogs, and multiple guns involved.

These particular dogs were the type that I referred to as 'maniacs' and Frank called, "lawn mowers on the loose." They were high energy, muscular, male dogs who weighed about sixty to eighty pounds each. These three dogs could have really hurt someone if they were running and slammed into someone's leg, which had happened to me regularly.

The rule was, if one of the dogs ran in and didn't want to come out and hunt, and you happened to be standing near the disobedient dog, you ignore him until the hunters can get his attention and get him focused on hunting and back out into the field. My mom had taught me that rule when I was about eight years old because, if you talk to or pet the dog, he'll never remember to return to hunting.

However, my mom had forgotten the rule, and when one of the maniacs ran up to her, she started trying to walk him back out toward us. The dog knocked her down into the mud and started jumping all over her. Another of the hyper dogs found this to be interesting, so he started to playfully jump all over my mom, who could not catch her breath, get the dogs off her, or stand up.

I was running through the field from about fifty yards away to help her, and when I got up to where she'd fallen, I grabbed one of the dogs by the collar and went to hook him up, thinking that Frank would be right behind me to get the other dog off his wife–his sick, weak, sixty-five-year-old wife, who was lying in the mud being jumped on by a seventy-pound dog. He was not behind me. He stayed in the field with the other three men. Four grown men watched this happen.

I caught the other dog, hooked him up, and helped my mom up. I sat her on the bench to clean her up, I gave her my water bottle and got the mud off her face.

When Frank and the customers walked back over to us, Frank asked my mom, "What's the matter, dear? Sick of standing around?" and the men laughed.

They made me sick. I had a difficult time holding my tongue. I wanted to call these men's wives and tell them congratulations on their despicable choice in Neanderthals.

Frank's friend Clark would show up randomly, and I was always happy when he was there because the two of them would spend the entire dog working day talking instead of torturing dogs or torturing me. Frank would share details of my mom's dementia with Clark that he would not open up about with anyone, including me. Even though I was right there listening, I was invisible if a man ever came to see Frank. This became beneficial to me because I could not only learn things about how to make Frank do things, but I could also make a fool of Frank, and he could not retaliate.

If they were not discussing my mom and her outbursts, they were feeding off one another's asinine views of the world. "Women should not be allowed to be in the military," was a favorite topic. It made all of them sick to see women in the military.

"For one thing," Frank said, "women should be home raising their children. You should absolutely, positively, not be allowed to be deployed or overseas if you are a mother with young children at home. That's what's wrong with this country. Mothers don't raise their own kids anymore. They're off having careers," he rambled.

This was too perfect an opportunity for me to pass up. "I'm glad you feel that way now, Frank, since you didn't see it that way between 1993 and 2008," I said.

"Nineteen ninety-three and 2008?" he asked, perplexed.

"Yeah, the years Ruby and I did not have a mother to raise us," I said, and they went back to their conversation.

Even though I knew it never did any good to say those things to someone who was in a permanent state of denial, I still said it. It helped the six and sixteen-year-old versions of me get some closure. I said it for Ruby and Amelia.

Clark was as closed-minded as Frank socially and politically, but he at least was in touch with reality enough to see how gone my mom was and that Frank needed to take some steps to ensure her health and safety.

One afternoon after Clark left, Frank asked me, "Did you know I could get in trouble if something happened to your mom?"

I was walking to my car to leave for the evening and wondering where my mom was at the moment. "Yes!" I answered him emphatically. "I have been telling you that for almost a full year. It's called neglect and elder abuse." I could not believe he had never heard me.

"That's exactly what Clark called it," he said. "I could go to prison?" He was amazed.

"I have been telling you that for a year." I was annoyed and still looking around for my mom before leaving her to be with him until it was time for me to get her ready for bed, and then I heard her screaming. I ran to her. Frank did not follow to help. He just stood there in the driveway next to my car.

I went behind his house where my mom was frantically screaming, "Ow!" and "Help!" When I got to her, I saw Oreo, one of the brood mommas, had gotten loose. When my mom tried to catch her, she got her fingers twisted all up in Oreo's chain collar. My mom was screaming, and Oreo was hopping around, pulling on my mom's twisted fingers even harder.

I couldn't breathe. The stress, the urgency, and the fact that I wasn't strong enough to undo the chain and hold the dog still at the same time had caused me to start to sweat and panic. This was a two-person job.

I hollered, "Whoa!" to Oreo, which means 'stop,' to a bird dog.

By some miracle, Oreo, who hadn't been hunting in years, remembered the command and froze. My mom slipped her fingers out from under the collar, and I put Oreo away and walked back over to Frank next to my car. He simply told me to have a good rest of my evening, and he'd see me at, "getting Mom ready for bedtime," as he called it.

Those horrible days slid into each other, and I became lost in them. Without my friends there in my phone listening to me tell my story and offering me emotional support, I would not have made it. I would have taken my own life. Charlotte and I would often discuss how my brain was changing due to being yelled at and belittled by Frank and how chronic stress was the fastest way to lose brain cells. We would talk about how that was exactly what had happened to my mom's brain and how being treated like shit would make anyone's brain turn to mush. People need kindness, love, peace, and rest. I had not had a moment of rest in years.

On days when I was late getting home because a dog had gotten loose, or my mom had run off because she was upset, or she'd gotten hurt, my teenager would have to watch my baby for longer. I do not blame Ella in the least for talking back, complaining, and even throwing tantrums. She was thirteen and constantly working too. If she wasn't watching her two-year-old brother or both her brother and her grandma who had a disease that caused her to wander around and pace, making my daughter very anxious, she was being asked to mow, wash kennels, or help with the horses or housework.

We needed help, or my mom needed to go to a facility where she could be cared for and nurtured. Where she was not getting knocked down, jumped on, or otherwise hurt by dogs. Where she could have peace and no longer be tortured by Frank.

I sat down one evening and composed a letter to my mom's doctor, whom she'd been seeing once a year. It had been six months, and we had six months more to go, but I was completely convinced that my mom had a urinary tract infection and that she needed an antibiotic for that and other things that she needed. I had researched dementia, and I believed she needed speech therapy, rest, nutrition, hydration, and someone to help her in the bathroom. I could not be there all the time, and she was like a baby now. I tried to explain to Dr. Spiva in my letter about how Frank was controlling, in denial, and very uninformed. I tried to explain that giving instructions to Frank about my mom's health was not ever going to benefit my mom.

As I folded the letter and put it in the envelope, I remembered a time one of the "lawn mowers on the loose," had pissed Frank off. The dog was just too stupid for me to see any reason to continue to try to train him, and to me the best solution for those dogs was to find a nice family who liked dogs but didn't want to hunt. We could give the dogs away to nice families if they weren't going to train.

Frank said we couldn't do that because we'd get the reputation of a kennel that throws junk and couldn't make any good, intelligent, well-bred pups.

I said, "Or, we'd have the reputation of a kennel who doesn't shoot their dogs in the head simply because they don't like birds." Of course, I was ignored.

This particular maniac could not, for the literal life of him, figure out that when Frank blew his whistle, that meant to come here. Instead, the dog would run away. He was a pretty fella with a dark brown saddle, white legs with ticking on them, and he was muscular, healthy, and nice looking. He was just dumber than a brick.

Frank blew his whistle, pulled on the check cord while saying, "Here," and drew him in. Then, he would let him go. After repeating this several times, usually a pup of this age, about eight months old, would understand.

The pup kept running away. I wondered if maybe some dogs just didn't like Frank, and often, they would come to me and not him. We would both remark on how this must be the case, but not with this puppy. He wouldn't come to me either. He just wasn't getting it, and the longer Frank stood out there in the August heat, blowing his whistle at a dog who was ignoring him, the more enraged he became.

"You can take a break, Amelia," was a phrase I hated to hear. That phrase meant Frank was going to hurt a dog and didn't want me to be involved.

Frank picked the dog up by the collar, dangling him in the air, cutting off his oxygen, and kicking him in the gut the entire way over to the pond, Frank kicked the suffocating dog, whose eyes were starting to dim, in the stomach once more before throwing him into the pond. That day was hot and humid. All of the dogs were panting. It was at least 100 degrees outside, and this dog was already unable to breathe and at death's doorstep when he was thrown into the water. Now, he was drowning.

Frank pulled him back up, gave him mouth to mouth, waited for the dog to come to, and then started to whip the fire out of him with the end of the check cord. At this point, Frank had to catch his own breath, and after he recovered, he started the whole process over. He lifted the dog by the collar until he couldn't breathe, kicked him the whole time, and threw him in the water again. This time, he left him out there in the pond longer. He reeled him in, gave him mouth to mouth, let him regain consciousness, and whipped him senselessly with the end of the check cord. About two more times of this, and Frank dragged the nearly dead puppy over to the bench to get himself a cup of coffee.

"You know why I had to do that, don't you?" he asked.

I wanted to say, "Because you are actually a demon, and for some reason, I can see you? You're not even human. There's no way you're human," but I couldn't breathe either.

The puppy was foaming at the mouth and did not even look like a dog any longer. He looked like something that had been dead in the hot sun by the side of the road.

"I had to completely break him and show him who's in charge. Some of them you have to almost kill. I brought many a dog back from the dead with CPR," he said.

I took the letter I'd written to Dr. Spiva and threw it in the trash. It was too scary. It was too risky. What if the doctor didn't believe me or was too chauvinistic to believe me over the patient's husband? After being around Frank for so long and seeing the true horrors that he was capable of with my own eyes, I was too afraid to run away. I was too scared to send a letter.

I was always terrified.

# CHAPTER NINETY-ONE

In the evenings, when I would drive down the road to Frank and my mom's house to get her ready for bed, I would instantly know how their house was going to smell before I even got out of my car. If there was a pair of Frank's jeans draped over the porch railing, it was going to smell like pure shit in their house when I walked in the door.

He would be sitting in the living room in his underwear, after shitting himself, taking his jeans off, changing his drawers and then going out to the yard to hose off and air out the soiled clothing. He would then be so exhausted from the episode, that he didn't have the energy to redress himself and would usually be dozing off in the chair in his underwear when I walked through the door.

The dog Frank had tried to break by almost drowning repeatedly had somehow recovered and lived to see another day, but as I predicted in the first place, eventually, a couple of weeks later, it was culled, or shot in the head for not training out. I asked my daughter Ella if he'd ever choked out or nearly drowned a dog in front of her, done CPR only to re-suffocate the animal again, and she said the first time he had done that in front of her, she was six or seven years old.

"He does that when he feels out of control. He does that to dogs because it makes him feel like a big, powerful man when he can't control the rest of his life. He actually enjoys it," my teenager, who was wise beyond her years, explained.

If I had known Frank was doing things like that in front of her, we would have never stayed another second. Unfortunately, he had brainwashed her into never telling me anything. Unfortunately, there are evil, and yet strangely powerful, people who can convince our children not to tell us things even when we ask all of the right questions. Throughout her childhood, I asked Ella about abuse regarding Frank and Chad. Frank had trained her never to tell me, her mom, the person she trusted the most.

Now, Ella not only has to process the abuse, the horrors, she saw, heard, felt, and endured at the hand of Frank, but she also has to learn how to talk about her emotions. She has to learn how to voice especially negative emotions. Currently, she explodes and tries to find blame in other people when something goes wrong because as a small child, emotional pain was something she was trained to hide from and to hide from me. Therapy, helping her and loving her through it, a lot of time and patience, will turn her into a healthy, well adjusted, woman, a woman that I already admire and can see her becoming, but her childhood was rotten and unhealthy, and for that, I can never apologize enough.

Out of control. I really can't think of anything that would make me feel more out of control than shitting my pants every day and not having a strong enough grasp of human anatomy, nutrition, proper diet, or the humbleness to just wear an adult diaper so I didn't make an enormous mess. I walked into their house knowing it would stink because that evening there were two pairs of jeans air drying on the porch, but I wasn't prepared for the mess I was walking into.

Frank was on his hands and knees in the hallway leading to the bathroom, trying to clean up his own poop with paper towels. I couldn't get my mom ready for bed without walking down that hallway, and I knew she was probably seconds away from stepping in poop as it were, simply because she was like a toddler now, and she wandered around like a two-year-old. Frank looked up at me from the floor wearing nothing but his underwear, and I felt like lecturing him on modesty and asking him why it applied only to women and children but not to him.

Instead, I said, "I'll clean this up if you keep her out of it while I do."

I got a bucket of scalding hot, soapy water and the cleaning gloves I left under their sink from when I cleaned out their nasty, moldy, fridge and their inches of caked-on greasy stove. I knelt in the hallway and scrubbed up poop. I vacuumed. I got my gloves that I kept under their bathroom sink and the cleaning products I used to scrub their bathroom and cleaned up the mess he made on his way to the toilet.

Often, when someone who's had colon cancer goes to the bathroom, they'll make a mess all over the walls. I had started cleaning up poop messes off the toilet and walls around the toilet daily because, for one thing, it was incredibly embarrassing when a customer would ask to use the restroom, and secondly, my mom shouldn't have to use a disgusting bathroom when she spent her entire life cleaning up toilets for other people. So, I cleaned up his literal shit, and yet, he wouldn't even call and make his wife a doctor's appointment.

Each morning when we would begin to work dogs, Frank would look more and more tired and worn out. Neither he nor my mom were sleeping at night because my mom would get up and wander around the house. She would get up in the middle of the night, put on her clothes, and ask if it was morning yet. She would bang on the walls, demanding food. She tripped and fell, hitting her face on his desk. She could not be still at night, and he would ask me what to do about it but never liked my answer.

"Can we like, wear her out more during the day or something?" he'd ask.

"She has an infection." I would try again. "She has an infection and maybe even other things wrong with her that we don't even know about. She's said she can't see out of her right eye a few times lately, and I know she has a urinary tract infection."

"Oh malarkey! No more of this UTI crap!" He was yelling now.

"It's not crap! They hurt. It's not a women's issue. Men can get them too. They hurt, they can cause a fever, they irritate you, they can make you really tired, and they drive you nuts." Now, I was yelling. "She's needed to see her doctor every six weeks for at least a year because she can't tell us what's wrong with her anymore. He can do tests and check."

"Do you wanna know whose health you should really be worried about, Amelia?" he asked. "Your own!" I could tell by his tone and facial expression that he really thought he was about to school me. "You're gonna have a heart attack or a stroke walking around here looking like a fat clown. Look at yourself! What do you weigh? Four hundred pounds?" He was serious.

"Oh, you want to talk about my weight?" I asked. "I started to gain weight when I was little and taken away from my mom. I comforted myself with food because I didn't have a mom. I was never taught to eat right as a child because I was feeding myself every day and not old enough to cook."

*"Why am I saying this? I am playing into his game."*

"Yeah. Sure. Okay. Keep telling yourself that. You need to put down the fork," was his response. "Look how fat you are and how you dress like a clown. It's actually embarrassing. It should embarrass you. It embarrasses me when customers see you." His insults sounded like something a thirteen-year-old boy would say, and for some reason, I still don't know why, I answered him.

"My weight embarrasses you in front of customers, but the actual poop all over the walls in your bathroom doesn't?" I asked. "Customers go in your bathroom, and they see the poop sprayed all over the walls, and all you would have to do is wipe that off, but my weight is what embarrasses you?"

"Why do you keep bringing that up? I had cancer. There's nothing I can do about going to the bathroom the way I do," he said.

"You can clean it up…." I trailed off, realizing for the first time that he was misunderstanding me. I was not giving him a hard time for being sick or having cancer. I was saying my weight should be less embarrassing to customers than poop all over the walls of the bathroom. "I've tried to lose weight my entire life. If you don't like me working here, I would be happy to never set foot on this place again," I said.

"Well, why don't you just stop eating for a while?" he asked.

"You want me to get up at five o'clock every morning, feed your wife breakfast, feed, water, and clean up after one hundred and fifty dogs, train dogs for six hours in the August heat in the field, put the dogs and the birds away, go home and take care of a toddler and a teenager, make their meals, clean their house, run their errands and do their laundry, then come back to your house, get your wife ready for bed, do some of your housework, laundry and paperwork, without eating?" I asked.

"That's what I do when I start to notice I've put on a few pounds. You can do it." He was serious. "I'll make a track for you around the field, and you can start jogging," he said.

"You think that I don't *move* enough? You think the problem is that I need to *move* more? I walk ten miles even before noon every day," I said.

"Well, look at how you walk, Amelia. You don't walk. You waddle," he said.

"Figure it all out yourself, Frank," I said. Then I got in my car and left.

On the way home, the two-minute drive, I cried. I was not crying because I was called fat. I've been called fat a billion times in my life. I was not crying because he had taken the real issue, my mother's health, and turned it into something about me so he could upset me enough that I dropped the real problem.

I was not crying because I had told him over and over that I had a crack in my pubic bone from having a ten-pound baby, and it was difficult to run, step sideways, or even walk straight, and he'd ignored me every single time I had mentioned that injury. I was not crying because essentially, I had been asked to starve myself, exercise more, and called a fat clown that waddled.

I was crying because the battle was becoming so clearly impossible to win on my own, and I knew I was going to have to call a professional or call the police, and I didn't want to have to do it that way. I just wanted him to take her to the doctor!

When I pulled into my driveway, Frank had driven his truck through the field and was at my house before I was.

"So, you're just gonna quit? You're gonna give up?" he asked.

"I can't do this anymore, and if I'm such an embarrassingly fat clown, I'm probably not necessary around here anyway," was my response.

"Well, what will you do then? Go live in one of those apartments for Black folks in the city?" he asked.

"Frank, I don't know what that means, but insulting an entire race of people and me? I guess? By comparison? I guess that's what you were trying to do? But comparing me to Black people is not an insult to me. I wouldn't want to be compared to you, but you can compare me to any race of people all day, and I would not mind. And it's absolutely none of your business where we go. Thank God I'm not married to you so you can't follow me around and bully me into coming back. I will leave, and I will immediately call the police and have them do a wellness check on Mom. They'll see that you can't do all of this by yourself, and she'll be put in a facility with doctors and nurses who will actually take care of her," I said, walking into my house and shutting the door.

About three hours later, my mom and Frank pulled into my driveway. He had taken her to the doctor and made her an appointment there and one with the eye doctor. Then he stopped at Pizza Hut and brought my kids and me a large pizza. Calling me fat and then buying me a pizza was something my mom would have done when I was in my twenties. Now, it was Frank doing it. I had no stomach for anything more that day, but I decided to go ahead and go to work the next morning. Maybe with more prayers, things would be sorted out.

It turned out that Mom did have a very severe UTI and kidney infection. Frank was shocked, asking me how I could have known that, and still not listening to anything I said. I knew he was not ready to hear that her current doctor was simply a general practitioner and that Mom needed a specialist who dealt with dementia, but I decided to lay the foundation for that topic while he was being cooperative and somewhat listening to me so that I could build on that subject later.

Had she had a specialist, they may have warned us not to let her be put under anesthesia unless it was life or death because every time someone with dementia is put under, they don't come back the same. We had spent too much of our time and resources being in denial and arguing, so we didn't know that, and neither did the doctor who did her eye surgery. Her eye doctor could not get her to be still and stop moving, and even though people are not normally put under for that type of procedure, Mom was moving around and talking too much, so they put her to sleep. When she came to, she was so much worse than before.

# CHAPTER NINETY-TWO

The long black T-shirt and baggy black sweatpants tucked into mud boots that I had worn to work every single day for five years had been meticulously chosen, as was anything and everything worn in front of Frank. I had chosen baggy clothing because I had been told by him my entire life that tight jeans and shirts were immodest. I knew I would be lectured about modesty enough while working with him. I didn't want for it to be about me.

However, I knew from day one that I would also be made fun of by him at some point for my clothes being too baggy. I just didn't realize it would be in an argument where I was pleading for him to take my mom to the doctor and he was calling me, "A fat clown."

Frank took her to the doctor, who prescribed her an antibiotic for her UTI and nothing more because all they had done were a couple of tests. Frank had not brought a list of questions with him about what she should be doing during the day, what she should be eating, how long she should be sleeping or when she should be sleeping, whether or not she needed to be supervised or facilitated, whether she needed therapy or speech therapy, or why she was panicking and walking around at night. So, he came back from her doctor appointment smug about the fact that the doctor hadn't really said much, and none of our issues or problems had been solved.

I had called my brother Chad and told him the details of the "Fat clown," argument and the doctor's visits. I told Chad that Mom was starting to rapidly get worse. I didn't know at the time that she was getting worse because of the anesthesia, but she was getting worse so quickly, I didn't have time to try to understand why she was constantly wandering off or why she was becoming violent, even with Ella and me. When we were trying to redirect her from doing something dangerous, she'd yell and even try to hit us. When I tried to get her to eat or drink something, sometimes she'd cuss me out and yell at me. Frank said she was foul-mouthed and up all night cussing, yelling, and trying to run away. Chad said that he would go talk to his dad about putting her in a nursing home or getting her a nurse.

One morning at breakfast, I noticed that she could not remember what she was doing even long enough to eat an omelet. "Pick your fork back up, Mom. We're eating breakfast, and I've got to go out and do chores here in a minute," I said.

She could remember to take a bite, but then she'd set her fork down and forget what she was doing. I sat at the dining room table and fed her breakfast like a baby.

That table was where my very first memory in life took place. I loved that table back then. I was about two, maybe three, and I was sitting on top of the table in our dining room in the house where I lived with my mom, dad, and older brother and sister. Ruby had not even been born yet, and I was sitting on this very table, watching "Hey Dude" on the living room TV while my mom spoon fed me beef and vegetable soup. She was standing in front of me in a pink T-shirt, and I was gobbling up the soup. We were happy.

Another memory I had at that table was of my childhood birthday parties. One year, I sat there with my cake in front of me while everyone sang "Happy Birthday," and I thought to myself, even at three or four, *I hate this part!* The next year when they sang "Happy Birthday," I cried. I started to sob. *I hate this part because everyone is looking at me, and that is too much for me!"* I thought, but my mom thought I was crying because I'd gotten my leg stuck in the opening of the back of the chair. She bent down to rub my leg and hugged the tears off my cheeks. I sat up and ate my cake, perhaps in this very chair I was sitting in now.

I had memories of the weird meals my mom would prepare when I was little, back when she was Libby. She would give us food she liked, and it always turned out to be yummy. I was five, and it was lettuce wrapped chicken nuggets, or my first taste of tuna fish, or the time I was allowed to go get grapes out of the fridge by myself and oh, so many pizzas after church when even Jordan and Mellissa were there.

Then, one day, that table was in Frank's house instead., The table my dad bought. The table where I turned one, two, three, four, and five was now Frank's table, and he had to sit at the head of it no matter what. Even if he wasn't sitting at the table. Even if someone was sitting there to do a puzzle or to do the kennel paperwork, everyone knew better than to sit in Frank's chair at the head of the table. Now, I was spoon-feeding my mom, and there was no joy to be found in that situation no matter how hard I looked.

My mom still went grocery shopping with Frank, and for some reason, one week, he stopped at a health food store. He was all excited the next morning when we started working dogs because he thought that Jesus had sent angels to provide him with a cure. On their way out of the grocery store, a young man, presumably an angel, asked Frank if Mom had dementia.

When Frank told him yes, she did, the man gave him a business card and said, "I don't work for these people or anything, but you should give them a call," and walked away.

The card was that of a nutrition company called Youthclarity. The elderly lady on the phone, whom Frank also thought might be an angel, talked to Frank for three hours. She told him she was also a Christian and that she too had dealt with colon cancer, and she too had dementia. At one point, she asked Frank if my mom was dozing off.

"Actually, she's dozed off just now," he said. "How did you know that?"

The sales rep answered, "She's dying."

This response really took Frank by surprise. When I said it to him, it couldn't be true but when an elderly angel tells you over the phone, well, it has to be. So, he bought $3000 worth of Youthclarity. He bought hundreds of different vitamins and supplements that the woman told him he could put in a blender with fruit and milk and give my mom as a smoothie. The salesperson told him he could put all of the supplements in the same blender at once because Frank had complained about measuring and reading ingredients.

At this news, I started to cry. He thought I was crying tears of joy because Mom was finally going to be cured. I was crying because I knew that I was about to have to argue with a seven-year-old about giving my mom a lethal dose of the same vitamins.

A few days later, box after box of supplements began to show up. All of them had B12 in them. Most of them had vitamins A, B, C, D, and E in them. I tried to explain to him that we couldn't just give her sixty pills and three packets a day. The elderly angel of a saleswoman had even told him that he could just empty the capsules and pour the contents of the pills into her smoothies, every variety, at once. Most of the packets and supplements contained the same vitamins. I tried to explain that her body would not be able to handle that because her kidneys would shut down. He ignored me.

I went home, and this time, instead of calling Chad, I called his wife, Karen. I thought, *"She's a woman. She has a mom. Maybe she'll have enough empathy to make her husband go talk to his dad."*

I explained to both Chad and Karen on the phone that Frank was going to have me start making Mom smoothies every morning with way too many doses of the same vitamins in them and that the thought of accidentally killing my mom was making me vomit, shake, and I even had a fever.

"If he wants her to start taking supplements that's great, but she can't take sixty of the same vitamins in a smoothie and certainly not every morning and every night," I said.

They promised they would go talk to Frank, and when I showed up too, the three of us sat down and showed him the doses and percentages of each vitamin.

"That could kill her. It could cause her kidneys to shut down," I said.

"Honestly, I don't think it's possible to overdose on any vitamin other than B12," Chad chimed in. "So just be careful how many doses of B12 you give her."

I could not believe Chad could not participate in reality enough to see that encouraging his dad, who did not even want to read the ingredients of the supplements and had never been smart enough to handle figuring out each dose, was a horrible idea.

"They all have B12 in them, and normally, I would agree with you, but this is so many doses of the same thing that her kidneys will immediately start to pee out the leftover, extra vitamins, which will cause her to not only have accidents, but she'll become dehydrated, and because I can only be here to make sure she is drinking three glasses of water a day, her kidneys could shut down, and she could die. If she is given too much water to flush out the vitamins, what is the point? And if she is given too much water, it could also flush out the nutrients from the food I give her," I said.

Even as I write this two years later, my cheeks flush with fury. I can feel how tired I was and how much I was still trying to hold on to my mom and save her.

The decision that was made that night was to ignore me and go ahead and make the smoothies as long as Frank made sure she drank a lot of water throughout the day. The next morning, I caught myself pouring out half of the smoothie mixture when Frank wasn't looking and replacing it with milk before giving it to my mom. I felt like someone who would do something like pour half the wine out of a glass and replace it with juice before giving it to their child rather than to continue to argue with the world's most simple-minded narcissist, just like when I was a kid and I could not figure out why she wouldn't stand up for me. Sometimes, standing up for someone doesn't work. Sometimes prayer is the only thing that works.

The first morning after drinking the smoothie, my mom was outside following me around while I did kennel maintenance, and she peed and pooped her pants. "Oh no! I'm sorry! I didn't mean to! Oh, no, I've done it now! I'm horrible and awful!" She was shaken up.

"It's not your fault. It's not your fault," I tried not to cry as I held her hand and as we walked into the house, the big bad wolf was on our tails.

"What's going on in here?!" he yelled through the bathroom door, mad at me for going inside the house rather than working.

"The smoothie made her poop her pants, and I'm giving her a shower," I told Frank. He said nothing and went back outside.

While they were at church each week, I would slip out of church, drive to their house, open their extra fridge where he'd mixed up two gallons of smoothies for her for the week, pour them out and replace them with supplement free smoothies or smoothies with the right amount of supplements if I had time to measure before church let out.

I understood why my mom had chosen being sneaky and lying to him all of those years, but I didn't want to live my life that way. We had to get away.

# CHAPTER NINETY-THREE

The first time I met Chad's new wife Karen, I'd learned all I needed to know about her. I try not to judge books by their covers, but she willingly told people everything about herself in heaping doses. The first time I met her, my brother Chad yelled at me, called me names, and disrespected me in front of both of my children, his new girlfriend, and her infant.

Her baby, Sara, was only three months old when she met Chad, and despite having just been in an abusive relationship and just having a baby, Karen was not only ready to date again but ready to become pregnant by a guy who yells at his sister. She also found out in the middle of that conversation that he'd stolen $1500 from his sister, who was on maternity leave from her job and the sole provider for two children.

However, Karen didn't find out until well after she became pregnant with Chad's baby that he was still married to another woman, with whom he had a child and who had abandoned and not seen in five years.

Chad and Karen had another little girl, Becky, who was only fifteen months younger than her older sister Sara. As soon as Karen found out that Chad was still married to someone else, she didn't run away as fast as she could. No, she made him get a divorce so she could immediately get married to him.

Karen often bragged about not ever having read a book. She loudly told people at the most random and unrelated times that her own father was a pedophile and she had "drama of all dramas," written all over her. I tried to steer clear of her if at all possible, but because I needed my brother Chad's help, sometimes she was unavoidable. Somehow, she got the idea in her mind that we were friends, and she started asking me if I could watch her daughters, who were now one and two, while she helped Chad at work with a small business he was starting.

They lived in her family's house on her family's farm, and Chad had been using his father-in-law's equipment and heavy machinery to start up an excavation and demolition company. Sometimes, he needed Karen's help running one machine while he was running another, and they would leave their two girls with me even though I had a two-year-old too. I thought that if I helped them by watching the girls, they'd eventually help me when I called for help. Family used to mean something to me. I'll never be fooled by that with Chad again.

I remember back when my mom was Libby, I was little, Ruby was a baby, and we would take walks around our neighborhood with Ruby in the stroller at dusk. The sounds of frogs and cicadas used to be so soothing to me. I associated them with my mom, comfort, security, and serenity. We would walk home, and Mom would put on a movie she liked.

It seems like our dad, Jordan, and Mellissa were never home back then. I'm sure they were, but I only ever remember it being Ruby, our mom, and me. We watched *Dirty Dancing*, *Pretty Woman*, *The Bodyguard*, really anything with Kevin Costner, *Dances With Wolves*. We were too young to be paying attention to those movies, and all I knew was that I thought Whitney Houston and Julia Roberts were beautiful. I wanted to learn how to dance like Penny from *Dirty Dancing*. When Ruby and I got bigger, we'd practice The

Lift, but it never worked out, and we'd both fall down in a pile of giggles.

I remember the way I'd sit on my mom's left knee to get my right earring in and switch to her right knee to put my left earring in like clockwork before school every morning. She put me in outfits that matched perfectly. I remember Mrs. Cherryvale giving me the 'Most Fashionable Award' in kindergarten, and who could blame her? My mom had put me in a hound's tooth top and skirt combo with red trim and red earrings.

My mom cared. She poured every ounce of herself into her children, and then somehow, she just gave it all away. The combinations of reasons why she would do that would race through my mind as I'd help her change out of her pajamas into her clothes every morning and into her pajamas every night. *"Why did you do that, Mom?"* I'd always wanted to ask her, but now I knew I never could. No one will ever know.

She'd lost so much weight that when I found one of Ella's yellow T-shirts from when she was about ten in my mom's drawer, I went ahead and put it on her. It fit. Before I put it on her, I'd held it up to my own body just to get it ready to put over her head. She looked up at me and started to laugh hysterically. It did look silly held up to me as I was about four times too big for that T-shirt, but seeing her realize that and laugh about it made the two of us start laughing together.

That was the last time we ever did that, so I cried the two-minute drive home, knowing we'd never share a laugh again.

Something that really bewildered and impressed me was that I didn't have to help her put on her pantyhose before church on Sunday mornings. Somehow, women who were in their prime in the 1980s and 1990s, when shoulder pads and pantyhose roamed the earth, can put on a pair of hose in their sleep.

That's what her brain was doing. It was falling asleep. Even though every alleyway and avenue of her brain had been putting up road closing signs, she could still remember by muscle memory, or perhaps in the way that women have to do so many monotonous things all their lives, and we just turn our brains off to be able to get through them, she could still stick on a pair of pantyhose.

Yet, she started biting her lips more and more often. She bit her lip and drew blood while I was brushing her teeth one morning, and I felt terrible. I felt like I had accidentally hurt a child.

It had been a full year since I'd received any child support from Ella's dad and six months since I'd called him asking for it. He had told me then that he'd informed the HR department that he was supposed to have his wages garnished for child support, but because of Covid, they were behind. I had too much going on in my life at the time to chase that money around, no matter how desperately we needed it.

Now, Ella was telling me she was going to call him herself because she needed new clothes, and I simply could not afford them. If I had had the $4000 in child support that he was behind, or any help from him at all, I would have been able to buy her everything she needed, but without his help, I was living paycheck to paycheck without anything left over at the end of buying groceries, gas, and paying bills.

When Ella called her dad and explained she needed socks, underwear, and some new jeans he asked, "Why don't you guys do what you always do and get ol' what's her ugly to pay for it?"

He was referring to my mom, who had always picked up his slack when raising his daughter was not important enough to him.

Ella explained to her dad that her grandma had dementia, that she was having to work at the kennel sometimes, watch her brother every day, watch my mom every afternoon, and do her schoolwork. She explained to her dad that she was worn out, tired, and just needed new clothes.

Her dad said, "I hope that bitch dies, and I'll piss on her grave too!" about my mom, and Ella hung up on him. That was the first time my daughter, fourteen at the time, blocked her dad from her phone.

When I think about how much I let Ella down when I settled on her dad and made a baby with someone who was too selfish to ever be a good person, let alone a selfless dad, I feel enough guilt to weigh me down forever. I have to forgive myself daily for making babies with men who are not here to be dads. I chased my mother's love around until I could no longer, and I never caught it, but my children will love themselves enough to be complete without the love and attention of their fathers.

We work on healing and loving ourselves every day.

# CHAPTER NINETY-FOUR

I remember the very first time Chad ever yelled at me. It had taken me by surprise because I had never been in an argument with a sibling before, at least not as adult. He was calling me out for leaving Ella with my mom on nights when the band I sang with for extra money played or nights when I had a date.

I was twenty-five or twenty-six, at the time, and I thought my mom loved Ella and was taking good care of her. I thought Frank had changed now that he was in his sixties. I saw no reason for him to lecture, yell at, endanger, or otherwise abuse my daughter. I knew that when he was younger, and I was my daughter's age, he saw me and my sister as a threat he needed to eliminate. I had not yet worked with him at the kennel, so I thought that he must have matured enough in twenty years that he no longer needed to compete for the attention of my mom with a five-year-old. I didn't think he'd lecture Ella about modesty or fornication because she was five, and who would feel the need to do that?

When I asked my mom and Ella, they both said she had a great time, watched movies, ate popcorn, and helped with whatever puppies my mom had in the house, nursing them back to health. I had no idea until Ella was fifteen that she was crying and wanting me to come and get her because Chad was picking on her, locking her in buildings and pretending to leave, hurting her physically, and that Mom and Frank were ignoring her unless Frank was lecturing her.

When Chad yelled at me that first time, he didn't tell me any of that. He told me she was crying her eyes out and wanting to go home, but I thought that was what every normal young child did when they missed their mom. I had to work. Sometimes it had to be at night. I went out once a week and made it count.

I had a rule: I would only go out if it would potentially find Ella a dad or if I could make money. So, I went on tons of dates, and I went out to bars and sang with a band. I would often make more money gigging in one weekend night than I would doing hair at the salon all week. So that's what I told Chad, and he didn't elaborate. He didn't say, "My dad and I are bullying your kid." He just told me how bad of a mother I was for leaving her with them.

The only exception I had to this rule was when I fell in love with a guy in a band. All the other bands paid me to sing, but these guys did not, and because I thought we were friends, I was okay with that. I was twenty-three, and he was twenty-eight when we met. He was the front man of a band, and I was completely in unrequited love with him, and he knew that. I told him often. I wrote songs about him and then shared those songs with him when we would sit on his couch having songwriting sessions.

He told me he did not feel the same way I felt, but he would ask me to sing a handful of songs with his band on stage and then take me home with him after every show. I was confused for about five years because I could not fathom sleeping with someone I was not in love with, especially if I knew they were in love with me. So, I thought he must love me too. I even tricked myself into feeling his love, many times.

I could not fathom that he did not love me because he carried my heart around in his back pocket and then brought it out to play with when he was lonely. At the time, I was in my twenties and had just been cheated on by my husband and left to raise a baby alone. Then my dad died, and my heart was unraveling, there, in this musician's back pocket. When that guy would get it out to play with, it felt good even when it felt bad, just to have someone acknowledging that I was alive and had a heart.

I kept expecting that all of that time and energy I was spending with that man would have to either turn out to become a musical collaboration or a romance. It never did, and it took five or six years, but eventually, he stopped asking me to sing with him, started making fun of me in front of his friends, and then he started dating other women. I deeply regret all of the time, money, and energy I wasted chasing what I thought was something and was really nothing at all. I should have been home with my daughter those nights.

Chad was right. I didn't know it at the time, but it was incredibly immature and selfish of me. Not the going out part but the ever letting my mom, Chad, or Frank be around my children in the first place. Ella has to undo all the horrible things being at their house did to her brain and the way she reacts to disappointment. She has a long way to go, but with therapy and healthy outlets, she is trying to make new, healthier habits stick. I hope she and I can both forgive me for letting her be around very toxic people for far too many hours.

I hope that one day we can forgive Ella's dad for only being there on the weekends he was supposed to have her a handful of times in the ten years we lived there and not even one single Wednesday night, which was a night he was supposed to pick Ella up and spend time with her. I should have been able to date and find someone to be with the way he had. I should have been able to have a side gig or weekend job to make extra money, the way he had the freedom to do. He should have been there for his daughter. If he had been, she would have never had to have been around Frank.

Someday, I would also like to be able to forgive Chad. That first time he accused me of being a terrible mother, he was sixteen and had been a father himself for a full year but had not even spent one night with his daughter or stayed up with her when she cried in the middle of the night. He had not even changed one diaper. I listened to his spewing of hate and judgment of my ability to parent and thought, *"For one thing, he's a child, so I don't care what he thinks. He's never been left to raise a child alone, and for another thing, he's a hypocrite. He's currently leaving someone with a baby to raise alone."*

I let it go, but I took note of how quick he was to have a full opinion of me without knowing what he was talking about whatsoever. He thought I was just going out for fun. He didn't know I sang with a band and was making money while my daughter slept so that I could spend more time with her while she was awake. He barely knew anything about me, and he was so ready with a list of things he hated about me and a list of flaws he thought he should tell me about.

It seemed odd to me at the time because I knew my older brother and my three sisters knew me far too well to ever judge and yell at me or accuse me without asking me first and finding out what was actually going on. Chad did not care enough about me to ask, and I kept that in the part of my heart where I prayed for my brother.

Ten years later, Chad and Karen had decided that when they were around my children and me at family gatherings, they were going to teach me how to raise and discipline my son. They had two toddlers who were both girls and listened to their parents very well. When Ella was a toddler and a small child, she listened very well. When Alexis, my niece, who was chauffeured between her parents Chad and Fannie, Fannie's grandparents, and my mom and me, raised by six to eight different people and had very little structure, she too listened to rules and instructions fairly well. Not every little girl is well behaved, and not every little boy is disobedient or difficult to keep focused, but, in my experience, little girls are a bit more easily wrangled than boys, and this was definitely the case with our three toddlers.

Chad and Karen thought I needed help figuring out how to discipline my son, never mind the fact that I just raised a child for fourteen years by myself. Chad and Karen knew better.

My son, Henry, is a wild one. Even before birth, he had far too much energy for one body to contain. When he was a toddler, I noticed that he was different from other children. He learned all his letters, pointing to the letters on his alphabet mat or handing me the correct foam letter I'd request, as young as nine months old, before he could even talk. However, he could not seem to listen to any instructions. He was very snuggly and kind, but he did not understand danger, bodily harm, or consequences. Sometimes when playing, he'd push or hit other children and sometimes adults.

He did not act this way out of anger or tantrums but because he genuinely did not realize what would happen, and he was curious. When my daughter was younger, she would play with other kids, and it was a dream. I could talk to another adult or even look at my phone for a second. When Henry would play with other kids at that age, he'd throw things at their faces, grab them around the neck and push them over, and I had to constantly be on my toes.

I was already stressed out from trying to learn how to keep him and other children safe, how to explain to him that he hurt someone and that he couldn't keep doing that and say those things without sounding like a helicopter mom. He is now five and a half, and it has taken me working with him every day of his life, since he was able to walk, to get him to stop tackling, pushing, and hitting other kids. He still hits, kicks, and bites me. He is a lot of work, and he has a lot of developmental delays we are working on, but back when he was two, I was still just learning that he was different and learning about what worked for him. Now, he is in therapy, and I dedicate most of my time and energy to helping him understand his emotions and curiosities so that he does not hurt anyone.

When Henry was two, Chad and Karen invited us to their house for dinner one night, and both of them asked simultaneously if I wanted them to show me how to get Henry to do what he was told. I have been given parenting advice in condescending fashion due to being a single mom numerous times in my life. People offer single moms advice in ways that they would never say if the husband and father were there. This time took first prize.

Chad and Karen were looking at each other like this was the whole reason we were there at their house that night. Like they had invited me over to teach me how to parent. Chad would have known if he'd ever been around his own son that boys are different.

They both started telling me what to do, telling Henry what to do, yelling at him, and looking at each other with disgust after he would not comply. They looked at my son like he was vile. In that moment, I had decided to never go to their house for any reason ever again. Ella and I looked at one another, and we both decided that my children weren't allowed to be around them ever again, especially not my son.

I had always assumed and hoped I would be able to save Chad from turning out like his dad, but he had been allowed to walk away from his responsibilities and never had to pay the consequences of his actions. He'd been bailed out over and over just like his dad, and it created a monster who could never deal with real problems. Money problems? Sure. You just leave your kids with a woman and go to work, but real, emotional battles where you have to admit that you don't have an answer, that you feel pain deeply, that you feel remorse for something you've done? He could never do that.

# CHAPTER NINETY-FIVE

Every year, in order to keep a show dog kennel license, the kennel had to host field trials. These were held on Saturday mornings during the spring and fall months. Frank, his friend Clark, previous assistant Travis, Chad, and many, many other customers and friends would show up at daylight for biscuits and gravy for breakfast, hot dogs for lunch, and friendly competition to see whose dog could find the most birds.

Basically, there were two dogs, two hunters, and a judge in the bird field hunting at any given time, all day long. Ella and her black and white pointer, Moose, and whomever she had picked to partner up with for the day, had even won a couple of times. I was very proud of her for helping train her own dog and for being such an excellent shot.

At first, before my mom got sick, field trials were fun. The weather was usually too chilly, or it usually started to rain, but people were together, talking, laughing, and complementing one another on their dogs. When my mom started to become increasingly obviously not okay, the field trials became a huge source of anxiety for Ella and me.

Frank was like a child in a candy store with his friends. He was never going to give up his favorite thing in order to check on my mom and make sure she was okay every few minutes. He was paying absolutely no attention to her at the field trials. My mom was not only becoming ruder and more belligerent when speaking nonsense to customers, but she was always constantly in danger.

At the last field trial she was allowed to walk around at, she stepped behind a truck that was backing up, and Karen had to pull her out of the way at the last second, or she would have gotten backed over. At that same field trial, Mom kept walking out into the field, and someone had to drop their gun at the last second when she stepped in the way, right before they shot her.

Ella had been trying to get Frank to keep her grandma from getting hurt the whole day, but after she almost got shot, and Frank wasn't even watching, had not even noticed, Ella went out into the field to retrieve my mom. That is when my mom punched Ella.

Ella walked home immediately, sobbing. "I still had one activity that I like! I had to give up all of my other activities and lessons, and now I can't even do field trialing because I can't watch my grandma get shot or backed over by a truck! I quit!" she cried.

I put my children in the car and drove down the road to the field trial to see what was going on. I wanted to find out why Chad and Karen couldn't be the ones watching my mom and keeping her safe instead of my child. Chad and Karen had already left for the day, leaving my mom with Ella, and now my mom was screaming at some strangers that this was her house, and they had to leave. Frank's friend Clark looked absolutely mortified. He was trying to get my mom to calm down and leave those people alone, but anytime my mom saw Clark, she'd start telling him that Frank was trying to kill her.

Frank was off in his own little world and didn't even notice. I told him I was taking my mom and my kids to my house, and I'd bring my mom back after the field trial was over. She paced in my living room, yelling and trying to leave, for three more hours before it was over, and I could bring her home.

The Monday morning after, Clark came by to tell Frank that he thought my mom needed to have a supervisor or a nurse. He also briefly mentioned putting my mom in a facility, but Frank had spent so many hours telling us both that he was absolutely never, ever, ever going to do that, that Clark focused most of the conversation on at least having someone keep my mom safe.

Frank sat there wide eyed and shocked when we told him all of the numerous ways and times Mom had nearly gotten killed or badly injured at the field trial. He was even more shocked to learn about Mom's mouth and the way she was acting like a mean drunk and had offended customers and guests, causing them to leave. Again, Clark was trying to get Frank to understand that if my mom got hurt, he would be legally responsible. By the end of the conversation, we decided that during the next field trial, my mom would come to my house with Henry and me and that way Ella could participate, and my mom would be safe.

I had turned on a show my mom liked where the dialogue and laugh track were not too overwhelming, gave the baby some letters to play with, and went to make both my mom and my baby a late breakfast when Karen popped her head into my living room. The baby and my mom had been fairly calm, and I'd gotten them set up even though he was two and a crazy monkey in general, and my mom was worried she was not supposed to be at my house. In spite of all of that, they were both being pretty chill until Karen got there.

Karen was talking with me about something I was only half listening to because I was really hoping she'd leave. Her energy was triggering my mom, and therefore me, and I was asking my toddler to sit down and eat breakfast. Karen started to yell at him and put him back in his chair, which was something no one had ever done before. I don't yell at or hit babies. I don't understand how anyone thinks that will help them learn.

Since we had never treated him that way, his eyes filled with tears, and he said, "Mommy?" which caused my mom to start yelling at Karen to leave him alone.

Karen was telling my mom, "It's okay, Elizabeth. He needs to learn to listen to his mom, and his mom wants him to sit down." Then to my son, "Sit down, Henry!"

My mom stood up to get in Karen's face and yelled something that made no sense, but it still made more sense to me than an adult simultaneously yelling at a developmentally delayed toddler and an elderly woman with dementia. Karen yelling at my mom and my baby went on for a few moments before I got Karen out of my house, but it seemed like the interaction went on for years of my life. Everything felt like it was in slow motion as Karen yelled at my baby and my elderly mom. My baby crying, my mom very upset, screaming, and trying to leave and some lady I wasn't allowed to yell at or hit, standing in my living room yelling at my entire world—it is baffling to this day. If I had threatened Karen or told her what I really thought of her, I would have had to contend with Chad.

The rest of the day of the field trial, after Karen left, my mom stood at my front door trying to get me to let her leave, and I had to juggle a toddler who was getting into everything while I was trying to keep my mom safe and inside the house. My entire life was chaos.

# CHAPTER NINETY-SIX

When someone raises one hundred and fifty dogs a year, losing a puppy or even a couple from each litter is commonplace. At first it's sad, but I had become very used to finding puppies their mommas had laid on and crushed. I would find puppies that were too small to keep up with littermates. We didn't have heated whelping boxes, so, occasionally, puppies would get too cold even inside the puppy room, under the heat lamps and with their moms and brothers and sisters.

My mom had been the queen of nursing puppies back to health. She could take a frozen puppy or a crushed little pup, and in a couple of days, my mom would bottle feed and keep it on a heating pad until it was back out with its litter mates. Now that it was no longer my mom's job, having a human baby myself, and Frank being too lazy to try, puppies who were goners usually stayed that way.

My mom had gone back to following me around in the mornings while I did chores instead of staying in the house because she was having a lot more trouble sitting still. She could no longer read, focus on a movie, do a puzzle, or any of the things one would do to entertain themselves indoors. So, she wandered around, usually following me.

One morning, I brought a dying puppy, who was only about three days old, to Frank to ask him what we should do for the pup. It was late November and already very cold, below freezing at night and because the puppy's momma knew that particular puppy was weak, she kept tossing it to the side at night to die so as not to take up any warmth or milk from the stronger puppies. Our breed often had up to twelve puppies per litter, so it was common that they wouldn't care for a weak pup.

I thought Frank was going to tell me to give it to a different momma who didn't have as many in her litter, as we often did, or to run it down to Ella and have her try to warm it up on a heating pad. Instead, he told me to give the puppy to my mom.

I looked at him like he was insane. Currently, my mom was incapable of brushing her own hair, and he wanted me to give her a three-day old puppy that was dying? Not only that, but he thought she could make it into the house with the pup and get herself set up with some warm milk, a towel, a syringe and a heating pad? Even though she had no idea where or what any of those things were? If I had asked her to tell me where my car was, she would not have been able to do that even as we walked past it, and he thought that this was a solid plan?

No one wants to argue with Frank that early in the morning, so I took my mom into the house and set her up with items she'd need and left her at the table with a puppy that I knew would be dead when I got back inside the house. I went back out to finish my work, and about an hour later, I came inside to check on my mom and the puppy. My mom was asleep in the chair and the almost dead puppy was in the trash can.

As completely fucked up as it may seem, I actually started to laugh. None of this was even believable. I felt like I was on the set of a Will Ferrell movie where instead of the stepbrothers coming up with asinine ways to destroy shit, it was the parents who were acting like seven-year-old sociopaths. A grown man who knew his wife had advanced dementia handed her a puppy to resuscitate, and she threw it in the trash can under the kitchen sink and took a nap in the recliner! It was too sad, crazy, and bizarre not to laugh about and text and tell everyone I knew who knew my situation well enough to understand. I told Chad and Karen, hoping they would see just how 'out there' and on the edge the whole situation was becoming.

Frank was complaining more and more about their lack of sleep. My mom was pacing all night, banging on furniture and walls, yelling nonsense, trying to leave, and one night she even dumped over the chair where Frank was asleep, waking him up as he fell to the floor.

A sliver of me wanted to laugh at that and say, "You did this to her! I hope she picks up your gun and shoots you in your sleep tonight," but I knew there was really nothing funny about any of it.

"You need to make a list," I said, handing him a pen and paper, "of things to ask Dr. Spiva about next time you're there."

"I kind of want to see if he can see her today. This not sleeping crap is awful. I can't keep doing this," Frank said.

We were about to hook the dogs to the roader, but because of his sleep deprivation, I was able to convince him to go in the house and make my mom an appointment. I helped Frank make a list of what to ask Dr. Spiva, including the way Mom was starting to speak to people. After I got the kennel chores done, I went back home because instead of working dogs, Frank was taking my mom to the doctor.

About an hour later, Frank called me asking if I could come back and give him a hand. My mom was refusing to get in the truck and go to the doctor. Frank was hoping I could talk her into getting into the truck.

"He's gonna kill me!" she said.

I could see terror in her eyes. "Well, what if I take you? Will you go with me?" I asked.

I finally got her into my car, and then I had to call Ella and tell her I would be gone a couple of hours, and she would have to watch her brother all morning, after all. Ella never took it well when I told her she'd have to watch her brother while I did things for my mom, and I do not and did not blame her. Her brother should have had another parent present. She should have had another parent to ask for help, and it was my fault that was not the case. I'd beat myself up about it the entire time I was helping with my mom. I was also dealing with the hard, increasingly bolder evidence that my mom was dying, and there was nothing more I was allowed to do for her. Guilt roared through me all day, every day.

When we were walking into the doctor's office, Frank said to me, "I think she knows something's about to happen."

"What do you mean?" I asked.

"I think she knows she's getting worse and that we can't handle her anymore."

"What makes you say that?" I asked.

"Because every once in a while, she'll start crying and saying she's sorry and ask me not to give up on her," he replied.

I almost vomited. How tragically sad that the person who repeatedly forgave him, took him back after he had robbed her of her children, physical safety, and comfort, security, well-being, spirit, personality, and mind, was having to ask *him* not to give up on *her*.

Frank wanted to speak with the doctor in private first and go over the list of questions and issues we were having with Mom while she and I waited in the waiting room. She sat next to me, shaking like a leaf. She couldn't stop shaking, and I could feel the fear and anxiety radiating off her. She looked so small, meek and fragile. I held her hand.

She looked at me with teary eyes and said, "I'm not going to get better, am I?" If it were possible for a human to throw up their own heart, I would have.

When the nurse, who was around my mom's age with fashionable glasses and a trendy hair cut, called us back, we had to follow her down a very, very long hallway.

"Elizabeth Hudson… Libby? Is that you?" she asked. "I remember you! It's been so many years! I was in your younger sister Cathy's grade." She went on, but my mom didn't know who Aunt Cathy was any more. She barely even knew her own name.

The nurse was only about two years younger than my mom. Here were two women in their mid-sixties, and yet, (I'm willing to guess due to how they were treated by people) one of them was there at work, and the other one was there to be put on medications so that she could sleep at night rather than yelling and banging on the walls.

# CHAPTER NINETY-SEVEN

My mom's doctor had prescribed her sleeping pills and a pill to give her during the day to make her less agitated but did not even bother to see if she had another UTI, which I was certain she did. I brought it up at the appointment along with my concerns about her needing constant care.

"The reason I know she has another UTI is that I can't always be with her to help her get clean in the bathroom, and I know she's forgetting to wipe based on the absence of toilet paper in the toilet and the presence of excrement in her undergarments every time I change her clothes, which is two or three times a day," I said.

Frank changed the subject, and both he and the doctor ignored me. When they were done, I brought it up again. "Isn't she going to need constant care soon?" I asked.

"That's very possible," was the doctor's response, and I could tell he did not really care and had not really been listening since every-thing we told him pointed to the fact that my mom had needed constant care for years. I was glad I had not sent the letter I had written to the doctor. It would have done absolutely no good.

When we got back from my mom's appointment, Frank asked me

if we should go ahead and give her two or three of her daytime pills, which she was only supposed to have one a day. My stomach had become so used to these asinine suggestions it forgot to turn over.

I simply rolled my eyes and told him in a tone that let him know that I was completely done with his shit, "If you want to go to prison for overdosing your wife on narcotics, give her two or three. I'll give her one, and if I were you, I wouldn't go near any of her pills. Taking too many of these could kill her, and this is the only time I'm going to say that to you. If the next time I say it, it's to the police, that's your fault."

Fortunately, one pill was enough to calm my mom down for the most part, and Frank didn't consider giving her more that first week. Unfortunately, he completely ignored Ella and me when we tried to explain object permanence to him and how if he moved something that had always been in a certain place, it would agitate and confuse my mom, causing her to go into a rage or have a fit.

There was a large, empty, bird cage that had been in the corner of the dining room next to the table for years, and Frank moved it into the back room because it was empty and taking up a lot of space. Immediately after he relocated the bird cage, my mom would either quickly pace around the house, frantically searching for it, or if she realized it was in the back room, she would push it around the house. She knew it belonged somewhere else but could not remember where it belonged.

People with dementia need certainty, security, and routine. When things are moved or change, it becomes overwhelming and sets off alarms in their heads. My daughter and I tried to explain that to Frank, but as with anything that he had not experienced in his own mind or body, it could not be true. So, he not only ignored us, but he asked us every day how to get her to stop messing with the bird cage. Eventually, he decided to buy some new birds and put them in the cage in the living room for her to watch. He thought it would be peaceful for her. He thought she would sit and watch the birds, but she did not notice the birds at all.

Mom started to pace more, making less and less sense, especially if there were customers or company over. She would flat-out tell people to leave. Mom was becoming embarrassing enough in front of "important" people that Frank called Chad, Karen, and me over for a meeting. Even Frank was finally saying the 'no no' words, "nursing home," after four and a half years of refusing to even discuss it as an option.

"The only thing she ever begged me for was not to put her in a nursing home," Chad said.

"She begged me to never put her in a nursing home from the time I was six years old and could understand what a nursing home was," I said. "Then, she refused to take care of herself and lived a life that was completely over the top filled with stress. So here we are."

I was talking to Chad, but Frank was who responded. "How was her life over the top full of stress?!" he asked. "Your mother lived a good life here, Amelia." He was serious.

Chad and I just rolled our eyes. We weren't there to argue with a delusional monster, and we both knew this was no place for our mom to live her last moments.

"She needs to live in a facility with nurses. I am not going to watch my mom die. I'm not a nurse, and even if I were a nurse, no one should have to watch their own mom die. We need help. There are too many animals and people here for me to take care of all by myself every day." I could have gone on, but they were finally in half-hearted agreement. Frank was exhausted, and Chad did not actually care.

That was the conversation where I found out that Chad thought Mellissa was our oldest sibling. I just cannot fathom having my head so far up my own ass my entire life that I didn't know which of my siblings was the oldest. I was completely done with these people. My children needed me, and for fuck's sake, I needed me.

That meeting took place a week or two before Christmas, and even though Frank had not only never celebrated Christmas but had never allowed my mom to celebrate either, he decided to invite us all to Christmas Eve dinner at his house. I still can't see why he would want to do something like that, and I knew it was going to end up devastatingly sad, or chaotic, or both.

The days leading up to Christmas Eve, I could feel tension building in the air, and my 5:00 in the morning sessions with Jesus became more focused. "Lord, please let this explode and pop and be over!" I'd beg, and I knew it would not be long before He answered my prayers. Jesus was making ways where there were roadblocks before.

Frank drove down the field on the four-wheeler more often, asking me for help because my mom was, "going berserk," as he would put it. I would drive down in my car to help him calm her down. She was completely confused, screaming, throwing things, and cursing.

"She has another UTI," I said after finally getting her to sit down.

"Now, how could you possibly know that?" he asked.

I was done repeating myself and arguing with him. It had been almost five years of the same arguments, illustrations and examples.

"I'm going home to my kids. I'll be back down to get her ready for bed," I said, and I left him with the mess he created. Abuse someone for thirty years and then wonder why they lose their shit on you.

A few days before Christmas Eve, Chad and Frank decided to remove the hedges that had surrounded mom and Frank's yard for twenty-seven years. When I drove down to see them ripping the bushes out of the ground, I laid my head on my steering wheel and softly sang a verse of, *"Because I know He holds the future and life is worth the living just because He lives,"* thanking Jesus that the stupidity of two ignorant morons who couldn't see or hear anyone but themselves would be the catalyst that finally rewarded my mom the care she deserved.

They had listened to nothing Ella and I had said about object permanence, and the fires burning the bushes were the fires that would ignite a rage in my mom strong enough to get herself out of the prison that is Frank Hudson.

For days on end, all day and all night, Mom looked out the

window, confused, ranting and raving about going home. "I wanna go home!" she'd scream.

"You are home, dear," Frank would answer. He tried to explain why it looked different outside, but even I, someone without dementia, had a lot of trouble adjusting to the overwhelming difference in the way the yard looked. There had been a neat, tight, uniform hedge all the way around their yard for nearly three decades, and simply because Chad wanted to play with some equipment, it was gone, and my mom could not adjust or understand.

Christmas Eve dinner was a catastrophe. Frank had never once had dinner done and ready even remotely close to the time when he had invited guests, and the 450 degree oven full of ribs and baked potatoes was still blazing and baking when Ella, Henry, and I got there. Chad and Karen had left their two toddlers with Karen's mom, thankfully, otherwise, I would have been guarding three babies from being burned by the hot oven.

Frank said there was about an hour left before dinner would be done cooking, so I stood near the stove for about fifteen minutes, shooing away my three-year old, who absolutely could not remember that the stove was hot. Even though Ella was trying to distract him, he was too interested in what was inside the oven and on top of the hot stove.

As I stood there, my feet began to hurt. I had done all of my usual jobs that day. Twelve hours of either messing with dogs, chasing my toddler, or doing something for my mom, and I was tired. I considered for a moment moving Frank's chair out of the way, getting a different chair and setting it near the oven so I could keep Henry away while sitting down, but I thought that was ridiculous. *I'm just going to sit in Frank's chair to keep my baby from burning himself since Frank's chair is right here.*

Frank got up and walked into the kitchen to yell at me to sit somewhere else. The utter audacity. Can you imagine allowing someone to wipe your wife's ass but not sit in your chair? Clean up your poop off the hallway floor, bathroom walls, and toilet, but not sit in your chair? Your empty chair? Forcing someone to clean up your dogs' shit until they are covered in it head to toe, every day for five years, but not let them sit in your chair? The chair my dad bought!

*"YOU NARCISSISTIC PIECE OF SHIT!"* I wanted to scream!

Chad must have recognized that I was about to kill Frank with my bare hands and stepped in, offering to guard the oven for a couple of minutes while I sat on the couch with Ella and Karen. Henry almost burned himself several times because he has developmental delays, and one of them is understanding consequences of actions. He does not understand that if he does something, something might happen or hurt him. Also, he had just turned three, and three-year-olds forget instructions and warnings and get hurt.

Finally, we were sitting down to eat, but my son, as usual, did not want to eat. He wanted to go back to playing, and I couldn't let him do that without following him around because the kitchen stove and oven were still hot. I started to beg everyone to just let me take Henry home. I told them that I didn't have an appetite, and Henry wasn't going to sit down and eat because he never did and never had before.

Instead of just letting me leave, Chad decided he was going to try to do what Karen had tried to do a few weeks prior and yell at my son until he sat down to eat. Only, my son has no idea what being yelled at is trying to accomplish in him, or even that they were trying to get him to do something. It was not working, but it was making my mom anxious and upset because she thought I was yelling at my baby.

Chad kept yelling at Henry to sit down and eat. Henry kept trying to wiggle out of my arms and get down.

Karen said to Chad, "It's not going to work. I tried the other day, and all it did was make your mom upset," referring to the field trial day when she yelled at both my mom and my baby at the same time.

Finally, my mom stood up to scream at me to leave the baby alone and threw her steak knife at the table in front of my plate. Ella took the knives away from the table.

"I'm going to take the baby home. Do you want to stay and eat or go home with me?" I asked Ella.

She wanted to stay and protect my mom from whoever was going to yell at her for her outburst, and sadly, we did not know which of the three of them it would be.

"Will you be okay?" I asked Ella.

She nodded yes, and once I got in my car, I texted her that if anyone threw anything else, she needed to walk home.

About twenty minutes later, Ella was walking home. My mom had thrown her entire plate of food.

"Why did Frank even want to have that dinner?" Ella asked, crying.

"No one ever knows the reason Frank does anything," I replied.

The next morning, I went to the kennel to do chores before daylight with a flashlight lighting the way, as I did every Sunday morning. Before church I took care of the bird dogs every Sunday morning in the dark so that I could spend my Sunday with my kids after church. I decided to do that on Christmas as well, as it happened to fall on a Sunday. I was happy, even though my kids were only getting three presents each because that's all I could afford because at least I would be able to spend the day with them. If Christmas had fallen on a Monday through Saturday, I would have had to work training dogs with Frank. Frank never let me have Christmas off unless it was a Sunday.

I got everything done before dawn and was just getting out of the shower so that my kids could open their Christmas presents when I heard the four-wheeler. Ella started to cry. We had had enough. Frank was there to see if I could get my mom to calm down. She'd been ranting and raving all night about wanting to go home. I went and tried to calm her down. Frank had even called Chad and Karen.

"Take her to the emergency room," I said.

When Frank finally agreed to take my mom to the emergency room, I asked Chad, "You got this from here?" implying that I was not going to the hospital.

"I guess?" he half asked, half answered.

"My kids only have me. Your kids have a mom and other grand-parents," I told Chad. "Make sure you tell them she has a UTI when you get to the emergency room," I said to Frank.

"I'm not dealing with that women crap, I told you!" he said.

"You are going to have to grow up! She's your wife! It's an infection! It's not— it's what–" I gave up.

I turned to Chad and Karen. "She has a urinary tract infection, and she's freaking out about the hedges. Good luck," I said.

Then I went home to the saddest Christmas of my life.

# CHAPTER NINETY-EIGHT

Christmas evening, around dark, Frank stopped at my house on his way home from the emergency room to give me an update. "You'll never guess," he started.

"What, she had a UTI?" I interrupted.

"Yes, she had a really bad UTI and a fever, but what I was gonna say is you'll never guess what Karen told those doctors over there," he said. "Karen told those dang people that your mom had taken a puppy, the family pet, outside this morning to go potty and wrung its neck. Broke its neck and threw it away in the trash can before coming back inside the house."

I put my hands over my face and put my head in my lap. It was completely clear that Karen was even crazier than my mom and that no one should ever tell her anything or listen to anything she said.

"Did they believe Karen?" I asked.

Now I was sick to my stomach again. I knew I should have gone to the emergency room and done everything myself. I just didn't want to leave my fourteen-year-old and my three-year-old alone all day on Christmas Day.

"They put it in her file," he said.

"You should have clarified and told them what really happened!" I said. "They could deny her access to nursing homes because she's violent based on a claim like that. She could have to stay in a psych ward instead, based on some something like that!"

Before, I was worried, and now I was petrified concerning my mom's well-being in a medical capacity. Why would Karen say something like that? I understand some people need constant attention and aren't happy unless they're getting the biggest reactions from people, but could she not consider how the people she's embellishing stories about might be affected?

Certainly, if it had been her mom, she would not have made such an absurd claim, but because it was Chad's mom, and she wanted all of this to be over so that she did not have to be involved in the misery of it any longer, she lied so that my mom would have to stay in the hospital for longer. Chad and Karen were so worried about my son, who didn't understand the consequences of his three-year old actions, and yet, they never considered the consequences of their own.

My mom stayed in the hospital that night and around eight o'clock that evening, the dogs started to howl down at the kennel. I started to tense up, and then I took a deep breath.

*"He can't kill her tonight,"* I thought.

It was the first night since I was six years old that I didn't have to worry that he was going to kill her. It was the deepest breath I have ever taken. A feeling of elation passed through my every cell from head to toe. Even though she was hospitalized and very ill with many ailments, at least he could not beat her to death.

The doctors at the hospital decided my mom needed to be psychologically evaluated. She needed specialists, all five of her medicines adjusted, antibiotics, speech therapy, and talk therapy. She needed constant care and all of the things that I had been begging Frank for and asking Jesus for, for five years. She was finally getting what she needed, but it was far too late.

They moved my mom to a facility where she could be evaluated and put on the right track toward at least having a healthier body and less mood swings. She was to stay at the facility for two weeks while

Frank got her set up with Medicaid, Medicare, and a rehabilitation facility or nursing home.

Over the course of those two weeks, multiple times, Frank asked me what would be wrong with culling my mom. In complete seriousness, he would look at me and say, "She can't work no more. She's never gonna be able to work again. That's what we do when something's at the end of their road around here. We need to just dig a hole and cull her."

Travis, his former assistant, had come back around needing his old job back and wanting to be a friend to Frank while he was going through such a hard time. Frank even said that in front of Travis, whose eyes could not have been wider. Having worked with Frank for many years, Travis had heard all of the hate, racism, sexism, and heartlessness that had come out of Frank's mouth and even he could not believe Frank would talk about putting his wife down in front of her daughter.

I could believe it. Men like Frank, Chad, and Tyler only use people. They do not love people. They're incapable of love. They try to love their own children, but it's not real love. It's simply an extension of narcissism. They definitely can't love anyone but themselves. They use people, and now that my mom was no longer being useful to Frank, she was in his mind ready to be culled. I believed he would say it, and I believed he would do it if my mom came back home, but I could not believe that he'd say that to my fourteen-year-old daughter.

Ella had felt pity for Frank. Even though she knew every bit of what I knew of him at that point, she'd grown up around him, and he had told her all of the stories where he thought he sounded like a cool hero, but he was actually a disgusting murderer. Even still, Ella felt sorry for him and sometimes would walk down and eat dinner with him so he didn't have to eat alone every night. He even said to Ella that he wished he could just go ahead and cull her Gram. That was the last time my daughter was around that toxic dump.

One morning after my mom had been in the hospital for about a week, I was washing kennels, and Frank asked me if I would mind if he called his ex-wife Nina and remarried her. I wanted to laugh.

*"Sure, Frank. Remarry the woman whose baby you killed forty-five years ago. I'm sure she's got her dress all picked out and can't wait to see you. She's probably been pining away for you this whole time."* I thought. I said, "Why would I mind?"

I was in constant prayer that my mom would be able to go to a nice facility with good nurses so she could live out the rest of her days in peace, and I would never have to worry about Frank hurting her ever again. The Medicaid and Medicare situations looked like they were going to work, and Frank had even found a lawyer to help him navigate the process.

We wanted my mom to go to a really nice facility called Shady Village, but because my mom had that bit about cracking a puppy's neck with her bare, sixty-six-year-old hands in her file, Shady Village would not accept her. She was a liability near the other patients. The only place that would take her was in the town where my mom had gone to high school. In the small town she had met my dad and raised Jordan and Mellissa. The rehab facility had been disgusting and dilapidated the last time I had been inside of it, and that was twenty years ago. It was called Jefferson, and I prayed that it had gotten better over the years. I knew that either way, it was better than my mom being with Frank.

Two days before we were to move my mom from the psych hospital to Jefferson, the nurses called us to let us know that she had contracted Covid while she was in the hospital and that we needed to see if it was still okay with Jefferson for her to arrive infected with the virus. Fortunately, Jefferson was still happy to have our money and said she could be admitted.

Frank didn't want to be the one to leave my mom at the nursing home, so he asked me to do it. He also didn't know what to pack for her or how to pack, so as I folded her clothes and put them in her bag, I began to cry. I looked like I was a mother packing my child's luggage for camp, and yet, I was a child packing my mother for the nursing home. Frank was watching me, and even though I had always tried to hide my emotions from him, I could not. I started to wail. Pain was loudly thundering out of me.

"I'm sorry, Amelia," he said.

He was apologizing for my current pain, but not for the seed he had planted thirty years ago, causing it to grow. He was not taking responsibility for any of this, even though it was he who drove her to this condition, and yet he could not drive her to the facility.

I knew that given her current options, it was the best place for her, so I drove to pick my mom up, confused and sick. I drove her all the way to Jefferson nursing home. That day destroyed me. Holding my mom's hand felt no different than holding my toddler's hand. Leaving my mom at Jefferson felt no different than leaving my baby at daycare, only babies are picked up at the end of the day. Babies grow up and learn, and my mom was never going to learn anything ever again.

She had no idea who I was or where she was and because she had Covid, they didn't have her room ready when I got there. Just a chair, next to a bed, with a roommate who had Covid too. They were just as disorganized and in just as much disrepair as they had been before. They were understaffed and underpaid. I kept trying to go back to her room to look at her, so tiny and frail, sitting in her chair, one last time, but because she had Covid, they would not let me.

I walked back out to my car and looked across the street at my best friend Sam's mom's house. I told Jesus, "Thank You for letting my friends have healthy parents who can still love me through their children. I'm going to need that love."

Then I drove to my dirt road, stopped on the bridge a quarter of a mile away from my house, and put my car in park so that I could scream as loud as I could before going inside to mother my children.

## CHAPTER NINETY-NINE

The winter before my mom went into the nursing home was fiercely cold. For two weeks straight, we were in negative temperatures, and everything was frozen. At the kennel, when everything is frozen, it makes taking care of the dogs, even just general maintenance, so much more difficult.

Usually, it warms up in the afternoon, the dog's water thaws, and they can get a drink. Then I can wash the kennels that were too frozen to wash in the morning. That winter, the negative temperatures went on for two weeks without letting up. Snow was up to my knees. I wore two pairs of pants, two pairs of socks, and my clothes were still frozen to my skin.

When I went inside, I noticed my nostrils had frostbite, and my jaw hurt from the way one holds their face when they've been outside in minus twenty-degree weather for six hours. Usually, it took me an hour and a half to two hours to take care of the dogs, but with everything frozen, it took six hours. The faucets were frozen. The hoses were frozen. I had to carry buckets of water from the only faucet that was thawed out to each kennel. I had to give each dog a drink before their water froze again within a couple of minutes. I had to take each dog who did not have the energy or the will to get up and brave the cold by the collar and force them to drink. Otherwise, their water would freeze, and they would go without drinking.

I shoveled frozen dog poop out of the kennels into buckets and then hauled the frozen dog poop filled buckets to the dog poop pond instead of washing kennels. I put straw inside everyone's kennels. I tried to make the expectant mommas drink more, knowing how thirsty I was when I was carrying one baby, and they were carrying at least four.

By day three or four, all of the dogs' water buckets were full of ice, so I had to carry everyone's buckets into the puppy room, wait for them to thaw, and then go put them all back. Then I had to walk around with five-gallon bucket of water, giving every dog a drink, refilling my bucket hundreds of times and walking back through the knee-deep snow to each individual dog.

I knew the dogs needed more than one sip of water per day, especially in negative temperatures, so after I finally got done, I'd start over. I'd carry water buckets around, trudging through the snow, and give them all another drink before I left. I did that every day for fourteen days straight, and one of those days was my birthday.

My brother Chad, whom I was doing this for because he was going to inherit the business, ignored every voicemail I left about coming to help me. I know that he was inside his warm house in his dry socks, playing video games, and relaxing because his job is an outside job too. He took off work when it was too cold because he could not dig into the frozen ground anyway, and it was just too cold to be outside. I begged him to come and help me, saying that if he could come over and help, I could be out in the cold for three hours instead of six. Chad just blatantly ignored me.

My friend Charlotte asked me why I was even still doing any of it. She asked why I was even still there. At the time, I believed so many things that were untrue. I believed Chad was my little brother and that I needed to keep his inheritance afloat for him while he was off ignoring his responsibilities and making bad choices. I believed it was my responsibility to keep the business afloat so that my mom and Frank had an income. I had to stay there until I finished paying off the car that I drove but was still in Chad's name because I did not want to ruin his credit. I believed I deserved everything that my life was dishing up and serving to me, including frozen tears streaming and then shortly sticking to my face on my birthday as I trudged around with gloves stuck to bucket handles.

Frank did not come out and help until it was afternoon, and I was almost done. Each day, I had a pile of puppies who had not made it through the previous night. It started the very first day when I told Frank our oldest stud dog was not getting up and was too cold to get a drink. His tail had even frozen to the concrete, so when I picked him up and carried him to my car, I left a piece of his tail behind. I carried the ninety-pound dog up my porch steps and into my house.

He spent a couple of weeks in my house, recuperating. After I got done with all my work the first day of negative temperatures, I went inside Frank's house where he had stayed warm all day and told him that if we didn't either bring all of the pregnant females inside or find them somewhere else to stay, they were going to die of dehydration.

"I've been pregnant before," I said. "I know how much water they need and how much blood and energy they are losing by being pregnant out there. It's going to be minus twenty tonight."

Frank scoffed and ignored me. He put up a tarp to block the wind, but that was all he did. We lost seven pregnant females in two weeks. One of those days, early on in the winter storm, Frank's friend who had previously owned a kennel with heated whelping boxes and indoor, heated facilities offered to load up all of our dogs and put them in his kennels until the cold spell passed.

Frank was too prideful to accept. We lost dog after dog, and I braved each morning knowing I would not only be outside for hours but that I would have to peel dead bird dogs from their concrete kennels, all because Frank was too lazy and prideful to do anything, and Chad was too arrogant and lazy to help.

Chad made me feel so worthless and alone when he ignored my begging for help.

Each evening, I would pray that my furnace would continue to work because every winter that I had lived there, it ended up quitting and needing repairs. Frank would always hire an elderly man who did more talking than fixing, and it would always take weeks to fix. The year of the storm, I'd bought space heaters for just such an occasion. We were blessed with having our furnace through the storm, but a couple of weeks later, before winter was over, our heater broke. It took weeks to repair.

That summer, the air conditioner broke, and it was so hot that summer that we spent a couple of nights in a hotel room. Charlotte insisted and even paid for the room. I was so used to enduring horrendous conditions and being uncomfortable, I never would have considered staying in a hotel. Fortunately, I still had friends like Charlotte who reminded me that my children and I were human.

My mom was in the nursing home with Covid, and I was waiting for her two weeks of quarantine to be up so that I could go see her. Finally, at the end of January, I was able to go to Jefferson and see my mom. It seemed like much longer than it had actually been since I'd seen her. Christmas Eve's fit, the emergency room on Christmas Day, two weeks in the psych ward and then two weeks with Covid at Jefferson but now, I could finally go see her.

I took a shower after work and then immediately got in my car to go to Jefferson. Ella was staying home with Henry because children weren't allowed inside the nursing home at that time due to Covid restrictions.

As I drove to see my mom, I decided to stop at Sonic and get her a burger, fries, and a cherry limeade. I knew it had to be better than the food there. I brought her lunch and sat with her, helping her remember to eat. She knew my name that day, and I thought she might actually be getting a tiny bit better now that she had full-time care. I brought her snacks and toiletries, which Jordan, Mellissa, and Ruby had helped me pay for, and I left a card on her dresser for the nurses.

In my card, I wrote that leaving my mom with them was the most difficult thing I'd ever had to do. I told them I had taken care of her like she was my baby for the last couple of years and thanked them for taking over for me, telling them how very much her five children and many grandchildren appreciated them and their care.

My mom kept asking me when we were leaving and telling me she was ready to go. She thought I was there to come and get her. When I had to leave to go home and take care of my kids, it broke my heart again. Leaving her there was horribly difficult as I knew it was not the best facility we could have chosen. There were sinks with plumbing cracks dripping underneath into buckets. There was dust and dirt. There were sick people hollering and moaning for far too long without any available staff to help them. There was a permanent urine smell. That nursing home always had a poor reputation, and I was deeply apologetic to my mom for leaving her there while simultaneously praising Jesus that she didn't have to be at home with Frank any longer.

On the way home that first time, it occurred to me that I finally had a free moment without my baby, my daughter, my mom, Frank, or any animals needing my help for the first time in years, and I could use that time to call child support enforcement. It had been a full year since I'd received any child support from Ella's dad, and his excuse was that he had told the HR department where he worked, but they couldn't get a hold of child support enforcement because of Covid and everything being behind.

First, I looked up the name, location, and mailing address of the company Tyler had been working at for the last fourteen months, and then I called child support enforcement. The representative answered. I told her I was calling to ask why I hadn't received any child support in fourteen months. She told me that Tyler had been unemployed and that they could not garnish wages that did not exist. I told her where he'd been working for fourteen months and gave her the address. She sounded like she might have been almost as upset as I was that he had been lying to both of us.

He'd lied to them about not having a job, and he had lied to me about them not doing their jobs. She said she was going to make my case her priority and get the information sent over to the HR representative at Tyler's company as soon as possible. She said she would get me my child support money as soon as possible, and she did. The very next month, child support started back up like clockwork.

While I was on the phone with child support enforcement, I asked about the money that he was behind. "How will I receive all of the thousands of dollars he's not paid over the last year?"

She said each of his checks would be garnished the usual amount plus a percentage of what he owed from the last year and that his tax refund would be garnished to make up for the remainder of the $4600 he owed me.

Driving home hurt extra badly. I felt the pain, the betrayal, in my chest. My mom was in the nursing home dying of dementia, and my ex-husband, who hadn't seen his daughter in years, was gaslighting me about child support. He told me multiple times that the system was just behind, that he wanted to pay it, but that child support enforcement and his human resources representative just didn't have their shit together.

He lied because he knew I was distracted by my mom's poor health, my baby, the kennel, Frank, and raising Ella by myself. He took my vulnerability and used it to withhold child support. When I got home, I told Ella, and once again, her dad's actions, or inaction rather, made her pretty face fall and her young heart break.

# CHAPTER ONE HUNDRED

I tried to go see my mom at the nursing home every afternoon after work, but a couple of obstacles made that impossible. No matter how much I tried to explain to Ella that her gram needed me to feed her at least one meal a day, Ella still didn't want to have to watch her three-year-old brother all day while I worked and then all afternoon while I was at the nursing home.

"Gram can't remember what she's doing well enough to eat, and they don't have enough nurses to spoon-feed her like I do," I said, trying to plead with my teenager. Both of us knew it should not be her responsibility to be her brother's other parent.

"The nurses have to feed the people that absolutely can't feed themselves, and because Gram can kind of pick at her food, they don't help her, but you've seen her. She forgets to eat. I'm afraid her blood sugar is going to be too low. She needs to be fed at least one meal a day." I tried, feeling guilty for leaving my baby with my child and for leaving my mother with strangers.

Ella would not let me go every day, but she agreed to three or four days a week. On my second trip to Jefferson to see my mom, one of the nurses who was very kind asked me if I was the one who left the card. I told her I was, and she said, "Well, tell me a little bit about your mom."

I blurted out a five-minute-long summary about who my mom was and how Frank had treated her for the last thirty years. The nurse, who was only about fifteen years younger than my mom, asked, "Did you say she used to go by Libby?"

In my summary, I had mentioned that my mom had turned from a fun, confident, beautiful, funny, Libby into an Elizabeth who was controlled by her husband, causing her personality to change and her spirit to die. I explained that he had changed her personality starting with her name.

"Yes, she used to be Libby Boyd," I said.

"She worked at Walmart back in the eighties, didn't she?" asked the nurse.

We were from a very small town, and many people recognized me even if they had never met. It was not unusual for someone to recognize me asking if I was, "Jordan's little sister?" or "Libby's girl?"

"Yep. That was her," I said. "I'm so glad that someone here remembers her."

"Oh, I remember your mom from Walmart! She was always friendly and funny when you'd go through her line, and then she started working in the back so ya didn't see her as often, but anytime she'd see you back there, she'd talk to you. Always something witty or silly to say. That's what I remember about your mom—witty."

I was weeping. I didn't know if this kind nurse actually remembered my mom or if she was just trying to make me feel better, but it made me feel incredibly ill. That horrible feeling I get when the enemy's win overcomes me. Frank had completely burned out such a bright and positive candle. My mom's flame was completely gone forever.

"Well, your mom will never, ever have to be abused by that man again," the nurse said.

I prayed that statement was true, but the way life's paths curve, I didn't believe it yet.

Our brains are strange places. Before returning home that day, I had to stop at Walmart, and because my mind knew my mom was not home, where she had been almost every day for five years, and because I was actively trying not to think about anything, especially not the nursing home, I got that feeling I used to get when I was a little girl and I would look for her at Walmart. I turned the corner of an aisle thinking, *"Maybe she'll be here somewhere,"* and then I realized she'd never be anywhere like that ever again.

I felt like a heartbroken child, and the physical pain weighed on me. I had a fever and chills. I wanted to throw up. I had been chasing Libby my whole life. I just wanted Libby back. I had prayed so hard to have Libby back for thirty years. She was completely gone.

The only thing in my life that was starting to look up was that I did not have to work dogs with Frank anymore. When Travis, Frank's previous assistant, came to help those first couple of weeks that Mom was in the nursing home, he stayed and was back to helping Frank train dogs. I was back to doing everything else for the kennel. I did everything from cleaning to paperwork, but at least I didn't have to train dogs with Frank while he yelled at me and beat the animals.

I remembered one of the first times my mom ran away from Frank when I was a child. Her main condition upon returning home was that she never had to work dogs again. I remember thinking at the time, *"Why not have the only condition be that you get to raise your children? Or see them?"* but after helping him train, being yelled at and insulted every day, I realized that nothing is ever as simple as someone's outside perspective makes it seem.

He had called me a circus freak and a fat clown. He yelled at me for hours every single day. I understood why that condition was kept and why my mom refused to work dogs or work alongside Frank.

I was finally, finally, free of having to spend hours with Frank every day, and that made me feel almost new again. I was finally able to breathe again. At first, I did not even care that it meant Travis had to leave his four- and five-year-olds with me all morning while I did my work and all afternoon while he trained dogs. I happily accepted watching Travis's kids every day for free instead of being around Frank.

However, on days that I got to go see my mom and feed her, make sure she got enough to drink, clean her nails and sing to her, watching the kids meant Ella had to watch all three of them. A five, four, and three-year-old were too overwhelming for Ella, as it would be for any fourteen-year-old kid. It just was not working. I would go see my mom on Saturday and Sunday but would only go see her one afternoon each weekday.

When Karen realized I was watching Travis's kids for him, she started asking me to watch Sara and Becky more often too. The girls were only two and three. It started out that Karen needed to help Chad at work but then they dropped the little girls off with us so they could drive to Missouri and get tattoos. That time, Sara and Becky were with us for two days.

One Saturday, Chad and Karen asked if I could watch the girls, and because I thought it was so Karen could help Chad work, I said I would. I had wanted to go see my mom that day, so when they dropped the girls off, I asked, "When will you be back? Where are you guys going?"

Karen said, "Chad has a job to go do. I'm just gonna be home crafting. I can't sew when they're home."

It was difficult for me to not spring forward like a tiger with my claws out ready to scratch and bite her face off. I had to physically restrain myself and actually rocked back on my heels as her words sent me into a rage that I hid well. Chad didn't see it in my eyes, but I knew Karen could.

I wanted to scream at her that she was a stay-at-home mom and that I wasn't! I had to work all week at a physically demanding job where I physically labored so that she and her husband could inherit a profitable business! I wanted to scream that my only free time that I had had in five years was the ten-minute shower my teenager let me have every day while she watched my baby and that I couldn't remember the last time I got to do a hobby or a craft. I wanted to send her children home with her and tell her that when you have babies, you don't get to sew unless they're asleep. I wanted to remind everyone that I had been taking care of her husband's mom so long that I couldn't even remember the last time I had a free minute to eat a meal that was still hot, but by all means, go craft. Go home and sew!

How dare they not see me at all?

I didn't want to make a scene in front of my children or my nieces, so I watched them, and Karen went home to craft. I wondered how many times I would be able to eat Chad and Karen's shit before I unleashed how I really felt about them. I thought that I was strong enough to hold it in forever and be everyone's slave. I thought my self-esteem was low enough that I could just take it all and eat it all forever and obviously, so did they.

I was still juggling too much even without having to watch Sara and Becky. I wished that I had the energy to want to add two extra toddlers to mine and the two I was watching for Travis, but I did not have the energy.

I thought that once my mom was in a facility, I would be able to figure out a way to get a second income and pay off my car so that we could leave too, but I didn't want Ella to have to watch Henry all day and all evening while I worked a second job. We talked it over, and Ella wanted us to leave so badly too, that she agreed to watch her brother for however long it took each day for us to pay the car off and leave.

So, I took an evening job at a gas station in hopes of getting us away from there and those toxic people.

# CHAPTER ONE HUNDRED ONE

Throughout all of those years, I made all of those poor decisions, which landed me in places like twenty-two and raising a two-year-old alone. Living under Frank's thumb. Thirty-one, pregnant, and alone. Taking care of my mom and the kennel alone. Every bad choice, and everywhere I ended up, came to be because I trusted toxic people. Naivety tossed me into messes I had to clean up alone because I trusted people far too much. I have made terrible, horrible, mistakes, but I am a good person, and good people make the mistake of assuming others are as kind and loving as we are.

Even after having conversations with Frank, where he shared what a hideous monster he was and even after he would beat animals and abuse my mom in front of me, I still tried to take care of him. Even after my younger brother misused and abused my love and self-lessness, I still trusted him, loved him, wanted to do my part in helping him succeed and care for his young family. To this very day, I have to remind myself that asking my children's fathers for help is impossible because they plainly aren't going to help. I have to constantly remind myself of that because I can't fathom a world in which I create a baby and don't throw every ounce of myself into raising and loving that baby.

I often ask myself what the world would be like if instead of shaming, being ugly, violent and hateful to, and even killing homosexuals, some Christians had spent their time shaming and being more interested in correcting the behavior of men who abandon their children.

Moving forward, I pray that I can be less trusting of people and guard myself and my children more carefully. When I say that I am a good person, I don't mean that it has anything to do with me. I was not born good. I am not always good. However, since I was a child, I have asked Jesus to help me become more like Him. I have asked Him to be my constant friend and brother. I have asked Him not to leave me. I have asked Him for a relationship, and when I ask myself what He would do and how to be more like Him, it is impossible to not do good.

I don't always listen to Him, and I do not always choose Him first. During the mess my life was in when I had an infant and an eleven-year-old, and my mom had dementia, my baby was crying, Frank was yelling at me, and the stress of taking care of all the animals, I lost my temper several times. I am still trying to forgive myself for allowing Ella to be the target of those tantrums I threw. She was going through enough, and she did not deserve my fits on top of it.

When Henry was about six months old and Ella was eleven, I walked into Henry's bedroom, expecting it to be tidy, the way I had left it. I was just stepping in to grab his changing table. I needed to bring it into my room. Ella had been building with her Legos in the baby's room. His bedroom floor was covered in piles of Legos, and his changing table had the beginnings of whatever Lego set she had started to build. I was tired, my baby was crying, I had no help with him and no one to rock him while I cleaned this mess up, and absolutely none of that is an excuse for the rage I flew into. I don't even remember what I said or what I did with her Legos. I know I was yelling and picking up handfuls of them, tossing them back into boxes. I messed up her piles. I messed up her building. I hurt her feelings. I tore her heart apart.

That guilt from that fit and a couple of others I threw during the postpartum depression era I can't shake. It keeps me awake to think that I hurt Ella so much over trying to make our lives work there so that I could continue to chase my mom's love around. Like a broken record, some sliver of my heart is stunted in 1993, trying desperately to chase Libby. I tried to chase her to the point that I hurt my own daughter.

One summer when we were stuck in that disgusting, toxic life, I asked Ella to start mowing the yard while I watched the baby and then we'd switch halfway through. Her response was that I could, "Fuck right off."

My hand flew across her cheek before I could stop myself. I slapped her face. How dare I? How dare I treat her that way? How dare I not see her? I was vile, putrid. I refuse to ever be that despicable again. I will never allow the way a toxic person makes me feel dictate how I treat someone else, especially someone who is innocent. Ella has helped me more than anyone ever has in my life, and she has helped far, far more than she should ever have had to. Even though she is a child, she is selfless, she is patient, and she is kind. I take full responsibility for my part in all the chaos. I made many terrible choices.

The year my mom was in the nursing home, and I was working at the kennel and the gas station to pay my car off early so we could leave, I stupidly used my $5000 tax refund on the car. I put the whole thing on that stupid car so that I could pay it off instead of leaving Chad with a repossession. Still, even after putting all that on my car loan, I still owed $4000 on the car. It would be another year before I could pay it off, but my loyalty to Chad made it impossible for me to just give up and leave the car there for him to worry about. If I had left the car there and left, the tax refund could have set us up somewhere where no one was treating us poorly. Rather, I trusted and loved my brother, so we stayed.

My friend Avery had a home in a nearby town that was completely furnished and sitting empty. She had been living with her boyfriend for a couple of years and had no renters in her house. Many times while I was struggling with the disaster of my life, Avery offered to let my children and I live in her empty house. I never accepted the offer because I was terrified that my enormous monthly car payment would hinder me from being able to pay Avery rent and would damage our friendship. I was scared to move for so many reasons, but the more Avery offered for us to live in her empty house, the more I dreamt of living there.

I had asked Chad many times if we could transfer the loan into my name so that I could speak with the lender and ask about refinancing. I asked if there was a way to sell the car with the loan, as it was in very good condition and nearly paid off. Each time, I was dismissed. Chad never wanted to help me with anything because he had his own life, and while I understood that, I was trying to save mine and my children's.

In the meantime, I worked all morning at the kennel and worked evenings at the gas station. I went to see my mom on my days off from the gas station. I tried to figure out where my children and I would go when we left. I had heard a sermon about praying for your Abishai, about praying for someone to come and help you when you are fighting for your life. I was definitely in the battle of my life trying to run away from Frank, and I desperately needed an Abishai. I thought that maybe God would send me a husband and that might be my way out, but I knew I wouldn't find him at a gas station in Nowheresville, Iowa. So, I decided to make a dating profile.

I had not dated since Henry's dad left me four years prior, and I couldn't even remember what dating felt like. I would spend my mornings at work at the kennel staring at my phone, weeding out the trash. I would spend my break at the gas station talking to whomever I had decided was worth talking to that week. By the end of February, I had made a friend I met on a dating app.

Rob is fifteen years older than me. He is intelligent, kind, warm, an amazing listener who didn't make me feel crazy or dramatic, even when I explained where I was in my life and how I had ended up there. He also lived an hour and a half away, and I didn't have the time or freedom to meet him. So, for the first month of our friendship, we just texted almost all day every day, about everything from pop culture, our favorite movies and music to literature and history. We talked about it all, and he let me vent about my life. He listened to hours' worth of voice texts about my mom, my kids, the way Frank treated me, and how Chad and Karen kept leaving their children with me even though I was struggling as it were.

By the end of March, I was asking Ella if she'd watch her brother while I went to meet Rob. Ella had not been to a friend's house in years, and her cousin Alexis was the only one she had left. Even so, she was selfless and kind enough to let me go.

I got dressed up and went to meet Rob, who had made dinner. I had never had a man make me dinner, and what he had cooked was unbelievably delicious. In person, he was charming, a great conversationalist, and he treated me like I was me. He wasn't asking me to do anything for him. He wasn't taking advantage of my kindness. He wasn't demanding anything of me. He wasn't screaming, or crying, or barking, or making messes. He poured *my* drink. He cooked *me* dinner.

When I left, I was ecstatic. I had made a friend who was not only interested in treating me the way I'd always deserved to be treated, but even better, he seemed like he might even be interested in helping me rediscover how I was supposed to treat myself.

As I drove the hour and a half home, I reflected on the last time that I had treated myself well. *When was the last time I had even a shred of self-esteem? Before I met Tyler? Nearly fifteen years ago? Back when I was in high school. Back when I surrounded myself with kind, wonderful, people who were uplifting, positive, and loving. That was the last time I was kind to myself.*

I also wondered how I was going to be able to continue to see Rob without it being a huge burden on my still very young teenager. I felt guilty for leaving my baby to watch my baby, and I felt guilty for never allowing myself any time for myself. I tried to focus on the good feelings from the evening and made it home, grateful to have a new friend.

# CHAPTER ONE HUNDRED TWO

A couple of months after starting my second job at the gas station, I had to quit. Watching three-year-old Henry for up to twelve hours a day while I was at two different jobs was too much for Ella to handle at fourteen years old, and I knew it would be, but I desperately needed to get my children and myself away from Frank.

I was willing to try anything. I put my entire tax refund on the car that was still in Chad's name, hoping to pay it off and drive away from Frank and the kennel forever, but even after putting all my money on that car, I still owed $4000 and did not see a way of coming up with that amount of money for at least another year. So, I worked at the kennel all morning while watching Travis's kids and then took them home with me to watch them and feed them for free while Travis worked dogs with Frank.

Every ounce of my being was happy to be away from Frank and that he was Travis's problem now, but at the same time, I was still being taken advantage of. I was still being paid too little and still living in a house that was not only in shambles, but it was next door to Frank and owned by him, and therefore, we were still his property. We were still to be bossed around and subjected to his temper.

When Frank told me I was going to have to take him to his routine colonoscopy, to ensure his cancer had not returned, I called Chad to see if he would take his dad instead. *Why should I have to take him when it was his selfishness that caused me to have to drive myself to and from my tonsillectomy and drive myself to go have a baby?*

Chad didn't answer his phone and had not been to see our mom at the nursing home at all. I could see he was completely abandoning his family and his responsibilities. I started to wonder if when I paid off the car, would it be mine or Chad's new wife's new car?

After Frank's colonoscopy, he loudly yelled through the hallways to the doctor, "Why did you put my butthole up so high?" which I wish I could blame on the anesthesia, but he had asked me the same question after his first surgery.

The doctor and I both ignored his moronic question, but unfortunately, the doctor continued to show me photographs at the inside of Frank's colon, explaining what we were viewing as though I was family, as though I cared. I did not listen to the doctor. Somehow, his words had become a rhetorical question, "Why are you so insistent on eating these people's shit that you're actually climbing up inside this guy's asshole? Now get out!"

It was early April. Rob and I had been friends for a couple of months when I asked Ella if she minded watching Henry on a Saturday evening while I went to Rob's for dinner. She agreed that it would be good for me to go somewhere other than home, church, the nursing home, or work. Rob was a fantastic cook. I've never eaten food as incredible as his. He listened and was a good conversationalist, funny, kind, comforting, and warm. Before I realized what was happening, he helped me change my view of myself.

While he cooked dinner, he would let me take a nap in his bed. No one, not even my parents, had ever treated me that well. I was eating delicious meals at Rob's house, but I was inhaling heaping spoonfuls of self-esteem.

Offhandedly, I mentioned my lip color was Revlon 425 Soft Silver Red. The next time I was at his house, there were five Soft Silver Reds on his bathroom sink. I started to simultaneously laugh and cry. This man did not have to choose me to show kindness to, and yet, he chose me. I had been married before, and I had never been shown such a romantic act of kindness and respect. Someone whom I respected, looked up to, and adored had taken the time to show me he was listening to me. He was showing me that what I said and how I felt mattered to him, even though he was receiving nothing but my friendship in return. So, I started to believe my friendship must be worth something, and therefore, I must be worth something.

All of the parts of my brain that Frank had darkened started to light back up. I wondered if my mom had had someone treat her so beautifully one of the times she had run away from Frank, if maybe she would not have gone back. If she had someone like Rob healing her with kindness and thoughtfulness, maybe she would not have gone back to Frank to have her mind evaporate.

I deeply regret not going to see her more often that spring. Most of my time, energy, and focus was on my children and myself. Each time I would go see my mom, she was farther gone. She stopped remembering both my name and her own. She stopped responding to my questions. She stopped asking to go home and would get up and pace around the hallways with the other patients with dementia.

Sundowning is what it's called when they wander around and pace at dusk. Only, when there are a lot of people with dementia in a small area, they tend to follow one another whether it's dusk or not. I would be sitting next to her trying to chat, simply to stimulate her mind so she'd feel less alone, and someone would wander by, so she'd get up and join them, leaving me sitting alone. Selfishly, I thought she didn't need me anymore because she did not even notice my presence.

My trips to Jefferson turned into once a week instead of three times, and then it was once every two weeks. Before I knew it, the receptionist was saying, "We haven't seen you in a while. Is everything okay?"

"It's just getting more and more difficult, watching her decline," was my response, and it should have made me feel horrible and ashamed that even the staff had noticed my absence, but it didn't. I had stopped chasing my mother's love and the notion that I could save her. Was it at an opportune time? No.

I probably should have stopped chasing Libby when I was six years old.

On a phone call with Mellissa from around that time, I asked her why she thought I had spent my whole life trying to help mom. My sister was ten years older than me, and I was not wrong in thinking she'd have some insight. When she answered my difficult question, I knew that her answer was not cruel but incredibly accurate.

She said, "I think it was because somewhere along the way, she convinced you that she loved you."

If Mellissa had said that five years prior or ten years prior, I would have felt insulted and angry, but after really seeing my mom's choices and taking a step back from her long enough to really see what happens when you choose a man over your children, your grandchildren, your friends, family, community, and yourself, I knew it was true. It was not because my mom didn't intend to love me that she never loved me. It was that she had never been taught how to love. She had never been shown love, and she did not love herself. My childish delusion that my mom had ever loved me had me try to be her hero at the risk of my own life.

I had to take my life back.

I had not been to see my mom in three weeks when Jefferson called me to tell me she'd fallen out of her chair at breakfast. They did not know why or what caused it and said that she may have had a mini stroke. They said that she was resting in her bed now and that Dr. Spiva was going to come and check on her later. I got off the phone, told Ella to watch Henry, and drove down the road to tell Frank.

I knew this episode was not a mini stroke and that it was my fault. "They don't help her remember to eat and drink," I told Frank for the eightieth time since my mom had been taken to Jefferson. "She didn't have a stroke. She's passing out due to malnourishment and dehydration," I said.

I had been asking Frank and Chad to go up to Jefferson around a mealtime to make sure that she ate or drank for the four months that she'd been there. Neither of them had been to see her even once. I suggested we make a schedule of people to go up and feed her. I offered that we could put her in a nursing home that knows she can't remember to eat and will feed her by hand like I did when I was there. Frank didn't believe me about the eating and the drinking and didn't seem to care. He constantly dismissed me when I told him she was not getting enough to eat or drink.

My brother Jordan was the only one who had visited her regularly, bringing her food and making sure she ate it. Ruby visited Mom a couple of times but realistically, Mellissa and Ruby lived too far away to be able to help with a feeding schedule.

I called Jordan the day Mom had her episode, and he met me at Jefferson. When we walked into her room, she was asleep with a onesie on and a fan blowing on her. She looked like a baby. She felt like my baby. I wanted to manifest a house in a town far away where she and my children were my only care, and I tended to them all day—healthy food, and lots of water, and peace. Rather, we were in a dirty nursing home where people were moaning in pain, and my mom wasn't getting enough to eat.

I explained to the nurses while shaking because I hate confrontation, that she had not had a mini stroke. She'd passed out due to low blood sugar and dehydration because she forgets to feed herself. I knew the nurses were understaffed and that they didn't care.

I started over, trying to balance going to the nursing home to feed my mom and also focusing on myself and moving on with my life, but those two pulled me apart. Feeling better about myself was something I had to do. Regaining my survival instincts after Frank had tried to piss all over them in order to keep me there caused me to pull farther away from anyone and everyone who had anything to do with my mom, and before I knew it, Jefferson was calling again with the same story. My mom had passed out and hit her face. This time, she'd been taken to the hospital. It seemed like "mini stroke," was their favorite code word for, "We forgot to feed your mom."

I called her doctor's office to see if they had any blood work confirming whether or not my mom was having strokes, and they had none. They had no information whatsoever. A nurse practitioner who was on call at Jefferson called me to try to smooth things over and sweet talk me into thinking they were doing the best they could. My use of the words, "malnourishment," and "dehydration," were scaring them, I could tell even over the phone.

The second time my mom collapsed, Frank asked me, "What is going on up there?"

"I told you. They are not feeding her enough. She's getting dizzy and passing out, just like you would if you forgot to eat except for two meals in a week, and I can only go up there two meals a week! I have kids!"

Frank decided to finally brave the nursing home. He would go and feed her lunch after church on Sundays. I went on Wednesdays and Saturdays, but it still wasn't enough, and we both could tell. So, we asked Chad and Karen if they'd take a turn one day a week, and we asked people at church if they would go up and feed her, but everyone had their own lives to live.

# CHAPTER ONE HUNDRED THREE

More often, I would find my afternoons were spent with both of Travis's kids and both Chad and Karen's toddlers at my house with my son Henry, of course, as well. I kept dancing between the feeling that I was helping Chad and Karen earn money to provide for my nieces, so it was okay but also feeling like I was being taken advantage of by my brother's manipulative wife, who saw my kindness as vulnerability.

I felt I would be a hypocrite if I told them I couldn't watch their children while begging them to go see and feed my mom who felt like my child. They never went to see her the entire time she was at Jefferson. By the third phone call I received from Jefferson regarding my mom falling, I was numb. I had spent four months' worth of sunrises thanking Jesus for her finally being removed from Frank and yet asking for her safety and health to be taken care of at Jefferson, and it felt like I could no longer worry about her.

I had been petrified that abuse and neglect were going to kill my mother for twenty-eight years with little to no rest from that anxiety. I was beginning to disassociate from my mother entirely. I was actively trying to convince myself that she was already gone and buried. Then, staff from Jefferson called to say she was being driven in an ambulance to a hospital in the city for hip surgery because this fall had broken her hip.

After I got off the phone with Jefferson, Frank called me from his truck on his way to the hospital to let me know what had happened. He told me he'd call me with updates as he found out more information. When I got off the phone with Frank, Chad's wife Karen called me. Frank had told Chad, and Karen wanted to sound concerned. She claimed she wanted to see if I was all right, but I knew her too well by now and wanted no part of any conversation with her. I told her I was fine.

"Are you going to go and see her?" Karen asked.

"No. I'm home with my kids and it's already 7:00 PM. There's nothing I can do tonight, and Frank is already there," I replied.

"I feel like one of us should be up there with her," she said.

I realized what she was doing. It entertained Karen to manipulate the stupid and the vulnerable. She was not smart enough to ever manipulate anyone with half a brain, so she had learned that it was fun to make people do things when they were either clueless or vulnerable and blinded by pain and trauma. A few times when I was so tired I was running on fumes, during the time where Mom was still home, and my list of beings and responsibilities was so great I had not had the energy to see Karen's manipulations, she'd been able to trick me into feeling sorry for her or excusing and ignoring certain insulting or inexcusable behaviors. This evening, she was using my mother's broken hip to test me. She wanted to see what she could make me do. She assumed too much about me. She assumed that I had such low self-worth that she could talk me into anything. It was her hobby to experiment with people's emotions and minds.

"One of us is up there with her. Frank is there, and she's probably asleep and on pain medication right now anyway," I said.

"But I mean one of us. Not Frank. Frank's not gonna do anything," Karen said.

"If you want to go up there, you can," was my response, and I had had about enough of this game. I was too tired to play, 'high school.'

"You need to go! What if she gets up to wander around like she does and gets lost?" Karen asked.

"She can't get up. She broke her hip," I said, making it clear that she had not met her match. I was done with her, and I was not her match. I was, and am, far, far, too good and kind of a person to be wasting time on scumbags like Karen.

The next evening, after my mom's hip surgery, I took my children to the hospital to see her. They had missed her. It was now May, and Ella and Henry hadn't seen my mom since Christmas Eve. I took a picture of my mom holding Henry's hand. She held his hand in hers with her hospital bracelet, and I had to take a picture to remind myself of the weight of the moment.

This is what my grandchildren will see and feel if I don't take care of myself. If I don't love myself, instead of playing basketball with Henry's children, they might be holding my hand after I've had hip surgery, after an accident, which was caused by my passing out due to forgetting to feed myself.

I must feed myself now–and only good things. I must feed myself now–and only healthy things. I must feed myself now–and only love.

The hospital staff told Frank and I that, undoubtedly, my mom's injuries were due to malnourishment and severe dehydration. They told us that my mom was starving to death, and that if we allowed her to return to Jefferson, she would most likely go into kidney failure due to not getting enough fluids. They didn't say it, but they strongly implied that if we were to send my mom back to Jefferson, they'd come after Frank for neglect, and then they gave him several options of facilities where she would receive better care.

Perhaps it was strange, but to me, this was an answer to prayer. I hated that my mom had been hurt, and it made me sick to think about her falling or going without food, but it was a way for her to be moved to a better facility and forced Frank to let her live somewhere that was clean and had better resources and staff. After a day or two of healing at the hospital, the ambulance moved my mom to a nursing home in a nearby town. Frank went to meet her there while I went and picked up her belongings from Jefferson.

One of the men who ran Jefferson helped me out to my car with my mom's boxes. I had grown up with him and knew him well, so when he said, "She's not coming back?" I knew he meant, "Are you going to sue us?"

I knew that if I said, "No, she's not coming back. You let her get in such abysmal shape that she was starving to death, so the hospital won't even allow us to let her come back to this wretched shithole," he would call me a bitch behind my back to people that I knew. So, I simply said, "Nope," and thanked him for helping me carry her things to my car.

As I unpacked my mom's belongings and put them away in her new room at her new nursing home, I thanked Jesus for getting her out of Jefferson. The new facility was cleaner. She had her own room. Nothing was broken, falling apart, or leaking, and the building smelled like disinfectant rather than urine. The staff not only understood that she needed to be fed by hand every meal, but there were enough of them on staff to actually accomplish that task. They seemed much more professional, and once again, I felt a touch of relief when I went home that night, hoping my mom would finally be safe.

# CHAPTER ONE HUNDRED FOUR

Frank said he saw the clothes my mom was wearing when she fell and broke her hip, and that they were, "covered in shit and blood." With the trauma of breaking her hip and the effects anesthesia has on the brain of someone with dementia, my mom could no longer speak at all.

Every time I went to see her at the new nursing home, she was silent, and she could not move or walk. Frank went every day and yelled at the staff that she needed physical therapy and that she should be up and walking. Ella and I all tried to explain to Frank that they would try, but that my mom most likely would never walk again.

My mom was weak, in pain, and did not want to get up and walk. She didn't even have the mental capacity to understand the concept of walking, let alone being able to accomplish it having just broken her hip.

"She will have to learn how to walk again," I said to Frank. "And do you know what the problem is with learning to walk again when you have dementia?"

Of course, he could not fathom the answer to my question, having yet to look up dementia in the five years his wife had been diagnosed. He had no response.

"She can't learn to walk again because she can't learn. Her brain is dying. The ability for her brain to learn is over. Gone." I went on, but he did not care.

Frank was still convinced that Jesus was going to completely cure my mom and that if he kept pushing her, she would go back to "her old self."

The new nursing home was feeding her regularly, giving her medications, and keeping her and her room clean. Those were answers to my prayers, but now I was afraid Frank yelling at the staff was going to get my mom sent back home to him. God bless the nurses who deal with people like Frank every day. I could never do their work.

The first time I tried to turn on our air conditioner in our trailer that summer, it was clear it was not going to work at all. I was in no position financially to fix, replace, or buy an air conditioner, so I went to Facebook with suggestions on how to survive the summer without one. Our house was basically a hot tin can soaking up the sun all day, and it was 110 to 120 degrees inside each afternoon. I took my kids outside because it was cooler and because my trailer was in such deplorable shape the windows didn't have screens, so there were fewer flies outside than inside my house.

Chad and Karen showed up one evening in late May with two window air conditioning units that they'd bought for us at Walmart. Chad installed them, and I thought, *"He is doing this so you will have to do whatever he wants all summer."* The old me would have thanked Jesus for a brother who was kind. The new me had experience with Chad.

In the middle of the night, I got a text from Chad telling me he overbooked himself at work and didn't have a babysitter for the next day, asking if l I could watch his girls so Karen could help him at work. I told him yes and asked him if Ella could go with them because she'd been wanting to get out of the house and wanted to learn from Chad and Karen how to operate the heavy equipment. Chad said Ella could go with them.

The next day, Karen dropped her girls off with me, Travis's kids, and Henry and took Ella with her. I asked Karen how long they would be gone, and she said she would be gone for two or three hours. She said she would be gone longer than Chad because he was at a different job site, and he'd be there to pick up the girls in about two hours.

I told Karen, "It's really difficult for me to watch five kids under five years old by myself. Are you sure it will only be a couple of hours? Otherwise, I'll need Ella to stay here."

Karen promised Chad would be there to get the girls in a couple of hours. About an hour after Karen and Ella left, Ella texted me that Karen was not working or at a job site. Ella was sitting at a nail salon while Karen got her nails done. Ella was crying because she hadn't brought anything to read or do because she thought she'd be helping Karen work and that she was very hungry, but that Karen was ignoring her.

I was furious. Not only had they lied to me, taken advantage of my kindness, and used me again, but they had taken my helper. Not only had they treated me like absolute garbage again, but also Ella was hungry, disappointed, sad, and bored and there was nothing I could do to help.

For three hours while Karen got her nails done, Ella texted me begging me to come and get her because she was so hungry she felt like she was going to pass out. I had to tell her I had five little kids with me and no way to take all of them with me into town. I had been promised that Chad, who was not answering his phone, would come and get his daughters within two hours and it had been three.

"How is she even still getting her nails done?" I texted Ella.

"She's getting designs on every single one of them!" she replied back via text.

I was irate. It is incredibly expensive to get a design on every nail and here I was, having trouble paying my bills and buying groceries because I worked at the kennel Chad and Karen were inheriting. I ate nothing but canned vegetables for dinner most nights because I had a $500 car payment that was still in Chad's name and because I didn't want his future business to go under. I wanted to do the right thing and pay off the car that I had already paid $27,000 on and still had $4000 left to go but didn't want a repossession on Chad's credit.

I was in an abusive situation, and I had not been in a financial situation where I could go get my nails done in five or six years, and even if I had the money, I had a toddler, so I still would not be able to go get my nails done.

All I felt was rage.

When Chad finally answered his phone, I asked him why he was an hour and a half late and why he had lied to me about where Karen was going. He threw the air conditioners in my face, just as I knew he would when he brought them into my trailer.

"How about I'm the only reason you and your kids aren't melting right now and you watch my kids?" Chad yelled and hung up on me.

My limit to picking up everyone's slack had been hit. When Karen finally showed up four hours later to get her daughters, I told her everything I thought of her and her lazy, lying, and manipulative ways. I told her I was never going to watch her kids again and asked her if she could imagine how Ella felt.

Karen started to cry and asked me, "Why are you even still here if you are clearly so miserable?"

I said, "I'm trying to pay this car off before I leave because I don't want to ruin Chad's credit, but I'm not even sure if he'll let me keep it after I pay it off. I'm here because I want the business that Chad inherits to be prosperous so he has something to fall back on if what you guys are currently doing falls through. I'm here because I want to raise my kids showing them that you don't abandon family."

Karen's response was just the right straw. "Amelia, you aren't family. You won't ever be treated like family here. If you were, you'd be living over there," she said, pointing to the empty mansion behind her. Pointing at the house Frank had built for Chad that sat next to my old trailer. The house that sat empty for nearly a decade next to my mouse, wasp, and spider-infested trailer with the broken air conditioner, furnace, and toilet.

An outsider was pointing out that I had been working there all those years while having to look at that nice, new, giant, empty house next door. An outsider was pointing out that even she could see that I was being used and abused, and that was my last straw.

After making Karen cry, I knew from experience with Chad and calling him out in a lie that he would be mad enough to give me the speech he had in his back pocket, listing everything I had ever done wrong in my life.

Rather than calling me and yelling at me so I could respond and defend myself like the previous times he had screamed at me, he wrote his speech in a text.

"Okay, here's the deal, Amelia. You need to have a grown up lesson. People have babied you your whole adult life. I know you don't see it that way, but that's how it is. You live rent and bill free. You act like you are a put-upon mother, but you chose to have a second kid by yourself. You make Ella watch him, and she will never have kids or any chance at a normal life.

"When you want things in life, you have to work for them. I worked forty hours a week, and another 80 at the quarry for six months to get far enough ahead. You have to do unpleasant things in life. I chose for Karen to stay home with our kids. If she wants to get her nails done it's because she's taking care of our kids, maintaining our home, being my secretary. If I had to pay someone to do all of those things it would cost me $1200 a week. She's very underpaid. She's also the person who tries to get other people to do things to help you.

*"You probably didn't want to lose her as a friend, but no one has an obligation to be your friend. When you burn bridges in real life, that's how it works. People are gone. Ella doesn't need to be apologized to by anyone but you. She's well aware of how things work at our house. When she's with us, if she's hungry, she'll ask. She's like another kid when she's here. She also knew where she was going before they pulled out of the driveway. She could have stayed home, but she wanted a vacation.*

*"We will most certainly find someone else to watch them from now on. I could be irate that you have the audacity to yell at my wife in front of my kids, but I'm sure you're aware of all of the things I would say. You are in your position in life because of choices you've made. This is another one. I'm not sure why you think I'm so violent and unhinged, but I'm not. I had to grow up and learn to control my emotions when I'm upset. There's nothing wrong with being upset, but you handled it very poorly, and that's only on you.*

*"I don't have a lot more to say to you. I'm not interested in your car. It's worth less than you owe on it, and by the time you pay it off, it will be worth like 4500 bucks. I don't need 4500 bucks, and if I did,, I wouldn't steal your car. I have watched your son push my daughters down on concrete, and you do nothing. If I was going to hit him at any point, I would have slapped him then because he needed it. Your kids are always safe and welcome here, and you know that, and I will continue to help you as I can because of your kids, but Karen isn't obligated to put up with abuse from you, for any reason, especially not because she took the time to do something for herself.*

*"She hadn't even talked to me and was totally unprepared for you to explode on her. That was unnecessary, uncalled for, and childish. We were like an hour and a half late. I'm sorry if that caused you any inconvenience. It won't be an issue in the future. I'm going to hang out with my family now. I've had to take 45 minutes of my time with my daughters to calmly type this out for you. I won't answer you again tonight, so don't bother sending me a book or calling me."*

Before I even read his message, I had decided I was abandoning the car, the kennel, my younger brother, and his family. Karen's disgusting way of lying and manipulating had knocked that sense into me, and so, as I read Chad's unkind words, I knew I wouldn't respond. I knew I would be blocking him and moving on.

But if I had responded I would have asked, *"How have I been babied my whole adult life? By whom? I've been left alone to raise two kids by two different men. My dad died when I was 25, and my mom was diagnosed with dementia the same year my second baby was born. I had to take care of both of them, our mom, and your kennel completely alone. I had to go to battle over and over for our mom's health and well-being at the risk of my own! I have cleaned up both of your parents' poop. I have driven both of your parents to medical procedures, multiple times. Anyone who knows me knows how tragically difficult my life has been. You don't even know me at all, do you? I live rent and bill free in a trailer that has been falling down and crumbling around me for a decade. I live there because the two people that let me live there were brainwashing me into thinking I had to and could not do better. You don't even know me at all, do you? You said I act like I'm a put-upon mother who chose to have a second baby by myself. How is this a sentence someone has said to me? Is there a way to force men to come back and be a dad? Is there a husband and father store I can go buy someone at? Do you even know what you are talking about?*

*"I did force parenthood on Ella, and Ella has had a lot of hurt and trauma because of my actions. I try every second of every day in every way that I can to show her how wrong I was to do that. I will never stop trying to show her I'm sorry and help her make much better choices than I have. You're right, it's my choices that have put me here. You talk about work and doing unpleasant things. There's nothing more unpleasant than being around your dad, Frank Hudson, and you and I both know that. I woke up every day for five years and worked with him at a business I was trying to keep alive for you. I worked there cleaning up dog poop, then I cleaned up your dad's poop off the bathroom walls, and then I cleaned your mom's poop up off her body. Do you really think I don't know about unpleasant? Do you even know who I am?*

*"You talk about all of the things Karen does for you and that you want her to stay home to raise your kids, be your secretary, and keep your house clean. Do you realize that I go to work just like you do, and then I come home and do all of the types of things that Karen does for you and your chil-*

*dren by myself? That would be fine and wonderful except people drop their children off with me, and I watch them for free, and then they don't come and pick them up on time, and I become overwhelmed with all of the work at my actual job, all the of the work taking care of your dad's laundry and housework, going and seeing our mom, and then all of the work of running my own household. That is why I have been asking for your help for years.*

*"In the same message where you ask why I think you are unhinged, you talk about slapping my three-year-old son. You insinuate that he should have been slapped for pushing another toddler. If you had bothered to raise your own son instead of abandoning him, you'd know that boys are different than girls. They often play rougher. I'm working on it with Henry, but how do you teach a baby not to hit by hitting them? Do you have any mind of your own or did you turn into a clone of your dad?*

*"To the parts about my friendship with Karen being over, I won't even really respond. I was never friends with her. Again, who do you think I am? She was the only person trying to get you to help me? Well, that is very sad, Chad. No one should have had to advocate for your sister to get help with your business, your mom, your dad, your niece and nephew. You should want to help, but it seems like you don't even know me, let alone love me.*

*"At the end where you say you spent forty-five minutes texting this out to me, and you wanted to spend that time with your family, just think if you'd wanted to spend that time with your family earlier when you were hours late picking up your kids. You asked me not to respond with a book because you don't want me to point all of these things out to you, and you didn't want to spend any more energy on me. You wanted to use me for as long as you could, just like everyone else who is unfortunate enough to cross your path. When you were a teenager it was for borrowing cash and stealing my jewelry for random girls. You stole three months' worth of my car payments when I had a newborn. The last few years, you used me for everything from taking care of the kennel and taking care of your parents to taking care of your kids.*

*"I thought you loved me. Maybe not as much as I loved you, but I did think that you loved me, and now I finally see that you don't even know me."*

Chad's message made me sob for so many reasons. He talked about my mishandling of my emotions and how it was okay to be upset, but that I handled it poorly. Chad, Frank, and Tyler all liked to use that insinuation. By the time I had asked for help with something for years and finally did it in a way that they couldn't ignore, usually by exploding in anger when my more ladylike attempts were ignored, they would claim I was crazy, violent, or otherwise wrong.

The only advice I have for someone who is asking for help repeatedly and being told no, and when their pleas become violent being told that they are in the wrong, is to get away from that person. Get away from that person long before your pleas for help become anger filled. They are never going to help you and they're only going to hurt you. You're better off completing the task alone.

After reading Chad's text, I called my older brother Jordan, who gave me the pep talk I needed. I needed Jordan to help me gain the momentum to put a plan into place to get myself and my children out of there.

# CHAPTER ONE HUNDRED SIX

When Ella was eleven and her brother was a newborn, I had her favorite little dog that she was best friends with put down. His name was Sir, and he looked like he was a Chihuahua mix but slightly bigger, about twenty pounds. I named him Sir the first night we brought him home, even though he was only ten pounds then. He followed me around the whole night, and I kept almost tripping over him. I had said, "Excuse me, Sir," enough times by the end of the night that it stuck.

I had not even realized that in the four years we'd had him that he'd become Ella's best friend. I knew she spent a lot of time with him, and he followed her around. I knew he'd wait for her to get home from school every day and lie on her pajamas until she returned. I knew he sighed like she did, mimicking her reaction to my asking her to do a chore. How I missed that she loved him, I have no idea. I prided myself on my attentive mothering. I thought I knew everything about her, and yet, I completely missed something so huge. I had not realized how much she cared for Sir until it was too late.

Sir had always been aggressive with men. He hated Frank and Travis, and he had tried to attack Chad. Sir growled and nipped at every mailman and UPS guy he got close to, and before I had my baby, I could call Sir off. He would either be in the house when the delivery man entered the yard, or I could call him as soon as I saw the UPS truck pull into the driveway and tell him to behave, but now that I was distracted with my newborn, I wasn't able to call him off. I didn't want Sir left in the house with the baby in case he decided that the baby was a threat. I didn't know if I could trust him and mentioned it to Chad, who hated the dog as he'd been bit by Sir. Chad voted to take care of him, or cull him, which is what happened to animals around there when they were either a threat or no longer useful. Ella told us she was okay with us putting Sir down because she didn't want anyone to get bitten, especially not the baby.

I should have figured it out. I should have been paying more attention to my daughter. I can't believe I didn't, and I don't know how I missed how much Sir meant to her. She dressed him up in doll clothes all the time, and he didn't even protest. He really was a good boy, he was just trying to protect us. I have no excuse. The toxic poisonous ways of the world we lived in seeped in through my postpartum depression, lack of sleep, and distractions with my baby, and all of that overtook the exhausted brain cells I had left.

I regret all of the times I let my daughter down. I wish I would have been more present and less judgmental with her. I wish I had known that, by accepting the people I allowed to be in her life, I was causing her to be unable to communicate, even with me. I can't imagine how bad that hurt to lose her dog, and what's more, I can't believe that under the stress I allowed myself to become a monster that allows dogs to be put down.

I sent the letter Chad wrote me, the one where he accused me of being babied my whole life, to the rest of my siblings. I'm sure they agreed with parts of it. I'm sure they thought I should not be living on Frank's property, whether rent free or not. I'm sure they thought, at times, over the years, that if I didn't need Mom's help as much financially, she would have been able to free herself and join us in the real world.

My list of regrets is unfortunately long.

I was twenty-two with a two-year-old when I showed up there, broken hearted and already tired. I lost my management position due to living too far away from the salon because my mom and Frank had moved us without even telling me. Three years later, my dad died, which threw me into such a deep depression I thought about suicide every day for five years.

When I finally started to get over my dad's death, I was left pregnant and alone the same year my mom was diagnosed with advanced phase dementia, and everything only got worse from there. I still should have made better choices. Part of me wants to say, "But you didn't choose suicide or meth. You didn't choose to abandon your children or your mom." Part of me wants to say, "But you did let depression drive a wedge between yourself and your daughter, yourself and any semblance of a good financial or romantic situation, and you chose poorly by sleeping with someone who didn't want to become a father."

I have made huge mistakes. I have made selfish, irrational choices. I have made my daughter help me raise my son. I have made her grow up far too quickly and did not understand her growing pains. I watched my mom make horrible choices when raising me, and then I let those toxins sweep me up and throw me into the same garbage.

I will spend the rest of my life making sure Ella and Henry are never hurt by my choices again.

After I read Chad's letter, I blocked him and his wife on any avenue of communication and called Jordan. My older brother Jordan gave me the pep talk I needed to convince me that I could, should, and would get myself and my children out of that horrible situation and away from Frank forever. After I got off the phone with Jordan, I called Mellissa to ask her if we could live with her and her family in Texas until I got on my feet.

Mellissa and her husband make a very handsome living and had enough space for my kids and me. While I knew her husband would not be thrilled about us staying with them, I knew Mellissa could, would, and will always help me in any way she can and that she wanted my kids and me away from Frank just as much as I did. She said we could spend at least six months living with them, so I began to make a plan for the next ten weeks.

I sold our belongings one small thing at a time. I knew that if Frank came inside of my trailer and noticed things were disappearing, we would be in danger. I thought he might actually even kill me if I tried to leave. I spent a lot of time in prayer and watched Jesus do something miraculous that summer. He built a wall around my home so that even though I sold at least fifty percent of our belongings including kitchen appliances and bedroom sets, Frank never noticed or saw anyone loading things into their trucks.

Frank never came inside my house or asked about our other dogs I had re-homed. I donated plasma and sold enough of our stuff to keep us on our feet while I searched for a job in Texas. I got a storage unit where I kept the things we couldn't part with selling and our keepsakes. I checked my credit score for the first time in my life and found out I had sparkling credit. When I went to the bank and asked for a car loan, I was accepted right away.

My mom and Frank had always told me my credit would be terrible and nonexistent because I had never had any credit, and that was one of the things I had just accepted about myself. I never even tried to improve my financial or romantic situations because I was constantly being told by my mom and Frank that I couldn't be successful in those aspects of life, and because I had enough on my plate, trying to be a good mother, I had never even checked my credit score.

I felt so alone every time I had considered leaving in the past, but this time, this move, I was not alone in executing. Jesus was with me now. I had a car waiting for me in Jordan's driveway so that Frank wouldn't see it and ask questions, and Ella, Henry, and I were counting down the days until Texas.

# CHAPTER ONE HUNDRED SEVEN

The car that was in Chad's name that I had already paid $27,000 toward, was no longer my problem and never was. I let go of the idea that I should be helping Chad. For one thing, he stole from me when I was on maternity leave, stealing out of the mouths of my children. For another thing, he tricked me into cleaning his house for free, the summer while I was pregnant. He had lied to me, stolen from me, ignored me, berated me, and he had never even gotten to know me.

I let go of all things Chad those ten weeks as we prepared to leave the kennel. As I write this, I feel nothing but sorry for him. He will ruin his life over and over, hurting numerous people along the way, just like his dad did with his life, and it is due to one solitary compulsion–that need to feed his own ego.

I feel badly for the ten-year-old version of myself who wanted so desperately to rescue her baby brother. In spite of every attempt I made, he still became his dad. I will always pray that he changes that about himself before it's too late.

Perhaps it was delusions of grandeur, but for some reason, I thought the day my children and I finally left and headed to Texas and freedom that everyone would be excited for us. For ten years, my friends and family felt we should leave and that we were enslaved by evil. Now that we were finally free, the few people who knew we were leaving that day forgot. No one texted us or checked on us. The parade I foolishly expected was absent.

We needed that parade. We were broken, lifeless, dying in a ditch, and we had dragged ourselves out of that ditch and to freedom and everyone had forgotten. Mellissa was there at her house to greet us, of course, and I am so grateful that she is my sister, and she loves me, but because she had not lived through what Ella, Henry, and I had lived through, she was not aware of how completely demolished we were. She was not aware of how badly we needed to hear that we were not going to die. It honestly felt like we were going to die, and we needed community around us telling us we were going to be okay.

We felt so alone.

Frank had no idea where we were, and we were safe. We had a place to sleep, but I doubted myself so strongly from all the years of abuse. I needed that parade. When people finally leave an abusive situation, they need a community of fireworks and hope. They need everyone they know meeting them with reassuring smiles because they've been told and sold on the idea that they are worthless garbage that can't make it on their own.

After a couple of nights in Texas, I wanted to go back to the abuse that I was used to. I was so sure I'd made a mistake in leaving, and everything was so expensive in Texas, I couldn't do it all alone. Everything was so overwhelmingly different, I was ready to go back to the kennel. I found out that in the wealthy area my sister lived in Texas, it was impossible for me to afford rent. Even if I worked two or three jobs, I would be barely making enough to pay bills and feed my kids. When I went to apply for housing assistance, I was told I needed to prove that I made a minimum of $2700 per month just to qualify for help! I didn't have a job yet, and $2700 a month was so much to me. I had only made $1200 a month at the most, before.

I was so discouraged. I'd made the biggest mistake of my life. After Henry went to sleep one night, I told Ella I was going to let her live with her dad, let Henry live with whichever one of my siblings would raise him, and kill myself. At the time, I truly felt that was what Jesus wanted me to do. I could not imagine why He had given me these children. I had made their lives so hard and we had come so far only to find out we were going to have to go back to Frank's.

I couldn't go back to Frank's. I would rather die. So, that was the choice I was making.

Ella cried and begged me to see how crazy I was being, but I could not think of another way. I was sure that my existence was the problem and that I was going to continue to ruin my children's lives. If Tyler had not ever told me how much of a problem my existence was, maybe I would not have felt that way. If Chad had not ever told me how much of a problem my existence was, maybe I would not have felt that way. I do not know. Maybe I would have felt that way anyway, but all I knew was that I had been told by both of them repeatedly that it was I who was not working hard enough.

It was I who was babied my entire life. It was I who was a terrible mother. So, I believed my existence was holding my children back from living the lives they deserved. I knew I couldn't live without them, knowing they were out there without me, and I wanted to just die.

I have wanted to die many, many times in my life, but in those moments in Texas, I was ready to go. I was too tired, broken and sad. I had no emotional support. I felt more worthless than I ever had before.

The next morning, I tried to find emotional support. I tried praying. I tried to find another way other than suicide. I texted and called everyone I knew, trying to find a place to stay back in Iowa where it was more affordable to live. I didn't ask Jordan or Ruby if we could stay with them and their families because I did not want to put them in a position where they had to say no to me and my three- and fifteen-year-olds.

When I asked her for advice, Ruby gave me the number of a person who might be able to help me in Kansas City with finding a homeless shelter we could stay at. I had never considered a homeless shelter in my life. Ruby told me to mention that we had been abused by Frank because it would move us up the list for places like shelters or battered women's shelters.

I called many homeless shelters and places for women and children who had been abused, and all of them in the area of Iowa where we were from had waiting lists. If there are so many men abusing women to the point that all of the shelters to protect women from those men are full, what does that say about us?

I called my pastor and his wife, who prayed with me but didn't offer us a place to stay. I asked if we could stay in the church while we looked for a place, and they told us we could not. I felt surely Jesus wanted me to end my life and let my children have a chance to live a better one without me.

I told my friends Charlotte and Avery how I was feeling because I didn't know if I could keep myself from hurting myself before I made arrangements for my kids to live with other people.

Avery said I was, "being crazy" and seemed too busy for me. She had an empty, furnished house back in Iowa that she had offered my children and me many times over the years because of our abusive living situation with Frank, but now that I desperately needed to stay there, even temporarily, she said she could not actually let me live there. She had been living with her boyfriend for years while her house sat empty, and we had been friends since we were kids, but when I really needed help, sometimes people are just too busy with their own lives.

Charlotte was very worried about me and told me to check myself in somewhere. I thought about how long I would be struggling in the courts to get my kids back if I had ever made it out of "somewhere." These friends were giving me clinical answers, not the answers they'd need to hear if it were they who were drowning, and yet, they had made better life choices than I had, and it was not their problem. I know that and do not blame them for anything they said or did not say because how can someone prepare you for helping your friend and her children when they are homeless?

Each night, I laid in bed listening to my teenager cry because she knew her mom was suicidal, and her options were going back to

Frank or be homeless with a suicidal mom. She could go live with her dad who did not love her and was not going to be good and kind to her, and she knew if she chose that life, she'd never see her mom again and would rarely see her baby brother.

Now, I know why my mom went back. Real life is not like the movies. There's no group of friends helping you out after you run away. There's no support system. Everyone just keeps living their life, and it's not their job to make sure that you're okay after you've screwed your life up. It's not their fault, and they don't have training on how to bring you out of your misery, the misery that you created for yourself.

You are all alone in this world.

I considered going back and begging Frank to let us move back into our trailer too many times to count. I considered killing myself even more. I completely traumatized my daughter by telling her that was our only option in a moment of shock and grief that led me to believe that it was true, that I should kill myself. I cried out to Jesus and begged Him to send me help. Just like the last time suicide beckoned to me when the postpartum depression and stress of having a baby who was not breathing on his own caused me to contemplate my own end, Jesus sent me my best friend Morgan.

CHAPTER ONE HUNDRED EIGHT

It is always Morgan whom I ask for help last because I always feel like I ask too often and too much from him. I tell him that every time, and he always says it's silly and to just go ahead and ask him first. I know he's right. He is so kind and will always be my best friend. When I called him for help, without hesitation he told me to come and stay with him while I figured it all out. He lives in Kansas City, and my kids and I had an eight-hour drive to get to him. My plan was to live with him while I found an affordable apartment in the more rural part of either Missouri, Iowa, Nebraska, or even Arkansas or Kansas. I didn't care where we lived as long as I could afford the rent.

Something most people don't really realize about being homeless with two children is that when you find yourself in that situation, you aren't only crushed under the guilt that your children are homeless and lacking stability, but you are also terrified someone will call the Department of Family Services and report you, causing you to lose your children entirely. All of this was a throbbing heartbeat feeding my idea that I was not a good mom and needed to leave my kids with other people and end my life. I am so ashamed that I told Ella how I was feeling. I am so ashamed that I scared her so badly. I am so ashamed that I let life, fear, and the enemy almost have me entirely.

I am so grateful and appreciative that I had Morgan. On our way to Kansas City from Texas, we needed to stop and spend a night in a small town in Missouri so that we could put in some applications at apartments in the area. By this time, a week into being homeless, I'd asked everyone I knew for leads on a place to live. My friend Sam's mom had been someone I contacted. She was kind enough to let us stay the night at her house one night on our way to Kansas City, and as I sat in her living room trying not to sob, I told her the whole story. She gave me those words of kindness and wisdom that I needed to put one foot in front of the other, the next leg of my journey.

Choking on my tears, I said, "Being homeless with two kids, I feel like I'm not a good mom."

Sam's mom said, "There are damn good moms sleeping in their cars tonight," giving me the encouraging bit of 'you care therefore you are,' and even though she's Sam's mom and not mine, once again, just like in my childhood when she saw I needed mothering, she mothered me. How could I argue with her point when she proved it with her life? Being a good mom is not getting it perfect every time. It's putting our kids first every time. It is in the trying.

The eleven days we spent at Morgan's were filled with highs and lows. Every apartment or rental home I could afford had a waiting list. We were overjoyed to be at Morgan's where we were getting the emotional attention we needed. We were getting that parade, the venting, the sharing, and the crying that I felt awkward trying to do with Mellissa in front of her children and husband. I am so relieved that I did not have an outburst at Mellissa's house and worry her kids or disrupt her family. I could explode in grief and pain in front of Morgan and no one else.

Henry and I went outside in the rain behind Morgan's building, and I sang Casting Crown's "Praise You in this Storm," thanking Jesus for the place we would live even before I was certain we'd live anywhere. Simply being in Morgan's presence had given me back my fight for life. Morgan's gumption had reminded me that Jesus could not possibly want me to die.

Morgan has the ability to make you completely forget about your worries, even if just temporarily, and it was those moments of joy and encouragement that I needed to keep going. One night we were looking at our yearbooks, and I had never, ever, read in the nineteen years that we had been out of high school what my dad had written to me in our senior yearbook. It had been twelve years since he had died. I didn't read it until the night I needed it the most.

All it said was, "Amelia, Psalm 91." I looked up Psalm 91 and felt the armor of the Lord envelop me. *My God protects me. My God will cover me with his feathers and His wings. In His wings, I will find refuge.*

The warmth and security of reading that verse and remembering that I had a dad who would be able to help me with reminding me of God's love and protection, even after he had passed away, gave me the motivation to get up and try again.

I haven't had to ask Morgan for help in a while, but he helps me every single day in the fact that I'm still alive. He saved my life and reminded me that I have a life worth living.

Someday, when we're old, Morgan and I will live together with a bunch of little dogs, and we will remember all the bullshit life threw at us. Occasionally, we'll reflect sadly on all the people who didn't understand that at the end of the day, life is not about being the sum of every good or bad decision we make, but life is about being understanding and empathetic enough to realize that shit just fucking happens.

Eleven days after calling every apartment Google had to offer in my price range and messaging every old friend I could remember, an old high school friend answered a text with, "Hey, do you mind living in Nebraska?"

"We're homeless. We will live anywhere. Why? Do you know of a place?" I replied with a bit of hope.

Natasha's mom was the property manager of an apartment in a small town in Nebraska. Natasha had told her mom our story, and she said to get our butts over to Nebraska. We could move in on Monday.

## CHAPTER ONE HUNDRED NINE

Between the time I was seven and twenty-two, my mom must have left Frank fifty times and talked about it hundreds of thousands of times.

"We'll go live in a small town in Missouri's boot heel where he will never find us."

"We'll go live in a small town in Nebraska called Oswego!" Oswego had a house she thought she could afford, and I remembered it because Mom said it sounded like, "Off we go!" and I wish we had.

I wish we could have ridden off into the sunset with her. I would have gone anywhere with her.

As a kid, I loved any and every song where the woman is running away from her abuser or even just a life she doesn't want anymore. Amanda Marshall's "Birmingham," Jody Messina's "Heads Carolina, Tails California," Martina McBride's, "Day of Reckoning."

My mom and I watched Whitney Houston's *The Bodyguard* a hundred times when I was a small child before she even knew Frank. The lyrics to "I Will Always Love You" still break my heart. If you really look at the lyrics, a romantic love is what it's written for, but for me, my story is the one that unfolds, talking about only being in the way if she stayed. And I will always love my mom, but I'm not so sure she ever really loved anyone.

I sat down at the piano a couple of days before I left the kennel so that I could try to create my mom a song to forgive her by. I wanted to write a song to tell her and the world that I knew she had tried, but that she was just never given the right tools. For one thing, she never loved herself, and I do not believe you can fully love anyone else until you've worked on forgiving yourself for cheating yourself and your own past. We have to learn from our mistakes but then forgive ourselves for making them, and my mom was too afraid to admit when she was ever wrong. She was stubborn, and she felt unloved. She was abused, neglected, and started to lose herself when she and I were both far too young. I want to forgive her with my song.

*What made her think that she could live out there on the edge for so long without ever coming in?*

*What made her want to stay as far as away from anyone and everything that she could be?*

*Think of all the lies she had to tell to stay way out there away from us.*

*Think of all the ways she had to feel to carry around all those lies.*

*She wouldn't have let you love her no matter how hard you tried.*

*She wouldn't even let you know her.*

*Sometimes she'd run, sometimes she'd hide, and you could never really have her.*

*You could never really have her. Do you remember long ago when she belonged to us?*

My mom spent her early adult life taking care of her home, husband, and children's needs. She was a single mother for a lot of that time who was drowning in the loneliness and betrayal of having been cheated on and left. Then, she spent the second half of her adult life in fight-or-flight mode running from an abusive narcissist, whether she was running mental circles around him in order to financially plan for her next getaway or actually physically running away from him.

When I was about ten, she'd run away, and at the time, Frank had a Bronco. Mom was always telling Ruby and me to keep an eye out for

Frank and his truck. Every time I would see a dirty white Bronco, I would get sick to my stomach. Now, in the little town I live in, someone drives a dirty white Bronco–and it's been two years since I have even seen Frank, and twenty-seven years since he drove a dirty white Bronco–but I still tense up and feel like I'm ten and that my life and my mother and sister's lives are in danger when I see that truck.

He was terrifying, and no one would admit it. Everyone just accepted his anger, his rage, his controlling, narcissistic bile. We not only tolerated it, but we let our children–I let my children–be around him. My dad let his children be around him. My mom let her children be around him and *made* a child with him. These cycles created in fear have to be broken. Someone has to be brave enough to leave, and we all have to stop accepting poison.

Was my mom's life a waste? All that time working and serving her children, nursing us and getting up with us in the middle of the night as babies, trying to be a good mom with absolutely no example... was it all a waste? When I left the kennel, my mom was in a nursing home unable to walk or talk. Was her life a waste? What are we doing here? Working forever, losing our minds, and falling apart? There must be something more.

My friend Natasha, whose mom was the property manager of some apartments in a small town in Nebraska, came through for us. I trusted it was Jesus and His miracles still in action when I realized the town was only fifteen miles from the storage unit I had randomly chosen to put our things in. It only took me a couple of hours to clean out the storage unit and move all of our stuff into our new two-bedroom apartment, which was great.

We had a playground right outside our front door, lots of kids in the neighborhood for Henry to play with, and everyone was friendly. We were closer to Rob's house, and he had stuck with me and texted me the whole time I was homeless and struggling, which ended up being almost three weeks.

Our new apartment didn't have beds or a place to sit because I had sold all of our furniture thinking we were going to live with Mellissa. As empty as the place was, I was elated. I felt so much hope, and I was beaming, singing, and spinning around the kitchen while I made my kids breakfast. I didn't have a job yet, we didn't have very many belongings, but we had a roof over our heads.

My friend Paul, whom I dated when Ella was younger and was still friends with, had supported me emotionally while I stayed at Morgan's place. Paul was the only guy I ever introduced Ella to because he is so good and so kind. The whole time I searched for a place to live and was at my lowest, Paul reminded me that I had been through worse and made it out alive because I was strong. He also promised me that no matter what, he would not let me take my kids to a homeless shelter. When I found my new place, he sent me $1000. His acts of kindness during our transition and over the last two years have been more than I could have ever imagined anyone doing for me. I can always call him. I can always vent to him. I can always ask him for help. I love him, and I know that he loves me, and that he has helped me heal because I was living in a world where I was unlovable.

I was so convinced that I was unlovable I accepted behavior from people that I should have never even been near in the first place. Paul showed me that I was lovable and helped me move on and heal.

The first week in our apartment, I asked some friends to help us buy beds for my kids because my kids had been through enough. They did not need to continue to sleep on the floor. My aunt told me where I could pick some beds up for free, but no one would help me move the beds, and my car was not large enough to transport beds. So, I asked if anyone would like to donate ten or twenty dollars to my "order my children beds from Amazon," fund, and some of my friends completely ignored me. Some of them sent money, and I was over-whelmed with gratitude. I was even more amazed by Jesus' plan when the child support money that had been garnished because Tyler was so far behind in his payments all rolled in at once, and it was enough to get us beds and a couch.

My friend Tori helped us with groceries and bills that I couldn't quite make that first year. Tori even bought us a freezer and filled my refrigerator, pantry, and freezer. I do not know how I could ever repay her for her kindness to me and my children.

We didn't have a washer and dryer or hookups in our apartment, and the laundromat was so pricey that I invested in learning to do our laundry with a washboard by hand. Every other weekend, Ella watched Henry while I took our bedding to Rob's to do laundry. Rob only lived an hour away from us in our new place, and I had to drive through Oswego to get to Rob's house. I smiled every time I passed the sign. My mom couldn't get away and go to Oswego, but I was long gone.

Our new place was amazing. I would randomly belt out, "Let freedom ring!!! Let the white dove sing!!!"

I finally had the life I had pictured since I was a little girl. It was a life that was finally judgment free because it was Frank Hudson free, danger free, anxiety free, worry free.

About a month after getting settled into our new lives, where I had found a job I liked, my kids were still homeschooled and we were happy and healing, we decided to go see my mom at the nursing home. When we got there, they told us her husband had come and picked her up and taken her home about a month prior. My heart broke again. There was nothing I could do.

I had known about and feared this possibility. Before I left, Frank kept talking about getting her a couple of nurses and bringing her home so she could relearn to walk and talk. Years of anxiety and fear, and I couldn't deal with it anymore. I had been chasing Libby for way too long, and she had been gone even longer still.

Libby was gone. Elizabeth was gone. My mom was gone, and I would probably never see her again.

I often wonder if I'll know when she passes away. I often wonder if I'll feel her spirit go. I spent my whole life trying to rescue her and rebuild our relationship, and I did not fully understand that we never had one to begin with until I wrote it all down.

The first year that we were away from Frank, Ella threw screaming fits almost every day, and I could not, and do not, blame her. Everything she'd been through from her dad abandoning us to having to be around Frank her whole childhood, her grandma having dementia, having to help raise Henry, running away and being homeless, watching me struggle with suicidal thoughts and more–I would have screamed even more than she did. But now, both of my children are in therapy, and both of them are starting to grow into well adjusted, happy, and carefree kids.

A year and a half into living in our new place, we were able to get a three bedroom with much more space for my kids. We are coming up on our two-year anniversary of leaving the toxic, narcissistic, waste dump that is Frank Hudson and that life, and I am the happiest I have ever been. I feel like I am finally in control of my life rather than playing a game of "how much happiness will Frank allow me to have today?" which I played every day of my entire life for thirty years.

That is how badly I wanted my mom. That is how long I let whether or not she was being my mom dictate my emotions. I had to write it all down to see it, and that is why everyone should go to therapy. Talking about our problems helps. It's not dramatic. It's not pitiful. It's necessary and cathartic.

I'm writing because I can't afford therapy, and it has helped me overcome issues I have had for three decades. If you write, paint, sing, draw, run, lift weights, play sports, cook, do whatever you do to get your emotions out productively, do it, but please do not keep your emotions inside. Process the emotions, go through them one at a time, face them.

We have to get to know ourselves and we have to love ourselves.

# CHAPTER ONE HUNDRED TEN

About six months after we ran away from the kennel, the tooth that I had to have crowned when half of it broke off when my dad died abscessed. My dad has been gone for twelve years, and that tooth had broken off when I lost him and stopped taking care of myself. I lost my dad and lost half the tooth, and then when I lost my mom it abscessed, and when the dentist asked if I wanted a root canal or I wanted him to pull it, I didn't even have to consider it.

"Pull it!" I said.

When the dentist pulled my tooth out, I felt a wave of serenity wash over me. It was not because I was no longer in pain. They'd given me antibiotics ten days prior to the extraction, and the infection and pain were gone. I believe the nirvana I felt when they pulled my tooth was a reaction to my letting go of the stress my parents had, however inadvertently, put on me my whole life in losing them and watching them lose themselves.

A year after we ran away from Frank, I started to write down everything he had done to me or had done to someone else in front of me. I wrote down every story he told me about how he hurt people I didn't even know. And as the stories flowed rapidly from my pen, I began to heal just like the hole where my tooth had been had healed.

I had always heard that journaling would help, but I never realized how true it was. Writing our stories down gives us the validation we need to say, "Yes, this *did* happen to me," and then we have the opportunity to sort it out and start the healing process. As each story landed in my notebook, it was removed from my heart.

I never thought there would be a day where I would not be scared or worried about my mom, and even though she's still alive, and even though I never got her away from her abuser, I finally understood that it was not my job to save her.

Oh, how I wish this story had ended differently. I often wished when I was changing my mom's clothes or giving her a shower that she would whisper, "I'm acting. I'm going to pretend I have dementia for a few years, shoot him in the head, and then plead insanity. Then we can finally be together without him as we always should have."

I know it sounds absurd, but it was just the type of plan she and I would have joked about when she still had control over her own mind.

I write songs about her, and I still cry about her and cry for her every once in a while, but I'm not letting my every decision or my every emotion revolve around her and breaking her out or helping her be happy. I could never do any of those things, and I wasted a lot of my life trying.

*What would we have done if we had met when we were both ten?*
*Would we have been friends?*
*I think you would have liked me.*
*Grass stains and bike wrecks.*
*Softball and summer afternoon adventure quests.*
*I'll try to come back someday and find you.*
*I hope you're still there and no one has harmed you.*
*I can't promise you anything that I thought I could.*
*I couldn't rescue you then, and I can't reach you now.*
*What would we have done if we had met when we were both seventeen?*
*Would we have been friends?*
*I think so.*

*I would have told you that you are worth way more than you ever gave yourself credit for.*

*Where would you be if you had loved yourself even half as much as I love you?*

*Where would you be if the world hadn't broken your heart?*

*Where would you be now?*

*I bet you would least be able to talk.*

*I bet you would at least be able to walk.*

*At least.*

*At least you'd be my friend.*

*If we'd have known what we know now back then, wouldn't you have chosen me?*

*Please tell me you would have chosen me.*

Maybe to some, myself included, sometimes these pages just sound like the whining of a brat who didn't have a perfect life, so she decided to write down every time someone was mean to her. I hope these stories help someone. That is the only reason I will share them with the world.

It's so easy to get wrapped up inside the control of a narcissist. You don't have to be married to them to be hurt by them. We move our children in with people because we don't want to be alone or because we think that we're in love. We think that our children won't be affected. Every decision we make affects our children.

My children will have to fight to heal the wounds Frank left them with, and the blood from these wounds is on my hands. I allowed them to be around him. Everyone accepted his treatment of me, so I accepted it for my children.

If someone reads this and wakes up and gets themselves out, gets their kids away from someone who is toxic, or if someone reads this and decides to choose better for themselves before she even goes down the path of a narcissist, it will have been worth it to share my story. I hope my words, stories, and emotional journey can help someone. I hope my experiences help my daughter every day, and I wish I could quantum leap into the past and save my own mom.

I have at least broken a cycle of accepting abuse. Henry and Ella will not choose to act like, or be around, the poison we used to live in.

What would my childhood have been like stress, anxiety, longing, and pain free? Where would I be now if I had not spent my entire life in fight-or-flight mode? If I had not had to worry about my mom, and then later myself and my children, being in danger every day?

Living that way caused me to believe that I was so unlovable, at times, I believed that God wanted me to give up and die. Living that way my entire life with no self-worth caused me to believe that no matter how hard I tried to be a servant of Jesus, something would cause Him in the end to say, "Oh, it looks like you tried, but you weren't even good enough for your own mom, so you're not good enough for Me."

Repeated neglect from people who should have been around caused me to believe that even Jesus thought of me as a burden. Now, after leaving the enemy and laying my trauma down on these pages, I'm going to work on building myself a life where Jesus is the center. I'm going to remember that it is not my earning it that will get me a seat at His table. I don't want to know Jesus so I can win a crown, a mansion, or a seat at His table in Heaven.

I'm His friend because He's shown me over and over that He is my friend. It is not by the merit of our actions that inspires this friendship to grow. It is constantly asking Him, "How can I be more like You?" When we ask Him to make us more like Him, and when we achieve being like Him, we find peace. My whole life has been chaos.

I'm ready for His peace.

Sometimes, we have to let go of people we really want to help because, no matter how badly we want to rescue them, they are just pulling us into their sludge. Whatever the issue causing me to feel down, alone, or anxious, I go to Jesus. And now I understand that it is not my earning of His love, His protection, or His peace that causes His miracles to appear in my life. The love of Jesus is never anything I could earn. God gave us Jesus because He already loved us enough. We cannot get better and become good enough for Jesus. It is He who makes us whole each day when we seek Him and ask Him for his likeness and His help.

I have forgiven Frank, Chad, Tyler, my mom, myself, and all of the circumstances that led me through shadows. I would remain sick and hurt if I did not forgive.

When I write down my stories, it is almost as though they never even happened.

Thank you for reading. If you or someone you know is suffering from abuse, please call the National Domestic Violence Hotline at 1-800-799-SAFE (7233).